Daniel Bros

Daniels Bros

Illustrated guide for amateur Gardeners

Daniel Bros

Daniels Bros
Illustrated guide for amateur Gardeners

ISBN/EAN: 9783741198960

Manufactured in Europe, USA, Canada, Australia, Japa

Cover: Foto ©Andreas Hilbeck / pixelio.de

Manufactured and distributed by brebook publishing software
(www.brebook.com)

Daniel Bros

Daniels Bros

Illustrated Guide

for AMATEUR GARDENERS

DANIELS BROS LTD
Seed Growers & Nurserymen
NORWICH

Spring 1921

THE ROYAL NORFOLK SEED ESTABLISHMENT,

NORWICH, ENGLAND.

Dead Office and Retail Establishment.
ROYAL ARCADE.
Telephone:—No. 38.

Seed Warehouses.
BEDFORD STREET
Private Telephone.

GOLD MEDAL AWARDED BY THE
ROYAL AGRICULTURAL SOCIETY.
JUNE, 1911.

Seed Grounds.
TUNSTEAD AND EATON.
Private Telephones.

Nurseries.
THE TOWN CLOSE NURSERIES,
NEWMARKET ROAD.
Telephone:—No. 38.

TERMS OF BUSINESS, &c.

All orders from unknown Correspondents must be accompanied by a sufficient Remittance or Bankers' Reference. To save the heavy cost of Booking now entailed, a Remittance should in all cases be sent with Orders under 20s. in value.

ACCOUNTS—DISCOUNTS.—All accounts are due net in three months; we however allow a discount of 5% on orders of 20s. and upwards, when accompanied by a remittance, or when paid within fourteen days of date of invoice, with the exception of "Collections," Cut Flowers and Floral Designs, all of which are strictly nett.

ADDRESSES.—Full Name and Address should be sent with every communication, and nearest Railway Station should be stated with every order, as much time is thereby saved, especially in our busiest season, when we often receive from 1000 to 1500 letters daily. In consequence of this large correspondence, we suggest that, at all seasons, Cut Flower Orders and other Urgent Letters should be so marked on the envelope.

CARRIAGE ON GOODS.—We pay carriage on the following Articles to any address in the British Isles :—
All KITCHEN GARDEN and FLOWER SEEDS of the value of 5s. and upwards.
SEED POTATOES, CULINARY ROOTS, HORTICULTURAL TOOLS and SUNDRIES (except Potting Soil, Sand, Manures, etc.), if included in a general Garden Seed order of the value of 40s. in all.
ROSES from the open ground, in quantities of one dozen and upwards.

We do not pay carriage on the following, owing to the heavy cost, in proportion to the value :—
SEEDS and ROSES of less quantities than those mentioned above.
TREES AND SHRUBS, FRUIT TREES AND BUSHES, PLANTS AND ROSES IN POTS.
POTATOES AND HORTICULTURAL SUNDRIES, of less value than mentioned above, Manures, Mushroom Spawn, Silver Sand, Peat and Loam, Mats, Tools, &c., if ordered alone.
N.B.—Should the cost of Postage or Rail Carriage be increased during the currency of this Catalogue, we reserve the right to charge any difference.

CHANGE OF ADDRESS.—We shall esteem it a favour if our customers, on changing their residences, will kindly favour us with their new addresses, so that we may be able to send them our Catalogues as usual.

CHEQUES, MONEY ORDERS, AND POSTAL ORDERS.—Should be made payable to DANIELS BROS. LIMITED, and crossed "BARCLAYS BANK LIMITED," Norwich. Letters containing coin (or Treasury Notes) must be registered according to Post Office regulations.

CO-OPERATION IN SENDING ORDERS.—Cottagers, and those requiring individually but small quantities of Seeds if they join together in sending their orders, will be allowed a special discount of five per cent., to be taken in seeds, besides the usual discount of five per cent. for cash, thus :—for every 40s. remitted, 44s. worth of seeds may be ordered. No order can be recognised under these terms unless over the net value of Two Pounds, and accompanied by prepayment in full. Each order will be packed separately, and consigned in one package, but full name and address of each customer ordering under this arrangement should be sent. Special terms will be quoted to the Allotment Holders' Societies on application from the Secretary.

CORRESPONDENCE. Most Important.—Our customers having occasion to write to us respecting any order previously sent by them, will much facilitate attention to their letters if they will kindly state the date on which the order was sent, and if remittance was enclosed name the amount; this will enable us more readily to identify their orders on reference to our Registers.

PACKAGES.—All packages are charged at the lowest cost price, and are not returnable, unless sent back in good condition, and Carriage Paid, within fourteen days of receipt of goods. Customers are particularly requested to put their name and address on each package, and to advise us by post when returned, or they cannot be credited.

PRICES, ALTERATION OF.—Owing to the uncertainty of procuring further supplies of Vegetable Seeds and Potatoes, the prices quoted in this Catalogue may be cancelled at any time after March 31st, 1921.

PACKETS.—Will our customers kindly note that, in all cases where Seeds are quoted by the "Packet," this is the minimum quantity that we can supply; smaller quantities or half-packets are not sold by us.

RECOMMENDATIONS.—The many kind recommendations to new customers with which we have been favoured in the past have been very gratifying. Should any of our customers have friends requiring Seeds, Plants, &c., to whom a copy of our *Illustrated Guide* would be acceptable, we shall feel much obliged by an intimation of the fact.

WARRANTY.—DANIELS BROS. LIMITED, NORWICH, give no warranty, expressed or implied, as to description, quality, productiveness or any other matter connected with seed or seed grain supplied by them, beyond the analyses required in accordance with the "Testing of Seeds Order, 1918," nor will they in any way be responsible for the crop. It must therefore be clearly understood that if the purchaser does not accept the goods on these terms, they are at once to be returned.

Telegraphic Address :—DANIELS, NORWICH. Telephones—38 & 39 Norwich.

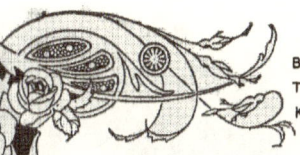

SEEDSMEN
BY APPOINTMENT
TO HIS MAJESTY
KING GEORGE V.

NURSERYMEN
BY APPOINTMENT
TO HER MAJESTY
QUEEN ALEXANDRA.

To·our·Customers

There are signs on every hand that the greatly increased interest in Horticulture aroused during the War is likely to be permanent, but there is yet abundant scope for extension in the cultivation of Vegetable and Potato crops by Amateur Gardeners. Nothing is more conducive to the health and happiness of the nation than the cultivation, in the leisure afforded by shorter working hours, of gardens and allotments.

The additional warehouse accommodation provided by us during the past two years to meet the greatly increased demands in our Potato and Kitchen Garden Seed Departments, although giving us double the space previously available, was utilised to the utmost capacity last Spring, but we were able to give prompt service to our customers, and our arrangements for the coming Seed Season will ensure a continuance of the same. Our new Seed Farm at Tunstead, occupying 225 acres of the finest arable land in East Anglia, has enabled us to produce largely increased crops of many of our own well-known Specialities in Vegetable and Flower Seeds.

KITCHEN GARDEN SEEDS. The past Summer was an exceedingly anxious one for all Seed Growers ; the long spells of cold, sunless weather in the height of the growing season was very trying for all crops. East Anglia was, however, more fortunate than most districts, and we are again able to offer full ranges of all Vegetable Seeds at the same prices (with a few minor exceptions) as last season.

SEED POTATOES. We have secured from our growers in Scotland a supply of all the best varieties, for which we enjoy a big demand ; our stock includes all the best Immune sorts, which have given good results in our trials for cropping and cooking. We shall carefully hand pick and grade our supplies, as has been our custom in the past, these selected tubers giving our customers heavier crops of best quality.

FLOWER SEEDS. We have this Summer had most successful results in the selection and improvement of the popular varieties of Choice Flower Seeds, and we offer the finest strains procurable in ASTERS, STOCKS, ANTIRRHINUMS, and all the popular annuals. We devoted a larger area than ever before to the cultivation of the very choicest varieties of SWEET PEAS, and on pages 54-56 will be found the pick of the best kinds. As we anticipated, last Spring witnessed a greatly increased demand for Flower Seeds, and we have made full provision for a further increased demand in the coming sowing season.

NURSERY STOCK. In this important branch of our business we offer a wide range of all the varieties of ORNAMENTAL TREES & SHRUBS, FENCING & HEDGING PLANTS, FOREST TREES, Etc. We transplant our stock regularly, and it is always in excellent condition for moving.

FRUIT TREES & ROSES. The demand for these has again been a very heavy one this Autumn, and whilst we are able to offer comprehensive lists on pages 76-83, we would ask our customers where feasible to leave the selection of sorts to us. As the season advances it is certain that many sorts will be sold out ; having, however, rigidly cut down the number of varieties, so that only the very best of each class are cultivated, we can promise that where the selection is left to us no indifferent kinds will be sent.

NORWICH,
Jan. 1st, 1921.

DANIELS BROS., Ltd.

A fine
collection
grown from Seeds
supplied by
DANIELS BROS
LIMITED
NORWICH

KITCHEN GARDEN SEEDS.

Our large experience in this department has enabled us to select the finest possible stocks, the same being grown on our own grounds or under our personal supervision. The growth of all seeds is carefully tested before sending out, and customers ordering from us may thoroughly rely on being supplied with the best and newest varieties, all of good growing quality.

DANIELS' COMPLETE COLLECTIONS OF CHOICE VEGETABLE SEEDS.

All Package and Carriage Free.

These Collections, of which we annually sell immense quantities, are carefully made up with seeds of finest quality in best varieties from each class with a view of furnishing an ample supply of Choice Vegetables throughout the year, and will be found extremely valuable for those who have not sufficient time or experience for making their own selection.

As our Collections are made up on a most liberal scale, intending purchasers will kindly bear in mind that it is only by having Seeds specially grown, and by preparing the packets beforehand in large numbers, that we can be so liberal in the quantity of the Seeds supplied for the amount charged, and that by ordering our selections, instead of making their own, will reap an advantage of at least 25 per cent. below the general Catalogue prices. We therefore wish it to be understood that no reduction, alteration, or substitution can be allowed in any of the collections. When ordering please quote Number and Price of the Collection required.

No. 1.	Contains 16 quarts of Choice Peas	And all	-	£5	5	0
No. 2.	Contains 12 quarts of Choice Peas	other	-	£4	4	0
No. 3.	Contains 8 quarts of Choice Peas	Seeds in	-	£3	3	0
No. 4.	Contains 6 quarts of Choice Peas	proportion	-	£2	2	0

No. 5. Daniels' Complete Collection, 30s.

Package and Carriage Free. All the best kinds for succession.

3 pints	Peas, Early, Medium, and Late	2 pkts.	Cauliflower, Autumn Giant, &c.	2 ozs.	Onion
2 pints	Broad Beans	2 pkts.	Celery, Giant Red and White	2 ozs.	Parsnip, Hollow-crowned
1 pint	French Beans	½ pint	Cress	3 ozs.	Radish, Long and Turnip
1 pint	Runner Beans	2 pkts.	Cucumber, Frame and Ridge	4 ozs.	Spinach, Summer and Winter
1 pkt.	Beet, Daniels' Green Top	1 pkt.	Endive	2 ozs.	Turnip, Snowball and Golden
1 pkt.	Borecole, Curled	1 pkt.	Gourd or Pumpkin		Ball
1 pkt.	Brussels Sprouts, Colossal	1 pkt.	Leek	1 pkt.	Vegetable Marrow, Large
3 pkts.	Broccoli, Early and Late	3 pkts.	Lettuce, Cos and Cabbage		Cream
3 pkts.	Cabbage, Defiance, &c.	4 ozs.	Mustard, White	3 pkts.	Herbs, Sweet and Pot
½ oz.	Savoy, Drumhead	1 pkt.	Melon, Choice	2 pkts.	Tomato
2 ozs.	Carrot, Intermediate, &c.	1 oz.	Parsley, Fine Curled	1 pkt.	Capsicum, Long Red

No. 6. Daniels' Complete Collection, 22s. 6d.

Package and Carriage Free. All the best kinds for succession.

6 pints	Peas, Early, Medium, and Late	1 oz.	Carrot, in 2 varieties	1½ ozs.	Onion
1 pint	Broad Beans	1 pkt.	Cauliflower, Choice	½ oz.	Parsley, Fine Curled
1 pint	French Beans	1 pkt.	Celery	1 oz.	Parsnip, Hollow-crowned
1 pint	Runner Beans	4 ozs.	Cress	2 ozs.	Radish, Long and Turnip
1 pkt.	Beet, Daniels' Green Top	2 pkts.	Cucumber, Frame and Ridge	2 ozs.	Spinach, Round and Prickly
1 pkt.	Borecole, Curled	1 pkt.	Endive	1½ ozs.	Turnip, Snowball and Orange
1 pkt.	Brussels Sprouts	1 pkt.	Gourd or Pumpkin		Jelly
2 pkts.	Broccoli, Early and Late	1 pkt.	Leek	1 pkt.	Vegetable Marrow
2 pkts.	Cabbage, Choice Sorts	2 pkts.	Lettuce, Cos and Cabbage	2 pkts.	Herbs, Sweet and Pot
½ oz.	Savoy, Drumhead	3 ozs.	Mustard, White	1 pkt.	Tomato

No. 7. Our Special Collection for Exhibitors, 15s. 6d.

Post Free. Contains the following liberal assortment.

4	pkts.	Peas, Choice	1	pkt.	Cabbage, Red Drumhead	1	pkt.	Onion, Choice
1	pkt.	Broad Beans, Daniels' Selected Long-pod	1	pkt.	Cauliflower, Daniels' King	1	oz.	Parsnip, Daniels' Improved
1	pkt.	Runner Beans, Giant	2	pkts.	Carrot, Telegraph and Scarlet Perfection	1	pkt.	Parsley, Daniels' Queen
1	pkt.	Dwarf Beans	1	pkt.	Celery, Exhibition Pink	1	oz.	Radish, New Scarlet Turnip
1	pkt.	Beet, Daniels' Green Top	1	pkt.	Cucumber	1	„	Best of All
1	pkt.	Brussels Sprouts, Colossal	1	pkt.	Leek	1	pkt.	Tomato, King George V.
1	pkt.	Broccoli, Daniels' Norfolk Giant	2	pkts.	Lettuce, Giant White Cos and Queen of Summer	1	pkt.	Turnip, Improved Snowball
2	pkts.	Cabbage, Defiance, &c.				1	pkt.	„ Orange Jelly
						1	pkt.	Vegetable Marrow, Large Cream

"This is the Third Collection I have had, and I am more than satisfied with results. I am sure every Seed came up."—Mr. W. STANLEY, S. Woodford.

"You will be pleased to know that I had splendid results from the Special Collection, every packet was the very best Seeds, in fact the best I have ever had." —Mr. F. WHITE, Edenbridge.

"I was highly satisfied with your No. 7 Vegetable Collection last year. I obtained very good results."—Mr. R. CHALLIS, Halifax.

No. 8. Daniels' Complete Collection, 11s. 6d.

Package and Carriage Free. All the best kinds for succession.

3	pints	Peas, Early, Medium, and Late	1	pkt.	Cabbage	1	oz.	Onion
½	pint	Broad Beans	1	oz.	Carrot	1	pkt.	Parsley, Fine Curled
½	pint	French Beans	1	pkt.	Cauliflower, Autumn Giant	1	oz.	Parsnip, Hollow-crowned
1	pint	Runner Beans	1	pkt.	Celery, Red and White	1½	ozs.	Radish, Long and Turnip
1	pkt.	Beet, Dark-leaved	2	pkts.	Cress, Plain	1	oz.	Spinach, Summer
1	pkt.	Borecole, Curled	1	pkt.	Cucumber, Ridge	1	oz.	Turnip, Snowball
1	pkt.	Brussels Sprouts	2	pkts.	Lettuce, Cos and Cabbage	1	pkt.	Vegetable Marrow
1	pkt.	Broccoli	1	pkt.	Leek	1	pkt.	Tomato
1	pkt.	Savoy, Drumhead	1	oz.	Mustard, White			

"The No. 8 Collection which I had last year gave me the greatest satisfaction, in fact the best I have grown for many a long day."—Mr. G. HARVEY, Banbury.

"I must congratulate you on the way you turned out your No. 8 Collection, especially the amount you sent in war time. I have now used your Seeds for the past eleven years. Thanking you for your past favours."—A. GOLDSTONE, Esq., Wanstead.

"Your No. 8 Collection has done remarkably well, I have drawn over 100 score of green plants from my bed."—Mr. F. YOUNG, Westbury.

No. 9. Daniels' Cottager's Collection, 7s. 6d.

Package and Carriage Free. This collection is of exceptional value.

3	pkts.	Peas, for succession	1	pkt.	Savoy, Drumhead	1	oz.	Onion
1	pkt.	Broad Beans	1	oz.	Carrot	1	pkt.	Parsley, Fine Curled
1	pkt.	Runner Beans	1	pkt.	Cauliflower	½	oz.	Parsnip, Hollow-crowned
1	pkt.	French Beans	1	pkt.	Celery, Mixed	1	oz.	Radish, Mixed Turnip
1	pkt.	Beet, Dark-leaved	1	oz.	Cress	1	pkt.	Tomato
1	pkt.	Borecole, Curled	1	pkt.	Cucumber, Ridge	½	oz.	Turnip
1	pkt.	Brussels Sprouts	1	pkt.	Leek	1	pkt.	Vegetable Marrow
1	pkt.	Broccoli	1	pkt.	Lettuce, Cos and Cabbage, Mixed			
1	pkt.	Cabbage						

"I am pleased to say your No. 9 Cottager's Collection which I had from you this year turned out very successful."—Mr. F. SMITH, Temple Balsall.

"I have the pleasure to let you know that your 7/6 Collection of Vegetable Seeds I had in 1919 have done well, I took 5 prizes out of 6 varieties. First each for Beet, Cabbage, Celery, Onions and Parsnips, all taken at our Local Show."—Mr. F. SUMNER, Clacton.

"Your No. 9 Collection was a complete success last year, so have pleasure in again ordering another, and thanking you for your prompt attention."—Mr. M. BAXTER, Dudbridge.

No. 10. The Cottager's Packet, 4s. 6d. Post free.

Containing fifteen varieties of choice Vegetable Seeds, including ¼ pint of Peas and fair quantities of Broccoli, Cabbage, Carrot, Lettuce, Onion, Radish, Turnip, &c.

This is a very cheap collection which can be highly recommended.

"I should like to say the Cottager's Collection which I had from you last year proved to be a huge success."—Mr. R. SKINNER, London, N.9.

"Have such a good result from your Cottage Collection last year. I never had a better show of Peas. All the other Seed gave a good return."—Mr. C. RAYNER, Spondon.

"I wish to express my satisfaction with the Cottager's Packet, especially the Peas, which were excellent."—Mr. L. RIBBONS, White Hart Lane.

PEAS.

Cultivation.—Peas form one of the most valuable of garden crops, and when once started into growth, require, under favourable conditions, little attention beyond the staking of such varieties as need support, and mulching and watering in dry weather. Peas require a good rich soil, which should be well trenched, and should receive a liberal supply of well-decomposed manure early in the season. They are essentially a moisture loving plant, and only when the ground is well prepared can really satisfactory results be assured. Given these conditions, it is possible by a succession of sowings to have a continuous supply of Peas for the table from June till October, or even later.

First early varieties should be sown from the middle of January onwards, and the best sorts in this class are Daniels' **Gem of the Season**, **Earliest of All**, and **The Pilot** ; if the seed is sown in boxes under glass in January, hardened off in a frame and planted out at the latter end of March or early in April, an advantage of ten days or a fortnight may be gained. Second early and main crop kinds should be sown in March and April, and for late use a succession of sowings at intervals from the beginning of May until the end of June should be made. For these sowings the tall varieties will be found more productive, and not so liable to mildew during hot weather. It should be borne in mind that although most of the Wrinkled seeded varieties may be sown in March, we do not recommend this unless the season is exceptionally favourable. We find from a careful record extending over ten years, that little if any advantage is gained by too early sowings, and that Peas sown at the beginning of April take less time to come to maturity than the earlier sown ones. If this rule was more generally followed, we should hear less about bad germination amongst this class of Peas especially in cold wet seasons. The seed should be sown in drills and covered about two inches deep ; allow four or five feet between each row unless it is desired to grow some other crop between, when the rows may be 12 to 15 feet apart. Let the rows run from north to south, thus allowing the plants to receive a maximum of light and air.

Peas suffer greatly from the depredations of all kinds of vermin, and it will always be found of advantage to give protection either by wire pea guards or some other means while the plants are growing. The rows should be earthed up before they are staked, and this should be done when the plants are about four inches high. If the tops of the sticks are cut evenly, and the pieces which are cut off placed between the large sticks at the base, they will prevent the plants from falling about, and give them an upward tendency from the start.

A good mulching of manure placed on each side of the row will help to retain the moisture in dry weather. Where this is not possible they must be regularly watered during dry periods, and liquid manure given once a week ; a mixture containing four ounces of Nitrate of Soda to one gallon of water will be found very useful for this purpose.

When it is desired to grow Peas for exhibition purposes the following points should be observed :—Sow the seed very thinly on ground that has been especially deeply trenched for the purpose, and which has been dressed with old farmyard manure or the remains of an old mushroom bed. If they are needed for early Summer Show it may be desirable to raise the seed on turves in a greenhouse and transfer them bodily to the border when about four inches high, but, generally speaking, if the seed is sown in rows in March and April it will be found early enough.

When the plants have shown about four blooms, pinch out the leader or top of the haulm. As soon as the pods have formed, choose the best shaped, and remove the others, leaving only two or three on each plant. Always select the strongest and healthiest plants for this purpose. When ready to gather, do not handle the pods, but cut off with scissors so as to retain their bloom.

NEW PEA, DANIELS' EXPRESS.

A grand new first early Marrowfat variety, growing to the height of about 18 inches, and of great productiveness, bearing a profusion of handsome dark green pods, 4½ to 5 inches in length, well filled with peas of the most delicious marrow flavour. In habit of growth it somewhat resembles Competitor, but the pods are much darker in colour and better filled. We can strongly recommend this as one of the finest first early varieties yet introduced. Per pint 2s. 3d. ; per quart 4s. 3d.

NEW PEA, DANIELS' LEADER.

A new first early dwarf Pea, of hardy constitution, very similar to the well-known Pilot, but growing only 12 to 15 inches high, thus requiring no sticking. The pods are equal to Pilot in size and at same time it is more prolific, and like that variety can be sown earlier than the dwarf wrinkled sorts with the certainty of a crop. per ¼ pint 1s. 6d. ; per pint 2s. 9d.

NEW PEA, HUNDREDFOLD.

A new early marrow of great productiveness ; it grows about 2 feet high, bearing a heavy crop of fine, handsome dark green pods 5 inches in length, well filled with fine peas of excellent flavour. This variety is well worthy of a trial, as it is sure to give satisfaction. Per ½ pint 1s. 4d. ; per pint 2s. 6d.

"I am more than satisfied with all Seeds supplied by you, the Daniels' Express Peas were first rate."—Mr. F. C. TUFFNELL, Luton.

"The Vegetable Seeds I had from you have exceeded my expectations, especially the Express Peas."—Mr. S. HENNELL, Brentford.

DANIELS' EXPRESS. *Reduced from a Photograph.*

PEAS.

Section I.—Earliest Varieties.

☞ DANIELS' SELECTED GRADUS.

This large-podded early wrinkled variety, is without doubt the finest and most distinct early Pea yet introduced. The haulm which grows to the height of three to four feet is well covered with large dark green pods, averaging five inches in length, and well filled with eight to ten fine Peas of the most exquisite flavour ; indeed, amongst the early varieties it has no rival in this respect. It is an excellent cropper, this combined with its earliness and grand flavour, has made it a favourite with all growers.

Per pint 2s. 3d. ; per quart 4s. 3d.

per quart—s. d.

DANIELS' SELECTED GRADUS. *Reduced from a Photograph.*

☞ **DANIELS' BEST OF ALL.** A very fine dwarf Early Marrowfat variety, growing only about eighteen inches in height. It is an abundant cropper, bearing quite a profusion of handsome pods of 3½ to 4 inches in length, each with seven or eight large finely-flavoured peas. It is as early as English Wonder, and will prove a splendid and profitable Pea for the market or private grower .. .. per pint 2s. 0d. 3 9

☞ **THE PILOT.** This valuable introduction has taken a leading place amongst the most useful varieties, both for market and private garden purposes. It is a first early cropper producing deep green pods of the well-known Gradus type, and on account of its hardy constitution and the seed being round it may be sown early with the certainty of a crop. It is a vigorous branching plant, growing three feet in height, bearing a large proportion of the pods in pairs, which contain fine deep green peas of excellent marrow flavour. per pint 3s. 0d. 5 0

DANIELS' GEM OF THE SEASON. The earliest Pea in cultivation, and very prolific. Is always the earliest, whether sown in Autumn, Winter, or Spring. Is also the hardiest, resisting frost better than any other kind, and is not affected by mildew. Being very prolific and of a most delicious flavour, will be found a most desirable variety for early work. Height 3 ft. per pt. 1s. 8d. 3 0

EARLIEST OF ALL. A round blue-seeded Pea of excellent and rich flavour ; very prolific, can be sown early. Ht. 2½ ft. pint 1s. 8d. 3 0

ENGLISH WONDER. One of the most useful of the dwarf varieties, of good constitution and very prolific, may be sown earlier than some of the wrinkled sorts. Height 1 ft. per pint 1s. 0d. 3 3

LAXTONIAN. A fine early wrinkled pea of dwarf habit and vigorous constitution. A very heavy cropper, the haulm being covered with fine dark green pods 4 to 5 inches in length, well filled with nine to ten large peas of the finest flavour. Can be highly recommended. Height 1½ ft. .. .. per pint 2s. 0d. 3 9

LITTLE MARVEL. A fine dwarf early variety of compact growth, and an exceptionally heavy cropper. The pods are of medium size and well filled with fine peas of excellent flavour ; a great acquisition to our first early sorts. Height 1 ft. per pint 2s. 0d. 4 6

THOMAS LAXTON. Award of Merit, Royal Horticultural Society. A large-podded first early Pea, coming in with Earliest of All, but with pods of double the size, and rich dark green colour. It is a true wrinkled Marrow, a grand cropper, and the flavour is of the best. Height 3 ft. .. .. per pint 2s. 3d. 4 3

WITHAM WONDER. A first-class early Dwarf Pea of hardy constitution, about same height as the well-known English Wonder, and like that variety an enormous cropper ; excellent for small gardens .. .. per pint 2s. 0d. 3 9

"I had some Pilot Peas sometimes ago, and they have been such a splendid Pea and grand cropper that I thought I would try them again."—Mr. T. RATCLIFF, Newbury.

"From the 1 pint of Peas, Gem of the Season, that I had in the spring, I have just finished picking, 5 pecks in all. No one that has seen them has ever seen anything like them."—Mr. JAS. GOULT, Gorefield.

PEAS.

Section II.—Second Early.

☞ DANIELS' DWARF PROLIFIC.

A grand second early dwarf wrinkled Marrow, of strong constitution and sturdy habit, growing about 1½ feet high ; it is enormously prolific, bearing a profusion of dark green, slightly curved pods, four inches long, well filled with eight to nine peas of excellent flavour, at the same time it is an excellent variety for forcing, being quite as prolific under glass as in the open. It is a very compact grower, and will be an acquisition to all gardens where space is limited, on account of the little room it occupies as compared with its heavy cropping qualities. **Per pint 2s. 0d. ; per quart 3s. 9d.**

DANIELS' DWARF PROLIFIC.

per quart.
s. d.

☞ **NEW PEA, ADMIRAL BEATTY.** A fine second early marrow pea, growing to the height of 3 to 4 feet, and producing an enormous crop of fine dark green pods 5 to 6 inches in length, and well filled with fine peas of excellent marrow flavour. This is without doubt a fine addition to our second early varieties, and when known is sure to be in great demand.

Per ½ pint 1s. 6d. ; per pint 2s. 9d. —

☞ **DANIELS' MIDSUMMER MARROW.** A grand early Marrowfat Pea of a good hardy constitution. It is an abundant bearer ; the pods, which somewhat resemble Gradus in shape, are 4½ to 5 inches in length and well filled with nine or ten fine peas of excellent flavour. We can thoroughly recommend this as a first-class variety for all purposes.
Height 3 to 4 ft. .. .. .. per pint 2s. 3d. | 4 3

☞ **LAXTON'S SUPERB.** A very early semi-wrinkled pea, carrying an immense crop of large dark green pods containing from nine to ten peas each, which have a very fine flavour. It is somewhat similar to Pilot, but with pods double the size of that variety, and is very hardy. Can be sown early, as the peas do not rot in the ground like fully wrinkled varieties. Award of Merit, R.H.S.
Height 2 to 2½ ft. .. .. .. per pint 2s. 3d. | 4 3

DAISY. A dwarf second early wrinkled Marrow of great merit. The haulm, which is very robust, is well hung with handsome pods four to five inches in length, well filled with large peas of excellent flavour. On account of its numerous good qualities it has been awarded a First Class Certificate by the Royal Horticultural Society. Height 1½ ft. .. .. per pint 2s. 3d. | 4 3

DUKE OF YORK. A fine wrinkled Marrow, of robust habit, pods five inches in length ; a very profitable bearer, coming in a few days earlier than Duke of Albany, and like that variety, A1 for exhibition. Height 3½ to 4 ft. .. .. per pint 2s. 3d. | 4 3

LYE'S FAVOURITE. Improved stock. A new selection of this fine second early variety, of hardy constitution and enormous productiveness, bearing a profusion of long, handsome, slightly curved pods, well filled with peas of excellent marrow flavour. Very useful for early sowing on account of its extreme hardiness. Height 3 to 4 ft. .. .. per pint 1s. 8d. | 3 0

SENATOR. A very prolific variety, bearing the pods mostly in pairs ; these are from four to five inches in length and well filled with peas of a fine marrow flavour. Height 3 ft. per pint 1s. 9d. | 3 3

WILLIAM THE FIRST. Selected stock. One of the finest early green Marrows, combining flavour and earliness, and produces a very heavy crop of slightly curved dark green pods, well filled with peas of excellent colour and flavour, and is one of the best varieties for market purposes. Height 4 ft. per pint 1s. 8d. | 3 0

This splendid maincrop variety continues to hold its position as first favourite for all purposes, on account of its heavy cropping qualities and excellent flavour. It grows to the height of 4 to 5 feet, the haulm being well covered with fine dark-green pods 5 to 6 inches in length and of splendid appearance, each containing 10 to 12 large Peas of the most delicious marrow flavour. It is the leading variety for exhibition purposes, having obtained numerous First Prizes in all parts of the country.

Per pint 2s. 3d.
Per quart 4s. 3d.

PEAS.

Section III.—Main Crop.

☛ DANIELS' SELECTED DUKE OF ALBANY.

A fine selected stock of this useful Main Crop Pea. It grows between 4 and 5 feet in height. The haulm being covered with a very heavy crop of long handsome dark green pods, averaging five inches in length, which are well filled with 10 to 12 large peas of the true marrow flavour. A splendid variety for exhibition, whilst its fine cropping qualities combined with its excellent flavour will recommend it alike to the private grower and the market gardener. **Per pint 2s. 0d. ; .per quart 3s. 9d.**

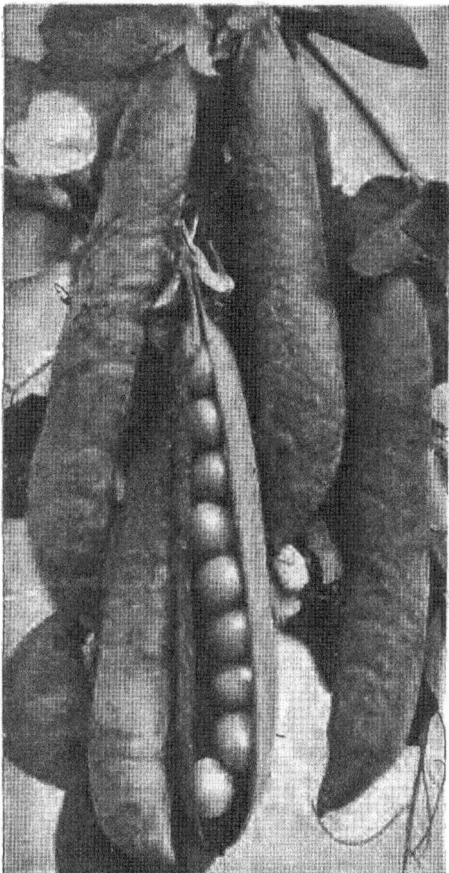

DANIELS' SELECTED DUKE OF ALBANY.

per quart.
s. d.

☛ **THE DANIELS',** An extra large podded Main Crop variety of great merit. It is of robust constitution, the pods are long and handsome, averaging five to six inches in length, and well filled with ten to twelve large peas of the finest marrow flavour. It is a very heavy and reliable cropper, and a most useful sort for exhibition ; strongly recommended for general crop. Height 4 ft. .. per pint 2s. 3d. 4 3

ALDERMAN. Received the highest award from the Royal Horticultural Society. In habit it is strong and branching, producing, a few days later than the Duke of Albany, very large, handsome, straight, deep green pods, five to six inches in length, containing 10 to 11 large peas of the richest Ne Plus Ultra flaveur and quality. Highly recommended for exhibition purposes. Height 5 ft. .. .. — — per pint 2s. 0d. 3 9

DR. MACLEAN. A fine wrinkled Marrow, of vigorous growth, wonderfully productive, flaveur of the first quality. Height 3½ ft. .. .. .. per pint 1s. 8d. 3 0

FILLBASKET. Very prolific. Height 3 ft. per pint 1s. 9d. 3 3

GLADIATOR. The plant is very robust and vigerous, stem branched, growing about three feet in height, exceedingly productive, bearing in pairs an abundance of long curved handsome pods, which are very closely filled with medium-sized peas of excellent quality. First-Class Certificate, R.H.S. Height 3 ft. per pint 1s. 8d. 3 0

MACLEAN'S WONDERFUL, or PRINCE OF WALES. Excellent cropping variety ef superior flavour. Height 3 feet .. — — .. — per pint 1s. 6d. 2 9

PRIDE OF THE MARKET. A fine dwarf variety, ef excellent cropping qualities. The dark green pods which are borne in profusion, each contain 8 te 9 peas, of good size and of the finest marrow flavour ; a grand sort for small gardens where space is limited. Height 2 feet .. .. per pint 1s. 8d. 3 0

" All the Seeds have given great satisfaction last year, the Carrots and Pride of the Market Peas gave enormous crops."—Mr. E. ATKINSON, Minster.

" Your Matchless Marrow Peas have turned out the finest I have ever grown."—Mr. E. BRADFORD, Hampden Park.

" I took First and Second Prizes with your Seeds at Wim Show with Peas and Dwarf Beans."—Mr. H. RAVENSCROFT, Wim.

" I am pleased to say the crops raised from your Seeds last season gave great satisfaction, especially the Matchless Marrow and Stratagem Peas, they were extra large."—Mr. F. GATCH, Beaumcote.

" I have great pleasure in thanking you for Seeds purchased from you : last year's success was great. I won First Prize with Duke of Albany Peas and First with Beet "—Mr. J. GARNETT, Coventry.

" I grew your Matchless Peas last year, also the Recorder, and I must say that they are the finest Peas I have ever grown."—Mr. C. SIMPSON, Luton.

" I had great success from your Peas last year—they were a picture. I have never seen Peas hung in such profusion before."—Mr. H. CARDER, Portland.

" We were delighted with the results we got from your Dwarf Prolific Peas, and only wish we had more garden to be able to grow more of them."—Miss H. LOVE, Skelton.

" Your Seeds were excellent last year, and I can tell you your Dwarf Prolific Pea was easily the best round here ; the Sensation Potatoes are grand croppers."—Mr. E. DUGGAN, Greet.

PEAS.
Section III.—Main Crop.
☛ DANIELS' RECORDER.

A grand long-podded Main Crop variety, growing about 3 feet high. The haulm, which is very robust, is well hung with large pods, which are of a deep green colour, averaging from 5 to 6 inches in length, and contain 10 to 11 fine peas of excellent colour and of the finest marrow flavour. Its great prolificness, combined with the large size of the pods, make it one of the most useful varieties, both for table and exhibition purposes. We can strongly recommend this fine variety to our customers.   Per pint 2s. 3d.   4   3

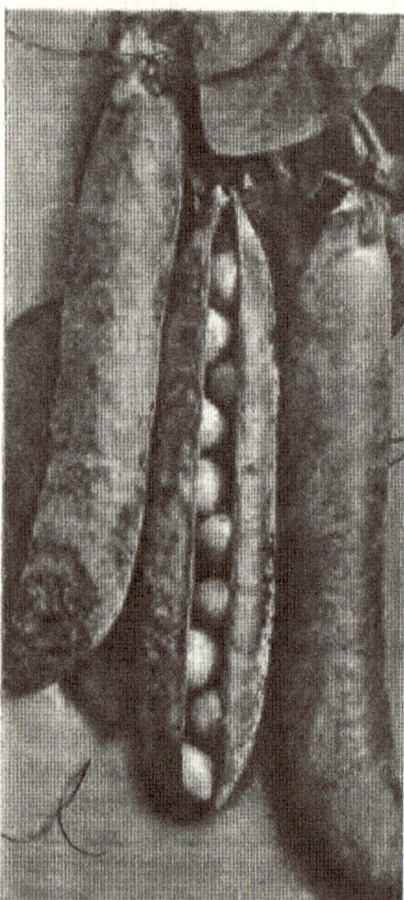

NEW PEA: DANIELS' RECORDER.

☛ **QUITE CONTENT.** This is undoubtedly the largest podded pea yet introduced. It grows to the height of 5 to 6 feet, bearing a great profusion of long, handsome, dark green pods, which are borne mostly in pairs, and average from 6 to 7 inches in length, containing large peas of excellent flavour. It is a most valuable sort for exhibition purposes, having gained numerous first prizes. It is a Main Crop variety, coming fit for use about the same time as Alderman, and somewhat resembles that variety in habit of growth.
(*Very Scarce*). In pkts. only, 1s. per pkt.   —

☛ **DANIELS' COMMANDER.** A superb dwarf Marrow-fat variety of robust constitution, with rich dark green pods and foliage, and is a splendid cropper. The individual pods are of large size, from 4 to 5 inches in length, containing on an average nine large peas of the finest marrow flavour ; will be found a most useful sort for all purposes. Height 1½ to 2 ft.   per pint 2s. 0d.   3   9

☛ **DANIELS' MAIN CROP MARROW.** One of the finest Marrow Peas in cultivation, and of the same flavour as the old Ne Plus Ultra ; but the pods are longer. It is very prolific, bearing a profusion of dark green, well-filled pods, each containing eight to nine large peas of exquisite flavour ; as a Main Crop variety it should be in great demand on account of its numerous good qualities   ..   ..   ..   per pint 2s. 0d.   3   9

STRATAGEM. This is a splendid variety, with pods five to six inches in length, containing eight to ten large fine flavoured peas. First Class Certificate, R.H.S. Our own selected and improved stock. Height 2 ft. ..   ..   per pint 1s. 9d.   3   3

TELEGRAPH. A hardy variety of first-class quality and strong constitution, pods large and well-filled ; also fine for exhibition. Height 4 ft. ..   ..   per pint 1s. 9d.   3   3

TELEPHONE. First Class Certificate, Royal Horticultural Society. This fine variety is good either for exhibition or market purposes. Height 4½ ft. ..   ..   per pint 2s. 0d.   3   9

TRIUMPH. A blue wrinkled Marrow, of exquisite flavour ; the pods are long and well filled, each containing nine to eleven large peas. In constitution it is robust and hardy. Height 2 to 3 ft. ..   ..   per pint 1s. 8d.   3   0

YORKSHIRE HERO. A fine dwarf Marrow Pea, of the Veitch's Perfection type, is very prolific, bearing a profusion of well-filled pods, containing six to eight large peas each ; flavour first-class. Height 3 ft. ..   ..   ..   per pint 1s. 8d.   3   0

" Your Matchless Marrow Peas were simply lovely again this year, 9 and 10 in nearly every pod ; there was none in Worcester Park like them."—Mr. T. LANE, Worcester Park.

" I should like to add that the Peas I had from you last year turned out a great success, much to the envy of all my amateur gardening friends."—H. W. SMITH, Esq., Bournemouth.

PEAS.

Section IV.—Late Varieties.

☞ DANIELS' DISTINCTION.

A very fine late variety which comes in about the same time as "Ne Plus Ultra," and which it rivals in its culinary qualities. The plants are of strong robust growth, attaining a height of about 3½ feet, and producing an abundance of handsome dark green, slightly curved pods, five to six inches in length, filled with large peas of the finest and most delicate flavour. We can highly recommend this as one of the very best for exhibition ; for a late crop it is unrivalled .. .. Per pint 2s. 3d. ; per quart 4s. 3d.

GLORY OF DEVON. Award of Merit, Royal Horticultural Society. A fine addition to our late varieties of Peas. It is of hardy constitution and a robust grower, the foliage being of a rich dark green. The haulm, which grows about four feet in height, is well laden with fine handsome pods, each containing eight to ten large peas of delicious flavour. For exhibition it is first-class .. .. per pint 1s. 9d. ; per quart 3s. 3d.

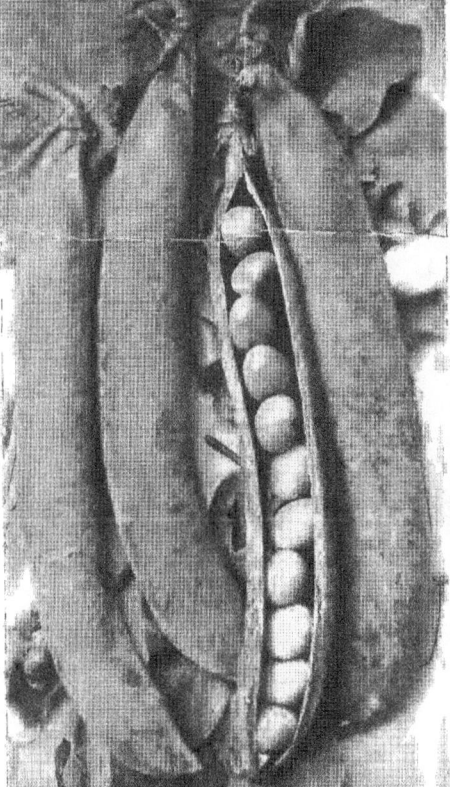

DANIELS' DISTINCTION. *Reduced from a Photograph.*

	per quart. s. d.
AUTOCRAT. First Class Certificate, Royal Horticultural Society. Is of exceedingly robust habit, much branched, foliage of a dark lustrous green. Owing to its strong constitution it is perfectly free from mildew, and is the best late Pea in cultivation. Height 4 ft. per pint 2s. 9d.	3 9
NE PLUS ULTRA. Extra select stock. Height 6 ft. per pint 2s. 0d.	3 9
NE PLUS ULTRA. Delicious Marrow Pea, very prolific, quality first-class, fine for general crop. Height 6 ft. per pint 1s. 9d.	3 3
VEITCH'S PERFECTION MARROW. Extra select stock. One of the best-flavoured of our Marrow Peas. Height 3 ft. .. per pint 1s. 9d.	3 3

TIME REQUIRED FOR PEAS TO COME TO MATURITY.

Taking the time of sowing from end of March to first or second week in April, the following are the approximate times they will take to be fit to gather.

First Early Varieties in about 11 to 12 weeks.
Second ,,   ,,   ,, 13 to 14 ,,
Maincrop   ,,   ,, 15 to 16 ,,
Late   ,,   ,,   17   ,,

In the Northern counties they will take a little longer.

DANIELS' SPECIAL COLLECTIONS
OF CHOICE PEAS FOR SUCCESSION.

We highly recommend these Collections to the notice of the Amateur. By successional sowings, in accordance with instructions, an excellent supply of fresh green Peas may be secured throughout the season.

	s. d.
12 quarts for succession, our selection ..	40 0
6 ,, ,, ,, ..	20 0
4 ,, ,, ,, ..	12 6
12 pints for succession, our selection ..	21 0
6 ,, ,, ,, ..	10 6
4 ,, ,, ,, ..	7 0

SPECIAL COTTAGER'S COLLECTION.

4 varieties. One pint each for succession, our selection, 6s. 6d.
4 varieties. Half-pint each for succession, our selection, 3s. 6d.

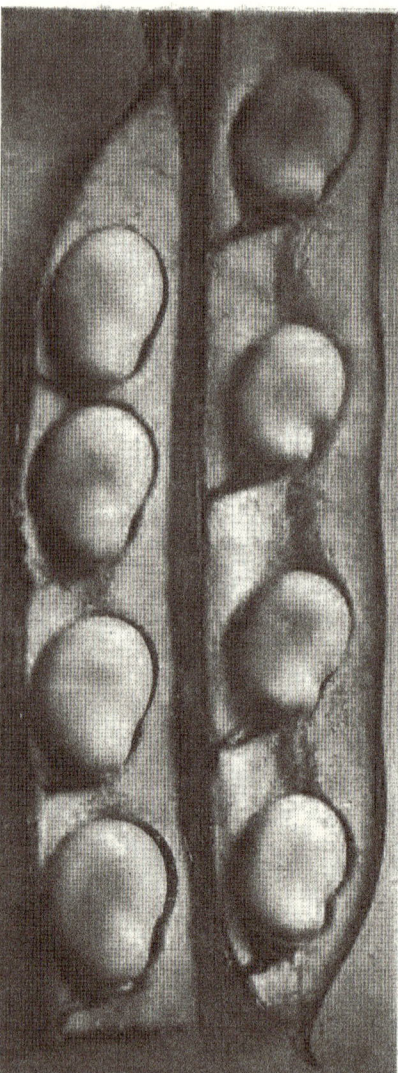

DANIELS' NORFOLK GIANT LONG-POD. *From a Photograph.*

BEANS—Broad.

Cultivation.—This highly nutritious vegetable grows well in any good garden soil, but responds readily to liberal treatment and should, therefore, when possible, be grown in well-prepared ground which has received a good supply of manure. The cultivation is of the easiest and everybody should be able to grow them successfully.

The earliest sowing should be made in February with our "**Selected Long-Pod**," this being one of the earliest and best sorts. For the main crop, sow in March and for a succession in April.

The seed should be sown in double rows 6 inches apart, with an intervening space of 3 feet between the pairs of rows; place the seed 6 inches apart in the rows, earth up the plants by drawing the soil around them, when they are about 6 inches high, give a good covering of ashes to keep off the slugs.

When the plants have made a good growth and set a nice quantity of bloom, the centres should be nipped out, thereby throwing more vigour into the pods.

A liberal supply of liquid manure given at intervals during the bearing season will add much to the size of the pods, as also will a mulching of decayed manure, if put on before the hot weather comes.

The Windsor varieties whilst not giving such long pods are of excellent flavour; the best varieties for exhibition purposes are Daniels' Norfolk Giant Long-pod, which produces the finest pods of any of the long-podded section, and Daniels' Mammoth Windsor, which is by far the best of its class.

WHITE-SEEDED VARIETIES.

per quart—s. d.

DANIELS' NORFOLK GIANT LONG-POD. The longest-podded Bean known, has been grown up to 18 inches in length. The pods are of very handsome shape and excellent quality. First-class for exhibition, having obtained numerous First Prizes per pint 1s. 9d. 3 3

DANIELS' MAMMOTH WINDSOR. The largest Broad Bean in cultivation. Very prolific, bearing a large quantity of fine broad pods, containing beans of exceptional size. These are of fine quality, and of flavour equal to the old Broad Windsor per pint 1s. 6d. 2 0

DANIELS' SELECTED LONG-POD. A grand selection of the Early Long-pod. Very prolific, pods larger and finer than the old variety; useful for exhibition .. per pint 1s. 6d. 2 0

BROAD WINDSOR. Fine selected stock .. per pint 1s. 3d. 2 3

HARLINGTON WINDSOR. Larger and finer pods than the old Windsor; very prolific .. per pint 1s. 4d. 2 6

JOHNSON'S WONDERFUL (Mackie's Monarch) per pint 1s. 3d. 2 3

MAZAGAN. Small, early, and hardy .. .. per pint 1s. 3d. 2 3

GREEN-SEEDED VARIETIES.

per quart—s. d.

DANIELS' IMPROVED GREEN WINDSOR. An abundant bearer, pods large; a great improvement on the old variety .. .. per pint 1s. 6d. 2 0

DANIELS' MAMMOTH GREEN LONG-POD. A very fine selection of this type, the pods being longer and much better filled than those of the old variety, and of excellent flavour .. .. .. per pint 1s. 6d. 2 0

BECK'S GREEN GEM. A fine dwarf bean, excellent for small gardens .. .. per pint 1s. 4d. 2 6

"The Long-Pod Beans did very well, every seed germinated, the crop being one of the earliest round here."—Mr. J. FAULKERS, Lound.

"I won First Prize with Long-Pod Beans, some of the pods over 16 inches long, and greatly admired."—Mr. R. JACKLIN, Binbrook.

"Your Seeds last season gave every satisfaction, especially Giant Long-Pod Beans, some of which were 12 inches long; also Matchless Marrow Peas could not met with describe can given, Brussels Sprouts were worthy of being photographed."—Mr. A. HOLMES, Howarden.

"I am pleased to say I am more than satisfied with garden Seeds supplied by you, which include Peas, Broad Beans, Parsnip, Carrot, and five kinds of Potatoes."—Mr. J. HARRINGTON, North Inticoton.

"I am pleased to inform you how successful I was at our Annual Show, Four Specials, Six Firsts and One Second."—Mr. B. ASHWORTH, Somersoat.

BEANS—Runner.

Cultivation.—Runner Beans form one of the most important and profitable of all garden crops grown for Summer and Autumn use, and yield a liberal supply of vegetables available for use after the main crop Peas are over.

They are easy of culture and may be grown as screens in small gardens, thus serving the double purpose of covering a trellis or wall and at the same time yielding a crop of delicious vegetables.

The ground should be prepared in the same manner as for other Beans, but Runners being somewhat tender the seed should not be sown until early in May.

Sow the seed in double rows 9 inches apart, and, if possible, allow a space of 12 feet between each double row, cropping the intervening space with other vegetables.

For a succession make further sowings in June and July.

When the plants are about 9 inches high, draw the earth round them, and place tall, strong stakes to the rows, taking care to make them very firm and able to withstand the wind. A good mulching of rotted manure during the cropping season will lengthen the period of bearing and give quality to the beans.

Where it is impossible to procure tall stakes, it is the practice to take out the leading growths when the plants are about a foot high, thus encouraging a spreading habit and in this way good crops may be grown and space economised.

The best varieties both for exhibition and general purposes are **Daniels' Giant White** and **Daniels' Giant Scarlet.**

per quart.
s. d.

☞ **DANIELS' GIANT SCARLET.** A grand variety both for exhibition and the table, and is at the same time one of the most prolific varieties with which we are acquainted. The pods are long, straight, and of excellent quality. Our own selected stock
per ½ pint 1s. 3d. ; pint 2s. 3d. 4 3

☞ **DANIELS' GIANT WHITE.** This is without doubt the finest type of Runner Bean extant, bearing in profusion long, green, thick, fleshy pods, upwards of twelve inches in length and nearly two inches in breadth. This variety, besides the best for culinary purposes, will also be found a grand exhibition kind
per ½ pint 1s. 6d. ; pint 2s. 6d. —

☞ **SCARLET EMPEROR.** A giant amongst Scarlet Runner Beans, producing fine straight pods fifteen inches in length, and is enormously productive. A grand sort for exhibition .. .. per ½ pint 1s. 3d. ; pint 2s. 3 9

BEST OF ALL. One of the longest-podded of the Scarlet Runners, very prolific. The pods, which are long, straight, and very handsome, are produced in large clusters. It is of excellent table quality, and one of the best for exhibition per pint 1s. 9d. 3 3

NE PLUS ULTRA. A fine variety for exhibition and main crop, producing a large quantity of fine pods of splendid form, from ten to fourteen inches long, and quite straight. To grow it to perfection each bean should be planted one foot apart in the row .. .. per pint 1s. 9d. 3 3

OLD SCARLET RUNNER. For general crop per pint 1s. 9d. 3 3

VEITCH'S CLIMBING KIDNEY BEAN. First Class Certificate, Royal Horticultural Society. This Bean combines the best features of the two types, Dwarf French and Scarlet Runner. It crops earlier than the Runners and has all the delicate flavour and quality of the Dwarfs ; height 6 to 7 feet per pint 2s. 0d. 3 9

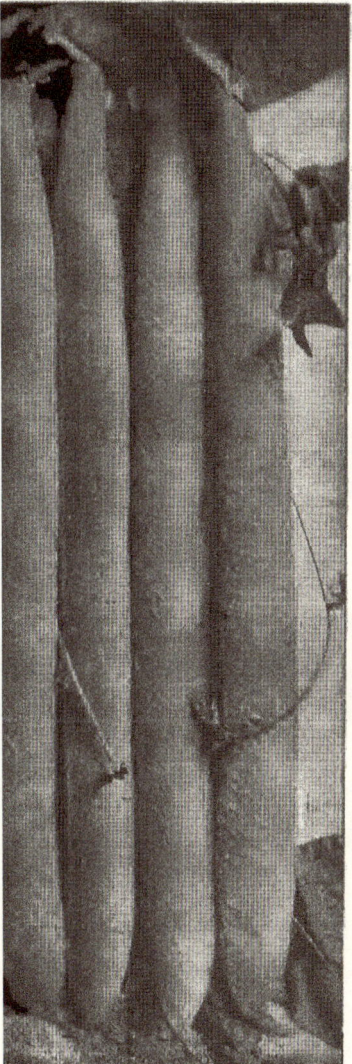

DANIELS' GIANT SCARLET. *Reduced from a Photograph.*

BEANS—Dwarf French.

Cultivation.—This useful vegetable may be grown by almost any one, as sufficient space for a row may be found in even the smallest garden. With attention to the preparation and manuring of the ground, there should be no difficulty in having a continuous supply of French Beans for a considerable portion of the Summer and Autumn.

The culture is of the simplest ; the ground having been thoroughly dug and manured in early Spring, the Beans should be planted about the end of April ; the rows should be 2½ feet apart and the Beans placed about 4 inches apart in the row, any gaps in the row may be filled up by transplanting the seedlings when just past the seed leaf.

The soil should be drawn round the plants to protect them from cold winds in Spring, and during the time of bearing occasional waterings with weak liquid manure will add much to the size of the produce and lengthen the period of bearing. Daniels' "Incomparable" can be highly recommended on account of its great prolificness and excellent quality.

Where greenhouses are available the earliest sowing may be made at the beginning of April and the young plants transferred to the outside border when large enough to handle. A crop may also be grown in the early months of the year in heated frames or greenhouses, the seed being sown in 8-inch pots half filled with good rich soil, and the pots gradually filled up with soil as the plants grow. It is most important that French Beans should be gathered as soon as ready, otherwise the plants will gradually give up blooming and the crop be much reduced.

DANIELS NCOMPARABLE. *From a Photograph.*

per quart.
s. d.

DANIELS' INCOMPARABLE. This splendid dwarf Kidney Bean since its introduction has fully justified our high opinion of it, both as regards quality and prolificness. The pods are of great length, straight, and of a rich clear green colour, very tender, and of the best culinary quality. It is of strong constitution, sturdy habit, and wonderfully prolific. It is quite distinct in the seed and has proved a decided acquisition .. per pint 2s. 0d. 3 9

DANIELS' WONDERFUL (new). This is without doubt the longest podded Dwarf French Bean yet introduced. The pods which are very straight and handsome, grow to the length of 10 to 12 inches, and are produced in great abundance. It is at the same time very tender and of fine quality. Excellent alike for exhibition and the table, and is highly recommended .. .. per pint 2s. 0d. 3 9

DANIELS' EARLY BLACK WONDER. We can highly recommend this splendid variety as one of the hardiest and most prolific French Beans in cultivation. The pods are long, of a light rich green colour, tender, and of fine flavour per pint 1s. 9d. 2 9

DANIELS' WHITE QUEEN. This may be best described as a sport from Canadian Wonder. The seed is white, whilst it quite equals that well-known variety in productiveness and quality. The dry seed is quite equal to the best Haricot Beans for cooking purposes .. .. per pint 1s. 9d. 3 3

CANADIAN WONDER. Abundant bearer, very fleshy and tender. The pods are long and of excellent shape and quality ; one of the best for general crop per pint 1s. 6d. 2 0

EARLY GOLDEN BUTTER. Pods thick and fleshy, nearly transparent, and of a bright yellow colour which is retained when boiled ; excellent flavour per pint 1s. 9d. 3 3

NEGRO LONG-POD. Useful variety, heavy cropper per pint 1s. 6d. 2 9

NE PLUS' ULTRA. The finest Kidney Bean in cultivation for all purposes. First-Class Certificate, R.H.S. .. per pint 1s. 9d. 3 3

ALL KINDS MIXED .. per pint 1s. 6d. 2 0

"I have had all my small Seeds from you this year, and I have got the best garden I have ever had—Onions, Carrots, Beet, and everything so splendid."—Mr. A. W. G. HAGGAR, Much Hadham.

"I am very pleased with the Seeds I had this year, they have all done remarkably well. I took one First and one Third Prize from our show this year."—Mr. T. JONES, Probus.

BRUSSELS SPROUTS.

Cultivation.—To grow Brussels Sprouts successfully the seed should be sown at the latter end of February or early in March on a sheltered border, or in a frame. Prick out the seedlings about four inches apart into seed beds as soon as they have made the first leaves, and directly the weather allows plant out permanently into well prepared ground, such as is used for general garden crops. For a later crop, a sowing should be made at the end of March, or early in April, and the seedlings planted as soon as possible; they cannot very well be planted out too early. Brussels Sprouts require plenty of room to develop, and therefore they should never be planted thickly. About 2½ feet apart in the row and 3 feet between the rows would be a suitable distance. Give a good supply of water when they are first planted, and keep the ground loose by frequent use of the hoe.

Brussels Sprouts thrive much better by themselves than when planted amongst other crops. In dry weather liberal supplies of liquid manure will be found of great advantage. Daniels' Colossal and Defiance are first-class stocks, and will be found the best for exhibition purposes and for general use.

per ox.—s. d

DANIELS COLOSSAL. *Reduced from a Photograph.*

DANIELS' COLOSSAL. One of the finest and best in cultivation, of very vigorous growth, bearing sprouts of a large, compact, globular shape all the way up the stem; these will be found of a more delicate and finer flavour than any other of the Cabbage tribe .. .. per pkt. 6d.   1 6

DANIELS' DEFIANCE. A finely selected stock of medium height, is exceedingly productive, the stem being well covered with large compact sprouts of the most excellent flavour. A very useful variety for exhibition purposes, and one of the best for general use .. .. per pkt. 6d.   1 6

AIGBURTH. A tall growing variety, of fine quality. The sprouts are of good size and very firm .. .. per pkt. 4d.   1 0

DALKEITH. A fine selected stock of medium height, the stems being well covered with solid sprouts of fine flavour .. .. per pkt. 3d.   1 0

SCRYMGER'S GIANT. An excellent tall variety; stems well covered with fine sprouts, of first-class flavour .. .. .. per pkt. 4d.   1 0

SOLIDITY. A fine dwarf variety, the stems being well covered with extra hard solid sprouts of medium size and of the finest quality per pkt. 4d.   1 0

" I am pleased to say the Seeds and Potatoes have turned out well, everything gave the greatest satisfaction. I have been dealing with your firm for 30 years, and your Seeds have never failed with me."—Mr. C. HOLLIDGE, Plumstead, S.E.

" I had excellent results last year from your Seeds. I had Brussels Sprouts (Colossal) 3½ to 4 feet high, covered with sprouts as big as my fist from the ground to the top of the stalk."—Mr. G. KIRTLAND, North Evington.

" I must say over again your Seeds are excellent, I had bumping crops, especially Brussels Sprouts and Kidney Beans."—Mr. A. PIDOUX, Staplehill.

BORECOLE or KALE.

Cultivation.—Borecole is of great value for providing a supply of tender green heads from Christmas onwards, during the very severe weather when Cabbages and Broccoli are not available. Many varieties of Borecole are quite ornamental and present most attractive objects in the kitchen garden. Sow the seed in April in seed beds, and when the plants are large enough transplant them into their permanent quarters about three feet apart. As an alternative they may be planted between Potato rows.

Borecole likes good soil, but does not require liberal treatment with liquid manure, etc., as many plants of the same family do. Give a thorough watering at the time of planting out. If there is any tendency to "clubbing" noticed in the garden, a dressing of lime applied in the Spring previous to planting will be found of great advantage. Daniels' Improved Drumhead can be highly recommended on account of its excellent flavour. It is much milder than some varieties. Daniels' Moss Curled Exhibition will be found invaluable for general purposes.

per ox.—s. d.

DANIELS' MOSS CURLED EXHIBITION. The finest strain of curled Kale in cultivation. It is of medium height, foliage dark green, and beautifully curled, is very hardy, and may be relied upon to stand the severest Winters. For exhibition it is unsurpassed .. .. .. per pkt. 6d.   1 6

DANIELS' IMPROVED DRUMHEAD. A valuable variety for Winter use. Hearts up like a Drumhead Cabbage with broad leaves; very mild and tender when cooked, and of the true Kale flavour per pkt. 4d.   1 0

COTTAGER'S. Exceedingly hardy .. .. „ 0 10

DWARF GREEN CURLED. A hardy dwarf-stemmed variety, of mild flavour, one of the best for general crop .. .. .. „ 0 10

TALL GREEN CURLED. The Tall Scotch Kale .. .. „ 0 10

VARIEGATED or GARNISHING. A fine curled-leaved variety, beautifully variegated, very useful and ornamental for garnishing, also valuable for Winter gardening .. .. per pkt. 4d.   1 0

ASPARAGUS KALE. Fine for winter use .. .. .. „ 4d.   1 0

BROCCOLI.

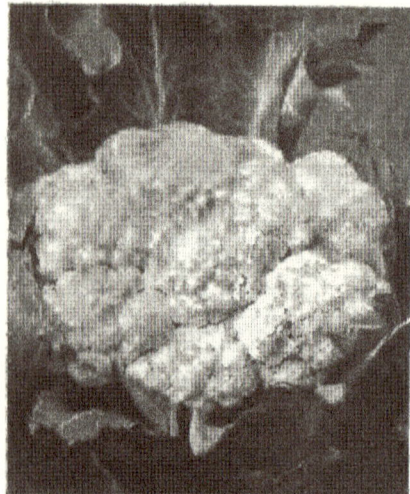

MICHAELMAS WHITE.

FIRST DIVISION.

Sow in April and May for cutting in September, October, and November the same year.

	per pkt. s. d.	per oz. s. d.
☞ **MICHAELMAS WHITE.** This is a most excellent variety for early use and invaluable as a succession to the Summer Cauliflowers. It is of quick growth, forming large firm heads of fine texture and first-class quality. If sown in March it will be fit to cut at Michaelmas	1 0	2 6
VEITCH'S SELF-PROTECTING AUTUMN. Extremely valuable to grow as a succession to " Autumn Giant " Cauliflower. The heads are well protected by the strong vigorous foliage, and, in some seasons, it may be had in good condition till nearly Christmas	0 9	2 0
WALCHEREN. A useful variety for early Autumn use. Heads of good size and of fine even texture	1 0	2 6
WHITE CAPE. A valuable variety for Autumn, coming into use in August and September	1 0	2 6

" I have just finished cutting the finest lot of Broccoli (over 200) I have ever grown, many of them weighing from 5 to 6 lbs. each."—Mr. W. BARTLETT, Redland, Bristol.

" I am growing Broccoli that is a treat to see anywhere. I have had one Broccoli from your seed that weighed 13 lbs."—Mr. I. DAVIES, Brynamman.

" I am cutting some splendid heads of Broccoli, Norfolk Giant, grown from your last year's Seeds. I also grow some splendid Alderman Peas, 70 pods weighing 1 lb."—Mr. A. E. JARVIS, Tottenham.

" I should like to say what grand Broccoli I have had from your Methven's June Seed."—Mr. E. LILL, Wadsley Bridge.

" I have taken Prizes with your Seeds every year."—Mr. J. ROWLES, Lessingham.

" The Seeds I had from you last spring have given me great satisfaction, I have taken four First, two Second and two Third Prizes."—Mr. T. STANTON, Carlton Scroop.

SECOND DIVISION.

Sow in April, May, and June, for cutting in January and February the following Spring.

	per pkt. s. d.	per oz. s. d.
☞ **DANIELS' NEW YEAR.** A vigorous, compact, dwarf-growing variety, with self-protecting foliage over-lapping snow-white heads, of excellent quality and flavour ; a most valuable variety	0 9	2 0
☞ **DANIELS' QUEEN OF SPRING.** This splendid variety comes in for cutting during February, is of dwarf compact habit, producing large snow-white heads of the finest texture. Its earliness, combined with its excellent quality, makes it a valuable addition to our Spring Broccoli .. .. .. In pkts. only	1 6	...
DANIELS' SELECTED SNOW'S WHITE. A fine selected stock of this well-known Winter Broccoli. The heads are large, firm and beautifully white, one of the most useful of the Winter varieties	0 9	2 0
ADAMS' EARLY WHITE. A strong growing variety of hardy constitution. Heads large pure white	0 6	1 6
MAMMOTH WINTER WHITE. Large pure white heads of the finest quality, coming into use in mid-winter, well-protected with long over-lapping leaves	0 9	2 0
PENZANCE EARLY WHITE. A useful early variety, producing fine large heads of excellent quality	0 6	1 6
ST. HILARY. A splendid Broccoli of hardy, vigorous constitution. Dwarf, compact growth, and large white heads, coming into use in January	1 0	2 6
WHITE SPROUTING. Produces a large crop of tender white sprouts of the most excellent flavour	0 6	1 6

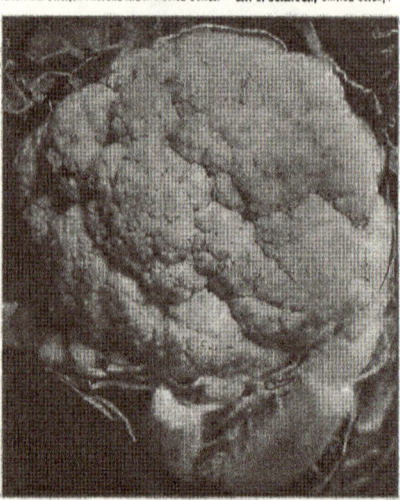

DANIELS' QUEEN OF SPRING.

BROCCOLI.

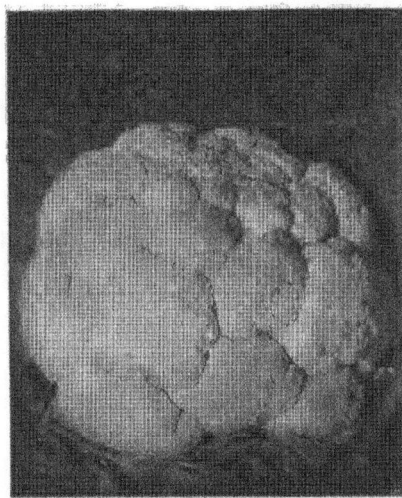

DANIELS' NORFOLK GIANT.

FOURTH DIVISION.

Sow in May and June for cutting in May and June the following season.

DANIELS' KING OF THE BROCCOLI. This splendid variety comes in for cutting from the beginning of May to the first week in June, and as a late kind cannot be surpassed. It is of a fine dwarf habit, and being well protected is exceedingly hardy. The heads are remarkably fine ... 0 9   2 0

DANIELS' LATEST WHITE. One of the best kinds for filling up the gap or period that occurs between Broccoli and Cauliflower 0 6   1 6

METHVEN'S JUNE. One of the latest Broccoli in cultivation, producing fine pure white heads till nearly the end of June 0 6   1 6

QUEEN. Very fine, heads well protected 0 6   1 6

Cultivation.—This excellent vegetable is of the greatest value during the Winter and early Spring, when Cauliflowers are not obtainable and vegetables generally are scarce. They like a good rich firm soil, which has during the previous Autumn been thoroughly trenched and liberally manured. If possible, choose a piece of land on which Celery has been grown. The earliest sowing of seed should be made at the latter end of March, and the principal sowings during April, whilst May will be soon enough for the late varieties. Sow the seed either in a warm sheltered border or in a frame, in drills eight or nine inches apart and one inch deep. When the plants are large enough to handle, lose no time in pricking them out, as they quickly suffer if allowed to remain too long in the seed bed, becoming drawn and weak. The final plantings should be commenced in May, and followed on as opportunity occurs until the end of July, and as land becomes available. Choose the strongest plants first, as by this means a much better succession will be obtained.

The most important point in planting out Broccoli is to be quite sure that the ground is very firm; the harder it is the better it will be for the plants, as they will thereby be able to withstand the Winter, therefore if the land was trenched and manured during the past Winter, do not have it dug again just previous to planting out. Make the rows about 2½ feet apart and place the plants about two feet apart in the row. Water the plants thoroughly after planting and keep the weeds down.

THIRD DIVISION.

Sow end of March and beginning of April for cutting in March and April the following season.

per pkt.   per oz.
s. d.   s. d.

DANIELS' NORFOLK GIANT. A magnificent variety of robust and compact habit, stem short, the flower heads are exceedingly large, beautifully white, and of the finest quality, being well protected by luxuriant, over-lapping foliage. The best and hardiest variety for general Spring use 0 9   2 0

EASTER DAY or SPRINGTIDE. A fine hardy variety of dwarf compact habit and vigorous growth, producing large, firm, white heads of excellent quality, which are well protected. One of the best kinds for maincrop in Spring .. .. in pkts. only 1 0

KNIGHT'S PROTECTING. One of the hardiest of our Spring Broccoli. The heads are well protected, large, and of fine quality 0 6   1 6

LEAMINGTON. Well-known hardy variety. Heads large and solid 0 6   1 6

PURPLE SPROUTING. Very hardy Winter variety, producing an abundant crop of Sprouts of excellent flavour 0 4   1 0

EVIDENCE OF QUALITY.

"I am well satisfied with all Seeds sent me last year, I cannot praise one more than another."—Mr. J. COLLOR, Dover.

"I should like to express the satisfaction received from Seeds; they were admired by everyone. I took First Prize for them."—Mr. F. WILKES, Hoole.

"The Seeds I had from you last year have yielded splendid crops." Mr. G. BATEY, Bexley Heath.

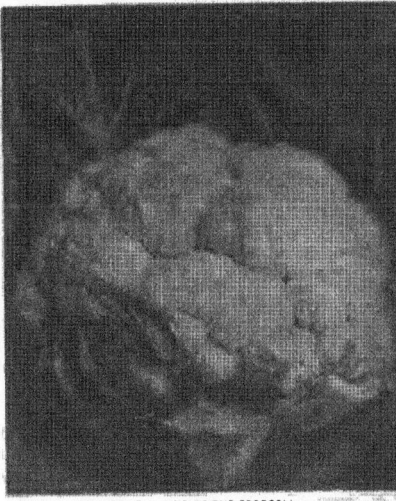

DANIELS' KING OF THE BROCCOLI.

BEET.

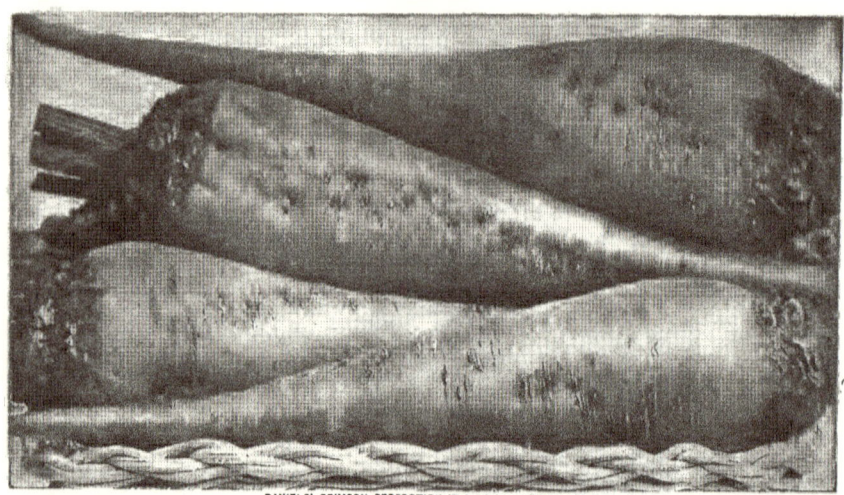

DANIELS' CRIMSON PERFECTION (*Reduced from a Photograph*).

Cultivation.—To ensure a crop of good Beetroot, it is of the highest importance that the seed should be of the very best strain procurable, such as offered by ourselves. Another very important point to observe is that the ground must not be specially manured for this crop, a good plan being to select a plot that has been cropped during the previous season with French Beans, Potatoes, or Celery. The soil should be a good light loam where possible, and in an open part of the garden; the ground should be deeply trenched (the deeper the better) quite early in the season. Before sowing, the ground should be made firm and level.

Sow the seed any time from the middle of April to the end of May. For an early crop New Red Globe is one of the best. Daniels' Crimson Perfection and Green Top will be found the most useful for a general crop. The seed should be sown in drills one inch deep and about 18 inches from row to row. A liberal quantity of seed should be used to ensure a good plant, and when the seedlings are nicely up, they should be thinned out, leaving them about 9 inches apart. As a rule those sown at the end of May produce roots of better quality. Keep the beds regularly hoed and weeded so that the soil may be free about the plants.

When specimen roots are wanted for Exhibition, it is the usual practice to make holes about 2 feet deep in the bed with a crowbar, and fill them with fine soil. The seeds are sown in these and thinned out, one plant being left to each hole. In this way splendidly shaped roots are grown. The crop should be lifted in October and stored in dry sand in a shed or cellar for Winter use. Care should be taken that the roots are not injured in any way, or they will bleed and lose quality; also the leaves should not be cut but twisted off with the hand. In this way the roots may be kept until the following Summer.

	per oz.—s. d.
DANIELS' CRIMSON PERFECTION SALAD. A grand dark-leaved variety of medium size and very symmetrical. The flesh, which is of the finest texture, is deep crimson in colour and of excellent quality. A first-class sort for exhibition. Owing to the fine deep colour of its foliage it is very valuable for ornamental purposes .. .. .. per pkt. 6d.	1 6
DANIELS' GREEN-TOP. This splendid Green-top Beet is chiefly remarkable for the fine deep colour of the roots, which are of excellent shape and of first-class quality and flavour .. .. per pkt. 6d.	1 6
CHELTENHAM GREEN-TOP. Roots very dark, of excellent quality; one of the best for pickling .. .. per pkt. 4d.	1 0
DARK RED SALAD. A very useful variety, roots a good colour	0 10
DELL'S BLACK. A fine dark-foliaged variety, roots small, but of exceptionally fine shape and colour .. .. per pkt. 4d.	1 3
EGYPTIAN DARK RED TURNIP-ROOTED. One of the best for Summer Salads, as it comes to maturity very early ..	0 10

	per oz.—s. d
DANIELS' INTERMEDIATE BLOOD RED. A new and distinct variety; the roots are of medium length and tankard shaped, a convenient size for boiling and no waste in cutting. The roots are of fine colour and excellent quality; it is as early as the turnip-rooted sorts, and can be pulled easily by hand. per pkt. 1s.	—
DANIELS' RED GLOBE. A valuable variety for early use. The roots are of fine globular shape, of rich colour and excellent flavour. It should be used early, if allowed to stand too long it loses as to quality. Useful for exhibition .. .. per pkt. 6d.	1 6
NUTTING'S DWARF RED. Fine dark foliage .. per pkt. 4d.	1 0
FRAGNELL'S EXHIBITION. A fine dark-leaved variety, roots very handsome and of good colour .. .. per pkt. 6d.	1 6
SUGAR BEET. Good stock	0 8

CARROTS.

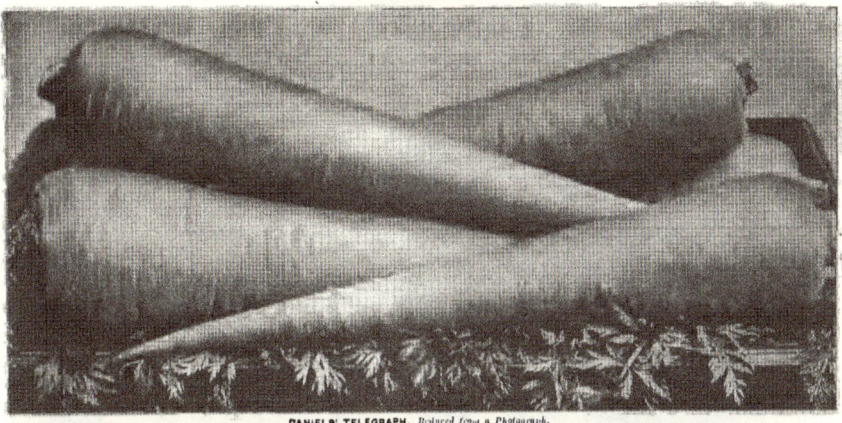

DANIELS' TELEGRAPH, *Reduced from a Photograph.*

Stump-rooted Varieties.

per oz.—s. d.

☞ **DANIELS' SCARLET PERFECTION.** A grand main crop variety of the intermediate type, and being stump-rooted, it is well adapted for growing on soils where deep culture is not possible. The roots are of a bright orange colour, very handsome and uniform in shape, with a fine clear skin, which makes it a most desirable sort for exhibition. It is one of the best flavoured and heaviest cropping varieties for general use, and one we can highly recommend .. .. per pkt. 6d.   1 6

DANIELS' NEW EARLY FORCING HORN. One of the earliest Carrots yet introduced. In shape it is nearly round. They can be left thickly in the row, and drawn for use as required pkt. 4d.   1 0

DANIELS' HARBINGER. A fine Carrot for early exhibition ; the roots are of good shape and excellent quality, averaging four to five inches in length, and three inches in diameter. It is a distinct and useful Carrot .. .. .. per pkt. 4d.   1 0

EARLY FRENCH NANTES. A medium-sized, stump-rooted variety of very fine quality .. .. per pkt. 4d.   1 0

EARLY SCARLET HORN. A stump-rooted variety. Very useful for first early crops .. .. per pkt. 4d.   1 0

Long Varieties.

per oz. s. d.

☞ **DANIELS' TELEGRAPH.** This grand Carrot is one of the best forms of intermediate yet introduced, being far in advance of the old James' Scarlet. It produces a heavy crop of roots, which are of uniform shape, attractive colour, and very clear in the skin. Where sufficient depth of soil exists it will prove one of the most profitable sorts to grow. It is unequalled for exhibition purposes, having obtained more First Prizes than any Carrot with which we are acquainted per pkt. 6d.   1 0

JAMES' SCARLET (Intermediate). Excellent for shallow soil. One of the heaviest cropping and most useful for general use .. 0 10

LONG RED ST. VALERY. A very choice stock, producing clean handsome roots and a great improvement on the Long Surrey. Fine for exhibition .. .. per pkt. 4d.   1 0

LONG RED SURREY or **LONG ORANGE.** Roots long, of good shape, and fine quality ; on a deep soil it will produce a very heavy crop 0 10

Cultivation.—By attention to a few points of importance, splendid clean straight Carrots can be cultivated without great delay. It is not necessary to manure the land for a Carrot crop, in fact, freshly manured land is a drawback ; the soil should be (where possible) of a deep light nature, and the land should, the Autumn previously, be deeply trenched two to three feet, and a quite light dressing of manure given at the same time ; land which has been recently used for Celery is excellent, and will not need specially manuring.

For the earliest crop, make a sowing on the hotbed in frames between the rows of early Potatoes, and pull the Carrots quite small. The first sowing of the outdoor crop should be made early in April on a warm border, Daniels' "Harbinger" or "Forcing Horn" being excellent kinds ; make other sowings in succession through the Summer until August, when the best kind to sow is "Scarlet Horn." For main crop, "Daniels' Scarlet Perfection" and "Telegraph" can be highly recommended.

Carrot seed should be sown on borders of finely worked soil, in drills about a foot apart. When the plants are nicely up, thin out gradually, leaving the smaller growing kinds, such as "Forcing Horn," to be pulled as required, and the larger kinds seven to nine inches apart. Keep the hoe going between the rows to ensure cleanliness, and nothing more is needed until the end of October, when the crop should be lifted, the tops carefully twisted off, and the roots stored in dry sand in a cellar, for use as needed during the Winter.

When specimen roots are wanted for exhibition, it is the practice to make holes with a crowbar, and fill with fine soil, sowing the seeds on the top and thinning out to one plant in each hole, as advised for Parsnips.

CHICORY.

per pkt.—s. d.

IMPROVED LARGE-LEAVED. Excellent for blanching 0 6

LARGE-ROOTED or **COFFEE** 0 6

WHITLOF. Equally good as a salad or boiled. Sow in June .. 0 6

CORN SALAD (Lamb's Lettuce).

per oz. s. d.

GREEN CABBAGING. A fine variety, rosette-shaped per pkt. 6d.   1 6

LETTUCE-LEAVED .. .. ,, 6d.   1 6

LARGE ROUND-LEAVED DUTCH .. .. .. ,, 6d.   1 6

DANIELS' DEFIANCE.
THE FINEST CABBAGE IN THE WORLD.

We highly recommend this magnificent Cabbage, which we claim to be the finest in the world. It is medium early, short-legged, and compact, and grows to a great size, at the same time retaining all the tenderness and delicacy of flavour of the smaller varieties. First-class for the private grower or market gardener. The seed we offer, which is our own true and original stock, has been carefully grown at our Seed Grounds from the stalks of fully developed and first-class Cabbages only, and owing to the many years of careful selection will be found of an unequalled and thoroughly reliable quality. Per packet 6d. ; per oz. 1s. 6d.

DANIELS' DEFIANCE. *Reduced from a Photograph.*

EVIDENCE OF QUALITY.

" I am delighted with the Defiance Cabbage, which has proved the best results yet on my plot."—Mr. L. DAVIES, Prithdir.

" You will no doubt be pleased to hear I have again got 1st First Prize for your Defiance Cabbage."—Mr. C. CATOR, Waterbeach.

CABBAGES.

per oz.—s. d.

DANIELS' LITTLE QUEEN. The earliest Cabbage in cultivation. It is distinct in appearance and of dwarf compact habit, with very firm heads. A most useful variety both for Spring and Autumn sowing. Our own selected stock .. .. .. **per pkt. 6d.** 1 6

ELLAM'S EARLY DWARF. A first-class Early Cabbage in all respects. Being very compact, they can be planted close together, thus growing double the quantity of plants on the same space than most kinds. A fine early market kind, and one of the best for Autumn sowing .. .. .. per pkt. 4d. 1 0

DANIELS' IMPROVED ENFIELD MARKET. A first-class stock, earlier and larger than the ordinary variety per pkt. 4d. 1 0

FIRST AND BEST. An early dwarf Cabbage of great merit ; heads very firm and compact, and of excellent quality per pkt. 4d. 1 0

ENFIELD MARKET. A most useful maincrop variety; heads large and solid, and of good flavour 0 10

EWING'S No. 1. A very fine early dwarf Cabbage per pkt. 3d. 1 0

FLOWER OF SPRING. An early variety of compact habit, heads solid and very tender. Very useful for Autumn sowing pkt. 4d. 1 0

NONPAREIL IMPROVED DWARF. Early variety, dwarf and compact ; very useful for market growers .. per pkt. 4d. 1 0

OFFENHAM. A fine variety of dwarf and compact habit, very useful ; one of the best for Autumn sowing .. per pkt. 4d. 1 0

ROSETTE COLEWORT. Very hardy ; the rosette-like heads grow to a nice size, and are very delicate eating .. per pkt. 3d. 1 0

ST. JOHN'S DAY. A fine, dwarf, very early variety of the Drum-head type, but much smaller and of fine quality per pkt. 3d. 1 0

WHEELER'S IMPERIAL. A fine variety of the Nonpareil type, heads very firm and of fine quality .. .. per pkt. 4d. 1 0

WINNINGSTADT. A most useful late variety, with pointed heads, which are exceedingly firm and keep sound a long time pkt. 4d. 1 0

CHRISTMAS DRUMHEAD. A fine, dwarf, compact Cabbage of excellent flavour, of a dark green colour. A splendid variety for culinary purposes .. .. per pkt. 4d. 1 0

UTILITY (new). A very dwarf early and compact variety for spring sowing, is of very rapid growth. Sown in March, it can be cut in July and early August .. .. per pkt. 4d. 1 0

DANIELS' EARLY DRUMHEAD. This variety does not grow quite so large as the ordinary field varieties, is of dwarf compact habit, with solid heads, and of mild flavour 0 10

" I am now cutting your Little Queen Cabbage, which was sown last August, and are very delicious."—Mr. W. DANIELS, Derby.

" Your Flower of Spring Cabbage were admired by all last year ; this is why my neighbours want some of the same kind."—Mr. F. J. BRADDISH, Sampford.

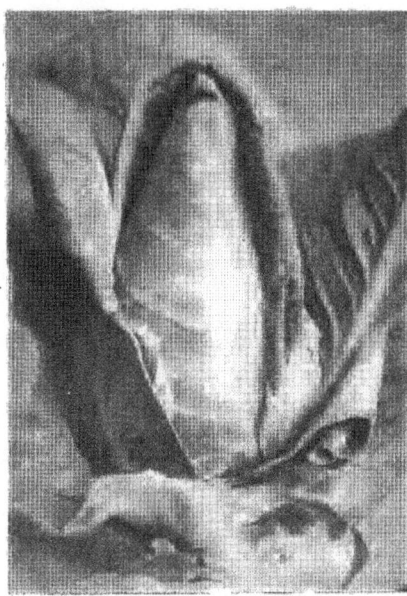

DANIELS' LITTLE QUEEN. *(Reduced from a Photograph.)*

Cultivation.- Cabbages are without doubt the most useful and at the same time the most easily grown of our Spring and Autumn Vegetables, and can be grown without much outlay by everyone possessing a garden or an allotment. They prefer a good rich loamy soil, and being what is termed a gross feeder will respond well to good cultivation, and will repay any extra outlay in this direction, as under these conditions they will heart up quicker and are consequently much more tender and of excellent flavour. The seeds should be sown on moderately poor soil as the plants are thus more stocky and hardy, and when transplanted into good soil will respond more readily to this treatment.

For Summer and Autumn use sow the seed in March and for a succession in April and May if required. They are greatly improved by being pricked out into nursery beds as soon as large enough and finally transplanted into rich, well-manured soil. The smaller varieties, such as " Little Queen " and " Ellam's Early," plant out in rows 18 inches apart, and 15 inches from plant to plant ; the larger and stronger growing sorts such as " Defiance," " Enfield Market," etc., in rows 2 feet apart and 2 feet from plant to plant.

In the kitchen garden should occupy the moistest and coolest positions, except the early Spring kinds, which require a warm sheltered spot. The ground should be deeply dug, plentifully manured, and kept free from weeds.

Cabbages are highly appreciated in the early Spring, and for this crop seed should be sown in the Northern Districts in July, and in the Midland and Southern Districts during August. These succeed excellently planted out on firm ground, such as an onion bed, or other ground previously occupied by surface-rooting plants that have not impoverished the ground too much. Do not dig over but hoe and clean before planting.

Manuring.—The hoe should be kept going every week on the beds, and an occasional application of nitrate of soda or sulphate of ammonia, at the rate of one ounce to the square yard, is recommended before the hearts form, or when procurable an occasional watering with liquid manure of medium strength will be found very beneficial.

Cutting.—A little attention in this direction will prolong the period of usefulness for this valuable crop. When cutting Cabbages do not cut off too low, always leave a few bottom leaves on the stem. The plants will then break again, producing a cluster of young succulent heads, which heart immediately and prove a very useful continuation of the crop.

" I have had a splendid lot of Cabbage from the Seed I had from you last autumn."—Mr. J. PENTER, Polnaan.

" Your Defiance Cabbage has done splendid with me, they were sown last autumn. I have the finest Cabbages on the field of over 100 plots."—Mr. W. WILSON, Newington.

" I am very pleased to inform you that I have had the finest Defiance Cabbage that has ever been grown."—Mr. J. PORTER, Ilkeston.

" I would like to mention that the Ailsa Craig Onion and the Defiance Cabbage I purchased from you last year have turned out very well, several of the Cabbages weighing over 10 lbs., yet having a good flavour and being very tender."—Mr. H. HOSKIN, Exeter.

" The Defiance Cabbage Seed obtained from you last year have proved very satisfactory, everybody admires them, I can well say they all weigh over 11 lbs."—Mr. W. GLAVIN, Merthyr Tydvil.

SAVOY CABBAGES.

SAVOY CABBAGE 'DANIELS' SELECTED DRUMHEAD.

	per oz.	s. d.
☞ **DANIELS' SELECTED DRUMHEAD.** A fine variety for general use, producing large firm heads of exceptionally good quality ; very hardy		0 10
BEST OF ALL. A fine variety of the Drumhead type, but not so large as that variety ; comes into use earlier, is beautifully curled and of fine dark colour. One of the best flavoured amongst the Savoys .. per pkt. 4d.		1 0
NEW YEAR. A grand late variety, keeps fit a long time after attaining full growth. The heads are large, solid, of a fine dark green colour and splendidly curled .. per pkt. 4d.		1 0
DWARF GREEN CURLED. Heads of fair size and very solid ; one of the best for general use ..		0 10
DWARF ULM. Early, very dwarf .. per pkt. 4d.		1 0
ORMSKIRK. A fine hardy variety, heads very compact, and beautifully curled. The leaves are of a fine dark green ; a grand market variety. One of the best for general use ..		0 10
TOM THUMB. A fine early variety, of dwarf compact habit, and finely curled foliage ; a most useful sort for small gardens pkt. 4d.		1 0
VICTORIA Large and of fine quality .. per pkt. 4d.		1 0

RED OR PICKLING CABBAGES.

	per oz.	s. d.
☞ **DANIELS' DWARF BLOOD RED.** A dwarf, compact-growing variety, coming early into use ; heads of a fine deep blood red colour, and very firm ; can be planted much closer than the other sorts .. per pkt. 6d.		1 0
☞ **DANIELS' INTERMEDIATE RED.** A fine type of Red Cabbage with medium sized heads, which are very firm and of a good deep colour. It is of medium height and very compact in growth ; fine for exhibition .. per pkt. 4d.		1 0
DANIELS' GIANT RED DRUMHEAD. A fine variety, grows to a large size, very firm, and of fine deep colour, and is undoubtedly the finest Red Cabbage known ; excellent sort for Autumn sowing .. per pkt. 4d.		1 0

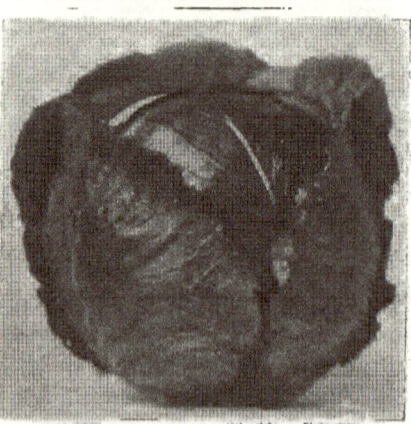

DANIELS' DWARF BLOOD RED. *Reduced from a Photograph.*

CAULIFLOWERS.

DANIELS' KING OF CAULIFLOWERS.

per oz. s. d.

☞ **DANIELS' KING OF CAULIFLOWERS.** The earliest variety in cultivation, of very dwarf and compact habit, the heads beautifully white and of the finest texture. Seed raised in frames in February, and planted out as soon as the weather permits, will produce some fine heads in June. One of the best to sow for succession through the summer .. per pkt, 1s. 6d. and 2s. 6d.

DANIELS' SNOWBALL. An invaluable early variety of dwarf compact habit, producing fine white heads of excellent quality. Ready to cut in four months from time of sowing
per pkt. 1s. 6d. and 2s. 6d.

DANIELS' DWARF MAMMOTH. A very superior dwarf early variety, grows to a larger size than Daniels' King, and forms a good succession to that variety; heads large, white, and compact. Also useful for forcing .. per pkt. 1s. 3d. .. 2 6

ECLIPSE. This is an excellent large Autumn variety, and very useful for Market purposes. By successional sowings it can be had from August to Christmas .. .. .. per pkt. 1s. .. 2 6

EARLY LONDON WHITE. Useful variety, growing to a large size, heads very white and firm .. .. per pkt. 1s. .. 3 0

SELF-PROTECTING AUTUMN GIANT. A fine late variety coming into use directly after Veitch's Autumn Giant. The heads are well-protected by luxuriant over-lapping foliage. May be had in good condition up to Christmas .. .. per pkt. 1s. .. 2 6

VEITCH'S AUTUMN-GIANT. The most useful of our Autumn Cauliflowers and most valuable for general crop. It is very distinct in appearance, producing splendid large heads, beautifully white and firm, and of the finest texture .. per pkt. 6d. .. 2 6

WALCHEREN. Sow under glass in February, to succeed the Spring Broccoli, and in beds from May to July for succession per pkt. 1s. .. 2 6

☞ **DANIELS' AUTUMN QUEEN.** A grand variety, coming in fit for use three weeks earlier than Veitch's Autumn Giant, is very short-legged and compact; the heads are beautifully white and of the finest quality.
per pkt. 1s. 3d. .. 3 6

Cultivation.—The Cauliflower is one of the choicest of our vegetables, and requires much care and very liberal treatment. Cauliflowers are very liable to bolt if any check occurs in their growth, and therefore every care should be taken that they grow on from start to finish without a break. It does not much matter whether the soil on which Cauliflowers are grown is light or heavy, so long as it is thoroughly trenched, and a very liberal quantity of farmyard manure applied. To get the earliest Cauliflowers, the seed should be sown in September in the open, and transferred when big enough to cold frames for the Winter months. Early in March select a warm border and plant them out when a very early crop will be secured.

The earliest Spring sowing should be made in February in boxes on a hotbed, and the plants moved to frames and gradually hardened so as to be ready to plant out in May. A succession of sowings should be made in March in frames and in the open during April, May, and June, so as to secure an unbroken supply. Cauliflowers are most highly prized in Autumn when the Summer crops are over, and it is as well to have more than one batch. When planting and also during dry weather, great care should be given to watering. Frequent applications of liquid manure will give size to the heads for exhibition purposes.

Cauliflowers are particularly subject to white fly, which causes the plant to become blind, and any suspicion of this should be met with a dressing of soot upon the leaves in the early morning. The beds should be regularly gone over to ensure the heads being cut before they get too old, as they soon get past their best. For early work, Daniels' King is undoubtedly the best, followed by **Dwarf Mammoth** and **Autumn Queen**. For general crop, **Autumn Giant** will be found the most useful.

VEITCH'S AUTUMN GIANT.

CELERY.

Cultivation.—This very important vegetable is one that fully repays a liberal outlay both of labour and manure. Being a moisture loving plant and a gross feeder, it should, if possible, be raised in soil where, during the growing period, copious supplies of water can be applied. For the earliest crop sow the seed about the middle of February, giving some heat, and when the plants have made their seed leaves, have them pricked off into boxes or frames, giving if possible a gentle bottom heat to keep them growing. Make a further sowing in March in a similar way, and, if necessary, another in April in an open border; these later sowings will give some useful Celery for cooking. It is an excellent plan to get the Celery trenches ready quite early in the season, so that advantage may be taken of the first favourable showery day to put out the plants when large enough.

In making the trenches throw out the soil 12 or 14 inches deep and 18 inches wide, and be careful to retain the top soil so that it may be placed in the bottom of the trench; mix with it a good dressing of farmyard manure and in this mixture the young plants should be placed; the rest of the soil taken out of the trench should be piled up on the sides and used, when the time comes, for earthing up the Celery; allow a space of three or four feet between the trenches.

In planting the Celery in the trenches, place the seedlings about nine inches apart, in a single row for the earliest crop; for the main crop they are often planted in double rows. In dry weather give liberal supplies of water or liquid manure to keep the plants growing, as if they get a check they are liable to bolt.

It is a good plan to give a sprinkling of soot over the foliage, while damp with the early morning dew, in order to keep away the Celery fly and snails.

The greatest care should be taken in earthing up Celery. As soon as the plants are about nine inches high, go over them and thoroughly clean off all side shoots, and tie the growth loosely with Raffia. Choose a fine day, and gradually work down some of the finest soil round the bases of the plants, being most careful not to allow any of the soil to get between the leaves; do not make the soil too hard, or it will stop the growth. Continue to earth up as the plants grow. The final earthing should form a ridge as a protection. In very severe weather it will be found an advantage to give a slight covering of straw or bracken over the top of the row.

WHITE VARIETIES.

per pkt — s. d.

☞ **DANIELS' EARLIEST WHITE.** This fine white Celery has now firmly established its reputation as one of the very best for early work, and has become highly popular. Sown at the same time, it is ready for use quite six weeks earlier than any other variety. The heads, which grow to a large size, are very firm and solid, and of a sweet nutty flavour . . 1 0

☞ **DANIELS' GIANT WHITE.** This grand Celery is undoubtedly one of the largest and best white varieties in cultivation. The heads are very solid and of excellent flavour. Very fine for exhibition 1 0

SANDRINGHAM DWARF WHITE. Useful early variety 0 6

SEYMOUR'S SUPERB WHITE. Heads very solid, fine flavour 0 6

SILVER PLUME. A fine, white-leaved variety. It blanches well by simply tying up the plants with matting 0 9

RED VARIETIES.

☞ **DANIELS' EARLIEST PINK (new).** This grand new Celery is a useful companion to our Earliest White, and like that variety comes into use quite six weeks earlier than the old varieties. It grows to a large size, the heads being very solid and of excellent flavour. A most valuable variety for early shows 1 0

☞ **DANIELS' GIANT RED.** The largest red variety grown. The heads are of splendid colour, very solid, and of fine nutty flavour, one of the very best for exhibition purposes. The seed offered is saved from carefully selected heads only . . 1 0

☞ **DANIELS' EXHIBITION PINK.** A very fine Celery, producing large solid heads of a delicate rosy pink colour. A fine variety for exhibition, and of excellent flavour . . 1 0

CLAYWORTH PRIZE PINK. Heads very large, solid, and of a beautiful rosy pink colour. A most useful variety for general crop 0 6

MANCHESTER FINE RED. Large, solid heads 0 6

STANDARD BEARER. Heads firm, solid, and of an attractive nutty flavour; fine exhibition variety 0 6

MIXED RED AND WHITE. Useful for Cottagers 0 6

CELERIAC, or TURNIP-ROOTED CELERY. Very useful for flavouring soups, &c. 0 8

"You will be interested to know that I have again been highly successful on the Exhibition benches with your Seeds. For the last three years I have taken a much greater number of Prizes than any other exhibitor."—Mr. F. W. FOREMAN, Tyne.

"You will no doubt be pleased to hear that I gained seven Prizes at our Show from Seed purchased from you last Spring."—Mr. A. E. TAPPIN, Forest Hill.

DANIELS' GIANT WHITE. *Reduced from a Photograph.*

DANIELS' LORD ROBERTS.

CUCUMBERS.

per pkt s. d.

☛ **DANIELS' LORD ROBERTS.** An exceedingly handsome variety, the result of a cross between Royal Osborne and Lockie's Perfection. The fruit which are longer than the last named variety, are of a rich dark green colour, of splendid shape, with no neck, and are borne in the greatest profusion. It is useful either for Winter or Summer cultivation.

1s. 6d. and 2 6

☛ **DANIELS' LORD KITCHENER.** This grand new Cucumber is one of the most prolific, bearing 4 and 5 fruit at a joint, and at the same time is of strong, robust constitution, producing a heavy crop of fine straight fruit 20 to 24 inches in length, with very little neck. It is a black-spined variety, and very handsome in appearance. A most useful variety for all purposes .. .. 1s. 6d. and 2 6

☛ **DISEASE RESISTER.** A very prolific variety of similar type to the Amateur, but a stronger grower. The strong leathery leaves resisting all kinds of disease much better and it keeps in bearing for a long period .. 1s. 6d. and 2 6

☛ **THE AMATEUR.** This can perhaps be best described as a very finely selected stock of The Rochford or Covent Garden type. It is enormously productive, bearing 3 to 4 fruit at a joint. The fruit, which are of handsome shape, average about 20 to 24 inches in length, are slightly spined and of fine colour .. .. 1s. 6d. and 2 6

☛ **DANIELS' IMPROVED TELEGRAPH.** A great improvement on the old Telegraph, bearing clean, straight fruit twenty to twenty-four inches long, an abundant bearer. Our own selected stock, all saved from picked fruit 1s. 6d. and 2 6

☛ **DANIELS' DEFIANCE** (early prolific). A variety of hardy, robust constitution, producing in great abundance very short-necked and elegant fruit of a rich dark green colour, from eighteen to twenty-four inches in length, straight and uniform 1 6

DANIELS' DUKE OF ALBANY. This is the finest Cucumber ever introduced for exhibition, having obtained numerous First Prizes. The fruit are long, straight, and of a beautiful dark green colour, very handsome, and of the finest quality 1 6

DANIELS' DUKE OF EDINBURGH. A beautiful, white-spined variety of fine, robust constitution and habit, its fruit growing rapidly to the length of thirty to thirty-six inches 1 6

EVERY-DAY. This fine Cucumber is of medium size, the fruit being dark-skinned, very handsome in shape, most prolific, and of splendid flavour. First Class Certificate, R.H.S. 1 6

THE ROCHFORD. A most prolific bearer. The fruit are slightly spined, eighteen to twenty inches in length, of a beautiful fresh green colour, and of the most handsome form 1 6

LOCKIE'S PERFECTION. The fruit, which are of medium size, are produced in great abundance 1 6

ROLLISSON'S TELEGRAPH. Very prolific 1 0

TENDER AND TRUE. Superior quality and flavour 1 6

RIDGE CUCUMBERS.

per pkt —s d.

☛ **DANIELS' PERFECTION RIDGE.** The longest and best out-door variety in cultivation, is very hardy and prolific, bearing a heavy crop of nice shaped fruit, averaging fifteen to twenty inches in length and of superior flavour 6d. and 1 0

JAPANESE CLIMBING. A most useful variety for growing on trellis work, &c., being very ornamental. It produces a good crop of fruit, averaging from ten to twelve inches in length .. .. 6d. and 1 0

LONG PRICKLY. A very useful variety of fine flavour 0 6

SHORT PRICKLY. Very hardy, fine for pickling 0 6

STOCKWOOD. Fine selected stock 0 6

PROLIFIC PICKLING. The most prolific out-door variety; very hardy .. 0 6

CRESS.

CRESS, GROWING IN BOX.

	per oz.—s. d.
PLAIN. The best for early salads per qt. 3s. 9d., per pint 2s. 0d.	0 4
CURLED. For salads in the second leaf ,, 3s. 9d., ,, 2s. 0d.	0 4
AUSTRALIAN or GOLDEN. This valuable Cress is a most desirable addition to all salads	0 8
DANIELS' GARNISHING or PARSLEY-LEAVED. Useful alike for salads and garnishing	0 6
AMERICAN or LAND. Eaten as Water Cress in Winter	0 6
SORREL-LEAVED. The largest-leaved of all, dark green colour, and good flavour. A most useful salad	0 8
WATER. Sow in a moist shady place per pkt. 6d. and 1s.	—

Cultivation.—Cress is one of the most useful salads grown, and it is quite easy to keep up a continual supply. as no expensive appliances are needed. If a greenhouse is available, fill boxes with good soil to within about half inch of the top, pressing the soil firmly, then sow the seeds thickly and evenly but do not cover them with soil. Put the boxes in a dark place and give a good watering; in about a fortnight the cress will be ready to eat. By repeating this process a succession can be maintained throughout the early Spring.

During Summer a shady border should be selected, and the soil raked fine and pressed firm. Sow the seeds and press down with a board, giving good waterings and protection with mats until the seed has germinated. To keep up a constant supply a sowing should be made every week.

American or Land Cress is most useful for mixed salads, and is quite easy to grow; sow the seeds from March onwards on a north border and thin out to allow about four inches between each plant, using the outside leaves only.

Water-cress can be grown in ordinary garden soil provided a shady border is chosen and copious waterings given. The seed should be sown in April, and the plants thinned out, leaving about six inches between each. Keep the plants pinched to prevent them from flowering. In Autumn fill pans half full of soil and place some of the plants therein. Put them in a greenhouse and keep thoroughly watered, and a supply of good tender Water-cress will be available all the Winter.

ENDIVE.

Cultivation.—A deep and rich soil is the most suitable for growing good Endive, and abundance of water should be given in dry weather. For early use, sow under glass or on a warm border in April, and make successive sowings at intervals of about three weeks. The best Endives are however grown in Autumn, and for these a first sowing should be made early in July, and successional sowings to the end of August. For these later sowings select a warm, sheltered position, a south border that has carried a crop of early Potatoes or Peas being very suitable. Sow in shallow drills about one foot apart, and transplant or thin out nine inches or one foot apart in the row. The broad-leaved varieties are best blanched by tying, but the finer curled-leaved sorts should have inverted flower-pots placed over them, with the holes stopped, or they may be blanched by pieces of slate being laid on them, and by other similar methods. Blanching takes about ten days, and only sufficient should be done at one time to meet requirements. The latest crops may be stored at the end of October for Winter use, in cool pits or frames, where protected from frost, and by this means may be had in use till Spring Lettuces make their appearance.

	per oz.—s. d.
DANIELS' SUPERB CURLED. The best of all the Curled Endives, it bleaches well, is of first-class quality per pkt. 6d.	1 6
GREEN CURLED. Extra ,, 6d.	1 6
WHITE CURLED. Useful variety ,, 6d.	1 6

	per oz.—s. d.
DANIELS' PRIZE MOSS CURLED. A splendid variety for exhibition, leaves beautifully curled, is very hardy per pkt. 6d.	1 6
BATAVIAN GREEN. Broad-leaved, very hardy, and desirable for Winter cultivation, tie up for blanching per pkt. 6d.	1 6
EXTRA BROAD-LEAVED. An excellent variety ,, 6d.	1 6

GOURD or PUMPKIN.

The seed should be sown in heat, in April, and the plants gradually hardened and transferred to their growing position during May. Give a little protection with a handlight or branches of fir for awhile, and also liberal supplies of liquid manure while the plants are growing. per pkt. s. d.

DANIELS' YELLOW MAMMOTH. Seed from large handsomely netted fruit, weighing one hundredweight or more 6d. and	1 0
POTIRON JAUNE or MAMMOTH. A giant variety 6d. and	1 0
COMMON PUMPKIN. Very useful for pies and preserves in Winter	0 4
VARIEGATED TURK'S CAP. Striped orange, green, and white	0 6

INDIAN SUGAR CORN OR MAIZE.

This is now being largely grown in this country as a vegetable. The cobs or heads should be gathered when just passing out of the milky state; if boiled and served up like asparagus are a great delicacy. Sow in April in a gentle heat, grow on in pots and plant out in June three feet apart. It is at the same time a most graceful plant in the garden. per oz.—s. d.

EARLY SWEET CORY. Extra early	0 8
EARLY SWEET MINNESOTA. Very useful sort	0 8
EARLY KENDALL'S GIANT. Very early and large cobs	0 8
EXTRA EARLY PREMO. The earliest of all, very suitable for this climate	0 8

LEEKS.

Cultivation.—The Leek is one of the most nutritious vegetables cultivated, and although to produce exhibition specimens much care and attention is needed, still a thoroughly good crop for cooking purposes can be grown quite easily. Leeks are gross feeders and therefore require well tilled and liberally manured ground; the best plan is to give the land a thorough dressing of well-decayed manure in Autumn and trench it deeply, allowing it to remain rough for the Winter. The seed should be sown in drills in March for the main crop, and care must be taken to keep the ground thoroughly clean from the outset in order to give the seedlings a good start.

The easiest mode of culture is to dibble the young plants when about six inches high into holes made about twelve inches deep, giving occasional dressings of liquid manure. In September draw the earth round the plants. It is best to defer using Leeks till as late as possible in the Autumn, as the flavour improves.

When it is desired to grow Leeks for exhibition, a good plan is to grow them in trenches in the same way as Celery, allowing two feet between the trenches; for this purpose the seed should be sown on a gentle hotbed in February, and the seedlings pricked off into boxes when big enough; it is important that the young plants be thoroughly hardened, as they will not stand coddling, but cold draughts should be avoided. When the plants have made about six inches of growth, plant them into trenches, allowing about 15 inches between each plant; lift the plants out of the box with a trowel, to ensure getting a good lot of roots. As the plants grow, the soil must be carefully and firmly worked round the roots, and this process continued all the Summer at intervals, giving frequent waterings of liquid manure. Some growers place collars of brown paper round the stems before commencing to earth up the plants as this excludes all light and is a great aid to blanching.

There is every encouragement to grow Leeks to a large size, as the flavour of the finest specimens is superior to the smaller ones. This is not so in most vegetables, but is certainly the case with Leeks.

per pkt.—s. d.

► **DANIELS' CHAMPION.** This is undoubtedly one of the finest Leeks in cultivation. It grows to a large size, and is unsurpassed for exhibition purposes, having produced specimens with 18 inches of blanched stem, and of perfect shape. It comes early into use, and is of exceptionally mild flavour. It has obtained First Prize at a great number of Shows on account of its extraordinary clearness of skin and handsome appearance. We strongly recommend this variety to intending exhibitors, as one likely to give the greatest satisfaction .. .. **per pkt. 1s.** 2 0

AYTON CASTLE GIANT. Remarkably large and good, may be grown ten to twelve inches in circumference, and with one foot of blanched stem   per pkt. 6d. 1 6

CONQUEROR. First class; very superior either for competition or culinary purposes. It is of large size and blanches for considerable distance up the stem; highly recommended .. .. per pkt. 1s. 2 0

HENRY'S PRIZE. Exceedingly large, blanches well, flavour mild, fine for exhibition .. .. per pkt. 6d. 1 6

LONDON FLAG. Large, broad-leaved. A good old variety possessing many excellent qualities 1 0

LYON. One of the largest kinds grown and excellent in every way. A kind much in demand for exhibition purposes .. per pkt. 9d. 2 0

MUSSELBURGH. Extra broad-leaved, blanches to a large size, flavour mild, highly esteemed for soups. A well-established kind of considerable merit and hardiness; grand stock .. .. .. per pkt. 6d. 1 6

MUSTARD.

per oz.—s. d.

WHITE. For early salads .. .. per quart 3s. 9d.; per pint 2s. 0d. 0 4
CHINESE. Fine salad variety 0 0

Cultivation. The Common or White Mustard is much used for saladings, and is generally used with Cress. Out of doors, any cool, moist place is suitable for sowings, which should be made at regular intervals during Spring and Summer. When sown under glass in Winter and early Spring, no better way exists than that recommended for Cress.

EVIDENCE OF QUALITY.

"The Seeds I had had year proved satisfactory. I am pleased to tell you I took twenty-five Prizes at our local show, mostly with produce of your Seeds, in open Amateur and Cottagers' Classes. I took premier honours in classes mentioned with your Distinction Peas, and they commanded admiration of the whole public."—Mr. W. WITHINGTON, Shifnal.

"You may be interested to know I took three First Prizes and Challenge Shield at an open Show, all Vegetables, etc., grown from your Seeds."—Mr. C. DIVER, Merton.

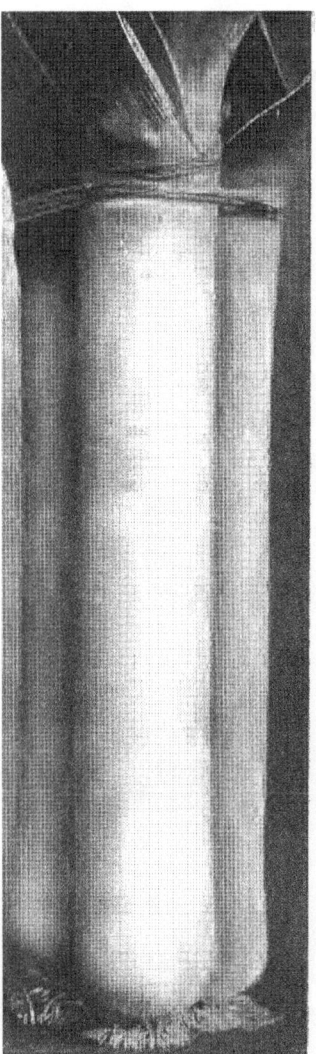

LEEK, DANIELS' CHAMPION.
Reduced from a Photograph.

LETTUCES—Cabbage Varieties.

DANIELS' CONTINUITY LETTUCE.

Daniels' Continuity.

The Longest Standing Cabbage Lettuce in the World.

This fine Cabbage Lettuce is remarkable from the fact that not even in the hottest and driest season does it even run to seed, the heads remaining firm and crisp long after all others have bolted or decayed. A bed of these sown or planted will keep up a supply of good Lettuces for a long period, one sowing of these being equal to three or four sowings of other varieties. Per pkt. 6d. ; oz. 1s. 6d.

	per pkt. s. d.	per oz. s. d.
DANIELS' EXHIBITION GIANT (new). One of the largest Cabbage Lettuces yet introduced, and grows to an enormous size without becoming coarse. The heads are very firm, crisp, and of excellent flavour. For exhibition purposes it is unrivalled, and is one of the best for Salads	0 6	1 6
DANIELS' MAGNUM BONUM. A splendid Cabbage Lettuce growing to a large size, the heads being very firm and crisp and of excellent flavour, stands well ; a useful variety for exhibition	0 6	1 3
DANIELS' GOLDEN BEAUTY. A grand Summer Lettuce of fine appearance ; the leaves are of a light golden colour, very crisp and solid, stands the drought well	0 6	1 3
DANIELS' MAMMOTH GREEN WINTER. A fine large Cabbage Lettuce. The heads although large are very firm and crisp ; an excellent variety for Autumn sowing	0 6	1 3

	per pkt. s. d.	per oz. s. d.
DANIELS' QUEEN OF SUMMER. This is one of the finest Summer Lettuces yet introduced. It is remarkable for its large size, splendid appearance, and for withstanding the drought. It produces fine, crisp, and tender Lettuces in the driest season	0 6	1 0
DANIELS' TENDER AND TRUE. A fresh, tender lettuce, about the size of All the Year Round, with a slight tinge of red on edge of leaf ; it is very delicate eating in the driest season	0 6	1 0
DANIELS' GIANT WHITE. An exceedingly large and fine variety, crisp and tender and of fine flavour, stands a long time without running to seed	0 6	1 0
DANIELS' BLACK-SEEDED TEXTER. Large, compact, and solid, one of the most splendid varieties in cultivation	0 4	1 0
ALL THE YEAR ROUND. One of the best for general use ; very hardy	0 4	1 0
DRUMHEAD or MALTA. Well known	0 3	0 10
LARGE WHITE WINTER. The best for Winter use ; heads large and solid	0 6	1 3
STANSTEAD PARK. A fine variety for sowing in Autumn to stand the Winter	0 6	1 0
NEW YORK. The heads attain a large size, and are very crisp and tender ; grand variety for exhibition	0 6	1 3
NEAPOLITAN. Leaves beautifully curled and tender, one of the finest Summer sorts	0 4	1 0
WHEELER'S TOM THUMB. The earliest variety grown, heads small, and very solid and tender	0 4	1 0
MIXED CABBAGE VARS.	0 4	1 0
MIXED. All kinds, Cos and Cabbage	0 4	1 0

"I had First Prize given by our Allotment Association, which is due to the Seed supplied by you last year. I have dealt with you for 32 years and I have never had anything to grumble at over the Seed you sent me."—Mr. J. PICKEN, Oldbury.

DANIELS' QUEEN OF SUMMER.

LETTUCES—Cos Varieties.

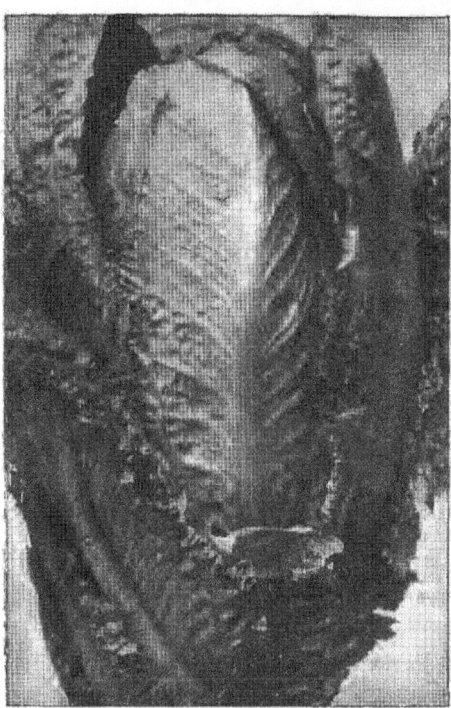

DANIELB GIANT WHITE COS LETTUCE.   *Reduced from a Photograph.*

	per pkt. s. d.	per oz. s. d.
DANIELS' GIANT WHITE. The finest and largest Cos Lettuce in cultivation, very tender and crisp, with fine solid hearts, and will stand a long time without running to seed ; should be grown in all gardens ; unrivalled for exhibition purposes	1 0	2 6
DANIELS' DREADNOUGHT. One of the largest Cos Lettuces in cultivation, the heads being very solid, crisp, and of fine flavour. An invaluable variety for exhibition	1 0	2 6
DANIELS' ALL HEART. A fine Cos Lettuce growing to a large size, the leaves folding well over the hearts, which are very solid and of fine flavour	0 6	1 6
DANIELS' LITTLE GEM. A very early Cos Lettuce, coming into use at the same time as the Cabbage varieties. It is very dwarf and compact, the heads, which are self-folding, require no tying	0 6	1 6
DANIELS' SELECTED PARIS WHITE. Self-blanching, tender, and mild flavour ; useful exhibition variety	0 6	1 6
DANIELS' GREEN WINTER. An excellent and hardy kind, valuable for Winter and early Spring	0 6	1 6
DANIELS' SOLID BROWN. A medium-sized Lettuce, outer leaves brown, hearts very solid and of a beautiful creamy yellow ; very crisp, requires no tying. An invaluable variety for Winter use .. pkts. only	1 0	—
HICKS' HARDY WHITE. A superior variety both for Summer and Winter use	0 6	1 6
PARIS WHITE. Best for general use	0 4	1 0
MIXED COS VARS. All the best for succession	0 4	1 0

" The Giant White Cos Lettuce I had this Spring are a great success both in size and eating qualities."—**Mr. J. KINGSTON**, Wellingboro'.

" I enjoy no Lettuce like the **Continuity.** For an early Lettuce it is the praise of the neighbourhood."—**Mr. C. PIGGOTT**, Cottenham.

" Referring to your Winter White Lettuce I have grown it with success for many years ; out of nearly 150 plants I only lost 4 plants."—**Mr. B. ROGERS**, South Wigston.

MELONS.

	per pkt.—s. d.
EMINENCE. A fine variety, raised by Mr. A. McKellar, The Royal Gardens, Windsor. Received an Award of Merit from the Royal Horticultural Society. The fruit is rather large, roundish oval, skin bright yellow and beautifully netted, flesh white, thick. Very melting and of delicious flavour	1 6
EMERALD GEM. A very handsome melon. Flesh unusually thick and of rich green colour and first-class flavour	1 6
DUCHESS OF YORK. A cross between Best of All and Hero of Lockinge ; fruit medium-sized, thick in the flesh, and of delicious flavour ; white-fleshed	1 6
GUNTON SCARLET (S.F.). A very superior scarlet-fleshed Melon of medium size, oval in shape, and finely netted. The flesh is very deep and the finest flavour of any Melon with which we are acquainted. Highly recommended	1 6
HERO OF LOCKINGE. Fine exhibition variety ; very prolific ; white-fleshed	1 6

	per pkt.—s. d.
MELTON HYBRID (S.F.). The fruit is large and handsome, and nicely netted. The flesh is thick, of rich salmon colour, juicy and melting, and of fine flavour	1 6
'ROYAL SOVEREIGN. A grand white-fleshed variety. Raised at The Royal Gardens, Windsor ; has received Award of Merit from the R.H.S. It has a robust constitution, and is a free setter. The skin is of a beautiful golden colour, slightly netted, flesh white	1 6
ROYALTY. A new variety of strong constitution, vigorous growth, and a free setter. The fruit is very handsome, round, yellow, and beautifully netted. The flesh pale green, melting, and juicy	1 6
SUPERLATIVE. A very prolific variety, medium size, almost round, and handsomely netted. Flesh scarlet and very thick and of exceptionally fine flavour	1 6
CANTALOUP. This variety may be grown in a cool frame, and is very prolific. The fruit can be grown up to four and six pounds	1 0

ONIONS FOR SPRING SOWING.

DANIELS' SELECTED AILSA CRAIG. *Reduced from a Photograph.*

DANIELS' SELECTED AILSA CRAIG. This grand Onion has now taken its place as one of the largest and most useful varieties for all purposes. It is very good sown either in Spring or Autumn, and produces a heavy crop of fine handsome bulbs, which are unrivalled for exhibition purposes. They have been grown to the enormous weight of 26, 28, 30, and 34 lbs. per dozen bulbs. Our own selected stock grown from picked bulbs. Per pkt. 1s. 3d. ; per oz. 3s. 0d.

AILSA CRAIG. Ordinary stock. A good useful stock of this fine variety .. .. .. Per pkt. 1s. ; per oz. 2s. 6d.

per oz.—s. d.

ROUSHAM PARK HERO. A magnificent variety of the White Spanish type. The bulbs, which are very solid, grow to a large size, producing a heavy crop of excellent quality and fine appearance. It is a grand sort for exhibition purposes, and an extra good keeper .. .. per pkt. 9d.   2 0

CRANSTON'S EXCELSIOR. A superior variety of fine globular shape, very deep, with fine skin ; has been grown two to three pounds in weight, is very mild in flavour ; a good keeper and excellent exhibition variety .. .. .. per pkt. 1s.   2 0

COCOANUT. This fine Onion has been grown to the weight of three pounds each. The skin is a very delicate pale straw colour, flesh white and mild ; one of the best for exhibition. per pkt. 1s. 3d.   3 0

per oz.—s. d.

DANIELS' NEW RED GLOBE. The finest Red Onion in cultivation. The bulbs are large, of a fine globular shape, and of a beautiful dark crimson. Besides being very attractive in appearance, it has the mild flavour and good keeping qualities of the very best of the White Spanish type. Will often produce a good crop on poor stony ground, where other varieties have been known to fail .. .. per pkt. 9d.   2 0

UP-TO-DATE. A fine new variety of globular shape. It is very solid, and has a well developed shoulder, and will therefore produce a heavier crop than the older sorts. The skin is a bright straw colour. It is an excellent keeper, and will be found a useful variety for exhibition .. .. .. per pkt. 9d.   2 0

EVIDENCE OF QUALITY.

"The Ailsa Craig Onion I had from you turned out quite a success with remarkable results."—Mr. A. JOPE, Hove.

"Pleased to let you know all the Seeds we had are doing very well; also the Ailsa Craig Onion have done very well indeed."—Mr. W. EATON, New Leamington.

"I may add that I again did very well indeed with your Seeds last season, in fact, many of my crops caused people to stop and look at them, the Onions especially."—Mr. R. FRYER, Boundary Road, N.22.

"I should like to say how very pleased I was with the Onions I had last year, they were absolutely splendid, the finest in the village."—Mr. P. COWGILL, Mossley Common.

"I had very great satisfaction with your Seeds last year. I took First Prize with the Onions I had from your Ailsa Craig, also Carrots. They gave me very great pleasure, for which I am now thanking you."—Mr. HAYES, Skelton.

"I took First Prize last season at our local Horticultural Show with your Ailsa Craig Onions."—Mr. H. RISBRIDGEN, Meadvale.

"I am pleased to let you know that I have received two First Prizes for Onions this year, one on the 26th July at Pears' Vegetable Show, the other at the Allotments Association of Isleworth, on the 30th August, from the Ailsa Craig Onion Seed I bought of your firm last year."—Mr. W. CLIMPSON, Isleworth.

"Have got a grand bed of Ailsa Craig Onion which I had from you last year."—Mr. W. HENSBY, Inchbeck.

"Have won First Prize at our local Show with Onions grown from your Seeds."—Mr. S. DAVIES, Haverfordwest.

"I have a grand lot of Onions this year from your Seeds."—Mr. CLARKE, Dosing stoke.

"I have a splendid lot of your last year's Red Italian Tripoli, both in colour and in size."—Mr. J. HARDING, Peterboro'.

"I won with your Giant Rocca at our Show, and I am well satisfied with all Seeds I had from you last year."—Mr. W. SMITH, Skelton.

ONIONS FOR SPRING SOWING.

DANIELS' IMPROVED WHITE SPANISH. *Reduced from a Photograph.*

▶ **DANIELS' IMPROVED WHITE SPANISH.** This grand stock of Onion has been carefully selected by us for a great many years, and we have no hesitation in recommending it to our customers as one of the very best of its type ; grows to a large size, very even, and it is unequalled for mildness of flavour. It is a heavy cropper, a grand variety for Exhibition purposes, and is sure to give satisfaction.   Per pkt. 1s. ; per oz. 2s. 3d.

▶ **BEST OF ALL (new).** This variety is the result of many years patient selection, the bulb of almost perfectly globular form, with very slender neck and bright straw-coloured skin. One of the chief points is the unusual weight and solidity of the bulb and the large size to which it can be grown. A grand keeper, will keep solid till the following April and May   Per pkt. 1s. 6d.

JAMES' KEEPING. A most valuable sort for Spring sowing ; it produces a heavy crop of onions of globular shaped bulbs of fine quality, and is at the same time an excellent keeper.   Per pkt. 9d. ; per oz. 2s. 0d.

BEDFORDSHIRE CHAMPION. This well-known variety is one of the best for general use. The bulbs are of good globular shape, and are fine keepers. It is at the same time a heavy and reliable cropper.   Per pkt. 9d. ; per oz. 2s. 0d.

Silver Skinned or Pickling Varieties.

EARLY WHITE GEM. One of the earliest in cultivation, three weeks earlier than the Queen, and comes to maturity from eight to ten weeks from time of sowing. Very useful for pickling   per oz.—s., d.   per pkt. 9d. 2 0

EARLY QUEEN. Remarkably quick-growing, may be sown in July and will ripen the same year   per pkt. 6d. 1 6

SILVER SKIN. Of very quick growth, best for pickling   9d. 2 0

ONIONS FOR SPRING SOWING.

DANIELS' GOLDEN GLOBE.

☞ **DANIELS' GOLDEN GLOBE.** One of the finest types of Globe Onion in cultivation. The bulbs are of true globular shape with bright golden yellow skin; the flesh is very solid and of mild flavour. It produces a very heavy crop of fine, handsome bulbs, and is one of the best keepers. A most useful variety for all purposes. Per pkt. 1s.; per oz. 2s. 3d.

	per oz.—s. d.
NUNEHAM PARK. Much recommended, bulbs of fine globular shape and of good keeping quality .. per pkt. 6d.	1 6
BROWN GLOBE. Very useful, heavy cropper .. ,, 6d.	1 6
DANIELS' BLOOD RED. Fine rich colour, very hardy .. ,, 8d.	1 9
WHITE SPANISH. Ordinary stock. A heavy cropper, flesh very firm, and keeps well .. .. .. per pkt. 6d.	1 6
STRASBURGH or **DEPTFORD.** Well known	1 4

	per oz. s. d
WHITE SPANISH, Portugal or Reading. A finely selected stock, producing a very heavy crop of handsome bulbs, of first-class keeping quality .. .. per pkt. 9d.	2 0
ZITTEAU GIANT YELLOW. A magnificent variety with fine yellow skin, and grows to a large size, the bulbs are of handsome appearance and excellent quality, remains sound till June. May also be sown with advantage in Autumn per pkt. 9d.	2 0
MIXED, all sorts for Spring sowing .. .. ,, 6d.	1 4

Cultivation.—There are few vegetable crops upon which so much care is expended as the Onion, and during recent years its culture has received much more attention than was formerly the case. When the seed can be raised in January in heat (thereby obtaining an early start) it is possible to grow bulbs of equal size to those grown from seed sown the previous Autumn; about the last week in January is the time for the earliest sowing.

Sow the seed in boxes or pots in fine soil, a good mixture being two parts of good loam to one part of decomposed manure, or leaf soil. When the young plants are about three inches high prick them off into boxes, and give all the light possible, gradually admitting air, and hardening as the days lengthen, until the time arrives for planting out in the beds about the middle of April. The earliest sowing out of doors should be made in February and the main sowing of all kinds in March.

The greatest care should be taken in preparing the Onion bed, the ground being thoroughly raked over, all the stones cleared off, and a perfectly fine surface obtained and the soil made quite firm. Sow the seeds very evenly in shallow drills about eighteen inches apart and carefully cover the seed by putting the soil from the side of the drills with the feet. The whole bed should then be well trodden down both down the bed and across as well, after this again rake the soil level and little further work is necessary beyond keeping the hoe going and thinning out the plants when the time arrives. Unless especially fine bulbs are required it is not advisable to thin too much. To prevent an attack of Onion Maggot in a dry season, a good watering with lime water will be found to be of much service.

Great care is necessary in harvesting the Onion crop. It is a good plan to bend over the tops of the plants in August by going over the plants individually, this will assist the ripening of the bulbs. Onions require to be thoroughly ripened before being taken off the ground and should, therefore, be pulled about the middle of September and turned over on the ground every two or three days for a fortnight, when they should be gathered into an airy shed in readiness for roping together, this being the best method of storing them for Winter use.

"My crop of Onions last year from your Golden Globe Seed was all that could be desired."—Mr. D. CHAPLIN, Haverhill.

"I have grown your Onion, Golden Globe, for several years now, and have had a splendid bed again this year. It is a fine keeper, of good shape and good quality."—Mr. A. WOODHOUSE, Letheringsett.

"It may interest you to know that I took First Prize at the Sudbury and Wembley Show with nine Golden Rocca Onions."—Mr. ROWLAND LANE, Wembley.

"I had quite a nice crop of Onions from the Autumn sowing this year; all the crops are very good."—Mr. J. SIMMONDS, Ventnor

ONIONS FOR AUTUMN SOWING.

DANIELS' GOLDEN ROCCA. *Reduced from a Photograph.*

☞ **DANIELS' GOLDEN ROCCA.** One of the largest and finest Onions ever introduced. Fine globular shape, golden yellow skin, mild flavour, and with careful cultivation comes equal to the imported Portugal Onions, and keeps sound till June. This variety is the best exhibition kind known, and has obtained more Prizes than any other Onion. If sown in Autumn, and kept under first-class cultivation, will grow bulbs two to three pounds each ; may also be sown in Spring, and will produce some fine bulbs. **Per packet 1s. ; per ounce 2s. 3d.**

	per oz.—s. d.
DANIELS' GIANT ROCCA. A splendid large globular variety of delicate flavour; grows to a large size .. .. per pkt. 9d.	2 0
DANIELS' WHITE ELEPHANT TRIPOLI. The largest and best of the Tripoli sorts .. .. per pkt. 9d.	2 0
SILVER SKIN. Very early, excellent for Spring use ,, 9d.	2 0

	per oz.—s. d.
TRIPOLI ITALIAN RED. Fine dark red skin ; a well-known and popular sort .. .. per pkt. 6d.	1 6
TRIPOLI ITALIAN WHITE. Similar to above, but milder ,, 6d.	1 6
LISBON WHITE. Very useful for pulling green for salads early in Spring	0 3

PLANTS.

Strong Autumn sown, to plant out for show purposes, can be supplied in Spring of the following kinds only :—

Ailsa Craig, Golden Rocca, Giant Rocca, White Elephant Tripoli, All Carriage Paid } .. .. **each sort 2s. 6d. per 100.**

The Autumn sowing of these, which offers many advantages to the cultivator, has very much grown in favour of late years. When sown in Autumn, Onions grow to a much larger size, and are milder in flavour than those sown in Spring, especially when transplanted, and being much less liable to attack from fly, are rarely destroyed by maggot. They are besides exceedingly valuable for the supply of fresh green Onions in early Spring which can always be relied on.

Cultivation. For securing specially fine Onions there is no doubt that it is much better to sow the seed in the Autumn. The ground should be prepared as for the Spring crop, except that the drills should be made a little deeper. Sow the seed any time from the middle of July to the end of August and treat in the same manner as advised for Spring sowing. Keep the ground clear of weeds, and give good soakings of water, if the Autumn is a dry one. If cooking size only is needed it will merely be found necessary to thin out the Onions and a good crop will be obtained, but if exhibition bulbs are required, the strongest must be selected in Spring, lifted carefully with a trowel, and transplanted nine inches apart on to a specially prepared bed of rich soil. Water thoroughly, at the same time making the soil firm round the bulbs. Keep the hoe going and excellent show specimens should be produced. A sprinkling of nitrate of soda (about a pound to the rod) in May or June, between the rows, is also very stimulating to the growth. Daniels' Norwich Fertilizer, applied at the rate of 4 ozs. to the square yard, in April or May, is also a first-class manure and is highly recommended. Soot is also an excellent stimulant for onions ; a light dressing about once a fortnight will add considerable bulk to the crop. This should be applied in damp weather if possible.

PARSLEY.

DANIELS' QUEEN OF THE PARSLEYS GROWING AT OUR SEED GROUNDS. *From a Photograph.*

DANIELS' QUEEN OF THE PARSLEYS. An extra selected stock carefully grown on our own Seed Farm. The most useful for garnishing, and extremely valuable as an ornamental plant for the flower-border　—　per pkt. 6d. 1 6

GIANT CURLED. A very handsome variety, leaves finely curled, grows to a large size, and is very ornamental ; this is the best sort to grow where Parsley is required in large quantities .. .. per pkt. 4d. 1 0

COVENT GARDEN GARNISHING. A splendid variety, beautifully curled 0 8

EXTRA-FINE CURLED. Fine for garnishing 0 8

Cultivation.—Parsley being a deep-rooting plant pays well for liberal cultivation ; it likes a good rich soil in a cool but not too shady position. Parsley is often grown as an edging to other kitchen garden crops and has a pleasing effect when thus used, and as it is in demand the whole year round it is an excellent plan to make a succession of sowings during the year to ensure a continuous supply. Make the first sowing in a box in February, and when the plants have been gradually hardened off they should be planted out during April in the permanent border, allowing about twelve inches between each plant. Another sowing at the end of March will be of value for a succession.

For a Winter supply, a sowing should be made in June or July, choosing a sunny aspect on a south border. The plants should be thinned out to prevent over-crowding; those taken out may be potted up and placed in a cold frame or greenhouse and will yield an excellent supply of leaves for Winter garnishing. In the event of severe weather it will be found advisable to cover the outside beds with mats or an old frame, and a sprinkling of soot in the early morning during the growing season will be found to have an excellent effect.

HERBS (Sweet and Pot).
Per packet 6d.

‡ **ANGELICA.** The mid-rib may be eaten as Celery, or when candied makes an excellent confection.

* **ANISE.** The seeds are much used for medicinal purposes ; the leaves for garnishing or seasoning.

‡ **BALM.** For making balm tea, which is invaluable in cases of fever ; makes also a fine-flavoured wine.

* **BASIL,** Bush. The leaves and tops impart the flavour of Cloves to soups, and are much used for seasoning.

* **BASIL,** Sweet. For flavouring salads and soups.

* **BORAGE.** The young leaves used as salad or pot herb

‡ **BURNET.** The young leaves have the flavour of Cucumbers.

† **CARAWAY.** For flavouring soups.

* **CHERVIL.** Very fine for salads.

* **CORIANDER.** The tender leaves are used for soups or salads.

‡ **DILL.** The leaves are used in soups, sauces, and pickles.

‡ **FENNEL.** Used in sauces for fish and for garnishing.

‡ **HOREHOUND.** Makes an esteemed well-known beverage.

‡ **HYSSOP.** Young shoots used as pot herbs.

* **MARIGOLD,** Pot. The flowers impart a beautiful colour to broths and soups.

* **MARJORAM, Sweet or Knotted** } Aromatic and sweet flavour, used in
‡ **MARJORAM,** Pot } soups and stuffings.

‡ **LAVENDER.** Cultivated for its flowers, which are very aromatic.

* **PURSLANE, Green** } The shoots and succulent leaves are cooling when used in Spring as salads.

‡ **RAMPION.** The leaves used as salads ; the roots, which have a pleasant nutty flavour, used as Radish.

‡ **ROSEMARY.** The leaves make a drink esteemed for relieving headache.

‡ **RUE, Broad-leaved.** Leaves used medicinally ; also used as a remedy for croup in fowls.

‡ **SAGE.** Used in stuffing and sauce.

* **SAVORY,** Summer } The tops being very aromatic are used in salads and soups ; they improve the flavour if boiled with Peas or Beans

‡ **SORREL,** Broad-leaved } The leaves are used in salads, soups, and
‡ **SORREL,** Lettuce-leaved } sauces.

‡ **THYME.** Broad-leaved. Used in stuffings, soups, and sauces.

‡ **WORMWOOD.** Fine tonic when taken as tea ; and imparts bitterness to drinks.

Annuals marked thus (*)　　　*Biennials* (†)　　　*Perennials* (‡)　　　*For Plants of most of the Perennial sorts, see page 47.*

PARSNIPS.

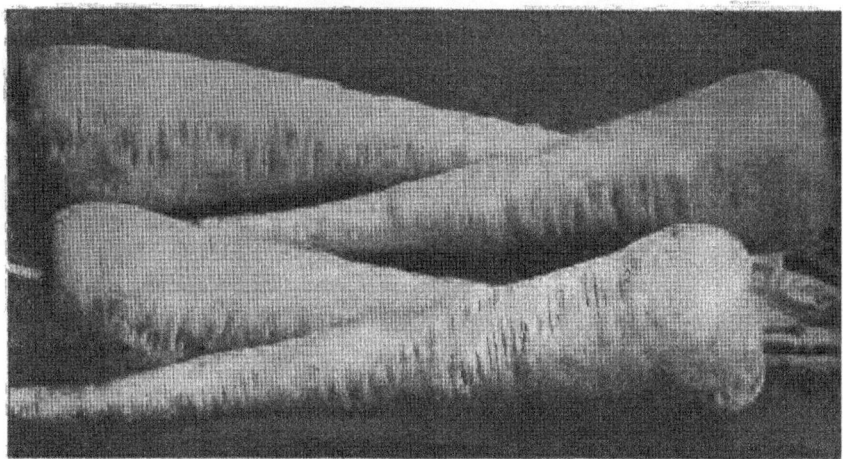

DANIELS' IMPROVED HOLLOW-CROWNED. *Reduced from a Photograph.*

per oz.—s. d

☞ **DANIELS' IMPROVED HOLLOW-CROWNED.** A finely selected stock of the Hollow-crowned variety. It grows to a very large size without becoming coarse. The roots are of grand symmetrical shape and very clear in the skin. It produces a heavy crop of even-sized Parsnips, and is the best variety for exhibition purposes .. .. per pkt. 3d. 0 9

GUERNSEY or JERSEY MARROW. A fine, large, and heavy cropping variety 0 6

HOLLOW-CROWNED. Largest and best for general use; a fine selected stock 0 6

THE STUDENT. A first-class variety, but requires a good depth of soil 0 6

TURNIP-ROOTED. Excellent for shallow soils 0 8

Cultivation.—Parsnips are amongst the most nutritious of vegetables, and are quite easy to grow; a good loamy soil free from stones being the most suitable. Have the ground thoroughly trenched (at least two feet deep) in the Autumn, and give a good dressing of farmyard manure, leaving it rough for the Winter. Early in February the bed should be levelled, forked down, and the seeds sown in drills about 1½ feet apart; thin the young plants out to about 12 inches apart as soon as it is possible to handle them, and be sure to keep the ground thoroughly clean between the rows by frequent hoeing.

When specimen roots are being grown for exhibition, holes should be bored three or four feet deep with a crowbar, and filled with carefully mixed soil, loaf mould, and wood ashes; sow four or five seeds in each hole and thin out the plants, leaving one to each; weed the ground carefully and apply a sprinkling of soot to keep away pests.

Parsnips are always better when allowed to remain in the ground and lifted when required for use, but when it is necessary to lift and store them, they should be placed in dry sand in a dark shed or cellar.

SPINACH.

per oz.—s. d.

LONG STANDING. A most valuable variety for Summer use, as it stands the dry weather and keeps longer fit for use than any other sort
per pint 3s. 6d. 0 6

NEW ZEALAND. Large and succulent 0 6

PERPETUAL or SPINACH BEET. Produces an abundance of green leaves close to the ground, as soon as these are cut fresh leaves appear, producing a supply during the Autumn and Winter 0 10

PRICKLY, NEW GIANT-LEAVED. A great improvement on the ordinary winter spinach. The leaves are much larger and of greater substance, and it remains fit for use for a much longer period .. .. per pint 3s. 6d. 0 6

PRICKLY. Ordinary stock for winter use .. .. per pint 2s. 6d. 0 4

ROUND. For Summer use; best for general crop .. .. per pint 2s. 6d. 0 4

Cultivation.—All kinds like a good rich soil; for the Summer Spinach select a warm border and sow the seeds in rows, where a little shade can be given; it is often grown between the rows of Peas and Beans. It is important that the plants should be thinned out so as to allow plenty of room for each to develop, and that the crop should be kept well gathered while young.

Winter Spinach should be sown in July or August in drills one inch deep, and twelve inches apart in a well-drained border, care being taken to thin out well, otherwise the leaves will decay, as they will also if grown on heavy, water-logged soil. New Zealand Spinach is a useful vegetable for the Summer, but will not stand the frost. Sow it on a warm border in April, and thin out the plants to about two feet apart.

RADISHES.

WHITE TURNIP.   DANIELS' BEST OF ALL.   DANIELS' EARLY SCARLET TURNIP.
FRENCH BREAKFAST.

LONG VARIETIES.

DANIELS' BEST OF ALL. A new and distinct long variety ; colour, beautiful bright scarlet, flesh pure white, very tender and crisp. It comes into use very early ; and will be found a most useful variety, its bright colour making it very attractive both for the table and market purposes   ..   per pint 5s. 6d.   0   8

DANIELS' LONG WHITE. A new variety of excellent quality. It is the same shape as the Wood's Frame, and pure white in colour. The flesh is exceedingly firm and crisp, and it keeps solid and in good condition a long time   ..   ..   per pint 5s. 6d.   0   8

DANIELS' LONG SCARLET. A fine select Stock, beautiful colour, and very crisp, best for general crop   per pint 4s. 0d.   0   6

WOOD'S EARLY FRAME. The best for early crop, forces well   per pint 4s. 0d.   0   6

SCARLET SHORT-TOP. Best for general crop and market purposes   per pint 4s. 0d.   0   6

OLIVE-SHAPED VARIETIES.

FRENCH BREAKFAST. Scarlet, tipped white, oval shaped, forces well, mild and crisp ; useful market variety   per pint 4s. 0d.   0   6

OLIVE-SHAPED SCARLET. Early, good forcer, very tender and mild ..   ..   per pint 4s. 0d.   0   6

OLIVE-SHAPED WHITE. Of quick growth, mild and crisp, handsome shape ..   ..   per pint 4s. 0d.   0   6

OLIVE-SHAPED MIXED   ..   ..   per pint 4s. 0d.   0   6

TURNIP VARIETIES.

DANIELS' EARLY SCARLET TURNIP. A very early variety, the roots are firm, solid, and of true globular shape. Colour, rich glowing crimson scarlet. This is unquestionably the earliest forcing Radish extant. It grows very rapidly, is of delicate flavour, and is fit to use in three weeks from time of sowing   per pint 5s. 6d.   0   8

SPARKLER (new). A quite distinct variety, the upper half of the root is bright scarlet and the lower portion pure white. The two colours are sharply defined and do not merge into each other. Has a most dainty appearance on the table   ..   per pint 5s. 6d.   0   8

TURNIP, Scarlet, White-tipped. Delicious and handsome   per pint 4s.   0   6

TURNIP, Scarlet ⎫ For Summer ⎫
   ,,   White ⎬   and   ⎬   .. per pint 4s.   0   6
   ,,   Mixed ⎭ Autumn use ⎭

WINTER RADISHES.

CHINESE ROSE-COLOURED. Of oblong shape and mild flavour ; for Winter use   0   8

BLACK SPANISH. For Winter salads ; sown in Autumn for Spring use   0   6

Cultivation.—The Radish is one of the most popular of all salads, and to be crisp and mild in flavour should be quickly grown. It requires a good rich soil and liberal supplies of water during hot dry weather. Care should be taken in making the sowings to ensure a continuous succession rather than a great quantity at one time. The earliest sowing (for which our new variety, "Best of All," is most suitable) should be made between the rows of early Potatoes or other vegetables grown in frames on the hot-bed. Be sure to admit plenty of air as they will not bear excessive heat.

From February onwards sowings may be made about every fortnight in a warm sheltered bed out of doors, making provision for covering the beds with mats or straw on cold nights. This covering must always be removed in the day-time. It is most important, however, that protection from birds be made in the day-time, and fish netting is generally used for this purpose. In the middle of Summer a north-east border will be found a most suitable position for Radishes. Sow the seed broadcast and evenly, so that they are not too crowded. For Winter work the varieties "Chinese Rose" and "Black Spanish" are the best ; they should be sown in August and the plants thinned out about four inches apart.

GARDEN TURNIPS.

WHITE-FLESHED VARIETIES.

DANIELS' IMPROVED SNOWBALL. *Reduced from a Photograph.*

YELLOW-FLESHED VARIETIES.

per oz. s. d.

GOLDEN BALL. Fine stock ..   ..   ..   per pint 4s. 0d.   0 6
ORANGE JELLY. Fine for late sowing   ..   per pint 4s. 0d.   0 6

Cultivation.—This most wholesome vegetable is a lover of moisture, and to be crisp and juicy (as it should be) must be grown quickly and not checked in its growth. Choose good rich soil which has been dug over some time previously, and if possible, in a slightly shady position, as during the Summer months Turnips become stringy and hard if exposed to the hot sun.

For the first crop sow Daniels' "Snowball" on a very warm border early in March, and a succession of varieties onwards until July. Thin out the plants when in the seed leaf, leaving the single roots twelve inches apart. Give occasional dustings with wood ash and soot in the early morning to ward off the deadly Turnip fly

For Autumn and Winter use sow in August and September either broadcast or in rows. Keep the hoe going and all weeds cleared off to hasten the growth and ensure crisp tender roots.

GARDEN SWEDE.

Sow in July in rows about 15 in. apart, and thin out to 9 in. apart in the row. A valuable crop for Winter use. They are highly nutritive and much superior to ordinary Turnips.   Per oz. 6d. ; per pint 3s. 6d.

DANIELS' GREEN TOP STONE.

SALSAFY.

per oz. s. d.

SANDWICH ISLAND MAMMOTH. Splendid variety per pkt. 6d.   1 6
COMMON ..   ..   ,, 4d.   1 0

SCORZONERA.

per oz. s. d.

RUSSIAN IMPROVED ..   ..   per pkt. 6d.   1 6
COMMON ..   ..   ,, 4d.   1 0

Cultivation.—Salsafy is a vegetable which deserves to be more grown, as it has quite a rich and distinct flavour. Being a deep rooting plant, it must have well-worked land. The seed should be sown early in May in drills about fifteen inches apart, and the plants thinned out to about nine inches in the row. If specimen roots are desired for exhibition, they may be grown in holes made by a crowbar and filled with fine soil as recommended for Parsnips and Beetroot ; a liberal supply of water should be given in dry weather and the soil kept loose between the rows by hoeing during the Summer. Salsafy should be lifted and stored in dry sand in a cellar for Winter use.

Scorzonera is a vegetable resembling Salsafy, being purple in colour. It requires similar treatment, but is somewhat hardier and requires a little more space in the drill.

TOMATOES.

DANIELS' LEIGH PARK.

per pkt.—s. d

☛ **DANIELS' LEIGH PARK** (new). This fine Tomato is the result of many years' careful selection, and will be found one of the most prolific. The fruit, which are of a rich glowing crimson, are produced in racemes or bunches averaging ten to twelve nice even-sized fruit on each. It is of good habit, short jointed and enormously prolific 2 6

☛ **DANIELS' KING GEORGE V.** This grand variety introduced by us some time since has proved itself one of the most useful sorts for all purposes. It is of strong constitution and a free setter. The fruit, which are of a rich glowing scarlet colour, are of perfect shape and of excellent flavour. For exhibition purposes it will prove a great acquisition — — — — 1 6

☛ **AILSA CRAIG.** A new variety of great excellence, bearing a heavy crop of fine shaped, grand coloured fruit, which are produced in great ropes and trusses. It is a very free setter, bearing up to eight and ten bunches on a plant. A good sort for pot culture and exhibition work — — — — — 1 0

KONDINE RED. A fine Tomato for early crop, and one that has become highly popular amongst market growers. The plant is of good constitution, producing a very heavy crop of grand shaped fruit, of pleasing colour and superb quality, and a most useful variety for all purposes. Succeeds well in the open ground — — 1 0

WINTER BEAUTY. A grand variety for growing under glass in Winter, it is of good strong constitution and an abundant bearer. The fruit are smooth and of a good deep colour and very firm. The quality is excellent. Also a useful sort for the open ground — 1 0

Cultivation.—One of the chief things which has contributed to the great popularity of the Tomato is the fact that it is so very easily grown. It is now generally recognized that Tomatoes can be quite successfully cultivated without such heavy dressings of manure as were used at one time, although there are certain periods when good liberal dressings of manure are necessary; but when the plants are young they do not need it.

For the earliest Spring crop the seed should be sown in January or early in February in pots or pans of light rich soil, and these should be placed on a shelf in the greenhouse; the vessel should be covered over with a sheet of glass to hold the moisture and kept at an even temperature until the seed has germinated. As soon as the plants have formed the seed leaf, have them potted off singly into three-inch pots and grow them on in a warm house, potting on into six-inch pots later, in which size they should remain until permanently planted out in the borders, or potted into the fruiting pots.

Many people prefer to grow their early crops in pots ten inches to twelve inches in diameter, claiming (we believe rightly) that they are better able to attend to the careful watering of the plants and thus avoid any injury to the roots. The treatment of young Tomato plants is pretty much the same as would be given to early Cucumbers, they should have a temperature of 60° during the day, and not less than 50°—55° at night. For a main crop sow the seed in February or March, then transfer into pots as before advised; it is of great importance that the plants be kept sturdy and therefore air should be given on all favourable occasions. The drainage of both the pots in which the young plants are grown on and the borders or boxes in which they are to fruit should be very carefully looked to, so as to allow of their receiving copious supplies of water, especially during the fruiting period. When planted out in the greenhouse border, the plants should be placed about 18 inches apart and supported either by means of a stake or tied up with soft string to the roof, all side growths should be cleared off as they appear, and only the main stem allowed to grow away, this being stopped when it reaches the glass, or when three or four trusses of fruit have been set.

The best soil for Tomatoes is a good rich loam to which has been added a light dressing of farmyard manure, say one-fifth of the bulk; many growers do not put any manure in the soil at the time of planting, leaving the feeding until the first truss of fruit has set, when they apply regular dressings of artificial manure, or give a mulching of well-decayed manure and water the same thoroughly in. In no case must the manure used be taken from a heap that is heated or the result will be disastrous.

TOMATOES—RED VARIETIES.

per pkt.—s. d.

THE DANIELS. The fruit are of good size, rather above the medium, smooth, brilliant scarlet in colour, of beautiful form, exquisite flavour, and remarkably solid. It is a robust grower, and a marvellously profuse and continuous bearer. A first-class variety for cultivation under glass 1 0

DANIELS' SELECTED OPEN-AIR. The heaviest cropping out-door variety with which we are acquainted. It is of hardy constitution, bearing large clusters of bright crimson fruit of medium size and good shape. Its distinct and delicate flavour will make it a favourite with all lovers of the Tomato 1 0

*DANIELS' SCARLET PERFECTION. Very handsome, perfectly round and smooth, firm and solid, flavour first-class and of a beautiful glossy scarlet colour; obtains first prize wherever exhibited 1 0

*DANIELS' HARBINGER. This variety, being very early and a prolific bearer, will be found extremely valuable for growing in the open air. The fruit are round, smooth, solid, and of a bright red .. .. 6d. and 1 0
*EARLY RUBY. Very prolific, is of dwarf habit, good shape, colour bright scarlet, flesh solid; succeeds well in the open air .. 0 6
*LAXTON'S OPEN-AIR. Very early and hardy 0 6
*LARGE RED. Very prolific and useful 0 4

per pkt.—s. d.

EARLY DAWN. The earliest Tomato we know, produces good even sized fruit in clusters of eight or nine, smooth skinned, a good colour and very solid excellent variety for indoor or open-air cultivation 1 0

*SUNRISE. This grand variety has received a First Class Certificate from the Royal Horticultural Society for its numerous good qualities. It is very early, a free setter, and enormously prolific, bearing ten to eleven even sized fruit in one bunch. Colour rich scarlet. It is equally prolific either in the open air or under glass 6d. and 1 0

SUPREME. Awarded Highest Marks, R.H.S. The fruit are medium sized, round, very smooth, and of a beautiful scarlet 6d. and 1 0
UP-TO-DATE. One of the heaviest cropping varieties, the smooth round fruit are of medium size and produced in clusters, bearing as many as twenty fruit at a joint; bright crimson 6d. and 1 0

YELLOW VARIETIES.

DANIELS' GOLDEN BEAUTY. A new and beautiful variety of splendid flavour. The fruit, which are freely produced in large clusters, are of good size, round, smooth, and of a rich bright golden yellow, occasionally flushed with a pale red .. 1 0
*GOLDEN EAGLE. This is the most prolific variety that we know, and there is none to equal it in flavour .. 6d. and 1 0
*LARGE YELLOW IMPROVED. A fine variety .. 6d. and 1 0

Those marked thus * are the best for open-air cultivation.

VEGETABLE MARROWS.

per pkt.—s. d.

DANIELS' EARLY WHITE. A long white variety coming into use before any other of the long kinds. It is very prolific, bearing its fruit immediately it begins to run 0 6

DANIELS' LARGE CREAM. One of the best Marrows in cultivation, grows to a large size, very handsome, and is an immense cropper, unequalled for general crop .. 0 6

DANIELS' GOLDEN CREAM. A very prolific variety, fruit medium size, and of a beautiful pale cream colour, flavour first-class 0 6

PEN-Y-BYD (The best in the World). Awarded two First Class Certificates. This distinct variety is enormously prolific and a continuous bearer. The vine is extremely short-jointed, setting a fruit at every joint. The fruit is of handsome appearance, almost globular in form, sometimes very slightly ribbed, averaging about six inches in diameter 0 6
CUSTARD-SHAPED. Prolific, ornamental-shaped variety .. 0 4
GREEN BUSH. Very prolific; compact habit of growth .. 0 4
LONG GREEN. Good variety, forms a striking contrast with other kinds 0 4
LONG WHITE-RIBBED, or BUSH. Good; a prolific kind .. 0 4
MOORE'S CREAM. Very prolific, delicious flavour 0 4
VEGETABLE MARROW and SQUASH. Various sorts mixed .. 0 4

Cultivation.—Vegetable Marrows are easy to grow, and it is possible in every garden to find a corner in which to grow two or three plants; they are often planted on old heaps of refuse, etc. It is not, however, essential that they should be planted on manure heaps, as they will grow quite well in the open garden in a hole which has been well manured, and in fact, they continue to fruit longer when so grown.

Copious supplies of water are necessary for Vegetable Marrows, and the fruits should be cut when young, as otherwise they become tough, and the plants cease bearing sooner. Sow the seeds singly in small pots, and plant out when about a foot high, giving protection for the first few nights. Another plan is to sow the seeds in the mound, where they are to grow, and to cover the plants with a hand-light, or some similar covering until frost has disappeared. Frequent waterings with liquid manure at the time of fruiting will add much vigour to the plants and size to the fruits.

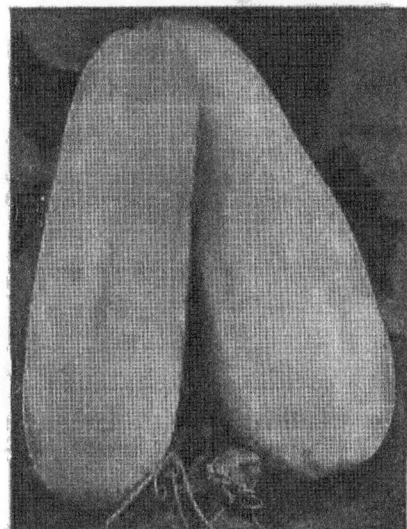

DANIELS' LARGE CREAM.

POTATOES.
FIRST EARLY VARIETIES.

DUKE OF YORK, *Reduced from a Photograph.*

DANIELS' DUKE OF YORK. This grand variety still holds its own as one of the best heavy cropping Earlies in cultivation. In habit of growth, it is very compact, the haulm being only a foot high. The leaves are smooth and of a rich glossy green colour, whilst the tubers cluster compactly round the stem, and are very easy to raise. The tubers are large, oval, smooth and handsome, and distinct in appearance, the eyes are few and quite even with the surface, ensuring a minimum of waste ; the flesh is dry and mealy when cooked, and of the most excellent flavour. (Originally raised by us and sent out in 1893.)   Scotch grown Seed. Per 14 lb. 7s. 6d. ; 56 lb. 27s.

SPECIAL NOTICE.

CARRIAGE OF POTATOES.

We pay carriage on a Potato Order when, either by itself or including other seeds, it amounts to 40/- and upwards. In the case of smaller orders we have, according to Railway regulations, to pay carriage in advance on all passenger parcels, and we therefore append a table giving such approximate charges, which amount should be added when remitting to the price quoted for the potatoes.

	28 lbs.		14 lbs.		7 lbs.
Up to 30 miles	1s. 9d.		1s. 4d.		1s.
„ 50 „	1s. 11d.		1s. 6d.		1s.
„ 100 „	2s. 1d.		1s. 7d.		1s.
„ 200 „	2s. 4d.		1s. 9d.		1s.
Over 200 „	2s. 11d.		1s. 11d.		1s.

When ordering quantities of 28 lbs. and upwards, the price for bags must be added as follows :—28 lb. bag 9d., 56 lb. 1s., 1 cwt. 1s. 6d.

Half quantities cannot be supplied at the whole quantity rate, even where several lots are taken, as each requires packing separately.

POTATOES.

FIRST EARLY VARIETIES.

EXPRESS. Reduced from a Photograph.

EXPRESS. A fine early White Kidney of handsome appearance and excellent cooking quality, and is at the same time a very heavy and sure cropper. We can strongly recommend this.   Scotch grown Seed. Per 14 lb. 7s. 3d.; 56 lb. 26s.

EXPRESS. A useful stock.   Class III. Seed. Per 14 lb. 6s. 3d.; 56 lb. 22s.

ARRAN ROSE (New and Immune). A useful early variety, tubers oval in shape, with pale pink skin, shallow eye, and white flesh. It is of robust constitution, with medium haulm; cooking quality excellent.
    Scotch grown Seed. Per 14 lb. 7s.; 56 lb. 24s.

DARGILL EARLY (New and Immune). This new early has been tested at Ormskirk and proved itself immune from Wart Disease. It is a white kidney with shallow eyes and pale yellow flesh, the haulm is medium and somewhat spreading. A very good cropper.   Scotch grown Seed. Per 14 lb. 6s. 6d.; 56 lb. 22s.

WITCH HILL EARLY (New and Immune). A beautiful, early White Kidney of heavy cropping qualities. The eyes are shallow, flesh white, and of excellent table quality; haulm medium. First-class Certificate, R.H.S.
    Scotch grown Seed. Per 7 lb. 4s. 6d.; 14 lb. 8s.

MYATT'S ASHLEAF, IMPROVED. This will be found a heavier and more reliable cropper than the old variety, and of exceptionally good table quality.   Per 14 lb. 7s. 3d.; 56 lb. 26s.

EARLY ECLIPSE. A handsome first early White Kidney of great productiveness with white skin and flesh, it cooks well early and late, and is in great demand as a market variety   Scotch grown Seed. Per 14 lb. 6s. 3d.; 56 lb. 22s.

EARLY ECLIPSE. A good useful stock   ..   .. Class III. Seed. Per 14 lb. 5s. 3d.; 56 lb. 18s.

SIR JOHN LLEWELYN. This splendid White Kidney, in consideration of its earliness, heavy cropping, good quality, and disease resisting properties, has become highly popular. The tubers are of good size and shape, and when cooked, white and floury. Award of Merit, R.H.S.
    Scotch grown Seed. Per 14 lb. 6s. 3d.; 56 lb. 22s.

EPICURE. A useful early white round potato of exceptionally heavy cropping qualities, and is at the same time a most excellent table variety.   Scotch grown Seed. Per 14 lb. 5s. 9d.; 56 lb. 20s.

ARRAN COMRADE (Immune).

ARRAN COMRADE.

ARRAN COMRADE (Immune). A fine second early variety with white skin and flesh ; it is oval to nearly round' in shape, and of fine appearance ; in fact one of the handsomest potatoes of recent introduction. The foliage is broad and spreading. It is an excellent cropper, having proved one of the best at the Ormskirk trials. If sprouted will come fit nearly as soon as the first earlies. We can strongly recommend this variety. Scotch grown Seed. Per 14 lb. 6s. 6d. ; 56 lb. 22s.

EDZELL BLUE (Immune). An early coloured round variety, eyes medium depth, skin reddish purple, flesh pure white, and of excellent table quality. The haulm is vigorous, somewhat spreading, bloom white. Crops heavily, quality very good when matured. Matures rather too late to be strictly classed as a first early.
Scotch grown Seed. Per 14 lb. 5s. 6d. ; 56 lb. 19s.

BRITISH QUEEN. A second early variety of great merit. The skin and flesh are white, and of extra fine table quality; this, combined with its great productiveness and good keeping qualities, make it a most desirable variety for all purposes. Scotch grown Seed. Per 14 lb. 5s. ; 56 lb. 17s.

KING GEORGE V. (Immune). A most useful early Main Crop variety, which we have grown for the past three seasons, and can thoroughly recommend. It is a handsome White Kidney, of vigorous constitution, producing a very heavy crop of large, clean tubers, with white skin and flesh, and a finely-netted skin, a sure indication of its good cooking qualities. A most useful sort for exhibition purposes. Scotch grown Seed. Per 14 lb. 5s. 3d. ; 56 lb. 18s.

KING GEORGE V. A good vigorous stock. Class II. Seed. Once grown from Scotch Seed.
Per 14 lb. 4s. 9d. ; 56 lb. 16s.

MAJESTIC (Immune).

MAJESTIC.

MAJESTIC (Immune). A fine Main Crop Kidney which has proved itself one of the heaviest croppers amongst recent introductions. The haulm is of medium height and moderately vigorous, flowers white. It is kidney shaped, with shallow eyes. Skin and flesh white, and of the most excellent table quality. Can be highly recommended.

Scotch grown Seed. Per 14 lb. 6s. 3d. ; 56 lb. 22s.

MAJESTIC. A good vigorous stock.   Class II. Seed. Once grown from Scotch Seed. Per 14 lb. 5s. 9d. ; 56 lb. 20s.

LOCHAR (Immune). A late white-skinned variety, roundish in shape ; eyes medium depth ; skin white with faint tinge of pink, flesh white and of excellent quality. Haulm upright, spreading, moderately vigorous. Produces a heavy crop of medium sized tubers of good appearance and fine table quality. Flowers creamy white.

Scotch grown Seed. Per 14 lb. 5s. 3d. ; 56 lb. 18s.

TINWALD PERFECTION (Immune). A fine late variety; the tubers, which are of white skin and flesh, are very handsome, and oval to oblong in shape. The haulm is of medium height, spreading and moderately vigorous ; leaves darkish green, flowers mauve, tipped white. On account of its handsome shape will prove a valuable sort for exhibition.

Scotch grown Seed. Per 14 lb. 5s. 3d. ; 56 lb. 18s.

KERR'S PINK (Immune). A late pale pink round potato of vigorous constitution, with strong upright haulm and white flowers. It is an extraordinary heavy cropper, flattish round in shape, white flesh, and of excellent cooking quality. Can be strongly recommended.

Scotch grown Seed. Per 14 lb. 6s. ; 56 lb. 20s.

IMMUNE VARIETIES. It should be understood that Potatoes classed as "Immune" are not always immune from the ordinary Potato Blight or Disease (*Phytophthora infestans*), but are only immune from what is known as Wart Disease or "Black Scab," caused by the fungus *Synchytrium endobioticum*. In all instances on ground where the latter disease has made its appearance, only varieties known to be immune should be planted.

GREAT SCOT (Immune).

GREAT SCOT.

GREAT SCOT (Immune.) A mid-season variety of vigorous habit of growth. Tubers round, large, eyes medium depth, skin of flesh white ; quality excellent. The haulm is tall, upright and vigorous, leaves dark green and glossy, flowers white, buds usually drop without opening. This variety is an excellent cropper, and may be grown as an early main crop. One of the best of the second early varieties ; most suitable for planting on light and medium soils.
Scotch grown Seed. Per 14 lb. 5s. 3d. ; 56 lb. 18s.

GREAT SCOT. A good vigorous stock. Class II. Seed. Once grown from Scotch Seed.
Per 14 lb. 4s. 9d. ; 56 lb. 16s.

ARRAN CHIEF. A distinct new Main Crop variety of Scotch origin. The tubers, which cluster compactly round the haulm, are very numerous, of good size, nicely rounded, and have comparatively shallow eyes ; they are of the very best quality, and make a splendid table Potato. The majority of the tubers are of good marketable size, with very few small, whilst its handsome shape will make it a fine addition to the exhibition table. It has been tested under various conditions for the past three seasons, and experts agree that it is one of the finest additions of recent years to our list of Main Crop Potatoes.
Scotch grown Seed. Per 14 lb. 4s. 6d. ; 56 lb. 15s.

KING EDWARD VII. A very fine Main Crop variety ; the haulm grows to the height of two feet, and is fairly robust, producing a large crop of handsome tubers. The skin is white, with a blotch of pink about the eyes, which gives it a very pleasing appearance. It is a good cooker, and free from disease ; for exhibition it is first class.
Scotch grown Seed. Per 14 lb. 5s. ; 56 lb. 17s.

THE ALLY. This is a grand cropping variety which has proved itself immune from black scab. It is an early Main Crop of vigorous constitution, producing a very heavy crop of handsome oval-shaped tubers with white skin and flesh. The eyes are few and shallow. We can recommend this as a thoroughly useful variety for all purposes.
Scotch grown Seed. Per 14 lb. 4s. 9d. ; 56 lb. 16s.

UP-TO-DATE. A large handsome potato of very heavy cropping qualities, tubers oval in shape, skin roughly netted, flesh white, dry, and mealy when cooked.
Scotch grown Seed. Per 14 lb. 4s. 9d. ; 56 lb. 16s.

DANIELS' SENSATION.

DANIELS' SENSATION. *Reduced from a Photograph.*

DANIELS' SENSATION. This grand Main Crop Potato is one of the heaviest-cropping and best varieties we have ever grown. It is of a good, robust constitution, the haulm growing about two feet high. The tubers are of good size, thick pebble-shape, with very shallow eyes, almost level with the surface ; the skin is white and slightly netted—a sure indication of good cooking qualities—the flesh being white, mealy, and of the finest texture. Its splendid cropping and good culinary qualities, combined with its very handsome appearance, have made this variety a great favourite alike with the cook and exhibitor.   Scotch grown Seed. Per 14 lb. 5s. ; 56 lb. 17s.

HINTS ON POTATO CULTURE.

Cultivation.—The varieties quoted in our list are the best in cultivation. It is most important that frequent changes of seed should be made, as Potatoes deteriorate if repeatedly saved from the same soil and district. For early work, "Duke of York," the well-known variety introduced by ourselves is still pre-eminent, and the increasing demand for this kind proves its superiority over all others as a first early.

Much depends upon the selection and treatment of the "sets " ; it is therefore necessary to secure good moderate sized Potatoes which should be set up on end in shallow boxes or trays, and allowed to sprout before being planted, as when this is done much advantage is gained both in the development of the plants and in the weight of the crops. Potatoes like a good open position in the garden, and the most suitable soil is a medium to light one in a well-drained position ; the ground should be deeply dug and manured in the Autumn. Where stable manure is available a good dressing should be given at the time of planting, placing a layer on the bottom of the trenches ; well-decayed leaf-mould, or the remains of an old mushroom bed are also excellent for this purpose.

When planting it is important that an abundance of room be left between the rows and the sets in the row ; allow a distance of two feet between rows for the early, and three feet for the late strong-growing sorts, and twelve to eighteen inches between the sets in the rows. Where the land is naturally low and wet it is a capital plan to elevate the rows by forming ridges and so planting the sets on about a level with the natural soil ; it is also good to keep the surface soil constantly stirred with the hoe until the earthing up commences.

When the young growths begin to push through the soil care must be taken to protect them from the frost by continually earthing up the soil round them (neglect of this has often resulted in the loss of a complete crop of Early Potatoes), and when it is desired to grow exhibition specimens only, one haulm should be left to a plant, all the weakest ones being drawn out as they appear. Slight dressings of soot or of "Norwich Fertilizer" during the growing season will be of much advantage. Immediately the growth is completed, the crop should be lifted ; choose fine weather for the work and store them after having had a few hours' sun on them.

Where small quantities only are grown it is much better to store Potatoes in a cool dry place where they can be easily got at, as they are not so liable to develop disease as when stored in a pit or trench.

☞ **IMPORTANT NOTICE.**—Seed Potatoes procured during the Winter and early Spring, when not required for immediate planting, should be taken out of the bag or package in which they are received and laid out in a dry, airy place protected from frost, or they will begin to sprout and a weakly growth will be the result.

DANIELS' SUPERIOR GRASS SEEDS FOR LAWNS, &c.

For many years we have given close attention to the selection of the most suitable Grasses for producing the best Lawns, Tennis Courts, Cricket Grounds, Golf Links, &c., and we have much pleasure in recommending the splendid mixtures we offer as the very best procurable for the purposes named. March and April are the best months for sowing in Spring. September and early October for Autumn sowing. For renovating existing lawns, lightly rake the worst places and bare patches, then sow our Peerless Mixtures (No. 5 or 6) at the rate of half-pound to the rod, or more thickly if the lawn is very bare; apply a thin sprinkling of finely sifted soil, and roll with a light garden roller; protect the newly sown parts from birds.

No. 1. DANIELS' SPECIAL MIXTURE FOR LAWNS.

This is a special mixture of the finest leaved dwarf evergreen Grasses, and will produce an extra fine close velvety turf. First-class for making new lawns or for renovating. Highly recommended.
Per lb. 3s., per bushel 60s.

No. 2. DANIELS' FINE MIXTURE OF DWARF GRASSES.

A splendid mixture of fine Grasses, suitable for Tennis Courts, Croquet Grounds, &c., also a most useful mixture for renovating bare and weak patches. Per lb. 2s. 6d., per bushel 55s.

No. 3. DANIELS' MIXTURE OF DWARF GRASSES.

A good cheap mixture for producing a fine close turf.
Per lb. 2s., per bushel 52s. 6d.

No. 5. DANIELS' PEERLESS MIXTURE

Without Perennial Rye Grass. FOR GARDEN LAWNS.
This mixture is composed of the finest dwarf-growing Grasses for producing a fine velvety Turf of extra good quality.
Per lb. 3s., per bushel 65s.

No. 6. DANIELS' PEERLESS MIXTURE

Without Perennial Rye Grass. FOR TENNIS LAWNS.
A mixture of fine Grasses for producing a close, dwarf, springy turf, most suitable for this purpose.
Per lb. 2s. 6d., per bushel 60s.

No. 8. DANIELS' SPECIAL MIXTURES FOR CRICKET & FOOTBALL GROUNDS.
Per bushel 52s. 6d.

Where larger quantities than those mentioned are required, we shall always be pleased to make special quotations.
N.B.—Where no definite instructions are given, we shall supply our Special Mixtures, containing Perennial Rye Grass.

MISCELLANEOUS PLANTS, ROOTS AND SEEDS.

ARTICHOKES.

DANIELS' WHITE MAMMOTH. This is a pure white skin variety of the Jerusalem Artichoke. The tubers, which are more regularly formed than those of the old variety, are somewhat globular in shape and of excellent quality. Per 14 lb. 3s. 6d.; 56 lb. 12s. 0d.
JERUSALEM. Good sound tubers
per peck (14 lbs.) 3s. 0d.; bush. (56 lbs.) 10s. 6d.

CHIVES AND GARLIC.

CHIVES. Fine strong clumps .. each 0d.; per doz. 7s. 6d.
GARLIC BULBS .. .. .. per lb. 2s.

SEA KALE (Seed).

ORDINARY .. .. per pint 2s.; per oz. 8d.
LILY WHITE (Special) .. per pint 3s. 6d.; per oz. 1s.
For Plants, see page 47.

SHALLOT BULBS.

CAPSICUM.

					per pkt.—s. d
RUBY KING	..	..	..	..	6d. and 1 0
CELESTIAL	..	..	..	..	0d. and 1 0
CHILI or BIRD	..	..	..	..	0 4
ELEPHANT'S TRUNK	..	..	..	6d. and 1 0
LONG RED	..	..	..	..	0 4
LONG YELLOW	..	..	..	..	0 4
PROCOPP'S GIANT	..	..	..	..	0 6
MONSTREUSE	..	..	..	..	0 6
SWEET GOLDEN DAWN	..	..	..	0 6
MIXED, all kinds	..	..	..	..	0 4

EGG PLANT OR AUBERGINE.
(Solanum Esculentum.)

		per pkt.—s. d
DANIELS' IMPROVED LARGE PURPLE. Fine handsome fruit; very prolific	..	6d. and 1 0
BLACK CHINESE. Very effective	..	6d. and 1 0
LARGE WHITE. A very useful variety	..	6d. and 1 0

SHALLOTS.

Cultivation.—Shallots should be planted as early in the new year as weather permits in good rich well-manured soil, use well rotted manure when obtainable as they thrive much better in this. It is still better if possible to plant on ground that was plentifully manured the previous year. Plant in rows about 1 foot apart and 6 to 8 inches apart in the row, do not bury deeply. It is essential that they should be kept free from weeds. When the leaves begin to wither about July, pull up and leave them to dry on the ground for a few days, after which store in a dry place, turn them over occasionally and remove any that show signs of decay. They are considered much superior to onions for pickling.

BULBS. Fine sound bulbs .. per 7 lb. 6s. 0d.; per lb. 1s. 0d.

"I have gained First Prize for the best cultivated allotment, and I took nine First, four Second, and one Third Prizes."—Mr. T. HEAVESLEY, Stockingford.

"You may care to know that I obtained five First Prizes at Elmswell Flower and Vegetable Show as follows: Peas, Sweet Peas, Red Cabbage, Vegetable Marrow and Beetroot, all from your Seeds."—Mr. H. MOGGS, Badwell Ash.

MISCELLANEOUS PLANTS & ROOTS

ASPARAGUS PLANTS.

An abundance of fine Asparagus may be grown with less than half the expense usually incurred in making costly "beds," and will succeed admirably on most soils when planted in lines or clumps on the Kitchen Garden borders, or amongst dwarf-growing Fruits where the space will admit, a liberal cultivation being all that is required to ensure the best results. The roots are liable to injury if removed during severe weather in Winter. They are best planted when growth has commenced in Spring, and when they can be carefully taken up and packed so as to travel a long journey, without injury. They should, however, in all cases be planted as quickly as possible after receiving them. We consider March and April the best months for planting.

CONNOVER'S COLOSSAL. Two and three years old   ..   per 100, 12s. 6d. and 15s.
TRUE GIANT. Two and three years old   ..   ..   per 100, 12s. 6d. and 15s.

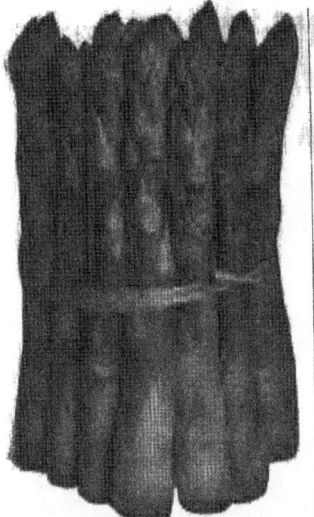

ASPARAGUS—CONNOVER'S COLOSSAL.

ASPARAGUS SEED.

per oz.—s. d.

TRUE GIANT. A fine variety, producing large heads of excellent quality   per lb. 6s.   0   6
CONNOVER'S COLOSSAL. A very large variety, very prolific, and of fine flavour per lb. 6s.   0   6
EARLY GIANT PURPLE (Argenteuil). As grown by the celebrated French growers for
   Paris Market ; robust variety of the most delicious flavour   ..   per lb. 7s.   0   8

RHUBARB.

One of the most useful, wholesome, and profitable of garden plants. The ground for this should be well broken up and manured, but it is not advisable to plant any of the stalks the first season for fear of unduly weakening the growth. A top-dressing of well-decayed manure in Winter is very beneficial.

CHAMPAGNE. Deep red stems, early, one of the very best for general use. each 2s.; per doz. 21s.
DAWS' CHAMPION. A fine new variety of great size and splendid colour. Very productive
     each 2s. 6d.; per doz. 28s.
DAWS' CHALLENGE. Largest kind known, large clumps   ''   ..   ..   each 3s. 6d.
VALENTINE (new). Very early, ready end of February   .. each 2s. 6d.; per doz. 27s. 6d.

SEA KALE.

This valuable esculent is easily forced if care is taken only to apply heat gradually, as it will not succeed if placed in too high a temperature at starting. Place several crowns a few inches apart in large pots, and stand them in a temperature of about 45 degrees, with an inverted pot placed over each to exclude light and insure blanching; a mushroom house, pit or cellar, will do well for this purpose. Sea Kale may also be easily forced in the open ground by covering it over with large specially made pots, and applying fermenting material. The heads should be cut when in about the condition shown in illustration, and taken off in the same way.

STRONG PLANTING ROOTS   ..   ..   =   per doz. 4s. 0d.; per 100, 27s. 6d.
GOOD STRONG ROOTS, for forcing   ..   =   per doz. 5s. 0d.; per 100, 30s. 0d.
EXTRA STRONG ROOTS, for forcing, very fine   =   per doz. 5s. 6d.; per 100, 40s. 0d.
SEED   ..   ..   see page 46

SEA KALE

SWEET AND POT HERBS.

We have a fine collection of these, including the following sorts:—

		per doz.—s. d.				per doz.—s. d.
BALM	—	each 1s. 10 6	ROSEMARY	—	— each 1s.	10 6
CHAMOMILE	—	,, 10 6	RUE	—	,,	10 0
HOREHOUND	—	,, 10 6	SAGE, Common	—	,,	10 6
LAVENDER	—	,, 10 6	SAVORY, WINTER	—	,,	10 6
MARJORAM, POT	—	,, 10 6	THYME, LEMON	—	,,	10 6
MINT, LAMB	—	,, 10 6	,, COMMON	—	,,	10 0
,, PEPPER	—	,, 10 6	WORMWOOD	—	,,	10 6
PENNYROYAL	—	,, 10 6				

The most useful varieties assorted, our selection, 9d. each ; per doz. 8s.; per 100 60s.

CAULIFLOWER PLANTS.

Ready about end of April and beginning of May.

DANIELS' KING OF THE CAULIFLOWER. *For description see page 23.*
     3s. 6d. per 100.

ONION PLANTS.

Strong Autumn sown, to plant out for show purposes, can be supplied in Spring of the following kinds only:—

AILSA CRAIG. GOLDEN ROCCA. GIANT ROCCA. WHITE ELEPHANT TRIPOLL.
    All Carriage Paid. Each sort 2s. 6d. per 100.

HOME-GROWN FARM SEEDS.

MANGELS.

Our stocks of these are all English grown, and can be fully relied on as really first-class. All growers of Mangels should give our Seeds a trial, as we feel sure the result would be most satisfactory.

per lb.—s. d.

DANIELS' CORONATION GLOBE. A new variety carefully selected by ourselves. It is of large size, perfect form, very solid, and of a feeding quality rivalling the famous Golden Tankard; a very heavy cropper 1 9

DANIELS' INTERMEDIATE or GATE-POST. A grand stock; one of the finest Mangels ever introduced, grows to a great size, with a uniform crop of very heavy, handsome, and clean roots, and of the finest quality 1 0

DANIELS' RED INTERMEDIATE. An improvement on the Long Red. Very useful for shallow soils. The roots are broader and shorter than that variety, and much easier to raise; can be used early 1 9

DANIELS' GOLDEN TANKARD. Specially selected for its yellow or golden flesh, its richness in saccharine matter, and handsome shape 1 9

DANIELS' CHAMPION ORANGE GLOBE. Our own unequalled stock, highly recommended for its neat top, fine clear skin, and tap root; a heavy cropper 1 6

DANIELS' SELECTED YELLOW GLOBE. Good stock 1 6

Price per Cwt. on application.

SWEDE TURNIPS.

per lb.—s. d.

DANIELS' NORFOLK GIANT PURPLE-TOP. The roots are somewhat oval, and of a deep rich purple. It is a heavy cropper and excellent keeper. All farmers should give it a trial .. 2 3

DANIELS' IMPROVED PURPLE-TOP. A carefully selected and splendid variety 2 3

DANIELS' DEFIANCE GREEN-TOP. A first-class variety for grazing purposes; very hardy 2 6

WHITE-FLESHED TURNIPS.

DANIELS' NORFOLK GREEN ROUND. Excellent for main crop, hardiest of the Globe varieties 1 6

DANIELS' PURPLE-TOP MAMMOTH. Early Turnip, very heavy cropper, large and handsome roots 2 0

BELL or DECANTER. Extra selected stock 2 0

YELLOW-FLESHED TURNIPS.

DANIELS' GREEN-TOP YELLOW SCOTCH. Grows a heavy crop, flesh solid and juicy, much relished by cattle 2 3

DANIELS' PURPLE-TOP YELLOW SCOTCH. A very superior variety, nearly equal to the Swede in quality 2 3

Price per Bushel on application.

CABBAGES.

per lb.—s. d.

DANIELS' CHAMPION DRUMHEAD. A very fine selected variety, producing extraordinarily large heads .. per oz. 6d. 6 6

DANIELS' EARLY DRUMHEAD. Comes into use some weeks before the larger varieties .. per oz. 10d. 8 6

ROBINSON'S DRUMHEAD .. .. ,, 6d. 5 6

THOUSAND-HEADED KALE, Selected stock .. ,, 6d. 2 0

KOHL RABI.

EARLY WHITE VIENNA. Best for garden per pkt. 6d.; per oz. 1s. 6d.

DANIELS' SHORT-TOP GREEN. For field culture 4 0

CARROTS.

per lb.—s. d.

GIANT WHITE BELGIAN. Grows to a large size, roots good shape; produces a very heavy crop of excellent feeding quality .. .. | All | 4 6

YELLOW BELGIAN. Best for general crop, roots large and of good shape; produces a heavy crop and is very useful for horses, etc. .. .. .. | Clean | 4 6

JAMES' SCARLET INTERMEDIATE. A well-known variety of fine shape, producing a heavy crop. One of the best for shallow soils .. .. .. | Seed | 3 0

CLEANED GRASS SEEDS & CLOVERS,

For all Soils and Situations, for Pasturage, Ensilage, &c.

Samples and Special Quotations on Application.

DANIELS' MIXTURES.

FOR ALTERNATE HUSBANDRY OR ROTATION CROPS.

DANIELS' SPECIAL PERMANENT PASTURE.

FOR LIGHT, MEDIUM, AND HEAVY SOILS.

DANIELS' SPECIAL RENOVATING MIXTURES.

RYE GRASSES AND CLOVERS OF THE FINEST QUALITIES.

Special Quotations on Application.

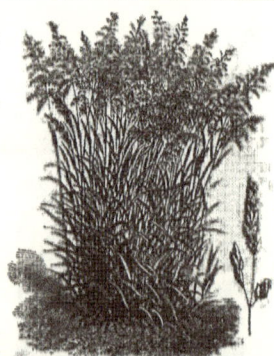

ROUGH-STALKED MEADOW GRASS.

Orders for Farm Seeds not less than 40s. Carriage paid to any Station in England and Wales.

OUR FARM SEED CATALOGUE FOR SPRING, 1921,

Will be published in Spring, and will be sent gratis and post free on application. If you are interested, let us register your name at once.

It contains a complete list of the choicest sorts of Mangels, Swedes, Turnips, and other Root Seeds, Clovers, Grasses, and other Forage Plants, besides many valuable hints on cultivation.

HORTICULTURAL MANURES, &c.

DANIELS' NORWICH FERTILIZER.

Part of a Crop of Grapes fed with Daniels' Norwich Fertilizer, grown by J. E. Moxey, Esq., Framlingham Hall, Norwich.

Without doubt the finest Manure for Fruit, Chrysanthemums, and all general Garden Crops, and we strongly recommend our Customers to give it a trial.

Prices per cwt., 36/-; ¼ cwt., 19/-; 28 lbs., 10/6; 14 lbs., 6/-; 7 lbs., 3/6.

DANIELS' DAISY DESTROYER.

For Destroying Daisies and Plantains and Broad-leaved Plants in Lawns

Various methods are employed to rid lawns of daisies, plantains, &c., such as grubbing them out and using poisonous liquids, &c., but the safest and most effectual way is to use a really reliable lawn sand, and besides it means a great saving of labour.

Daniels' Daisy Destroyer, when used carefully, and the application is followed by a short spell of dry weather, will be found to be a sure remedy. It may give the grass a scorched appearance for a short time, but it does no permanent harm to it. On the contrary, it is an excellent fertilizer. A dressing of about 4 ozs. to the square yard will be found sufficient, and the best time to apply it is in the Spring.

Prices per cwt., 32/-; ½ cwt., 17/-; 28 lbs., 9/-; 14 lbs., 5/-; 7 lbs., 2/9

DANIELS' SPECIAL LAWN MANURE

This preparation is quite simple to use, and if applied during showery weather in Spring it will have a very beneficial effect, giving colour and vigour to the finer grasses, ensuring a thick growth of rich velvety green turf.

A dressing applied in September with an equal bulk of fine soil will be most helpful to Tennis and Croquet Lawns, which have been much worn during the Summer.

One hundredweight will be found sufficient for a full-sized Tennis Lawn, and for smaller lawns it should be applied at the rate of 3 ozs. to the square yard.

Prices per cwt., 35/-; ¼ cwt., 18/6; 28 lbs., 10/-; 14 lbs., 5/9; 7 lbs., 3/3

We can supply a very useful book on the Care of LAWNS & GREENS. Post Free 4'-

SPECIAL POTATO FERTILIZER.

(A Splendid Manure also for Onions, Peas, Cabbages, etc.)

Specially prepared for Allotment and Garden Potato Growing. It is a high-class, valuable Manure, and of high guaranteed analysis.

We can very confidently recommend our Special Potato Fertilizer as the best Manure on the market, and one that will not only produce heavy crops but early crops of sound tubers. One of the most important functions that our Fertilizer performs is to assist in the formation of starch and sugar, or in other words, to fill the cells of the potato with nutritious matter, instead of water, thereby increasing the weight and soundness of the crop.

Directions for Use.—Six cwts. per acre; 6 lb. per rod; to be sown in the furrows at time of seeding, and well mixed with the soil. When the tops are through the soil a light dressing may be also applied during showery weather.

In Bags—7 lbs., 2s. 3d.; 14 lbs., 3s. 9d.; 28 lbs., 7s. 6d.; ½-cwt., 14s.; 1 cwt., 27s. Carriage Paid on 28 lbs. and upwards.

VARIOUS GARDEN MANURES.

CLAY'S FERTILIZER. Bags, 7 lbs., 4s.; 14 lbs., 7s.; 28 lbs., 12s.; 56 lbs., 22s.; 1 cwt., 40s.

ICHTHEMIC GUANO. Cartons, 9d. and 1s. 3d. Bags, 7 lbs., 3s. 6d.; 14 lbs., 6s.; 28 lbs., 11s.; 56 lbs., 20s.; 1 cwt., 36s.

THOMSON'S VINE AND PLANT MANURE. Tins, 1s. 6d. Bags, 7 lbs., 3s. 6d.; 14 lbs., 6s.; 28 lbs., 10s. 6d.; 56 lbs., 19s.; 1 cwt., 36s.

THOMSON'S CHRYSANTHEMUM MANURE. A special top-dressing manure. Bags, 7 lbs., 3s. 6d.; 14 lbs., 6s.; 28 lbs., 10s. 6d.; 56 lbs., 19s.

TOMORITE. A first-rate manure for Tomatoes. Cartons, 9d. and 1s. 3d. Bags, 7 lbs., 3s. 6d.; 14 lbs., 6s.

DANIELS' SPECIAL LAWN MANURE, Special sample packet, post free 1s. Bags, 7 lbs., 3s. 3d.; 14 lbs., 5s. 9d.; 28 lbs., 10s.; 56 lbs., 18s. 6d.; 1 cwt., 35s.

BONE MEAL. Bags, 7 lbs., 4s.; 28 lbs., 7s.; 56 lbs., 13s.; 1 cwt., 24s.

BONES. Specially prepared for Vine borders. 28 lbs., 7s.; 56 lbs., 13s.; 1 cwt., 24s.

BASIC SLAG. 1 cwt., 9s. 6d.; ½ cwt., 6s. 6d.; 28 lbs., 3s.; 14 lbs., 1s. 9d.

SUPERPHOSPHATE. 1 cwt., 12s. 6d.; ½ cwt., 7s.; 28 lbs., 3s. 9d.; 14 lbs., 2s.

SULPHATE OF AMMONIA. Per lb., 6d.; per stone, 6s.

NITRATE OF SODA. Per lb., 6d.; per stone, 6s.

When sending remittance for small quantities of Manures, extra should be enclosed for carriage, as per table of carriage on potatoes. See page 40.

POTTING MATERIALS.

CHARCOAL. In Lumps. 6s. per bushel.

COCOA-NUT FIBRE. 5s. per bushel.

LEAF SOIL. 3s. 6d. per bushel.

LOAM. Fibrous. 3s. 6d. per bushel.

PEAT. Best Orchid, 7s. 6d. per bushel. Ordinary Potting, 5s. per bushel.

SILVER SAND. Best coarse, 7s. 6d. per bushel.

SPHAGNUM MOSS. 3s. 6d. per bushel.

Prices subject to alteration without notice.

HORTICULTURAL REQUISITES.

FUMIGATORS.

XL ALL VAPORISING COMPOUND.
In bottles.

No. 1 for 40,000 cubic ft.	23s. 0d.
No. 2 for 20,000 „	12s. 3d.
No. 3 for 10,000 „	6s. 4d.
No. 4 for 5,000 „	3s. 4d.
No. 5 for 2,000 „	1s. 6d.

XL ALL VAPORISING COMPOUND.
In solid dry cakes. Supplied in same sizes and prices as the liquid.

FUMIGATORS. (*See Illustration.*) Complete for above. Price 2s. 3d. and 2s. 6d. each.
Postage extra on all the above.

XL ALL PATENT FUMIGATOR.

XL ALL FUMIGATING SHREDS. These are very effectual and simple to use. Packed in boxes, sufficient for 5,000 cubic ft., 3s.; 10,000 cubic ft., 5s. 3d.

McDOUGALL'S FUMERS. (*See Illustration.*) Complete in themselves and very efficient. A first-rate fumigator for the Amateur. In sizes, for 1,000 cubic ft., 1s. 3d. each, 15s. per doz.; for 2,000 cubic ft., 2s. each, 24s. per doz.

McDOUGALL'S SELF-ACTING FUMIGATING SHEETS. Sufficient for 1,000 cubic ft., 1s.; 12s. doz.
Postage extra on the above.

LETHORION VAPOUR CONES. A very convenient form of Fumigator for small greenhouses and frames. 10d., 1s. 3d. and 1s. 0d. each.

DANIELS' RELIABLE TOBACCO PAPER. Every packet is accompanied with full instructions for use. Per lb., 2s.; postage 5d. extra.

NICOTICIDE VAPORISING COMPOUND. In bottles.

No. 1 for 40,000 cubic ft.	20s. 0d.
No. 2 for 20,000 „	10s. 0d.
No. 3 for 12,000 „	6s. 0d.
No. 4 for 8,000 „	4s. 0d.
No. 5 for 2,000 „	1s. 2d.

FUMIGATORS. Complete for above, each 2s.

POTATO SPRAYING.

We cannot too strongly urge upon our customers the great advantage gained by spraying their growing crops of potatoes. It is quite clearly proved that potato crops which are sprayed at least twice—once early in July and again in August—give much heavier yield of better quality—the additional yield amply repaying the extra outlay on labour and material.

"BLIGHTY" BURGUNDY MIXTURE. One pound of "Blighty" Mixture is sufficient to spray 4 rods. Full instruction for mixing supplied with each packet. Cartons, 2 lbs., 2s.; postage 1s. extra. 4 lbs., 4s.; postage 1s. extra. Bag, 20 lbs., 12s. 6d.; carriage extra.

BORDEAUX MIXTURE. Complete instructions with each packet. 2 lb. packet 2s. 6d. each. Postage 1s. extra. This mixture is also excellent for the winter spraying of Peach trees, &c.

INSECTICIDES.

ABOL. A very safe and effectual insecticide for destroying all kinds of Aphis.

Per pint	..	..	..	..	2s. 5d.
Per quart	..	..	..	..	4s. 0d.
Per ½-gall.	..	..	..	—	6s. 6d.
Per 1-gall.	..	..	..	—	11s. 4d.
Carriage extra.

"ABOL" INSECTICIDE.

EWING'S MILDEW COMPOSITION. In bottles, 2s. 6d. each; postage extra.

GISHURST COMPOUND. A good winter dressing for Fruit Trees and Vines. In boxes, 1s. 3d. & 3s. 6d. each; postage extra.

HELLEBORE POWDER. For destroying Gooseberry Caterpillars. Tins, 1s. and 1s. 6d. each; postage extra.

"KATAKILLA" POWDER INSECTICIDE WASH. Non-Poisonous.
Exterminates Pests on Roses, Fruit Trees, and Vegetables, &c.
Ready measured, ready for use when mixed with cold water.

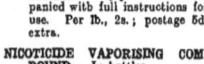

Non-Poisonous.—Fruit & Vegetables washed with "Katakilla" are in no way injured for use. In Cartons, to make 10 gallons of wash, 2s. each; postage extra. (Each Carton contains 4 packets for 2½ gallons of wash.) Large Cartons, to make 50 gallons of wash, 6s. each; postage extra.

KILSALL. Kills all insect pests. Packets for 3-gall. wash, 8d.; for 7-gall., 1s. 2d., post free.

MEALY BUG DESTROYER. In bottles, 1s. 6d. each. Postage extra.

McDOUGALL'S CARBOLIC SOFT SOAP. In tins, 2s. 9d., 5s. and 9s. 6d. each. Carriage extra.

QUASSIA CHIPS. Per lb., 1s. 6d.

QUASSIA EXTRACT. Per gallon, 8s.; half-gall., 4s. 9d.; tins, 1s. 9d. Carriage extra.

SLUGENE. A splendid remedy for destroying slugs. In tins, 2s. each.

SULPHUR, YELLOW. Per lb., 1s.

TOBACCO POWDER. In tins, 9d., 1s. 6d., and 3s. 6d. each. Postage extra.

V. I. FLUID. Winter Spray for Fruit Trees. It destroys all moss and lichens, the breeding grounds of insect pests. Re-invigorates the trees, and leaves them beautifully clean and healthy. Does not damage or clog the spraying machine. Does not burn the bark of the tree, or skin and clothes of the operator. One gallon of Fluid makes 100 gallons Spray Mixture. Price per quart, 4s. 6d.; ½-gall., 8s.; 1-gall., 14s. Carriage extra.

V. II. FLUID. Summer Spray for Fruit Trees. A splendid Insecticide, containing nicotine. For all kinds of summer pests. Per quart, 6s.; ½-gall., 10s. 6d.; 1-gall., 16s. Carriage extra.

VAPORITE. For destroying Wireworms, &c., in the soil. Tins, 1s. 6d. and 3s. 9d.; 14 lbs., 5s. 6d.; 28 lbs., 8s.; ½-cwt., 11s. 9d.; 1-cwt., 18s.

WORM DESTROYER FOR LAWNS. 14 lbs., 7s. 6d.; 28 lbs., 14s.; ½-cwt., 25s.; 1-cwt., 45s. Carriage extra.

XL ALL LIQUID INSECTICIDE. A well tested Insecticide for Fruit Trees and Roses. Per pint, 3s. 3d.; per quart, 6s.; ½-gall., 9s. 6d.; 1-gall., 18s. 6d. Carriage extra.

XL ALL MILDEW WASH. A certain cure for Mildew. Per pint, 3s. 9d.; per quart, 6s. 6d; ½-gall., 10s. 9d.; 1-gall., 20s. Carriage extra.

XL ALL WINTER WASH. For cleansing Fruit Trees of lichen, &c. In tins, 1s. 6d. each.

OSTICO. For banding Fruit Trees. Per tin, 2s. 6d. and 8s. 6d. Postage extra.

GREASE BANDS. In packets of twenty, 6d. per packet.

Prices subject to alteration without notice.

HORTICULTURAL REQUISITES.

STAKES, LABELS, TYING & PACKING MATERIALS, &c.

BAMBOO CANES. 4 ft., Thin. Per 100, 8s. 6d.
    ,,   ,,   ,, Med.   ,,   14s. 0d.
    ,,   ,,   ,, Thick.   ,,   17s. 6d.
    ,,   ,,   5 ft.   ,,   20s. 0d.
    ,,   ,,   6 ft.   ,,   22s. 6d.
ROSE STAKES. Painted green, tarred ends. 4 ft. Per doz., 7s. 9d.
    ,,   ,,   ,,   ,,   5 ft.   ,,   9s. 0d.
    ,,   ,,   ,,   ,,   6 ft.   ,,   11s. 0d.
LABELS, WOOD. Painted. In boxes of 100.
  4 in.   5 in.   6 in.   7 in.   8 in.   9 in.   12 in.
  1s. 6d. 1s. 9d. 2s.   2s. 3d. 2s. 6d. 2s. 9d. 3s.
LABELS, ZINC. For Roses and Fruit Trees. Write with Indelible ink. Will last for years. Per 100, 4s. 6d. for Roses; per 100, 7s. 6d. for Fruit Trees.
INDELIBLE INK. For above. Bottles, 9d. and 1s. 6d.
LABELS, ACME. *See illustration.* For Roses 2s. 6d., and for Fruit Trees 3s. 6d. per doz. Postage on 1 doz. 3d.
    Please give names of varieties wanted.
RAFFIA. Very fine quality. Per lb., 1s. 6d. Postage 9d. extra.
TARRED STRING. For tying up all kinds of Ramblers and Shrubs. Thin, Medium, and Thick. ½-lb. balls, 1s. 6d. ; 1-lb. balls, 3s. Postage 9d. extra.
SUMMER CLOUD, GREEN. For shading greenhouses. Packets, 1s. 3d. each. Postage 6d. extra.
SUMMER SHADING, WHITE. In tins, 1s. 6d. each.
TANNED NETTING. For protecting Strawberries, &c. In pieces, 50 yds. by 4 yds. Per piece, 35s.
TIFFANY. A very fine material for shading. In pieces, 20 yds. by 38 ins. Per piece, 9s.
WOOD WOOL. Price on application.
WADDING. For fruit packing. In sheets. Per doz. yards 8s. 6d.

MUSHROOM SPAWN.

Splendid crops of Mushrooms may be had all the year round by using

DANIELS' SUPERIOR MUSHROOM SPAWN.

The Mushroom Spawn we offer has been manufactured expressly for our Retail Trade, and may be fully relied on as the very best procurable. By successive plantings, a supply of Mushrooms may be had all the year round, but the best crops are usually grown from Spawn planted in Autumn.

Bricks, 9d. each ; 4 bricks, 2/9 ; postage on 1 Brick, 9d. ; on 4 bricks, 1/3.

Complete Instructions for Cultivation will be sent with every order.

TRUCK BASKETS.

Very strong, made of wood. The most useful basket for the garden. Various sizes. No. 5, 18 ins. by 9½ ins., 5s. 6d.; No. 6, 20 ins. by 10 ins., 5s. 9d. ; No. 7, 23 ins. by 12 ins., 6s.; No. 8, 26 ins. by 14 ins., 6s. 6d.

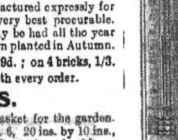

Prices subject to alteration without notice.

WATERING CANS.

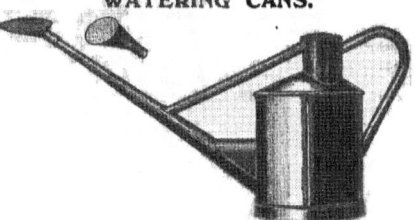

The "Ideal" Gardener's Can.

WATERING CANS. HAWES' PATTERN.
No. 2, 4 qts., 13s. 9d. No. 3, 6 qts., 17s. 6d. No. 4, 8 qts., 22s. In 3 sizes only.

MISCELLANEOUS REQUISITES.

APHIS BRUSHES. 3s. 6d. each.
BOUQUET WIRE. 7 in. and 12 in. lengths. 2s. to 2s. 6d. per lb.
BOUQUET WIRE. For binding. Reels 6d., 1s. 3d., and 2s. each.
BROOMS, BIRCH. 9d. each, 9s. doz.
DEAN'S MEDICATED SHREDS. In boxes of 100. 2 in., 9d. ; 2½ in., 1s. ; 3 in., 1s. 3d. ; 3½ in., 1s. 6d. per box.
GARDENERS' APRONS. Shalloon, light and durable, 12s. 6d. each. Blue Serge, very serviceable, 13s. each.
GISHURSTINE. A dressing for gardeners' boots. 9d. and 1s. 6d. per tin.
GRAFTING WAX. 9d., 1s. 6d., and 3s. per tin.
GARDEN WEBBER. For threading bushes with cotton for protection from birds. 15s. each ; extra spools of cotton 1s. 3d. per box of two.
LAYER PEGS, ZINC. In boxes of 100. 1s. 6d. each.
MELON NETS, STRING. 4s. 6d. per doz.
NAIL BAGS. Leather, best quality. 13s. 6d. each.
PEA GUARDS. 3 ft. long. 9s. per doz.
PENCILS, WOLFF'S GARDEN. 6d. each.
STYPTIC. For preventing bleeding in vines. 1s. 6d. per bottle.
TOBACCO POWDER DISTRIBUTORS, RUBBER. 4s. each.
    BELLOWS. 2s. 3d. per pair.
VERBENA PINS. For pegging down Verbenas, &c. Box of 1 gross, 1s. 6d.
WALL NAILS. French. 10d. per lb.
WALL NAILS, CHANDLER'S PATENT. A useful invention. Shreds not required. Boxes of 100. 1½ in., 7s. 3d. ; 1½ in., 8s. 3d.
WEED KILLER, McDOUGALL'S NON-POISONOUS. 1 gallon tin, 7s. 5 gallon drums, 27s. 6d.
WIKEHAM WEED ERADICATOR. Fill with Weed Killer, stab the crown of the weed and it will soon perish. 15s. 6d. each.
WIRE ALUMINIUM. 1s. 6d. per coil of 40 feet.
MEASURING TAPES. In strong leather case 16s. each.

THERMOMETERS.

THERMOMETERS, BOXWOOD. Reliable. 2s. 9d. and 4s. 6d. each. Packing and postage 6d. extra.
  ,, **METAL SCALES.** Enamelled white, especially adapted for the garden (Negretti and Zambra), each 7s. 6d. Packing and postage 9d. extra.
  ,, **MAXIMUM AND MINIMUM REGISTERING.** In metal case, zinc scales, complete with magnet for adjusting (Negretti and Zambra), price 13s. 6d. Packing and postage 9d extra.
  ,, **HOTBED.** For testing the temperature of Mushroom beds, &c. Metal scale in copper frame and brass stem 20 inches long, price 27s. 6d. Packing and postage 1s. extra.

SPRAYING MACHINES.

The Spraying of Fruit Trees has now for many years been recognised abroad and in our colonies as an operation indispensable to fruit growing if clean fruit and healthy crops are to be obtained. It is only during the last few years, however, that the necessity for spraying has begun to be generally recognised in Great Britain. Spraying, to be successful, must be done intelligently. The grower must know what to spray for, what to spray with, and when to do it. It is also most important that the right kind of spraying machine is used. The machines offered here we can confidently recommend; they will be found to be very efficient and durable.

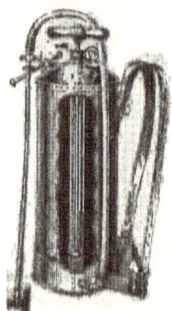

For the various kinds of Insecticides and Washes, see page 50.

TYPE B.B. MEDIUM KNAPSACK. Capacity full 2½ gallons, working 2 gallons. A medium size in every way, suitable for gardens, estates, and small holdings. Made in Virex Alloy with pressure gauge, 40 ins. hose, 20 ins. spray-rod, vaseline chamber, swivel self-cleaning nozzle, filling funnel. See illustration. Price nett, £5 18s. 6d.

TYPE A.B. STANDARD (GROWERS) KNAPSACK. Capacity 4 gallons full, working 3 gallons. Made in Virex Alloy and complete with fittings as above. Price nett, £6 18s.

BAMBOO LANCE. For use with above for spraying tall trees, 7 ft. long. Price nett, 20,-

THE HANDSPRAYER DE LUXE. TYPE D. Capacity 5 pints, working 3 to 4 pints. In Virex Brass Alloy. Strong and light. Complete with powerful self-contained pump, automatic valve giving instantaneous start and release of spray. Swivel "Mist" nozzle adjustable to front —up, down, or side. An absolutely perfect hand sprayer. Price nett, £3 3s. 6d.

SYRINGES AND DISTRIBUTORS.

"ABOL NEW PATENT." For distributing Insecticides and for ordinary Syringing. Each, 19s. 6d. and 24s. Bends for any size, 2s. 9d. extra. Postage 9d. extra.

THE "ABOL" SYRINGE,

SYRINGE, "FOUR OAKS." A first-class syringe, very strongly made, price 27/6 each.
,, GOOD USEFUL MAKE. For general spraying, price 11/-
,, PEERLESS THREE WAY. No bend required, price 19/6.
Postage on each Syringe 9d. extra.

GARDENING GLOVES.

	per pair—s.	d.
STRONG LEATHER. Best quality, very suitable for handling rambler roses, etc.	5	9
LAMBSKIN GLOVES. Natural fleece inside	7	9
MEN'S GARDENING. Very serviceable	5	6
LADIES' GARDENING GAUNTLETS. Splendid quality, handsewn	6	3
,, ,, GLOVES. Handsewn	5	6
WOMEN'S TAN GLOVES	3	6
RUBBER GLOVES. For use when using insecticides	12	6

When sending remittance for Gloves 3d. extra should be enclosed for postage

PORTABLE SPRAYING AND LIMEWASHING MACHINES.

THE "DUKE." Capacity 10 gallons. Fitted with powerful pump, 10 feet length of hose, and brass spraying lance. Complete with interchangeable nozzles for lime washing and fine spraying. Price nett, £12 15s.

THE "VISCOUNT." A very useful sprayer, holding 6 gallons. Complete with container and brass strainer, powerful pump and all accessories. Price nett, £5 7s. 6d.

THE "KITCHENER." A very convenient Bucket Sprayer. Holding 4 gallons. Complete with lime washing spraying nozzles. Price nett, £3 18s. 6d.

THE "EMPEROR." Can be used with any bucket. Price nett, 47/6

"FOUR OAKS" KNAPSACK SPRAYERS. As illustration. Price nett, £5 3s. 6d.

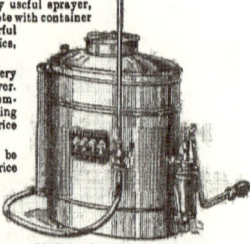

FOUR OAKS KNAPSACK SPRAYER.

BOOKS ON GARDENING.

		s.	d.				s.	d.
GRAPES, AND HOW TO GROW THEM	post free	4	0	THE AMATEUR'S GREENHOUSE	post free	7	3
LAWNS AND GREENS	,, ,,	4	0	PRUNING, BUDDING AND GRAFTING	,, ,,	3	0
ROSES, AND THEIR CULTIVATION ..	,, ,,	7	3	FRUIT, AND ITS CULTIVATION ..	,, ,,	8	3
ALLOTMENT AND KITCHEN GARDEN	,, ,,	1	11	TOMATOES, AND HOW TO GROW THEM ..	,, ,,	1	11

Prices subject to alteration without notice.

HORTICULTURAL REQUISITES.

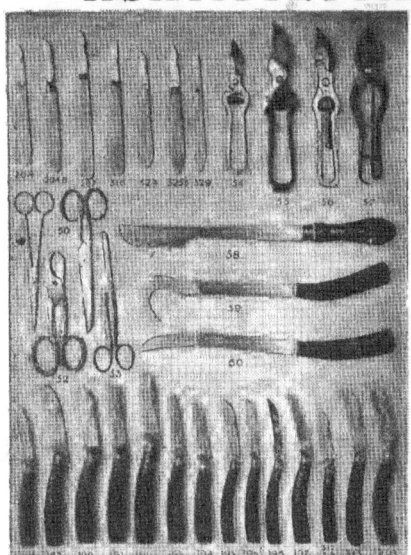

TOOLS AND IMPLEMENTS.

	s.	d.
AXES. A very useful tool for chopping down hedges. Medium size,		
with 24 in. handles	8	3
BILL HOOKS. Best pattern	5	6
DAISY GRUBS. For grubbing daisies and plantains from lawns	2	9
" " Long handles	3	6
DIBBERS, GARDEN. With spade handles, iron shod	5	0
EDGING IRONS. Handled	8	6
FORKS. Small hand weeding	2	6
HAMMERS, STRONG GARDEN	4	9
HOES, DUTCH. Best make, 5 in.	3	9
" " 6 "	4	0
" " 7 "	4	3
" **STALHAM.** Swan neck 4 in., 4/- 5 in.	4	3
" " 6 " 4/0 7 "	4	9
" " 8 "	5	0
MATTOCKS. Light garden, with handles	6	9
RAKES, IRON. 8 teeth, 2/9; 10 teeth, 3/-; 12 teeth	3	6
" **STEEL.** Fitted with ash handles, 8 teeth	5	0
" " " 10 "	5	6
" " " 12 "	5	9
" " " 14 "	6	6
RAKE AND HOE COMBINED. A useful tool	6	0
REELS. For garden lines	4	6
LINES. Best quality, 30 yards 3/-, 60 yards	5	9
SAWS, PRUNING. Double edge	5	0
" Curved pattern	5	0
SHOVELS. Best London	8	0
SLASHERS. Single cutting edge. Long handle	7	0
" Double	8	6
SPUDS. Best quality	1	9
TROWELS. All bright, polished handles, 6 in.	3	9
" " " 7 "	4	3
TURFING IRONS. Best solid blades	23	6
SCYTHE BLADES	11	0

Prices subject to alteration without notice.

BUDDING & PRUNING KNIVES. &c.

	s.	d.
BUDDING. Ivory handles, No. 204	6	3
" " " 204B. Brass bound	8	0
" " " 207	8	0
" " " 316	7	0
" " " 324	6	6
" " " 325½. Brass bound	9	6
" " " 329	5	9
PRUNING. Horn handles, No. 189	6	9
" " " 190	6	0
" " " 191	7	0
" " " 194	7	0
" " " 195	8	9
" " " 197	8	3
" " " 938	7	9
ASPARAGUS KNIVES. No. 58 in illustration	8	6
GOOSEBERRY PRUNERS	4	6
TREE PRUNERS. For pruning tall trees, 6 ft. handles	10	0
" " " 8 " "	11	0
" " " 10 " "	12	0
EXTRA BLADES FOR PRUNERS. Each	2	0

SECATEURS AND SCISSORS.

	s.	d.
SECATEURS. No. 57 in illustration, famous French pattern 6½ in.	9	9
" " 57 " " 7½ "	10	9
" " 56 " patent wheel spring, 7½ in.	7	9
" " 56 " " " 8 "	8	0
" " 55, spiral spring, very strong, 7 in.	6	0
" " 55 " " 8 "	6	9
SCISSORS. Grape thinning, No. 51, 6 in.	4	6
" " 7 "	5	0
" Flower gathering, No. 53, 6 in.	6	6
" " 7 "	8	0
" Pruning, No. 52, 5 in.	5	0
" " 52, 6 "	6	9

GARDEN SHEARS.

	s.	d.
SHEARS. For grass edges, long handles	15	0
" For hedge trimming with notch	10	6
" Pruning, takes off pieces 1 in. diameter	9	9
" Powerful lopping, for hard work, French pattern 27/6 and	35	0
" Ladies' size, for grass or hedge trimming	9	0
Carriage extra on all Shears 1s.		

SPADES AND FORKS.

	s.	d.
SPADES, NORFOLK pattern, half bright	10	6
" " all bright, very best quality	12	0
" **BORDER,** for ladies' use	7	0
FORKS. Best quality digging, 4 prongs	9	6
" " " 5 "	11	9
" **BORDER.** For ladies' use	7	6
" **FLAT PRONG,** for digging potatoes	8	0
Carriage extra on Spades and Forks 1s. 4d.		

CULTIVATORS.

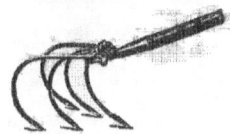

These Cultivators get deep down and loosen the soil, giving it oxygen. They clean out weeds by the root—they mean more flowers, more fruit, more vegetables, healthier shrubs and trees and a cleaner garden—with less labour. They are adaptable for all classes of soil—they do the work of hoe, fork and rake in less time and with fuller results.

THE "BUCO" has five prongs, with ash handle, 4½ ft. long. 8s. 6d. each. Carriage 1s. 4d. extra.

FLOWER SEED DEPARTMENT

NEW AND SELECT VARIETIES OF SWEET PEAS.
FOR EXHIBITION AND DECORATION.

Since the Spencer varieties of Sweet Peas were first introduced we have had on several occasions to report very short crops of seed, but we do not remember any year in which such a small crop of seed has been harvested as the present, many growers having saved practically no seed at all. We ourselves are large growers of the newest varieties, and though our crop is much smaller than usual, we hope to be able to supply all our orders in the present season. As some varieties, however, may be exhausted sooner than others, we shall be greatly obliged if any of our customers who desire special sorts will let us have their orders as early as possible. The following list, which we recommend with great confidence, represents the finest of the newer sorts, in addition to those which have obtained the highest commendation during the past summer, and are now offered for the first time.

1 **ANNIE IRELAND.** This is the very finest picotee-edged Sweet Pea yet raised; a strong grower with many four-flowered sprays. The colour is a clear white distinctly edged with terra-cotta pink. Award of Merit, R.H.S. ... 6d. and 1 0

2 **ATTRACTION.** Although there have been many new pink Sweet Peas introduced lately, this variety will be found well worth a trial. The very large flowers are of a deep shell-pink, suffused fawn. Many of the blooms have double standards, giving the sprays a most effective appearance ... 6d. and 1 0

3 **BLUE STONE.** A distinct and striking new variety of great value for decorative work. The flowers are of aniline blue, with a bluish-violet shading on the standards. Free-flowering & of vigorous growth 6d. & 1 0

4 **BROCADE.** A distinct and charming colour, of a pleasing satin rose tint with mauve shading, the base of the standard deeply suffused mauve. Of robust growth, with large well-waved flowers. Awards of Merit, R.H.S., Chelsea, Wolverhampton, and Manchester ... 6d. and 1 0

5 **DAISYBUD.** Beautiful soft, rich, rose pink on white ground. Exceedingly vigorous with many five-flowered stems. Of great merit, both as a decorative or exhibition variety. Award of Merit ... 6d. and 1 0

6 **DORIS.** A beautiful sunproof variety of a charming rich cerise cherry-pink. Flowering abundantly on long stems, large well waved flowers. Award of Merit, R.H.S., and Silver Medal, Chelsea ... 6d. and 1 0

7 **HAWLMARK PINK.** The richest coloured Sweet Pea ever seen, excelling Audrey Crier in depth of colour, absolutely fixed and true. Vigorous; producing an abundance of beautifully frilled flowers of ideal form of a rich bright rose-pink, flushed and shaded salmon. Awards of Merit, R.H.S., Chelsea, Wolverhampton, Manchester, and Belfast. Silver Medal, Chelsea ... 6d. and 1 0

8 **JACK CORNWELL, V.C.** A rich dark violet-blue self, fine robust habit, producing four-sprayed blooms; the best Sweet Pea in this colour ever raised. A distinct and most effective grower, will become very popular ... 6d. and 1 0

9 **MASCOTT'S HELIO.** A most vigorous grower, with long stems of well-placed flowers, giving plenty of four-bloomed sprays. The whole flower is of a pleasing shade of lavender suffused with bronze, deeper in the standards, but even on the wings the shading is noticeable. This variety was First in the seedling bunch class of the National Sweet Pea Society. Award of Merit, R.H.S. ... 1 0

NEW SWEET PEA—MASCOTT'S WHITE.

10 **MASCOTT'S WHITE.** This is the finest white Sweet Pea yet raised. The flowers are of the largest size and of great substance, giving a most solid glistening effect without the least trace of other colouring. The blooms are beautifully placed on long wiry stems, and in the raiser's opinion produces far more flowers on each plant than any other kind. Award of Merit, R.H.S. ... 6d. and 1 0

11 **MAGIC.** One of the most distinct Sweet Peas yet offered. The deeply waved standards are of a glowing rosy amethyst deepening to blue, the wings of an intense shade of blue overlying lavender. In a strong light the whole so changes in character that an adequate description is impossible, the standards having the appearance of liquid bronze. Unequalled for decoration, lasting well in water ... 6d. and 1 0

12 **MRS. TOM JONES.** A huge flower of great substance, beautifully waved and well placed on long stout stems—four-bloomed sprays predominate, with an occasional five. The colour is bright delphinium blue, deepening to amethyst blue as the flower develops. A most attractive and fascinating colour. Award of Merit, R.H.S. ... 6d. and 1 0

13 **PICTURE.** In the opinion of practically all the experts "Picture" marks the greatest advance up to date. The flowers are of enormous size and superb form, the outlines of the flowers being in every respect the most perfect in existence. The stems are of great length, and six perfect blooms on a spray occur frequently. The colour is a rose-flushed flesh pink, the whole suffused creamy apricot, a charming combination of colour. The fragrance is pronounced and very sweet. F.C.C., Shrewsbury. Award of Merit, R.H.S. Award of Merit, N.S.P.S. ... 1 6

14 **ROYAL SALUTE.** This is the finest sun-resisting orange-scarlet yet produced, the brighter the sun the more dazzling the colour becomes. Free flowering ... 6d. and 1 0

15 **ROYAL SCOT.** This is undoubtedly the finest scarlet Sweet Pea. The colour is the most brilliant scarlet, and does not burn or fade in hot sunshine. It is strong growing, with a profusion of four-bloomed sprays of beautifully waved flowers. ... 1 6

16 **SPLENDOUR.** This grand variety resembles "Warrior" in vigour of growth and size of flower. It is brighter in colour than that variety, being a rich red maroon, without a trace of purple. The finest in this colour yet raised 6d. and 1 0

NEW AND SELECT SWEET PEAS.

SWEET PEA—HAWLMARK PINK.

SCARLET AND CRIMSON.

per pkt.— s. d.

17 **ALEXANDER MALCOLM.** Superb new variety, flowers on long stems; cerise toned orange scarlet   0 6
18 **FIERY CROSS.** Colour brilliant fiery scarlet without any shading; does not burn even in long periods of intense sunshine   0 6
19 **KING EDWARD SPENCER.** Deep rich crimson scarlet   0 6
20 **KING EDWARD VII.** A grand crimson   0 4
21 **QUEEN ALEXANDRA.** Brilliant pure scarlet; one of the best   0 4
22 **SCARLET MONARCH.** Deep rich scarlet Spencer, equal in colour to "Queen Alexandra," but much larger   0 6
23 **SUNPROOF CRIMSON** (Maude Holmes). Flowers borne three and four on a stem. An improvement on King Edward Spencer   0 6
24 **VERMILION BRILLIANT.** Intense brilliant scarlet, quite distinct   0 6

DEEP PINK AND CARMINE.

25 **ANNIE BOWNASS** (new). Lovely deep pink. Very beautiful   0 6
26 **DECORATOR.** Large showy and useful decorative variety. Colour is a deep crushed strawberry   0 6
27 **DUPLEX SPENCER.** A beautiful shade of rich pink, large flowers with double standards   0 6
28 **JOHN INGMAN.** Rich rosy carmine   0 6
29 **MRS. ARNOLD HITCHCOCK.** Pink flushed salmon on cream ground   0 6
30 **MRS. G. W. BISHOP.** Soft salmon cerise, large flowers   0 6
31 **ROSABELLE.** Brilliant rose, lighter at the base of standard, a most beautiful variety   0 6

PALE ROSE AND PINK.

per pkt. s. d.

32 **AGRICOLA.** Pale blush suffused rosy lilac. A distinct and charming flower. One of the prettiest   0 6
33 **COUNTESS SPENCER.** (True.) A lovely shade of pink   0 6
34 **ELEGANCE.** Soft silvery pink, beautifully waved   0 6
35 **ELFRIDA PEARSON.** Light rosy pink self. Flowers large, and frequently four on a stem   0 6
36 **GLADYS UNWIN.** Lovely pale rosy pink   0 4
37 **HERCULES.** Lovely clear rose shading off to deep rosy pink at the edges   0 6
38 **VALENTINE** (new). Blush pink, large flowers on long stems   0 6

CREAM PINK.

39 **BERYL.** Charming, soft salmon pink, shaded buff, very fine   0 6
40 **EDITH CAVELL.** Rosy pink on cream ground, delightful fresh colouring   0 6
41 **GLADYS.** A grand variety of rich bright salmon-pink on a cream ground, with an abundance of four-flower sprays   0 6
42 **LILIAN.** A superb variety. Pale cream-pink, flushed buff   0 6
43 **MARGARET ATLEE** (new). Apricot on cream; a lovely flower   0 6
44 **MRS. HUGH DICKSON.** A beautiful pale salmon pink self   0 6
45 **SALENA** (new). Rich cream, edged and flushed rosy-scarlet   0 6

PURE WHITE.

46 **CONSTANCE HINTON** (new). A really grand new pure white   0 6
47 **ETTA DYKE.** Very large pure white flowers with bold wavy standards   0 6
48 **KING WHITE.** A magnificent pure white Spencer of immense size, producing four blooms on a stem; splendidly formed and of great substance   0 6
49 **NORA UNWIN.** A magnificent pure white, flowers of great size   0 4

PICOTEE EDGED.

50 **BLUE PICOTEE.** Large white flowers beautifully frilled and edged with violet blue   0 6
51 **EVELYN HEMUS** (syn. Mrs. C. W. Breadmore). Rich cream shading to yellow with a picotee-edging of bright terra-cotta red   0 6
52 **JEAN IRELAND.** Colour creamy buff, beautifully edged and shaded with carmine rose   0 6
53 **PICOTEE.** Pearly white, distinctly edged bright carmino   0 6

BLUE AND LAVENDER.

54 **ASTA OHN SPENCER.** Lavender tinted mauve, a magnificent variety with large splendid flowers   0 6
55 **FLORENCE NIGHTINGALE.** Flowers of great size, beautifully waved. Charming soft, clear, lavender blue   0 6
56 **LADY GRISEL HAMILTON.** Beautiful shining pale lavender   0 4
57 **LAVENDER GEORGE HERBERT.** Pale lavender beautifully waved   0 6
58 **LORD NELSON,** (Brilliant Blue.) Deep bright blue self. Very fine   0 4

BLUE AND LAVENDER—continued.

per pkt. s. d.

59 **ORCHID.** One of the most refined varieties, rich deep lavender delicately suffused rose-pink   0 6
60 **R. F. FELTON.** A strong growing variety, with lilac standard and French grey wings   0 6
61 **ROYAL PURPLE.** A true bright purple with handsomely waved flowers. Quite distinct   0 6
62 **WEDGEWOOD.** Blooms of great size, mostly four on a stem; a unique shade of Wedgewood blue   0 6

MAUVE AND HELIOTROPE.

63 **DOROTHY.** A gigantic rosy-lilac self, beautifully waved, mostly four on a stem   0 6
64 **KING MAUVE.** A giant rich rosy mauve, giving an abundance of four-flowered sprays   0 6

MAROON, CLARET, CHOCOLATE.

65 **BLACK KNIGHT.** Deep maroon self; one of the finest   0 4
66 **KING MANOEL.** Deep maroon, waved; a fine exhibition variety   0 6
67 **NUBIAN.** A magnificent chocolate Spencer, the finest of its colour   0 6
68 **WARRIOR** (new). Rich deep chocolate maroon. Very large blooms   0 6

CREAM AND YELLOW SHADES.

69 **CLARA CURTIS.** Beautiful primrose yellow, one of the best   0 6
70 **IVORINE.** Ground colour ivory, standard buff and a faint suggestion of salmon pink   0 6
71 **PARADISE IVORY.** A lovely shade of old ivory   0 6
72 **PRIMROSE SPENCER.** Large flowers of a beautiful primrose yellow   0 6

SWEET PEA—CONSTANCE HINTON.

NEW AND SELECT SWEET PEAS (continued.)

SWEET PEA—SUNPROOF CRIMSON.

SALMON AND ORANGE-RED SHADES.

73 **BARBARA.** A lovely salmony-orange self, with large, beautifully waved flowers 0 6

74 **EARL SPENCER.** Flowers of great size, colour a brilliant orange-rose 0 6

75 **HELEN LEWIS (The Orange Countess)** (true). Standards wavy and of rich orange colour, wings rosy 0 6

76 **ILLUMINATOR.** Flowers well placed and of fine substance. Glowing orange-scarlet 0 6

77 **ROBERT SYDENHAM.** Brilliant orange-scarlet, more intense in colour than Thomas Stevenson, 0 6

78 **TANGERINE.** Magnificent salmon-orange of an intense shade, the best in this class 0 6

SALMON AND ORANGE RED—cont. per pkt. s. d.

79 **THOMAS STEVENSON.** Brilliant orange-scarlet, large waved flowers 0 6

80 **THE PRESIDENT.** Intensely rich orange-scarlet. Free-flowering, on long stems 0 6

BICOLORS.

81 **MRS. CUTHBERTSON.** Clear rosy pink, white wings 0 6

82 **SPARKLER** (new). Bright rose-scarlet standard, cream wings shaded rose pink. 0 6

STRIPED VARIETIES.

83 **AURORA SPENCER.** Large waved flowers, white ground, striped bright salmon-red 0 6

84 **SENATOR SPENCER.** Rosy heliotrope striped chocolate 0 6

DANIELS' SPECIAL COLLECTIONS OF SWEET PEAS.

The following liberal collections include what we consider the best selection of varieties for exhibition or for cut flowers. Towards the end of the sowing season we may have to substitute some varieties.

Alexander Malcolm. Cerise scarlet.
*Beryl. Salmon-pink shaded buff.
‡*Blue Picotee. White, edged violet.
‡*Clara Curtis. Primrose yellow.
*Constance Hinton. Pure white.
*Dorothy. Rosy lilac.
*Earl Spencer. Orange rose.
*Edith Cavell. Rosy pink on cream.
Etta Dyke. Pure white.
‡*Fiery Cross. Brilliant scarlet.
‡*Hercules. Clear rose.
*Illuminator. Glowing orange-scarlet.

‡ Jean Ireland. Buff, edged carmine-rose.
*John Ingman. Brilliant carmine.
*King Edward Spencer. Crimson scarlet.
‡*King White. Pure white.
‡*Margaret Atlee. Apricot on cream.
*Picotee. White, edged carmine.
‡ R. F. Felton. Lilac and French grey.
‡*Royal Purple. Bright purple.
‡ Salena. Cream, flushed rosy scarlet.
*Sunproof Crimson. Rich crimson.
The President. Orange-scarlet.
‡*Wedgewood. China blue.

		s. d.
85	TWENTY-FOUR SPLENDID VARIETIES, as above ..	8 6
86	EIGHTEEN SELECTED VARIETIES, marked (*) ..	6 6
87	TWELVE SUPERB VARIETIES, marked (‡)	4 6
88	SIX FINE VARIETIES, Constance Hinton, Hercules, John Ingman, Jean Ireland, King Edward Spencer, Royal Purple	2 6

DANIELS' SPECIAL MIXTURE OF GIANT-FLOWERED SPENCERS.

We highly recommend this splendid mixture which we feel sure will give great satisfaction. The varieties included are all of the true Giant-flowered and Spencer types, and the colours include all the most brilliant and beautiful shades of scarlet, crimson, magenta, orange, salmon, pink, lavender, mauve, cream and primrose to the purest white. This will prove a first-class mixture where really good Sweet Peas are required for cut bloom.
89 Per pkt., 6d. and 1s.   90 Per oz., 1s. 9d.   91 Per 4 ozs., 6s.
92 Per half-pint, 10s. 6d.

LARGE-FLOWERED MIXTURE.

Splendid varieties in choicest mixture, including a good proportion of the light and delicately coloured sorts. Very highly recommended.
93 Per oz., 1s.   94 Per 4 ozs., 3s. 6d.   95 Per half-pint, 6s.
96 Per pint, 10s. 6d.

SWEET PEAS—ORDINARY MIXED.

97 Per oz., 8d.   98 Per half-pint, 3s. 6d.   99 Per pint, 6s. 6d.

LARGE-FLOWERED COLLECTIONS.

The sorts given in these collections are carefully selected to ensure the best possible variety for garden decoration, and also for cutting.   s. d.
100 12 CHOICE VARIETIES 3 0
101 6 ,, ,, ... 1 9

Cultivation. To grow really fine Sweet Peas, the ground should be deeply dug or trenched, and plenty of well-decayed manure with some coarse bone meal worked well in and to the bottom of the trench. This should be done in Autumn if convenient, or as early as possible in Spring.

For early blooming, sow the seeds thinly in pots or pans in January or February, and place in a gentle heat; harden off as soon as the plants are well up, and plant out as soon as convenient in March. As growth advances some weak liquid manure should be given once or twice a week, and if the weather continues dry, a mulching of some short, well-decayed manure should be placed on the surface about the roots. This will be of great benefit in stimulating a healthy growth, and some splendid flowers will be produced.

For later successive blooming the seeds may be sown out of doors at intervals from early March to the middle of May, giving them a similar treatment to that recommended above. Excellent results may also be had by sowing in October or November in a sheltered position in the garden. These, with a slight protection, will survive a moderately severe winter and furnish some nice blooms for cutting earlier than those sown in Spring.

If the blooms are closely gathered and seed pods not allowed to develop, the plants will continue in bloom for a much longer period.

SPENCER SWEET PEAS IN VASE.

DANIELS' SUPERB PRIZE ASTERS.

Cultivation.—Asters are alike useful for borders and as cut flowers, the single kinds being of especial value for the latter purpose. The seed should be sown in March or April in boxes of good rich soil, and treated in the same manner as other half-hardy annuals; give plenty of room between the plants, and place the boxes in a sunny position under glass, allowing abundance of air and water; after about three weeks remove the boxes to a frame where the lights can be lifted off during the day, and so gradually harden the plants in readiness for their removal to the borders. The greatest care should be exercised in transplanting from the boxes, so as to ensure the seedlings getting a good start.

ASTER—DANIELS' GIANT OSTRICH PLUME.

OSTRICH PLUME (Ordinary Class).

Charming varieties of exquisite beauty. The large flowers are borne on long stems, and the petals are beautifully curled and twisted, giving them somewhat the appearance of Japanese Chrysanthemums.

		s.	d.
102	AN ASSORTMENT OF SIX BEAUTIFUL VARIETIES	2	0
103	SALMON PINK. Very fine colour .. per pkt.	0	6
104	PURE WHITE. Splendid for cutting .. per oz. 10s.	0	6
105	CHOICEST MIXED .. .. ,, 8s.	0	6

IMPROVED PÆONY-FLOWERED.

12 to 15 inches. In many beautiful colours.

		s.	d.
106	Six Splendid Varieties .. per pkt.	2	0
107	Very Choice Mixed .. per pkt. 6d. and	1	0

SPECIAL NAMED VARIETIES.

		s.	d.
108	SALMON QUEEN. 18 inches. Beautiful bright salmon-rose flowers on long wiry stems .. per pkt. 6d. and	1	0
109	HERCULES, Pure White. 15 to 18 inches. Pure white blooms of immense size; very fine variety .. per pkt. 6d. and	1	0
110	HERCULES, Brilliant Rose. Identical, except in colour. per pkt. 6d. and	1	0

DWARF COMET.

		s.	d.
111	CHOICE MIXED. Only 9 inches high; very pretty per pkt. 6d. and	1	0

DWARF CHRYSANTHEMUM-FLOWERED.

A splendid dwarf-growing late-flowering variety for bedding or edging.

		s.	d.
112	VERY CHOICE MIXED .. .. per pkt. 6d. and	1	0

DANIELS' GIANT OSTRICH PLUME.

☞ We have much pleasure in recommending this grand strain of beautiful varieties; the very large handsome flowers, which are borne on long wiry stems, are of the true Ostrich Plume type, and of immense size—when well grown, frequently measuring six inches and even seven inches in diameter, whilst the colours embrace the most beautiful and delicate shades. These will prove a splendid class alike for garden decoration, as cut flowers or for exhibition. Height about 18 inches.

			s.	d.
113	A COLLECTION OF 8 BEAUTIFUL VARIETIES, DISTINCT		3	0
114	DANIELS' BRILLIANT ROSE ..	per pkt.	0	6
115	DANIELS' LILAC BLUE ..	Distinct and	0	0
116	DANIELS' PURE WHITE ..	beautiful ,, 6d. & 1	0	
117	DANIELS' AZURE BLUE ..	colours.	0	6
118	DANIELS' DELICATE ROSE ..	Specially ,,	0	6
119	DANIELS' ROSY LILAC ..	selected. ,,	0	6
120	DANIELS' BRILLIANT CRIMSON	,,	0	6
121	DANIELS' DARK BLUE ..	,,	0	0
122	DANIELS' CHOICEST MIXED. In splendid variety	,, 6d. & 1	0	

DANIELS' GIANT COMET.

An elegant strain of highly improved and beautiful varieties, growing about fifteen inches high, the individual flowers resembling those of the Japanese Chrysanthemum, and are of great size. The blooms are very useful for cutting, the pure white and the delicately-striped flowers being extremely beautiful.

			s.	d.
123	SIX BEAUTIFUL VARIETIES ..		2	0
124	WHITE. Very fine variety ..	per oz. 10s.; per pkt.	0	6
125	CHOICEST MIXED ..	per oz. 8s.	0	6

DANIELS' IMPROVED VICTORIA.

A magnificent class, growing about fifteen inches high, and producing an abundance of large, perfectly double and beautifully imbricated flowers, four to five inches across. One of the most splendid for garden decoration.

			s.	d.
126	AN ASSORTMENT OF SIX BEAUTIFUL VARIETIES		2	0
127	PURE WHITE ..	per pkt.	0	6
128	FINEST MIXED. In beautiful variety. per oz. 10s.; pkt. 6d. & 1			0

NEW TALL BRANCHING.

Beautiful late blooming varieties, growing almost two feet high, and branching almost from the base of the stem. The blooms are produced in the greatest profusion, and are borne on very long wiry stems, rendering them of especial value for cut flowers.

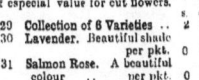

		s.	d.
129	Collection of 6 Varieties ..	2	0
130	Lavender. Beautiful shade per pkt.	0	6
131	Salmon Rose. A beautiful colour .. per pkt.	0	6
132	Pure White. Splendid for cutting .. per pkt.	0	6
133	Mixed. A grand variety of shades per oz. 6s.; pkt. 6d. &	1	0

GIANT RAY ASTER.

A showy type of Aster with large flowers composed of long needle-like petals. Height 18 inches to 2 feet.

		s.	d.
134	GIANT WHITE. Very fine	0	6
135	GIANT BLUE. Lovely shade	0	6
136	GIANT ROSE. Fine colour	0	6
137	GIANT MIXED. 6d. and	1	0

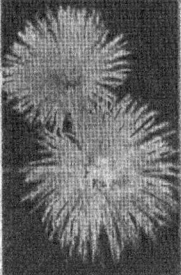

ASTER—DANIELS' GIANT RAY.

DANIELS' PRIZE ASTERS.

DANIELS' DWARF PERFECTION BEDDING.

These beautiful dwarf Asters, introduced by us a few years ago, have proved themselves by far the finest and best dwarf bedding varieties in existence. The plants grow only about 7 or 8 inches high, with stiff upright stems and branches, and form handsome circular bushy plants with the flowers well above the foliage. The blooms are of large size, perfectly double, beautifully imbricated and of the most perfect form. Planted in beds of distinct colours, or used as an edging, they are splendidly effective and continue in bloom for quite a long time.

	s. d.			s. d.
144 ASSORTMENT OF SIX VARIETIES .. 2 8		147 DANIELS' PURE WHITE per pkt. 0 6		
145 DANIELS' BRILLIANT SCARLET per pkt. 0 6		148 DANIELS' BRIGHT ROSE " 0 6		
146 DANIELS' DARK BLUE " 0 6		149 DANIELS' CHOICEST MIXED " 6d. & 1 0		

SINGLE-FLOWERED ASTERS.

All the varieties of Single Asters have attained great popularity during the last few years. They are extremely free-flowering, the flowers being borne on strong stiff stems making them very valuable for cutting. The blooms have small golden yellow centres, and the single row of petals gives them a light, graceful effect seldom obtained in Annual flowers.

Per pkt.—s. d.

150 APPLE BLOSSOM (new). A charming shade of rose shaded white, good border plant; compact habit. .. .. 6d. and 1 0

151 CINNABAR RED (new). Brilliant colour, valuable both for decoration and for cutting 6d. and 1 0

152 MAUVE BEAUTY (new). A great improvement on the old Single Mauve, having much larger flowers and wider petals, good branching habit, and excellent for cut flowers 6d. and 1 0

153 SINGLE MAUVE. Large, handsome single flowers having a single row of delicate pale mauve florets with golden central disc. First-class as border plant or for cut flowers .. 0 6

DANIELS' GIANT SINGLE. A fine showy class for garden decoration, and very effective when grown in large beds of separate colours. The flowers are produced on long wiry stems and are very useful to cut for decoration.

	Per pkt.—s. d.			Per pkt.—s. d.
138 BRILLIANT SCARLET (new) .. 0 6		141 PURE WHITE 0 6		
139 BRIGHT ROSE 0 6		142 DARK BLUE 0 6		
140 LIGHT BLUE 0 6		143 CHOICE MIXED per oz. 4s. 6d.; 6d. & 1 0		

DANIELS' GIANT SINGLE ASTERS.

DANIELS' SUPERB TEN-WEEK AND OTHER STOCKS.

GIANT ENGLISH BROMPTON STOCKS.

An exceedingly fine and useful class of Spring flowering plants of the old cottage garden type, producing large, handsome spikes of beautifully coloured and deliciously scented flowers in April and May. The seeds should be sown in May or June, and soon as the young plants are large enough to handle, prick them out about six inches apart on nursery beds in a sheltered position where they can remain during Summer. In September or October they should be planted out where intended to bloom in Spring. The plants grow about two feet high, and should be planted eighteen inches or more apart.

	s. d.
154 SIX CHOICE VARIETIES, Separate 2 6
155 DARK BLOOD RED, Splendid colour .. per pkt. 0 6
156 SNOW WHITE. Very fine .. " 0 6
157 BRILLIANT ROSE. Splendid variety .. " 0 6
158 DARK PURPLE. Fine colour 0 6
159 CHOICEST MIXED, In beautiful variety of colour 6d. and 1 0

Perpetual Perfection Ten-week Stocks.

A new and exceedingly valuable class growing to the height of about eighteen inches, and blooming profusely from July till late in Autumn.

160 CHOICEST MIXED 6d. & 1 0

Dwarf Bouquet Stocks.

A charming dwarf-growing class with compact heads of flowers. Useful for small beds and edgings.

161 CHOICE MIXED 6d. and 1 0

STOCK—DWARF BOUQUET.

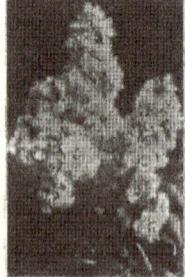

STOCK—NEW GIANT-FLOWERED.

NEW GIANT-FLOWERED STOCKS.

These magnificent stocks are of French origin, and furnish one of the most profuse flowering types of Stocks obtainable. The habit is strong and branching, and the flowers are of the largest size. Treated as Ten-week Stocks they will flower but little later; and will also furnish fine blooms in the conservatory or greenhouse if grown in the same manner as East Lothian Stocks.

	s. d.
162 SIX CHOICE VARIETIES 2 6
163 AURORA (new). A lovely shade of chamois, lightly shaded rose; a charming colour 0 6
164 ALMOND BLOSSOM. White, delicately shaded carmine 0 6
165 BEAUTY OF NICE. Delicate flesh 0 6
166 CRIMSON KING. Fiery crimson 0 6
167 MADAME RIVOIRE. Early-flowering, pure white .. 0 6
168 MAUVE BEAUTY. Pale bluish mauve 0 6
169 MONT BLANC. Very fine pure white 0 6
170 MONTE CARLO. Canary yellow 0 6
171 NUIT D'ETE (Summer Night). Deep blue 0 6
172 PARMA VIOLET (new). Charming shade of mauve .. 0 6
173 QUEEN ALEXANDRA. Soft rosy lilac 0 6
174 SOUVENIR DE CANNES. Rich shade of maroon .. 0 6
175 CHOICE MIXED. A grand mixture of this fine new class, including many beautiful shades .. 6d. and 1 0

CULTIVATION OF TEN-WEEK STOCKS.

Ten-Week Stocks are easily raised from seed, but require careful treatment when in the seedling stage, as they are liable to damp off if over-watered and kept close, but if they are given an abundance of air and kept moderately moist, nothing need be feared and sturdy plants are assured. Sow from February to April under handlights or in a frame close to the glass, use a light rich compost, prick out under handlights, &c., to strengthen, harden off by giving plenty of air, and plant out towards the end of April where intended to flower. For succession sow in April or May in a sheltered place, and thin out or transplant.

In planting out seedling Ten-Week Stocks, with a view to securing the largest number of double flowers, preference should always be given to those with a good share of fine fibrous roots, even if the plants are somewhat weaker; we have found from long experience that those having coarse forked roots invariably produce the largest percentage of single blooms.

DANIELS' SUPERB TEN-WEEK STOCKS

STOCK—Daniels' Large Flowered Ten-Week.

DANIELS' LARGE-FLOWERED TEN-WEEK STOCKS.

This is incomparably the finest strain of Ten-week Stocks in existence, and, where space is limited, should always be grown in preference to others. The plants which attain about one foot in height are of the same compact habit as the dwarfer varieties, but the flowers when well grown are nearly double the size of those of the old variety. The seeds of this always produce a high percentage of double flowers, whilst in substance of petal, brilliancy of colouring and richness of fragrance they are unrivalled.

		s.	d.
176	A COLLECTION OF 12 SUPERB VARIETIES. The most distinct and beautiful colours	4	6
177	A COLLECTION OF 6 SUPERB VARIETIES. The most distinct and beautiful colours	2	6

		per pkt.—s. d.			per pkt.—s. d.
178	BRIGHT ROSE	0 6	187	SULPHUR YELLOW	0 6
179	DARK PURPLE	0 6	188	BRILLIANT ROSE	0 6
180	PURE WHITE 6d. &	1 0	189	CHOICEST MIXED special large pkt.	2 6
181	LIGHT BLUE	0 6			
182	FLESH COLOUR	0 6	190	CHOICEST MIXED smaller pkt. 6d. and	1 0
183	BRILLIANT CARMINE	0 6			
184	DARK BLOOD RED	0 6	191	DANIELS' SPECIAL MIXTURE of the most brilliant varieties	1 6
185	DARK VIOLET	0 6			
186	CHAMOIS	0 6			

DANIELS' GIANT PERFECTION TEN-WEEK.

A grand class of tall growing, beautiful varieties. The plants attain a height of from 15 to 18 inches, are of a handsome pyramidal form with branching habit, and throw up long central spikes of large, beautifully double flowers. This is an exceedingly fine strain that we can highly recommend.

		s. d.			s. d.
192	SIX CHOICE VARIETIES, distinct	2 6	197	PURE WHITE per pkt.	0 6
193	CRIMSON per pkt.	0 6	198	ROSE "	0 6
194	CANARY YELLOW "	0 6	199	CHOICEST MIXED "	1 0
195	LIGHT BLUE "	0 6	200	" " smaller pkt.	0 6
196	DARK BLUE "	0 6			

STOCKS—DANIELS' SPECIAL NAMED VARIETIES

STOCK—Daniels' Giant Perfection.

		per pkt.—s. d.			per pkt.—s. d.
201	ALL THE YEAR ROUND (new). A beautiful dwarf-growing variety, very early and extremely free flowering. One of the most useful for cutting. Pure white 6d. and	1 0	205	MAUVE QUEEN (Heliotrope). A beautiful variety, 1 foot high, with flowers of a pale bluish mauve colour, quite a distinct and novel shade 6d. and	1 0
202	DANIELS' AZURE QUEEN (new). A charming shade of light blue, with very fine central spike. Height 2 feet 6d. and	1 0	206	PRINCESS ALICE. Pure white, deliciously-scented double flowers. The plant is of a branching habit. Height 18 inches 6d. and	1 0
203	GIANT WHITE PERPETUAL. Enormous spikes of double white fragrant blooms. Superb variety. Height 2½ feet 6d. and	1 0	207	DANIELS' QUEEN OF VIOLETS (new). Rich dark blue, deliciously scented. Height 2 ft. 6d. and	1 0
204	LLOYD GEORGE (new). Fine blood-red, large flowered. Excellent for cutting 6d. and	1 0	208	DANIELS' SALMON QUEEN (new). One of the finest Stocks of recent introduction. Grand spikes of lovely salmony-pink flowers shaded buff. 2 feet 6d. &	1 0

EAST LOTHIAN STOCKS.

This splendid strain of Stocks gives a longer succession of bloom than any other kind and has a very good percentage of doubles. Sown in February or March it flowers in late Autumn after the Ten-week Stocks are over. It is also very useful as a pot plant from seed sown in May or June, and when sown in July or August and wintered in a frame will give a magnificent display in the early summer months.

		s. d.			s. d.
209	SIX DISTINCT VARIETIES	2 6	212	SCARLET	0 6
210	LAVENDER	0 6	213	WHITE	0 6
211	ROSE	0 6	214	CHOICEST MIXED 6d. and	1 0

DANIELS' SELECT ANTIRRHINUMS.

ANTIRRHINUM—THE BRIDE.

The value of Antirrhinums for garden decoration is now evidenced by the great popularity they enjoy, the advance in a few years being most remarkable. A great deal of this is no doubt due to the fact that many charming new colours have been evolved ; also to their free-flowering habit and the trueness to colour now displayed by them. There is still some difficulty in getting the pink strains to flower perfectly true to colour, but this can easily be obviated by having a few plants in reserve. The cultivation is extremely easy. Seed may be sown from January to March in very gentle heat for flowering the same year ; or if extra sturdy plants are required, seed may be sown at any time during the Summer months, and planted out in Autumn or Spring in the beds.

TALL GROWING VARIETIES.

This class is more suitable for border decoration than for beds, most of them attaining the height of from 2½ to 3 feet. They add a long display of colour to herbaceous borders if planted in groups of several plants.

		per pkt.—s. d.
241	TALL VARIETIES. Six brilliant sorts, with names	2 0
242	BLACK PRINCE. Dark maroon crimson	0 6
243	CERISE KING. Cerise pink with white throat and lip	0 6
244	CORAL PINK. Bright rosy pink, beautiful	0 6
245	FAIRY QUEEN (new). Rich orange-salmon with white throat	0 6
246	FIRE KING. Brilliant orange scarlet, white throat	0 6
247	GOLDEN YELLOW. Very fine	0 6
248	LILAC QUEEN. White, suffused pale lilac	0 6
249	MONARCH (new). Gigantic spikes of blood-red crimson flowers on long spikes	0 6
250	MOONLIGHT (new). Golden apricot and old rose, charming	0 6
251	ORANGE BEAUTY (new). Lovely orange scarlet	0 6
252	PINK BEAUTY. Deep rose pink, a charming flower	0 6
253	PRINCESS PATRICIA. Beautiful pale rose self	0 6
254	PURE WHITE. Beautiful variety	0 6
255	ROSE DORE (new). Lovely salmon-rose shaded gold	0 6
256	ROSE QUEEN. Soft rose, a lovely self colour	0 6
257	SALMON PINK (new). Rich rosy pink with white throat	0 6
258	TORCHLIGHT. Large vivid orange flower with yellow centre, shaded carmine	0 6
259	VULCAN. Intense crimson scarlet	0 6
260	CHOICEST MIXED. In beautiful variety	6d. and 1 0

TOM THUMB VARIETIES.

Dwarf and compact, the plants are covered with bloom all Summer if planted early. The best for edgings, growing 6 or 8 inches in height.

		per pkt.—s. d.			per pkt.—s. d.
261	TOM THUMB. 6 brilliant varieties, separate	2 0	265 SCARLET KING. Beautiful		0 6
262	ANTIQUE ROSE. Fine colour	0 6	266 WHITE QUEEN. Pure white, splendid		0 6
263	CRIMSON KING. Intense crimson, very fine	0 6	267 YELLOW PRINCE. Bright golden yellow		0 6
264	ORANGE KING. Bright orange scarlet	0 6	268 CHOICEST MIXED	6d. and	1 0

SEMI-DWARF OR INTERMEDIATE.

This type is the best for bedding, the sturdy plants being from 12 to 18 inches in height, blooming from early Summer until late Autumn if the dead flowers are removed.

		per pkt.—s. d.
215	AMBER QUEEN (new). Canary yellow overlaid with chamois, strikingly handsome, large flowers	0 6
216	APRICOT QUEEN (new). Lovely apricot pink, white throat	0 6
217	COTTAGE MAID (new). Beautiful pale pink with white throat, distinct and beautiful	0 6
218	CRIMSON KING. Very fine	0 6
219	ELECTRA. Beautiful salmon-maize and orange	0 6
220	FASCINATION (new). Large beautiful flowers of a delicate soft pink, exquisite variety	0 6
221	FLAME (new). Brilliant orange scarlet, very striking and fine	0 6
222	FLAMINGO (new). Deep terra-cotta, white throat	0 6
223	GOLDEN GEM (new). Rich deep golden yellow, large flowers	0 6
224	GOLDEN QUEEN. Rich yellow, splendid	0 6
225	MAIZE QUEEN IMPROVED. Salmon-maize and gold	0 6
226	MAUVE BEAUTY (new). A lovely shade of pale clear mauve, quite a new shade of colour amongst Antirrhinums	0 6
227	MORNING GLOW. Bright terra-cotta orange, bold spike	0 6
228	NELROSE. Beautiful rich coral pink, the finest of all for winter blooming in the greenhouse	0 6
229	ORANGE QUEEN (new). Terra-cotta pink and gold, orange lip	0 6
230	PINK GEM (new). Lovely clear rose-pink with white throat	0 6
231	PEACE (new). Compact variety, large rose-pink flowers with salmon shading	0 6
232	PURITY (new). Pure glistening white, free flowering	0 6
233	ROSEBUD (new). Bright rose-pink, white throat	0 6
234	SCARLET KING. Brilliant scarlet	0 6
235	SILVER QUEEN (new). Clear silvery lilac, unique colour	0 6
236	SUNRISE. Old rose, suffused orange and terra-cotta	0 6
237	THE BRIDE. Pure white	0 6
238	THE FAWN (new). Terra-cotta pink and pale yellow	0 6
239	VESUVIUS (new). Deep orange scarlet	0 6
240	CHOICEST MIXED. In fine variety	6d. and 1 0

ANTIRRHINUM—NELROSE. IN THE GREENHOUSE IN WINTER.

ALPHABETICAL LIST OF FLOWER SEEDS.

Cultural directions will accompany all packets of Flower Seeds.

AQUILEGIA.

MRS. SCOTT-ELLIOT'S LONG-SPURRED VARIETIES.
This is undoubtedly the finest strain in existence of these charming hardy plants; most exquisite blendings

Per pkt.—s. d.
		s.	d.
269	Blue Shades. Lavender, mauve, &c., very beautiful .. .. 6d. and	1	0
270	Pink Shades. From pale pink to red .. 6d. and	1	0
271	White and Yellow Shades. Very delicate and graceful .. 6d. and	1	0
272	Choicest Mixed. Beautiful variety of colours 6d. &	1	0

AQUILEGIA—
LONG SPURRED HYBRIDS.

AUBRETIA. Dwarf-growing hardy perennials.
273	Leichtlini Rosea. Carmine-rose	1	0
274	Græca. Bright blue ..	0	6
275	Large-flowered Hybrids. Saved from named varieties ..	1	0

AGERATUM.
276	LITTLE BLUE STAR. Splendid dwarf bedder, pale blue flowers	0	6
277	IMPERIAL DWARF BLUE. Fine for bedding ..	0	4

ANCHUSA ITALICA.
278	DROPMORE VARIETY. Hardy perennial. Dark blue 6d. and	1	0

ANEMONE.
279	ST. BRIGID. A lovely strain of extra large-flowered varieties. Irish grown seed .. .. 6d. and	1	0

ACHILLEA.
280	PTARMICA, THE PEARL. Heads of small double flowers, very useful for cutting	0	6

ALONSOA.
281	WARSCEWICZII COMPACTA. Brilliant annual, 1 ft. high, covered with brilliant scarlet flowers ..	0	6

AURICULA.
Showy old-fashioned favourites, delightfully scented.
282	DANIELS' PRIZE MIXED. From a magnificent collection 1/6 &	2	6
283	ALPINE. Very choice mixed .. .. 6d. and	1	0
284	GIANT YELLOW. Large trusses of sweetly-scented flowers	1	0

ASPARAGUS.
285	PLUMOSUS NANUS (Asparagus Fern). Very useful for greenhouse and table decoration	1	0
286	SPRENGERI. Splendid pot plant .. 6d. and	1	0

ARALIA.
287	SIEBOLDI. Large fig-like foliage, new seed ready in April 6d. &	1	0

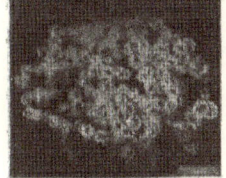

ALYSSUM—LITTLE GEM.

ALYSSUM.

288	COMPACTUM "LITTLE GEM." Charming little dwarf-growing annual, 4 or 5 in. high, bearing a profusion of pretty white flowers per oz. 3s.	0	6
289	PROCUMBENS (White Carpet). Dwarf-creeping continuing long in bloom	0	0
290	MARITIMUM (Sweet Alyssum). Free flowering, pure white; ht. 9 in. Good for edgings oz. 2s.	0	4
291	SAXATILE COMPACTUM. A fine hardy perennial, growing about 6 inches high, and quite covered with bright yellow flowers in Spring. First-rate for rockwork or borders ..	0	6

BALSAMS.

When well grown these form handsome objects for the decoration of the greenhouse or conservatory, where they will make a fine display for a long period. Balsams succeed admirably when planted out of doors in good soil, in a sheltered position. Sow the seeds in March or April in light rich soil, and place in a gentle heat.

DANIELS' CAMELLIA-FLOWERED.
Per pkt.
		s.	d.
292	AN ASSORTMENT OF SIX SPLENDID VARIETIES ..	2	6
293	SALMON QUEEN (new). Brilliant salmon-rose	0	6
294	SNOW QUEEN. Pure white. Splendid double	0	6
295	CHOICEST MIXED .. .. .. 6d. and	1	0

BEET.
Per pkt.
		s.	d.
296	CRIMSON WILLOW-LEAVED. Long narrow leaves of a splendid deep colour, fine for bedding	0	6

BROOM.
A beautiful hardy shrub. Seed sown in the early summer months will make fine shrubby plants for blooming the following year. Sow in light soil, covering the seed but slightly, and plant out as soon as large enough.

297	CRIMSON & YELLOW (G. Andreanus). A beautiful hardy shrub, carrying masses of bloom ..	0	6
298	WHITE PORTUGAL. Long sprays of flowers..	0	6
299	YELLOW SPANISH. Bright yellow	0	6

BALSAM—
DANIELS' CAMELLIA-FLOWERED.

BROWALLIA SPECIOSA MAJOR.
300	A charming plant for pot culture, growing about 18 inches high and producing large beautiful sky-blue flowers 6d. and	1	0

BEGONIAS.

Sow the seeds on the surface of well-drained pots or pans of light rich soil, press the surface firm before sowing and sprinkle with tepid water, cover the pot or pan with a sheet of glass to retain the moisture, and place in a heat of 65°. As the seed of Begonias does not germinate very quickly or evenly, and a long interval will often occur between the first and last plants coming up, the young seedlings should be carefully lifted as soon as large enough to handle, and pricked into pots or pans to grow on, and this will make room for the succeeding young plants. Those sown in February, if grown on freely, will commence blooming in June. Seeds may also be sown later, and will form nice healthy tubers before Winter.

301	DANIELS' PRIZE SINGLE. Carefully saved from a grand collection 1s. 6d. and	2	6
302	DANIELS' PRIZE DOUBLE. A superb strain, carefully hybridised, saved from finest varieties .. 1s. 6d. and	2	6
303	FRINGED, SINGLE. Beautifully fringed .. 1s 6d. and	2	6
304	FRINGED, DOUBLE. Elegantly fringed petals, splendid for pots 1s. 6d. and	2	6

FIBROUS ROOTED VARIETIES
This graceful class, with its bronze foliage and numerous small flowers is of great value for bedding, blooming well throughout the Summer.
305	GRACILIS LUMINOSA. Scarlet, bronze foliage 6d. &	1	0

BEGONIA—DOUBLE FLOWERED.
306	VERNON COMPACTA. Brilliant red flowers, deep red foliage 6d. and	1	0
307	SEMPERFLORENS, MIXED. Dwarf bedding varieties 6d. and	1	0

CALLIOPSIS OR COREOPSIS.

These beautiful free-flowering hardy annuals succeed almost anywhere, but are of especial value for growing in town gardens. They remain in bloom for a long period during the Summer and Autumn, and the blooms of all the taller growing varieties are useful for cutting. The Tom Thumb varieties are exceedingly pretty.

		Per pkt.—s. d.
308	DRUMMONDI. Golden yellow, with brown centre. Fine.	
	18 inches	0 4
309	MARMORATA. Peculiarly spotted yellow and brown	
310	TINCTORIA. Yellow and chestnut; showy. 2 feet ..	0 4
311	TALL VARIETIES. Choice mixed, including all the prettiest	

varieties. A useful selection for cutting

		per oz. 1s. 6d.	0 4
312	DOUBLE MIXED. Many fine colours, mostly double, and semi-double flowers		0 6
313	TOM THUMB (Mixed). Beautiful dwarf-growing varieties, about 1 foot high, and producing quite a profusion of pretty flowers		0 6
314	GRANDIFLORA. Handsome perennial variety, quite hardy, and growing about 3 feet high. Golden yellow flowers		0 6

CALLIOPSIS MARMORATA.

CANDYTUFT.

An exceedingly useful and showy class of hardy annuals that should be grown freely wherever a good display is desired. The beautiful variety " Rose Cardinal " is particularly fine, as are also those of the new dwarf large-flowered section. " Little Prince " is distinct and charming with its numerous trusses of pure white flowers.

		Per pkt.—s. d.
315	DANIELS' MAMMOTH SPIRAL, WHITE. Immense spikes of large pure white, very fine 6d. and	1 0
316	ROSE CARDINAL. Brilliant carmine rose ..	0 6
317	CREAMY WHITE. Large creamy flowers, beautiful	0 4
318	DARK CRIMSON. Selected, very fine colour. Height 1 foot	0 4
319	CHOICEST MIXED. A fine mixture, containing all the colours of the taller growing varieties. per oz. 1s. 6d.	0 4
320	LITTLE PRINCE. Six inches.	

CANDYTUFT—MAMMOTH SPIRAL.

	Per pkt.—s. d.
	Pure white flowers	0 4
321	LARGE-FLOWERED DWARF. A splendid new class of large-flowered beautiful varieties of a dwarf, compact habit. Very choice mixed ..	0 6

CENTAUREA CYANUS MINOR.
(CORNFLOWER.)

Highly popular showy hardy annuals. They are of the easiest possible culture, and are very useful to cut for decorative purposes, giving a profusion of bloom with little trouble. The plants grow about 3 feet high.

322	EMPEROR WILLIAM. Bright blue	0 4
323	BRIGHT ROSE. Beautiful colour	0 4
324	CHOICE MIXED. All colours .. per oz. 1s. 3d.	0 4
325	SEMI-DOUBLE VARIETIES. Choice mixed. A very pretty class ..	0 6

CORNFLOWER BLUE.

CANTERBURY BELLS.
(Campanula Medium.)

A beautiful class of free-flowering hardy biennials for garden decoration. Young plants potted up in early Autumn and stored in a cool pit for the Winter, may be brought into the greenhouse or conservatory in Spring, and will bloom beautifully without forcing. It should be borne in mind

that all the varieties have a tendency to sport and cannot be depended on to come absolutely true from seed, the best selected strains of doubles always producing some single flowers. All the sorts grow about 2 feet high.

		Per pkt.—s. d.
326	NEW PYRAMIDAL. Beautiful upright growing varieties. Very choice mixed seed 6d. and	1 0
327	SINGLE. Mauve, large-flowered	0 4
328	„ Pure white, very fine	0 4
329	„ Blue, large-flowered	0 4
330	„ Rose, large-flowered	0 4
331	„ Choicest Mixed	0 6
332	DOUBLE. Pure white, fine	0 6
333	„ Rose	0 6
334	„ Blue, extra select ..	0 6
335	„ Choice Mixed	0 6

DOUBLE CANTERBURY BELLS.

CALYCANTHEMA VARIETIES.
Cup and Saucer.

336	BLUE. Very large flowers	0 6
337	LAVENDER. Lovely shade	0 6
338	PURE WHITE. Very beautiful	0 6
339	ROSE. Handsome rose-coloured flowers of great size ..	0 6
340	CHOICE MIXED	0 6

CANTERBURY BELLS.
New Hybrids.

341	A very fine class of beautiful varieties. Shades of pink, lavender, mauve, blush, violet, white, &c. Very fine .. 6d. and	1 0

CALENDULA
(Scotch Pot Marigolds).

Showy hardy annuals, continuing in bloom for quite a long period; pleasantly scented, and very useful for cutting.

342	CHOICE MIXED DOUBLE. In beautiful variety of orange, yellow, primrose striped, and other shades	0 4

CANTERBURY BELLS, CUP & SAUCER.

CAMPANULAS.

Campanulas pyramidalis and p. alba form very useful pot plants for the cool greenhouse. The beautiful Persicifolia varieties are very fine and greatly prized for garden decoration. They are easily grown, and when in bloom are very charming. They will succeed almost anywhere, but generally speaking thrive best in a light rich sandy soil. Seeds sown from April to end of June.

343	PERSICIFOLIA GRANDIFLORA, MIXED. Fine hardy perennials with long spikes of bright blue and white flowers. 3 feet ..	0 6
344	„ MOERHEIMI. Long spikes of large semi-double pure white flowers. Superb variety. Hardy perennial. Height 3 feet	0 6
345	PYRAMIDALIS. Blue (the Chimney Campanula). Excellent as a pot plant for greenhouse. Half-hardy perennial. 3 feet	0 6
346	PYRAMIDALIS ALBA. Pure white	0 6

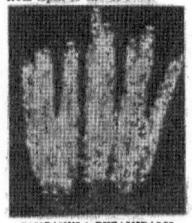
CAMPANULA PYRAMIDALIS.

CALCEOLARIAS.

CALCEOLARIA—
DANIELS' CHOICEST STRAIN.

We have much pleasure in offering our splendid strain of Calceolaria hybrids, which has been carefully saved from a magnificent collection during the past season. The flowers will be found of large size, beautiful form, and tigred and spotted with the most exquisite and brilliant markings.

Sow the seeds in well-drained pots or seed-pans; cover the drainage with rough fibrous loam, and fill up the surface with fine, light, sifted mould and silver sand; water with a fine rose water-pot, after which sow the seed, placing a piece of glass over the pot to retain the moisture, no covering of soil being required. Place the pots in a cool frame or under a handlight, taking care to shade from the sun. Prick off one inch apart into pots or pans made up as before, placing in a somewhat close situation, and when of sufficient size pot off singly, and treat in a similar manner to that recommended for tender annuals. Calceolarias should be always kept in a cool, moist position, a dry heated atmosphere being very prejudicial to their growth, and they should be kept well supplied with fresh air.

                                   Per pkt.—s. d.

347 **DANIELS' CHOICEST MIXED.** Beautifully spotted and marked; the most perfect type..   ..   1s. 6d. and   2 6
348 **BUTTERCUP.** An attractive new hybrid for conservatory or summer bedding. Seed may be sown in August for Spring flowering in the greenhouse or early in Spring for bedding out. Golden yellow flowers. Award of Merit R.H.S.   ..   1 6

CARNATIONS.

Carnation seed should be sown in well-drained pans of good rich soil, and kept shaded until the seed has germinated, when the plants should be gradually hardened off by admitting air and light. Prick off the seedlings about nine inches apart in boxes or prepared borders, and let them stay there until the Autumn, when they may be permanently planted in the positions they are to occupy.

The Perpetual or Tree varieties are a very valuable class, giving as they do a charming display in Winter, when flowers are so much valued.

The "Marguerite" Section is a special favourite with amateurs, as the plants when raised from seed early in the Spring, produce an abundance of flowers during the Summer; if sown in June, carefully lifted in Autumn and potted up, they will continue to bloom right into the Winter

SEEDLING CARNATIONS FROM OUR COLLECTION OF CHOICE VARIETIES.

                Per pkt.—s. d.

349 **DANIELS' CHOICEST MIXED.** A very fine strain of beautiful varieties, saved from stage flowers, and will produce a high percentage of double blooms   1s. 6d. and   2 6
350 **DANIELS' PERPETUAL or TREE.** A fine strain of beautiful flowers. Fine for pot culture   1s. 6d. and   2 6
                Per pkt.—s. d.
351 **AMERICAN PERPETUAL.** A fine class for pot culture, very choice mixed   ..   ..   1s. 6d. and   2 6
352 **DANIELS' NEW EARLY.** A beautiful strain of early flowering perpetual Carnations; large double flowers in splendid variety   ..   ..   ..   1s. 6d. and   2 6
353 **NEW PERPETUAL CARNATION, EXCELSIOR.** A new strain of perpetual flowering Carnations during the first year from seed. The flowers are very large, on strong stems, equalling the best of the named sorts; gives a good percentage of double flowers. Choicest mixed   1s. 6d. and   2 6
354 **PICOTEE. DANIELS' CHOICEST MIXED.** From stage flowers, in splendid variety   ..   1s. 6d. and   2 6
355 **MARGUERITE. NEW LARGE-FLOWERED.** Handsome, double, fringed flowers, deliciously scented. Sown early will bloom freely the first year. Very choice mixed   6d. and   1 0

CINERARIAS.

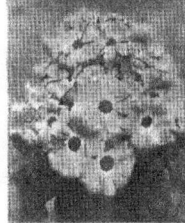

CINERARIAS—LARGE-FLOWERED.

When required for a general display in early Spring, the seed should be sown in July or early in August, and when for Winter blooming, a few should be sown in March or April.

356 **DANIELS' CHOICEST MIXED.** Splendid strain. Carefully saved from a fine collection of named and choicest seedling flowers, which we have every confidence in recommending as unsurpassable. The colours will be found varied and brilliant, combined with a faultless form of flower   1s. 6d. and   2 6
357 **BLUE.** Fine rich colour   ..   1 6
358 **WHITE.** Very useful 1 6
359 **ANTIQUE ROSE.** Most beautiful shades of rose   ..   1 6
360 **MATADOR.** Rich glowing scarlet   ..   1 6
361 **DOUBLE-FLOWERED.** Produces a large percentage of double flowers. Choicest mixed   ..   1s. 6d. and   2 6

CINERARIA STELLATA (New Cactus Varieties)

A splendid new strain, the petals of the flowers being elegantly twisted and fluted, and comprising a wonderful range of beautiful colours.
362 **CHOICEST MIXED**   ..   ..   ..   1s. 6d. and   2 6

CINERARIA STELLATA (Star Cinerarias).

Magnificent plant for conservatory or corridor decoration. Immense heads of star-shaped flowers are borne on long stalks, well above the foliage. Plants grow from 2 to 4 feet high.
               Per pkt.—s. d.
363 **CHOICEST MIXED** 1/6 &   2 6
364 **BLUE.** Various shades   1 6
365 **PINK.**   ..   1 6

CHEIRANTHUS ALLIONI.

366 A charming little hardy perennial, producing a profusion of brilliant orange flowers. 1 foot   0 6

CINERARIAS—NEW CACTUS.

CELOSIA (Feathered Cockscomb.)
               Per pkt. s. d.
367 **CELOSIA PLUMOSA. CHOICEST MIXED.** All shades of yellow and rose to brilliant crimson, etc. ..   ..6d. and   1 0

CONVOLVULUS.

A fine class of well-known beautiful annuals.
368 **MAJOR. CHOICEST MIXED.** In beautiful variety; rapid and graceful climbers   ..   ..   per oz. 1s.   0 4
369 **MINOR. CHOICE MIXED.** Beautiful hardy annuals, growing about one foot high   ..   ..   per oz. 1s.   0 4

COLEUS.

Sow the seeds in February or March in light rich soil and place in a good heat. Pot off singly into small pots, keeping near the light, and shift into larger pots as required. Those of about six or seven inches diameter being ample for a final potting.
370 **NEW LARGE-LEAVED HYBRIDS.** Choicest Mixed. This is a grand strain of brilliantly coloured varieties, invaluable for decoration of the greenhouse or conservatory. Seed offered will produce a splendid variety of beautiful foliage ..   1s. 6d. and   2 6

COLEUS—LARGE LEAVED.

CLARKIA ELEGANS.
NEW DOUBLE-FLOWERED.

CLARKIA QUEEN MARY.

The beautiful new double-flowered varieties mentioned below are especially worthy of notice, as they continue in bloom for quite a long time, and sown early under glass are excellent as pot plants for the greenhouse. Per pkt.— s. d.

		s.	d.
371	QUEEN MARY. A splendid addition to this lovely class. The stems and branches are studded with very double brilliant rosy-carmine flowers 6d. and	1	0
372	CHAMOIS QUEEN. Soft chamois rose	0	6
373	SCARLET QUEEN. Brilliant orange-scarlet double flowers; splendid ..	0	6
374	ORANGE KING. Brilliant orange red ..	0	6
375	ROSY MORN. Rose pink	0	6
376	DOUBLE WHITE Fine	0	6
377	SALMON QUEEN. Long sprays of double flowers	0	6
378	FINEST MIXED. per oz. 3s.	0	6

ANNUAL CHRYSANTHEMUMS.

An exceedingly useful and showy class of hardy annuals for garden decoration. The single-flowered varieties are especially valuable to cut for vases and large bouquets, and will last for a long time in water. Sow the seeds in March or April in the open ground and thin out to 6 or 8 inches. Per pkt.—s. d.

		s.	d.
379	MORNING STAR. Beautiful large pale yellow flowers	0	6
380	NORTHERN STAR. Soft yellow, clear white edges	0	6
381	EVENING STAR. Large, rich golden yellow flowers	0	6
382	DANIELS' CHOICEST MIXED. Single. Beautiful strain, splendid for garden decoration per oz. 2s. 6d.	0	6
383	DANIELS' CHOICEST MIXED. Double (new). A splendid strain ..	0	6
384	INODORUM, "BRIDAL ROBE." Double snow-white flowers. 6d. and	1	0
385	CHRYSANTHEMUM MAXIMUM. (The Speaker.) Hardy perennial. Very large, splendid pure white. Sown in March under glass will bloom beautifully out doors in the Autumn	0	6
386	CHRYSANTHEMUM FRUTESCENS. (Parisian Daisy.) Starry white, very useful for pots, window boxes, or bedding out	0	6

ANNUAL CHRYSANTHEMUMS— CHOICEST MIXED.

COSMEA (Cosmos).

COSMOS.

A beautiful class of free-flowering, showy, half-hardy annuals, growing about three feet high, with finely-divided, elegant, fern-like foliage. Seed sown in March under glass will commence blooming in July and continue into late Autumn.

		s.	d.
387	NEW GIANT HYBRIDS. A much improved strain; the blooms are larger and more numerous, ranging from crimson through all shades to white 6d. and	1	0
388	ROSE QUEEN (new). Soft rose, beautifully early flowers ..	0	6
389	WHITE QUEEN (new). Pure white, fine for cutting	0	6
390	CRIMSON QUEEN (new). A new double-flowered variety; about one-half coming true from seed ..	0	6
391	EARLY FLOWERING MIXED	0	4

CYCLAMEN.

CYCLAMEN—SALMON KING.

A beautiful class of plant for the greenhouse, blooming freely in Winter and early Spring. The seed should be sown in January or February in a gentle heat, for blooming the following year. For earlier flowering sow in November. Per pkt.—s. d.

		s.	d.
302	DANIELS' GIANT MIXED. A magnificent strain of a highly improved type. The blooms are of splendid size, each flower frequently measuring from 2½ to 3 inches in length .. 1s. 6d. and	2	6
303	SALMON KING. Large beautiful flowers of a clear salmon-pink colour.	1	6
304	DANIELS' GIANT WHITE. Pure white, large flowers. Splendid	1	6
305	VULCAN. Splendid crimson, large flowered	1	6

DAISY—Double-flowered.

Well-known useful hardy perennial plants for Spring bedding. Sow in March or April for blooming the same year, and sow in June for blooming the following Spring.

		s.	d.
306	GIANT WHITE. Large double pure white flowers	0	6
307	GIANT ROSE. Very large flowers; fine colour ..	0	6
308	CHOICEST MIXED, Double .. .. 6d. and	1	0

DAHLIA.

Sow the seeds of these in February or March in a gentle heat, pot the young plants singly into small pots and plant out towards the end of May. Will bloom from July till the plants are killed by the frost.

		s.	d.
399	LARGE-FLOWERED SHOW AND FANCY. Saved from our fine collection of choice named flowers	1	0
400	CACTUS-FLOWERED. From named flowers, very choice ..	1	0
401	COLLARETTE. Saved from the finest strain in existence ..	1	0
402	POMPONE. Fine varieties from choicest named flowers ..	1	0
403	SINGLE-FLOWERED. From a very fine collection 6d. and	1	0
404	PETER PAN. A charming miniature class, with anemone-shaped flowers; many combinations of colour	1	0

DIANTHUS.

One of the most brilliant and splendid groups of hardy biennials in cultivation. Sown in March under glass and transplanted they will bloom freely the first season and make charming beds.

DIANTHUS HEDDEWIGI, Double-flowered.
VERY USEFUL FOR CUT FLOWERS.

		s.	d.
405	PINK BEAUTY. Clear flesh pink, a delightful flower ..	0	6
406	FIREBALL. Dark crimson, splendid ..	0	6
407	SNOWDRIFT. Pure white, beautifully fringed flowers ..	0	6
408	FRINGED, DOUBLE. Splendid mixed. The petals of these are elegantly laciniated. Excellent for cutting ..	0	6
409	DANIELS' CHOICEST MIXED, DOUBLE. A charming variety of beautiful colours .. .. .. 6d. and	1	0

Single-flowered.

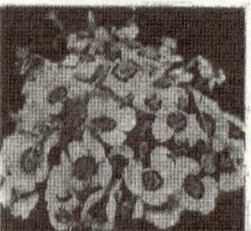

DIANTHUS—LITTLE GEM.

		s.	d.
410	LITTLE GEM. White with crimson eye ..	0	6
411	SALMON QUEEN. Brilliant salmon pink	0	6
412	CHOICEST MIXED SINGLE. Showy	0	6
413	CHINENSIS (Indian Pink). Finest double mixed ..	0	6
414	LACINIATUS, "The MIKADO." Free flowering, great variety of colour, beautifully tasselled ..	0	6
415	DIANTHUS CÆSIUS (New Hybrids). Beautiful new varieties of the Cheddar Pink, ranging in colour from rose-crimson, blush and mauve to white; deliciously clove scented ..	1	0

DELPHINIUM.

These beautiful hardy border perennials, when grown in clumps on the herbaceous border, are strikingly effective when in bloom. Their handsome spikes of flowers, ranging in colour from white through all the richest shades of blue and purple, furnish some rare colours not found in any other class of plant.

Per pkt.—s. d.

416 **BELLADONNA, CLIVEDEN BEAUTY.** Beautiful sky blue, a great improvement on the old Belladonna 6d. and 1 0
417 **REV. E. LASCELLES.** Rich dark blue, white centre, double 6d. and 1 0
418 **CHOICEST MIXED SINGLE.** In beautiful variety. From our fine collection of named flowers .. 6d. and 1 0
419 **DOUBLE - FLOWERED, CHOICEST MIXED.** Fine new varieties, magnificent strain 6d. and 1 0

DIMORPHOTHECA.

420 **NEW HYBRIDS.** Beautiful half-hardy annual, with showy flowers, ranging from white, lemon, maize, salmon, to deep orange 0 6

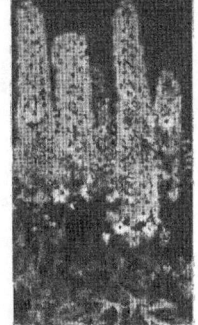

DELPHINIUM—SINGLE-FLOWERED.

DIGITALIS—Fox-Glove.

A very beautiful and showy class of hardy perennials, with long spikes of beautiful Gloxinia-like flowers that continue for a long period when the plants are partially shaded.

Per pkt.
s. d.

421 **DANIELS' SUPERB SPOTTED.** Magnificent varieties with large, Gloxinia-like spotted flowers .. .. 6d. and 1 0
422 **MONSTROSA.** Splendid mixed, beautiful shades 0 6

ERYSIMUM LINIFOLIUM.

423 A profuse flowering biennial, forming in June a mass of blossom of bright clear mauve, resembling, in colour and shape " Aubretia Græca " 0 6

ERIGERON AURANTIACA HYBRIDS.

424 Showy hardy perennial, ranging in colour from white to deep orange 0 6

EUCALYPTUS.

425 **GLOBULUS** (Australian Blue Gum). Glaucous green foliage, fine for sub-tropical garden 0 6
426 **CITRIODORA.** Lemon-scented foliage, makes a capital pot plant for the greenhouse. Deliciously fragrant 1 0

ESCHSCHOLTZIA.

A brilliant class of hardy biennials growing about one foot high. Sown and treated as hardy annuals will give a beautiful display within a few weeks of the seeds being sown. These are amongst the most delightful of our summer flowers and should certainly find a place in every garden.

427 **VESUVIUS** (new). Grand variety, inside of petals as brilliantly coloured as the outside; colour wallflower red 0 6
428 **ORANGE KING** (new). Flowers of a deep orange yellow, 2½ to 3 in. diam.; largest flowered variety .. 0 6
429 **MIKADO.** Intense crimson scarlet suffused with orange; fluted petals .. 0 6
430 **CARMINE KING.** Brilliant carmine, splendid colour 0 6
431 **CROCEA FL. PL.** Orange, double, resembling a Marechal Niel rose, very fine 0 6
432 **MANDARIN.** Orange scarlet 0 6
433 **ROSE CARDINAL.** Beautiful rose 0 6
434 **EXTRA CHOICE MIXED.** In beautiful variety .. 0 4

ESCHSCHOLTZIA—ROSE CARDINAL.

GAILLARDIA.

A splendid class of showy hardy perennials. If sown under glass in March, will bloom freely the first year from seed, and continue quite into late Autumn. First-class for cut flowers.

Per pkt.—s. d.

435 **LARGE-FLOWERED SINGLE.** Saved from our splendid strain of choice named flowers. 2 to 3 feet .. 6d. and 1 0
436 **LORENZIANA.** Double mixed. Very fine for cutting, fine annual variety 0 4

GLOXINIA.

These should be grown by every one having accommodation for them. Sow in February or March on a good moist heat, in the way recommended for Calceolarias. Pot off singly into small pots as soon as the young plants can be handled, and shift into larger as required. Treated in this way, a charming display of bloom may be had during July and August, and some really grand flowers will be the result.

437 **DANIELS' PRIZE MIXED.** A splendid strain of large beautifully coloured flowers, including the newest colours.

1s. 6d. and 2s. 6d. per pkt.

438 **GIANT-FLOWERED, MIXED.** Very large flowers, more than four inches across and of the most splendid colours, 1s. 6d. & 2s. 6d.

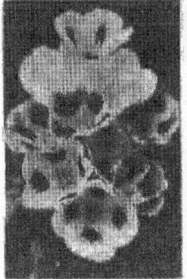

GLOXINIA—DANIELS' PRIZE.

439 **PURE WHITE.** A large flowered beautiful pure white .. 1 6

GEUM.

A very useful hardy perennial, growing about two feet high, with brilliant scarlet ranunculus-like flowers.

440 **MRS. BRADSHAW.** Beautiful double scarlet, fine variety .. 0 6

GERBERA—The Transvaal Daisy.

441 **JAMESONI.** New Hybrids. The flowers are of incomparable delicacy and richness, with almost an infinity of tints ranging from pure white through all the shades of yellow, orange, salmon, rose, cerise, scarlet, ruby and violet .. 1 0

GODETIA.

A magnificent class of brilliant, large-flowered, showy hardy annuals that should be grown freely in every garden where a bold display is desired. They are very effective for mixed beds or borders, and when grown in masses are very charming. For a general display sow thinly in the open ground from early in March to the end of April. If sown in Autumn and transplanted in Spring they will bloom much earlier and finer. The single-flowered varieties grow about one foot in height, and the double-flowered two feet.

442 **COLLECTION OF 6 SUPERB VARIETIES** 2 0
443 **BRIDESMAID.** Rose and white 0 6
444 **CRIMSON GLOW** (new). Intense dark crimson, splendid, very compact. Height nine inches .. 0 6
445 **DUKE OF YORK.** Vivid carmine, brilliant showy colour 0 6
446 **DUCHESS OF ALBANY.** Pure satiny white, beautiful bedder 0 6
447 **GLORIOSA.** Dark crimson, taller than Crimson Glow .. 0 6
448 **DANIELS' DOUBLE MAUVE.** Fine new colour 0 6
449 **DANIELS' DOUBLE ROSE.** Beautiful double rose .. 0 6
450 **DANIELS' LARGE-FLOWERED MIXED.** A splendid mixture in a variety of colours. per oz. 2s. 6d. 0 4

GODETIA—DANIELS' LARGE-FLOWERED.

GREVILLEA ROBUSTA.

Sow in pans of sandy loam, and place in a gentle hot-bed. Pot off as soon as large enough and transfer to the greenhouse shifting into larger pots as the plants require them.

451 Beautiful greenhouse shrub with handsome fern-like foliage — 0 6

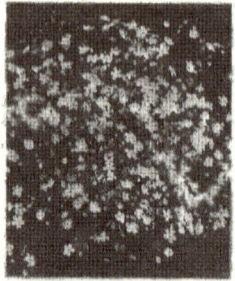

GYPSOPHILA ELEGANS GRANDIFLORA ALBA.

GYPSOPHILA.

This splendid hardy annual should be freely grown wherever cut flowers are in demand. It has a very graceful and pretty effect in association with Sweet Peas when used for table or other decorations.

per pkt.— s. d.

452 ELEGANS GRAN-DIFLORA ALBA. An exceedingly pretty hardy annual with finely branched elegant stems of white flowers. Splendid for bouquets, 18 inches, per oz. 2s. 0 6
453 „ ROSEA Rosy pink, very pretty 0 6
454 PANICULATA. A hardy perennial with elegantly branched panicles of small white flowers. Height 2 feet 0 6
455 PANICULATA DOUBLE. A beautiful double form of the preceding, about one-half coming true from seed 6d. and 1 0

HELICHRYSUM. (Everlasting.)

A brilliant and splendid class of showy hardy annual everlasting flowers. The flowers vary in colour from dark crimson or purple, orange scarlet and yellow, to delicate rose and pure white.

456 FIREBALL. Deep crimson red, fine. Height 3 feet 1 0
457 LARGE-FLOWERED. 6 separate varieties. Height 3 feet.. 1 0
458 „ „ Choicest mixed, all colours „ .. 0 4

HEUCHERA.

Charming hardy perennials, growing about 18 inches high, with long slender panicles of brilliant flowers.

per pkt.—s. d.

459 CHOICE HYBRIDS. Mixed 0 6

HELIOTROPE.

These deliciously scented and highly popular flowers bloom freely the first year from seed, and sown in February or early March in a gentle heat will commence blooming in July and continue to flower till late in Autumn. The plants grow about 18 inches high.

460 EXTRA CHOICE MIXED. Saved from a splendid giant - flowered strain, bearing immense heads of flowers of the most delicious fragrance 6d. & 1 0

HELIOTROPE.

HOLLYHOCKS.

Easily raised from seed sown in May or June out of doors, planting out in Autumn for blooming the following year.

461 PINK QUEEN (new). Double salmon-pink, very large flowers 1 0
462 SIX CHOICE VARIETIES. From a splendid collection .. 2 6
463 DANIELS' PRIZE MIXED. A superb strain saved from the finest type of Prize Double Hollyhocks .. 6d., 1s. and 2 6
464 SINGLE-FLOWERED. Attractive and beautiful class 6d. and 1 0

HONESTY.

Very useful early flowering hardy biennial. Fine for shrubbery borders, and valued for its dried silvery seed pods for Winter decoration.

465 CRIMSON. Bright red, very fine 0 6
466 MIXED. Various colours 0 4
467 ICE PLANT. A trailing half-hardy annual 0 4

KOCHIA TRICHOPHYLLA. (Summer Cypress, The True Variety.)

One of the most interesting plants of recent introduction. The plant attains a height of about eighteen inches. In the Autumn, the foliage changes to a bright crimson, when it has a novel and striking effect. Easily raised and grown as a half-hardy annual, or may be sown in the open ground in April, and thinned out or transplanted.

468 .. .. 0 6

LARKSPUR.

A very fine class of beautiful showy hardy annuals that are of great value for garden decoration. The tall-growing varieties are especially handsome, and the flowers being produced on long, graceful spikes, are very useful for cut flowers. The Stock-flowered varieties grow about 3 feet in height.

per pkt.—s. d.

469 STOCK-FLOWERED, CARMINE ROSE. Very fine. Height 3 feet .. 0 6
470 „ PALE BLUE (new). Beautiful colour .. 0 6
471 „ PURE WHITE. Fine for cutting .. 0 6
472 „ DARK BLUE. Very rich 0 6
473 „ ROSY SCARLET (new). Charming colour .. 0 6
474 „ CHOICEST MIXED. Fine, tall varieties .. 0 6
475 EMPEROR, CHOICE MIXED. Free-flowering. Height 2 feet .. 0 6
476 DWARF ROCKET, CHOICE MIXED. Beautiful early-flowering varieties. Height 1 foot 0 4

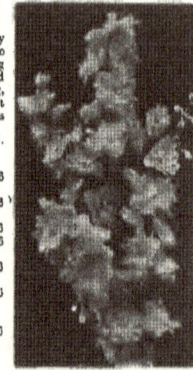

LARKSPUR—STOCK-FLOWERED.

477 LINARIA MAROCCANA. EXCELSA HYBRIDS. Splendid new strain, with spikes of small Antirrhinum-like flowers .. 0 6

LAVATERA.

Exceedingly beautiful and showy hardy annuals, growing about 3 feet.

478 SPLENDENS "SUNSET" (new). A very fine improvement; the flowers are exceedingly bright and of the most beautiful deep rose colour, and are very lasting when cut .. 6d. and 1 0
479 ROSEA SPLENDENS. Large bright rosy-pink flowers .. 0 6
480 ALBA SPLENDENS. Large glossy pure white flowers .. 0 6
481 LEPTOSIPHON. NEW FRENCH HYBRIDS. Free-flowering and exceedingly pretty hardy annuals, very useful for beds 0 6

LANTANA.

A half-hardy shrubby perennial, with heads of brilliantly coloured flowers, as showy as Verbenas. Excellent for bedding, or pot plant.

482 NEW DWARF HYBRIDS, MIXED. Height 9 inches .. 0 6

LINUM.

483 GRANDIFLORUM RUBRUM. Showy hardy annual, brilliant crimson-scarlet, 1 foot .. .. .. per oz. 1s. 0 4

LOBELIA.

Sow thinly in pans or pots of sandy loam, cover very lightly, and place in a heat of about sixty degrees, keep moist, and soon as the young plants can be handled, plant them thinly in shallow trays of rich soil, keeping in a gentle heat. These quickly produce a beautiful effect when planted out.

484 DANIELS' DARK BLUE. Very fine dark blue; compact .. 1 0
485 DANIELS' WHITE BEDDING. Pure white dwarf .. 1 0
486 ROYAL PURPLE. Deep rich blue with distinct white eye .. 0 6
487 BARNARD'S PERPETUAL. Bright blue 0 6
488 BLUE WINGS (new). Lovely ultramarine blue flowers .. 0 6
489 SPECIOSA (true). Fine dark blue 0 6
490 SAPPHIRE. A charming variety, with trailing sprays over 2 feet long, flowers dark blue with white eye; splendid for window boxes or baskets .. 6d. and 1 0
491 TENUIOR. A charming variety, growing about one foot high, with very large flowers, cobalt blue, with white centre .. 0 6
492 CARDINALIS VICTORIA. Beautiful half-hardy perennial, brilliant scarlet, Height 2 feet 1 0

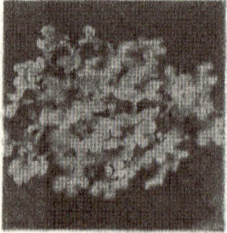

LOBELIA—WHITE BEDDING.

LUPINUS.

Showy hardy annuals and perennials that well deserve their high popularity. All the varieties are free-flowering and have a very pretty effect on mixed beds or borders.

		s.	d.
493	HYBRIDUS ATROCOC- Per pkt. CINEUS. Scarlet and white, very showy. 2½ ft.	0	4
494	ANNUAL VARIETIES MIXED per oz. 1s. 6d.	0	4
495	ARBOREUS (The Tree Lupin). Shrubby variety, flowers yellow. 4 feet	0	6
496	„ SNOW QUEEN. Pure white flowers, splendid variety. Height 4 feet	0	6
497	POLYPHYLLUS MOER-HEIMI. Fine spikes of rose and white	0	6
498	POLYPHYLLUS HY-BRIDS. A grand strain, with many new and charming colours	0	6

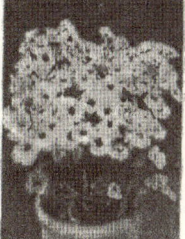

LUPINUS POLYPHYLLUS.

LYCHNIS (New Hybrids).

A splendid class of hardy herbaceous perennials. The flowers vary in colour from brilliant scarlet to the brightest orange and salmon shades; very effective. per pkt.—s. d.

499	HAAGEANA, CHOICE MIXED. In beautiful variety 1 foot	0	6
500	ARKWRIGHTII. A magnificent new strain, growing 18 inches to 2 feet high. Great range of colour 6d. and	1	0

MATHIOLA BICORNIS.

(Night-Scented Stock.)

501	One of the most deliciously-scented of all annuals, especially in the evening. Should be grown freely per oz. 1s. 6d.	0	4
502	MICHAELMAS DAISY. Perennial Asters. Saved from a grand collection of all the finest varieties 6d. and	1	0

MIMULUS.

503	DANIELS' LARGE-FLOWERED. A grand strain of large beautiful flowers of the richest colours. Height 1 foot 6d. and	1	0
504	MUSK PLANT, NEW DWARF. A fine compact-growing variety. Very free-flowering and powerfully fragrant	0	6

MAIZE.

505	VARIEGATED JAPANESE. A beautiful variety growing about 4 feet high, broad green leaves, elegantly striped with white. Half-hardy annual	0	4
506	NEW GIANT VARIEGATED. A fine variety with foliage handsomely striped with white, pink and yellow.	0	6

MIGNONETTE.

These well-known, deliciously scented, hardy annuals are extremely easy of cultivation.

507	ORANGE QUEEN (new). Immense spikes of bright orange-red flowers. Deliciously scented, magnificent variety 6d. and	1	0
508	YELLOW PRINCE. Numerous fine spikes of rich canary yellow, deliciously scented 6d. and	1	0
509	DANIELS' CRIMSON KING. About one foot high, with gigantic spikes of the darkest bright red blooms. 6d. and	1	0
510	DANIELS' GIANT RED. Grand variety, two ft. high, large spikes of red, highly-scented flowers 6d. and	1	0
511	DANIELS' GIANT WHITE. A superb variety, bearing very large spikes of almost pure white flowers 6d. and	1	0
512	DANIELS' GOLDEN QUEEN. Compact-growing, sweet-scented yellow flowers 6d. &	1	0
513	MACHET. A fine, sturdy, compact-growing variety	0	4
514	GIANT MACHET, SALMON-RED. Splendid variety 6d. &	1	0
515	A COLLECTION OF SIX CHOICE VARIETIES	2	0
516	LARGE-FLOWERED, oz. 1s.	0	4

MIGNONETTE—DANIELS' CRIMSON KING.

MALOPE.

Showy hardy annuals growing about 2 feet high. Very useful for large borders or beds. Similar in growth to Lavatera. 1 per pkt. s. d.

517	GRANDIFLORA ROSEA. Bright rose	0	4
518	„ CRIMSON	0	4
519	„ ALBA. Pure white	0	4
520	„ MIXED per oz. 1s. 3d.	0	4

MARIGOLD.

These fine half-hardy annuals should not be sown earlier than the beginning of April; planting out can only be done with safety when all danger from Spring frosts is over. Per pkt.

521	ORANGE AFRICAN. A magnificent selection, bearing immense, brilliant orange-coloured flowers	0	6
522	LEMON AFRICAN. The same as preceding, but varying in colour	0	6
523	DANIELS' STRIPED FRENCH (Scotch Prize). Beautifully striped flowers 1 foot 6d. and	1	0
524	TALL FRENCH. A very showy strain	0	6
525	DWARF FRENCH. Striped and blotched	0	6
526	„ Dark brown	0	6
527	LEGION OF HONOUR. Splendid bedder. Height 9 inches	0	4
528	SIGNATA PUMILA. Single, golden-yellow flowers	0	4

DANIELS' STRIPED FRENCH MARIGOLD.

MYOSOTIS. (Forget-me-not.)

A free-flowering and beautiful class of easily grown hardy perennials, which are in great request for Spring gardening. They will thrive in almost any soil, but prefer a partially-shaded and rather damp position.

529	DANIELS' SKY BLUE. A charming dwarf-growing variety, 6 inches high, lovely sky-blue flowers. A gem for pots 6d. &	1	0
530	DANIELS' INDIGO BLUE. Long sprays of deep indigo blue flowers. First-rate for cutting. Height 1 foot 6d. and	1	0
531	RUTH FISCHER. Large beautiful flowers, intense sky-blue	1	0
532	DISSITIFLORA, Large-Flowered. Sky-blue	0	6
533	PALUSTRIS SEMPERFLORENS. True marsh Forget-me-not	0	6
534	NEMOPHILA INSIGNIS. Lovely sky blue with conspicuous white eye. Charming. Height 6 inches per oz. 1s.	0	4

NIGELLA (Love in a Mist).

535	MISS JEKYLL. An attractive annual, growing 18 inches high, with lovely clear blue flowers; excellent as a cut flower	0	6
536	DAMASCENA FL. PL. Light blue double flowers. 9 inches	0	4

NICOTIANA.

Beautiful half-hardy annuals for pots, beds or borders, or for sub-tropical gardening. The hybrids are very fine. Height 3 feet.

537	AFFINIS. White flowers, deliciously fragrant at evening	0	4
538	„ NEW HYBRIDS, mixed. Beautiful shades of pink, violet, mauve, &c. Very sweet-scented	0	6
539	SANDERÆ HYBRIDS, Mixed. A splendid race of fine varieties. Colours from white, rose and lilac to dark crimson	0	6

NEMESIA—GRANDIFLORA.

NEMESIAS.

Magnificent half-hardy annuals, producing flowers of the most rare and brilliant colours. They are easily raised in boxes or pans of light soil in March. Plant out in May 6 inches apart.

540	GRANDIFLORA, DANIELS' ORANGE KING	1	0
541	„ SCARLET BEAUTY. Rich brilliant scarlet	1	0
542	„ Mixed. Beautiful shades of crimson, yellow, orange and rose to pure white. Ht. 12 ins. 6d. &	1	0
543	COMPACTA, BLUE GEM. Beautiful myosotis blue	0	6
544	„ FIRE KING. Brilliant scarlet	0	6
545	„ Mixed. A fine class of brilliant varieties. Height 9 inches	1	0

NASTURTIUMS.

An exceedingly brilliant class of easily grown half-hardy annuals. To obtain the best results the seeds should be sown in Spring on rather poor soil in the open ground, and in an exposed sunny position.

DWARF NASTURTIUMS. *Growing at our Seed Farm.*

TOM THUMB VARIETIES.

	Per pkt.—s.	d.
546 EMPRESS OF INDIA. Intense crimson scarlet, with dark leaves. Splendid variety of dwarf habit .. per oz. 1s.	0	4
547 SNOW QUEEN (new). Very compact and free-flowering variety. The blooms opening creamy and changing to pure white ..	0	4
548 QUEEN OF TOM THUMBS. Dark crimson flowers, with silver variegated foliage. Very pretty	0	4
549 CRYSTAL PALACE GEM. Primrose, spotted maroon ..	0	4
550 FELTHAM BEAUTY. Rich brilliant scarlet ..	0	6
551 FIREBALL. Brilliant orange scarlet ..	0	6
552 GOLDEN KING. Rich yellow with dark foliage per oz. 1s.	0	4
553 KING OF TOM THUMBS. Brilliant scarlet per oz. 1s.	0	4
554 VESUVIUS. Rich apricot with dark foliage per oz. 1s.	0	4
555 ROSY MORN. Beautiful rosy scarlet, quite distinct ..	0	6
556 CHOICE MIXED. Splendid variety .. per oz. 9d.	0	4
557 LILIPUT, MIXED. A charming race of very dwarf-growing Nasturtiums, with flowers well above the foliage..	0	6

CLIMBING VARIETIES.

Brilliant and rapid growing annual climbers of splendid effect. First class for walls or trellises or for covering rough fences or banks.

558 DEFIANCE. Brilliant scarlet ..	0	6
559 IVY-LEAVED. Brilliant scarlet	0	6
560 MIDNIGHT. Crimson maroon with dark foliage, splendid ..	0	6
561 MOONLIGHT. Pale yellow, beautiful ..	0	6
562 SUNLIGHT. Bright golden yellow	0	6
563 VESUVIUS. Deep apricot with dark foliage, very pretty ..	0	6
564 CHOICEST MIXED. Beautiful variety .. per oz. 9d.	0	4

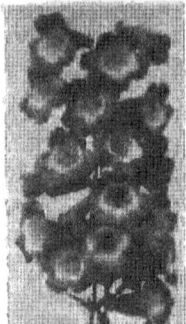

LARGE-FLOWERED PENTSTEMON.

CANARY-BIRD NASTURTIUM.

(*Tropæolum canariense.*)

565 Well-known useful annual climber ..	0	6

PENTSTEMONS.

These beautiful free-flowering plants succeed admirably when treated as half-hardy annuals, and sown in February or March on a gentle heat and planted out in May they will commence blooming in July and continue to throw up their lovely spikes of flowers till late Autumn. The new large-flowered hybrids produce some charming flowers, many of them being equal to the finest named sorts. The plants grow about 18 inches high.

566 NEW LARGE-FLOWERED HYBRIDS. Choicest mixed, from a magnificent strain .. .. 6d. and	1	0

DANIELS' SUPERB PANSIES.

These beautiful, free-flowering, hardy plants are easily raised from seed, and will richly repay the small cost and trouble required to grow them to perfection. Sow in February, March, and April in boxes of light rich soil placed in a gentle heat, and as soon as large enough, prick out about two inches apart on rich soil; finally plant out six or eight inches apart, in ground into which well-decayed manure has been worked. Pansies delight in a somewhat shady position, and plenty of moisture in dry weather. The finest blooms are produced the second year, and grand flowers may be had by sowing in July or August in the open ground, and planting out in the following Spring into good rich soil.

	Per pkt.—s.	d.
567 DANIELS' EXHIBITION GIANT. A superb strain of extra large and beautifully coloured flowers of the highest type, and including the most charming and richly coloured stained and blotched flowers. Many of the blooms from this strain will be found equal to the finest named varieties. Very choice mixed seed. Highly recommended	5	0
568 " " " "	2	6
569 " " " " smaller pkt.	1	6
570 DANIELS' PRIZE per pkt. s. d. BLOTCHED. A splendid strain of brilliantly coloured flowers, most exquisite shades of colour .. 6d. and	1	0
571 DANIELS' GIANT WHITE. Very large flowers, pure white, with dark purple eye; splendid ..	0	6
572 DANIELS' GIANT YELLOW. Very large, pure yellow, a very fine variety	0	6
573 DANIELS' GIANT PURPLE. Dark purple, very fine ..	0	6
574 DANIELS' GIANT STRIPED. Beautifully formed flowers, handsomely striped. The perfection of all striped varieties ..	0	6
575 BUGNOT'S CHOICE MIXED. Fine blotched varieties 6d. and	1	0

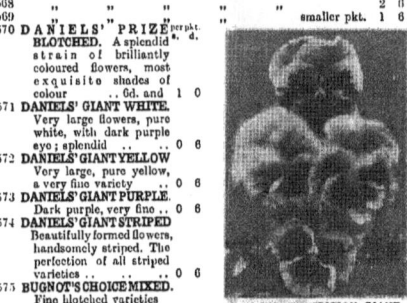

PANSIES—EXHIBITION GIANT.

576 CRIMSON AND BRONZE SHADES. Grand variety of red, bronze, crimson, and combinations of above shades ..	1	0
577 ORCHID-FLOWERED. Large beautiful flowers, including some rare and attractive shades .. 6d. and	1	0
578 GIANT PEACOCK. A strikingly handsome and very distinct variety. The upper petals are a beautiful peacock blue, the flower shading off to velvety maroon and crimson ..	0	6
579 TRIMARDEAU or GIANT. A fine strain of beautiful large-flowered varieties .. .. .. 6d. and	1	0
580 MADAME PERRET, or "The Wine Pansy." A quite distinct class that continue in bloom throughout the Summer. The colours may be described as a series of wine shades varying from deep port to claret, and delightfully fragrant 6d. and	1	0
581 MIXED. Ordinary class .. .. .. per oz. 3s.	0	4

BEDDING PANSIES.

582 COLLECTION OF SIX SPLENDID VARIETIES ..	2	6
583 CHOICE MIXED. Many good colours, mostly selfs 6d. and	1	0

PERILLA.

Valuable plants for bedding with richly coloured dark foliage.

584 ATROPURPUREA LACINIATA. Handsome laciniated foliage	0	4

PHACELIA CAMPANULARIA.

585 A showy hardy annual from California, growing about one foot high, with bell-shaped flowers of a bright blue colour, which continue for a long time	0	4

POLYANTHUS.

A beautiful free-flowering class of hardy perennials which has been highly improved of late years. The plants are about six inches high, and bloom about the same time as primroses. The large-flowered varieties in their many beautiful colours are very charming and should be used extensively for Spring gardening.

586 LARGE-FLOWERED, CHOICEST MIXED. A very fine strain of beautiful varieties, very free-flowering 6d. and	1	0
587 POLYANTHUS-PRIMROSE (bunch-flowered). Choicest mixed hybrids, special selection .. .. 6d. and	1	0
588 GOLD-LACED. Fine, from a choice collection 6d. and	1	0

PETUNIAS.

Petunias for indoor cultivation may be sown in January or early in February, but those intended for bedding out do not require to be sown before March. A soil composed of two-parts loaf-mould and one part loam, with the addition of a little sharp sand, forms an excellent compost for these, but the seeds being very small require special care in sowing. As soon as the young plants can be handled, prick them out about one inch apart to strengthen, when sufficiently advanced pot off singly into small pots, gradually harden off, and plant out about the middle of May, or shift into large pots as required. In planting Petunias, out of doors, ground should be selected that has not been freshly manured, otherwise a superabundant foliage will retard the flowering.

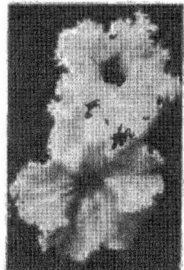

PETUNIA—DANIELS' SUPERB FRINGED.

DANIELS' SUPERB FRINGED.

A beautiful class, large and strikingly handsome flowers, the petals being elegantly laciniated or fringed.

	pkt.—s. d.
589 SINGLE, VERY CHOICE MIXED	1s. 6d. and 2 6
590 DOUBLE, CHOICEST MIXED	1s. 6d. and 2 6

HYBRIDA GRANDIFLORA.

Large-flowering varieties producing blooms of immense size and of the most charming colours; much superior to the old varieties.

	s. d.
591 AN ASSORTMENT OF 6 BEAUTIFUL VARIETIES ..	2 6
592 ALBA GRANDIFLORA. Immense pure white flowers ..	0 6
593 BRILLIANT ROSE. Very fine large flowers	0 6
594 CRIMSON. Splendid colour	0 6
595 VERY CHOICE MIXED, IN BEAUTIFUL VARIETY ..	2 6
596 „ „ „ „ .. smaller pkt.	1 0
597 „ „ „ „ .. smallest pkt.	0 6
598 DOUBLE, VERY CHOICE MIXED. Carefully saved from hand fertilized flowers, only a small percentage come double, but the plants thus raised are more vigorous than those taken from cuttings	1s. 6d. and 2 6

DWARF BEDDING.

A very pretty free-flowering class of dwarf compact-growing varieties, exceedingly useful for massing in beds, or as an edging.

599 CHOICEST MIXED	6d. and 1 0

PELARGONIUMS—GERANIUMS.

ZONAL PELARGONIUMS.

A splendid class of beautiful free-blooming plants, admirably suited for greenhouse or conservatory decoration; may be had in bloom nearly all the year round. Sow in February or March in pots of light rich soil, covering the seeds to the depth of about a quarter of an inch, and place in a heat of about sixty-five or seventy degrees. These will bloom the first year, and some really beautiful varieties may be expected.

	s. d.
600 FRENCH BLOTCHED or REGAL. Beautiful 1s. 6d. and	2 6
601 FANCY VARIETIES. Very choice mixed	1 6
602 ZONAL. Single-flowered, from finest named sorts ..	1 6

PHLOXES.

Seeds of these beautiful annuals should be sown from February to April, and as soon as the plants are large enough transplanted into boxes, finally planting out in May. Seeds can also be sown in the open during May, and will give a late display.

PHLOX DRUMMONDI GRANDIFLORA.

The grandiflora varieties form a magnificent class; the plants are robust in habit, and the flowers, which are of various rich and beautiful colours, have in many of the varieties large, conspicuous white eyes; the individual blooms are of fine substance and scarcely inferior in size to the perennial sorts.

	per pkt.—s. d.
603 A COLLECTION OF 6 SPLENDID VARIETIES ..	2 6
604 ALBA. Pure white	0 6
605 CARMINEA. Beautiful carmine, white eye	0 6
606 ROSEA. Rose, white eye	0 6
607 VIOLACEA. Violet blue, white eye	0 6
608 SPLENDENS. Fine vivid crimson	0 6
609 CHOICEST MIXED. In beautiful variety .. 6d. and	1 0

DWARF VARIETIES.

A charming class of beautiful dwarf-growing varieties. The plants grow 4 to 6 inches in height and 6 or 8 inches across, and are almost covered with bloom. Splendid for edgings or beds.

	s. d.
610 FIREBALL. An exceedingly free-flowering brilliant scarlet ..	0 6
611 SNOWBALL. Bearing a profusion of large, pure white flowers	0 6
612 EXTRA CHOICE MIXED. In beautiful variety 6d. and	1 0

PERENNIAL PHLOX.

Splendid hardy perennials for large beds or borders.

613 TALL VARIETIES. Very choice mixed. Ht. 3 ft.	1 0
614 DWARF VARIETIES. Choice mixed. Ht. 2 ft.	1 0

PHLOX DRUMMONDI GRANDIFLORA.

PEA, EVERLASTING.

615 FINE MIXED. Splendid hardy perennial climbers	0 6

PINKS—Garden.

616 MRS. SINKINS. A fine double-flowered pure white, deliciously scented; quite hardy	1 0
617 DOUBLE MIXED. Saved from a splendid collection of the finest varieties .. .. 6d. and	1 0

PRIMROSES.

Profuse flowering and very charming hardy perennials, growing six inches high, invaluable for Spring gardening. The hybrid varieties vary in colour from the palest and most delicate sulphur yellow, through all the soft shades of rose and purple to the most intense and brilliant crimson.

	s. d.
618 LARGE-FLOWERED HYBRIDS. Grand strain of beautiful high-coloured flowers, all of the true Primrose type, with the flowers large and brilliant; very fine	1 0
619 VERY CHOICE MIXED. From a good collection 6d. and	1 0

PYRETHRUM—GOLDEN FEATHER.

Exceedingly useful for bedding. Sow the seeds under glass in February or March, and plant out in May for the best results.

	s. d.
620 GOLDEN FEATHER. Selected. Height 6 inches ..	0 4
621 GOLDEN MOSS. The finest form for carpet bedding, very compact and good colour	0 6
622 SELAGINOIDES. Fern-leaved variety. Height 6 inches ..	0 6

PYRETHRUM HYBRIDUM.

Very fine hardy herbaceous perennials. Excellent for mixed borders.

	s. d.
623 DOUBLE-FLOWERED, Choicest Mixed. Double and semi-double flowers. Height 2 feet	1 6
624 SINGLE-FLOWERED. Splendid mixed, saved from a fine collection. Height 2 feet .. .. .. 6d. and	1 0

POPPIES.
ANNUAL POPPIES.

A brilliant and charmingly effective group of hardy annuals of great value for garden or shrubbery decoration. The single-flowered varieties are especially valuable as cut flowers, and if cut when the blooms are just beginning to expand, will retain their beauty for four or five days. The beautiful Shirley Poppy, sown at intervals from early Spring to the end of June, will give a charming display quite into the Autumn.

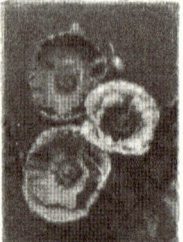

POPPY—DANIELS' SELECTED SHIRLEY.

625 **DANIELS' SELECTED SHIRLEY.** The fine strain we offer has been carefully selected and includes all the most brilliant and exquisite shades of colour. Highly recommended for cut flowers. Height 2 feet. Choicest mixed

		per pkt.—s. d.
	per oz. 2s. 6d.	0 0
626	SHIRLEY POPPY PICOTEE. A beautiful white flower with distinct carmine edge; coming very true from seed ..	0 6
627	COLLECTION OF 6 CHARMING VARIETIES OF SHIRLEY POPPIES ..	2 6
628	NEW DOUBLE POPPIES. RYBURGH HYBRIDS. A magnificent new strain of double-flowered annual poppies of bushy growth, carrying long-stemmed flowers of many charming shades of flesh, salmon, orange, rose and carmine. 6d. &	1 0
629	CARNATION-FLOWERED, Double. Fine double flowers in many brilliant colours. Height 2 feet	0 4
630	CHAMOIS-ROSE, Double. Large, beautiful double flowers of a lovely salmony-pink, handsomely fringed. Height 2 feet ..	0 6
631	PÆONY-FLOWERED, Double. Handsome double flowers in beautiful variety of colour. Height 3 feet. Choice mixed ..	per pkt.—s. d. .. 0 4

PERENNIAL POPPIES.

For blooming the same year from seed, these should be sown in February or March in a gentle heat, and planted out in May. The large-flowered Orientale varieties are best sown outdoors in May or June, and transplanted in Autumn or early Spring where intended to bloom. NUDICAULE (The Iceland Poppy).

632 **NEW EXCELSIOR STRAIN.** Many exquisite shades, a great improvement on the old varieties .. 6d. and 1 0

633 **ORIENTALE HYBRIDS,** Choice Mixed. Magnificent hardy perennials Height 3 feet .. 6d. and 1 0

POPPY—CHAMOIS-ROSE.

PRIMULA SPECIES.

The various species of Primulas are amongst the most lovely plants we possess. The Malacoides type can be flowered in four months from seed. The new Bullesiana and Japonica hybrids are perfectly hardy, and display a great variety of colour.

634 **BULLESIANA.** A charming new race of hybrids, perfectly hardy 1 0

635 **PRIMULA MALACOIDES.** Pale lilac flowers, very early blooming .. 0 6

636 " **ALBA.** A pure white-flowered variety of the above .. 0 6

637 " **SUPERBA.** Deep rosy-pink, a great improvement 1 0

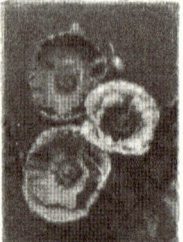

PRIMULA MALACOIDES.

638 **PRIMULA JAPONICA.** Fine hardy plant. Height 18 inches, with whorls of various coloured flowers. Choice mixed seed 0 6

639 " **KEWENSIS.** Beautiful half-hardy Winter bloomer for the greenhouse. Flowers bright yellow. Height 1 foot .. 1 0

DANIELS' SUPERB
FRINGED PRIMULAS.

The beautiful varieties of Primula sinensis may be sown in March, April, May, and June. Great care must be taken to have a well-drained pot or seed-pan filled to within half an inch of the top, with sifted leaf-mould; leave the surface rather rough, and sprinkle the seeds thinly upon it. The most successful raisers do not cover with soil, but after sowing the seed press down the surface tolerably firm, and place a square of glass over the pot. Place in a good strong heat, shaded from strong light, and water very gently when the soil becomes dry.

It is with very much pleasure that we offer the grand strains of Primulas named below, all of which have been specially grown for our retail trade, and will give the highest satisfaction. The flowers will be found of great size and perfect form, combined with the most brilliant and charming colours, and a habit of plant which leaves nothing to be desired.

PRIMULA—WHITE PERFECTION.

		per pkt.—s. d.		s. d.
640	"KING GEORGE V." (new). Very large, beautifully fringed flowers, of intense crimson.	1s. 6d. and	2 6
641	"QUEEN MARY" (new). A magnificent new variety of true giant type. A most lovely rose pink	1s. 6d. and	2 6
642	QUEEN ALEXANDRA (new). Pure white flowers of enormous size and substance; a great acquisition	1s. 6d. and	2 6
643	ORANGE KING (new). A superb new colour in Primulas. The beautiful orange colour in the bud and the orange-salmon shade around the edge of the terra-cotta coloured petals give the flower a most pleasing and distinct appearance	1s. 6d. and	2 6
644	NEW GIANT PINK. Bright rosy pink	1s. 6d. and	2 6
645	NEW GIANT SALMON. Beautiful salmon pink	1s. 6d. and	2 6
646	THE DUCHESS (new). Beautiful white, with rosy-carmine zone surrounding a yellow eye; splendid	1s. 6d. and	2 6
647	CRIMSON KING. The darkest of all	1s. 6d. and	2 6
648	DANIELS' WHITE PERFECTION. A beautiful pure white of the fern-leaved type, of splendid habit	1s. 6d. and	2 6
649	DANIELS' SUPERB BLUE. Deepest shade of blue	1s. 6d. &	2 6
650	DANIELS' CHOICEST MIXED. In beautiful variety. Including the very finest of the named kinds	1s. 6d. and	2 6

DOUBLE-FLOWERED FRINGED.

Exceedingly useful for flowering in the greenhouse during Winter.

651 **DOUBLE CHOICEST MIXED.** In splendid variety .. 1s. 6d. and 2 6

PRIMULA STELLATA
(Star Primula).

An improved form of the Star Primula, differing only in the formation of its flowers, which nearly equal the best of the Chinese varieties.

652 **KING OF THE STARS.** Magnificent variety, immense heads of deep crimson-carmine flowers 1 6

653 **CHOICEST MIXED STAR.** A charming mixture .. 1 6

654 **GIANT WHITE STAR.** The grandest White Star Primula .. 1 6

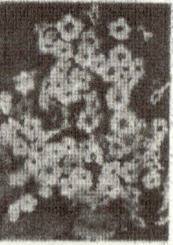

PRIMULA STELLATA.

PRIMULA OBCONICA.

A beautiful class of free-flowering half-hardy perennials, growing about eight inches high, admirably suited for pot culture in the cool greenhouse. The blooms are very useful for cutting.

655	ALBA GRANDIFLORA. Pure white, with small yellow eye	1 0
656	ROSEA. Large, finely-formed, bright rosy lilac flowers	1 0
657	VERY CHOICE MIXED. In beautiful variety	6d. and 1 0
658	PRIMULA OBCONICA GIGANTEA. Mixed. Very fine 1s. &	2 0
659	" " " Rosea. .. 1s. 6d. and	2 6

SALPIGLOSSIS.

A charming class of half-hardy annuals, exceedingly useful for cut flowers. The large blooms are beautifully veined, and vary from dark purple and crimson to orange, golden yellow and scarlet. Sow in the open in March or April, and thin out. Ht. 3 ft.

		per pkt.—s. d.
660	SIX BEAUTIFUL VARIETIES. Separate	2 0
661	VERY CHOICE MIXED. 6d. and	1 0

SALPIGLOSSIS.

SAPONARIA.

| 662 | SCARLET QUEEN. A compact-growing hardy annual, with numerous bright rosy scarlet flowers | 0 6 |
| 663 | VACCARIA. Delightful pink, most useful for mixing with Sweet Peas and other cut flowers | 0 4 |

SALVIA.

Beautiful free-flowering half-hardy perennials, splendidly effective for beds or borders in Summer and Autumn.

664	MINIATURE, New Dwarf. Splendid large pure scarlet flowers. First class for pot culture or for bedding. Height 1 foot	1 0
665	SPLENDENS GLORY. Brilliant scarlet. Height 2 feet	0 6
666	PATENS. Intense pure blue. A fine variety for beds. 2 feet	1 0

SILENE.

Brilliant, profuse-flowering hardy annuals of dwarf compact growth.

| 667 | COMPACTA, DOUBLE DWARF ROSE. Beautiful bright rose, very compact. The best for Spring bedding | 0 4 |

SWEET ROCKET.

Deliciously fragrant Spring-flowering hardy herbaceous perennial.

| 668 | MIXED. Sweet-scented varieties | 0 4 |

SCABIOUS—SWEET.

Beautiful hardy biennials with large fragrant flowers of many rich and beautiful shades of colour, blooming the first year from seed. Sow in March under glass and transplant, or sow in April in the open ground and treat as hardy annuals. Height about 3 feet.

669	THE BRIDE. Large double pure white flowers, very sweet	0 6
670	ROSE PINK. Lovely colour	0 6
671	MAUVE QUEEN. Beautiful lilac-mauve colour	0 6
672	SIX LARGE-FLOWERED VARIETIES. Separate. Our selection	2 0
673	LARGE-FLOWERED. Splendid double mixed.	0 4

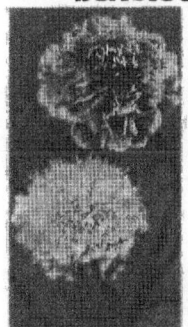

SCABIOUS—SWEET.

SCABIOSA.

| 674 | CAUCASICA. Splendid hardy perennial producing large bluish mauve flowers. Height 2 feet 6d. and | 1 0 |

STATICE.

| 675 | SINUATA HYBRIDA. Mixed. Charming easily grown Everlastings. Flowers mauve, white, and yellow; very fine. Height 18 inches | 0 6 |
| 676 | ,,　　,,　Mauve. Useful colour | 0 6 |

STREPTOCARPUS.

| 677 | DANIELS' LARGE-FLOWERING HYBRIDS. A very fine strain of large beautiful flowers, varying in colour through all the shades of pink, lavender-blue, purple, &c., to pure white. Greenhouse perennials. Height 9 inches 1s. 6d. and | 2 6 |

SCHIZANTHUS.

A beautiful class of half-hardy annuals of elegant growth which succeed well grown out of doors. They are also of great value for pots in the greenhouse where they are charmingly effective. The flowers vary in colour from delicate pink and rose to carmine-yellow, apricot, mauve, crimson and other lovely shades, the long sprays of bloom being very useful when cut.

For pot culture seed may be sown at almost any time, and splendid specimens may be had by sowing in Aug. or Sept. for Winter blooming, about five plants in a six inch pot being most suitable.

678	WISETONENSIS, PINK PEARL(New). This charming novelty produces sheafs of lovely flowers, and like its parent variety, makes an unsurpassed plant for conservatory decoration. The glistening white corolla is set off by a broad margin of rosy pink on wing and lip petals, wonderfully enhancing its beauty. 1s. 6d.	
679	WISETONENSIS. DANIELS' EXCELSIOR STRAIN. A highly selected and splendid class for pot culture. Very choice mixed 1s. 6d. and 2s. 6d.	
680	DANIELS' SELECTED STRAIN. Charming shades of beautiful colours, very fine. Ht. 18 ins. 6d. and 1s.	
681	HYBRIDUS GRANDIFLORUS. Very fine large-flowered varieties. 18 inches	4d.

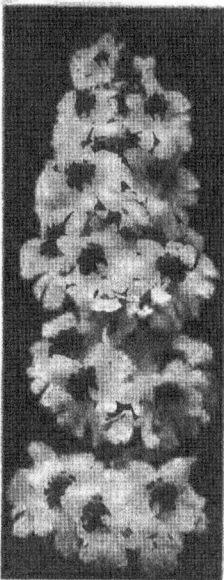

SCHIZANTHUS WISETONENSIS. DANIELS' EXCELSIOR STRAIN.

SUNFLOWER.

		per pkt.—s. d.
682	GIANT YELLOW, Double. Enormous flowers, very double	0 4
683	GIANT YELLOW, Single. Immense flowers, with black disc.	0 4
684	NEW RED. Large single, deep orange flowers, with bright chestnut-red rings. Height 5 feet	0 6
685	MINIATURE, Single. Small bright yellow flowers, very useful	0 4
686	STARLIGHT, Single. Pale primrose with pointed petals. Height 3 feet. Charming for cut flowers 6d. and	1 0

SWEET SULTAN.

Very fine hardy annuals, deliciously scented, and very useful for cut flowers, remaining fresh for a long time in water.

687	GIANT WHITE. A superb variety, with large pure white, sweet-scented flowers	0 6
688	GIANT BLUE. Large bluish mauve flowers	0 6
689	GIANT ROSE. Varies in shade, large flowers	0 6
690	NEW GIANT HYBRIDS (Centaurea Imperialis). A superb strain growing about 2½ feet high, producing very large, sweet-scented flowers of the most beautiful and novel shades of colour 6d. and	1 0
691	ORDINARY MIXED per oz. 2s.	0 4

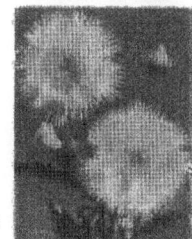

SWEET SULTAN—GIANT WHITE.

SWEET WILLIAM.

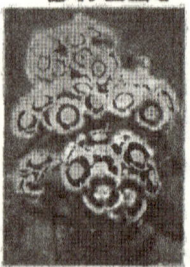

We have given great attention for several years past to our splendid strain of these, which we have much pleasure in offering. The flowers are beautifully formed, of good substance, and are almost invariably awarded First Prize wherever exhibited. Sow the seeds in May or June, and plant out one foot apart in August or September.

Per pkt.—s. d.

692 DANIELS' GIANT PRIZE AURICULA-EYED. A magnificent strain of Auricula-eyed varieties. Mixed Seed .. 6d. and 1 0
693 PINK BEAUTY. Large heads of lovely salmony-rose coloured flowers .. 0 6
694 SCARLET BEAUTY (new). Intense scarlet, very showy 0 6
695 DIADEM. Dark crimson flowers with white eye .. 0 6
696 MIXED. Beautiful varieties, including Auricula-eyed and self-coloured flowers 0 4

SWEET WILLIAM—DANIELS' PRIZE AURICULA-EYED.

VIRGINIAN STOCK.

697 CRIMSON KING. Bright rosy-crimson. Height 6 inches .. 0 4
698 WHITE. Large-flowered. Height 9 inches .. 0 4
699 MIXED. Various colours .. .. per oz., 1s. 3d. 0 4

BEDDING VIOLAS.

These profuse-flowering plants are great favourites with everyone. They bloom from early Summer to late Autumn, and are easily raised from seed. Per pkt.—s. d.
700 SIX BEAUTIFUL VARIETIES 2 6
701 JOHN QUARTON. Light mauve 0 6
702 KING-CUP. Pure yellow 0 6
703 KITTY BELL. Light lavender 0 6
704 WILLIAM ROBB. Deep lavender 0 6
705 WHITE QUEEN. Pure white 0 6
706 MIXED. From the finest Scotch strains 6d. and 1 0

VIOLAS—CHOICE BEDDING.

VERBENA.

Beautiful free-flowering half-hardy perennials, producing an abundance of bloom during the Summer and Autumn. Exceedingly useful for beds or borders. The plants grow about one foot high. Per pkt.—s. d.
707 ROSE QUEEN (new). The greatest advance in Verbenas. The colour is a lovely delicate rose, flowers 1 to 1½ inches in diameter, twenty or more on one head 1 0
708 SCARLET QUEEN (new). Another grand variety, colour vivid scarlet, large white eye .. 1 0
709 SNOW QUEEN (new). Pure snow white, very large flowers 1 0
710 HELEN WILLMOTT. A lovely bright salmon rose with white eye. This variety now comes fairly true from seed 0 6
711 EXTRA CHOICE MIXED, includes the most brilliant varieties 6d. and 1 0
712 AURICULA - FLOWER-ED. Large - flowered varieties, conspicuous white eyes. Choice mxd 0 6
713 LEMON SCENTED VERBENA (Aloysia Citriodora). A fragrant leaved pot plant 0 6

VERBENA—CHOICE MIXED.

WALLFLOWERS.

This beautiful class of hardy flowers should be freely grown. No plant is easier of cultivation. Their charming colours and delicious perfume, added to their profusion of bloom, renders them highly desirable for Spring gardening.

Per pkt.—s. d.

714 EASTERN QUEEN. Chamois, changing to salmon-rose .. 0 6
715 VULCAN. Large velvety-crimson flowers, splendid 0 6
716 PRIMROSE DAME .. 0 6
717 RUBY GEM. Ruby violet 0 6
718 HARBINGER. Dark brown 0 4
719 BLOOD RED. Daniels' Selected. Splendid colour 0 6
720 CLOTH OF GOLD. Dwarf, large-flowered 0 4
721 BLUE or VIOLET. Beautiful 0 6
722 FIRE KING (new). Vivid orange colour 0 6
723 PRIMROSE MONARCH. Beautiful pale primrose .. 0 6
724 ELLEN WILLMOTT. Ruby-red, distinct and beautiful 0 6
725 VESUVIUS (new). Orange scarlet buds, expanding a rich bronzy orange .. 0 6
726 ROSE QUEEN. Terra-cotta pink 0 6
727 WHITE QUEEN. Pale primrose changing to white .. 0 6
728 GOLDEN MONARCH. Large, rich golden yellow .. 0 6
729 DANIELS' CHOICEST MIXED .. per oz. 2/6; 6d. and 1 0

730 TOM THUMB. Golden yellow { A dwarf type, very } 0 6
731   „   Dark brown { useful for bedding. } 0 6
732   „   Choicest mixed { Height 9 ins. } 6d. and 1 0

DANIELS' DOUBLE WALLFLOWERS.

The Double Wallflowers produce grand spikes of handsome double blooms in April and May, but require a sheltered position.
733 AN ASSORTMENT OF 6 CHOICE VARIETIES. Separate .. 2 6
734 TALL VARIETIES. Splendid mixed. Large double sweet-scented flowers. Height 2 feet .. .. 6d. and 1 0
735 DWARF VARIETIES. Choicest mixed. Stout spikes of large double sweet-scented flowers. Height 1 foot .. 6d. and 1 0

VISCARIA.

Brilliant, free-flowering hardy annuals of easy cultivation.
736 CARDINALIS. Brilliant crimson-scarlet, very showy .. 0 4
737 OCULATA CÆRULEA. Bright, deep lavender blue, fine .. 0 4

ZINNIA.

Sow in pans or pots of light, rich, finely made soil, place in a moderate heat. Soon as large enough they should be potted off singly into small pots or pricked out into larger pots or pans to strengthen. Planting out should not take place till all danger from May frosts is over. An open sunny position with fairly rich soil should be chosen.
738 AN ASSORTMENT OF 6 DIFFERENT VARIETIES .. 2 0
739 BRILLIANT SCARLET. Splendid colour 0 6
740 STRIPED VARIETIES. Large blooms, handsomely striped .. 0 6
741 WHITE. Creamy white .. 0 6
742 DANIELS' CHOICEST MIXED. A splendid strain, including the most beautiful varieties per oz. 3s. 6d., 6d. and 1 0 Per pkt.—s. d.

DANIELS' GIANT-FLOWERED. Superb class of a robust habit of growth, producing beautiful double flowers of immense size and of the most charming colour. 2 to 2½ ft.
743 VERY CHOICE MIXED. Beautiful colours 6d. and 1 0
744 DWARF DOUBLE. Fine mixed, one foot high .. 0 6
745 ELEGANS ROBUSTA ACHIEVEMENT. Fluted petals like Cactus Dahlia; beautiful colours 6d. and 1 0

ZINNIA—LARGE-FLOWERED.

DANIELS' COMPLETE COLLECTIONS OF CHOICE FLOWER SEEDS

Specially adapted to the requirements of the Cottage, Villa, or large Garden.

COLLECTION "A"   Price 6/6, Post Free.

6 Distinct vars. Aster, Ostrich Plume
6   ,,   ,,   Stock, large-flowered Ten-week
4   ,,   ,,   Sweet Peas, Spencer varieties
1 Packet each Petunia, Phlox, Zinnia, Verbena and Lobelia.
12 Packets Choice Hardy and Half-hardy Annuals

COLLECTION "B"   Price 9/6, Post Free.

6 Choice varieties Giant Comet Aster
6   ,,   ,,   Stock, large-flowered Ten-week
6   ,,   ,,   Spencer Sweet Peas
1 Packet each Phlox, Marigold, Petunia, Zinnia
10 Packets Choice Hardy Annuals
10 ,,   Choice Half-hardy Annuals

COLLECTION "C"   Price 13/6, Post Free.

6 Choice vars. Victoria Aster
6   ,,   ,,   Stock, large-flowered Ten-week
6   ,,   ,,   Zinnia, large-flowered
6   ,,   ,,   Sweet Peas, Spencer
30 Packets Choice Hardy and Half-hardy Annuals

COLLECTION "D"   Price 25/-, Post Free.

6 Varieties Aster, Ostrich Plume
6   ,,   ,,   Tall Branching
6   ,,   Stock, large-flowered Ten-week
6   ,,   Zinnia, large-flowered, double
6   ,,   Phlox Drummondi Grandiflora
9   ,,   Choice Spencer Sweet Peas
32 Packets Choice Hardy and Half-hardy Annuals
12 ,,   Choice Hardy Perennials and Biennials

Other Collections of Choice Flower Seeds, 31s. 6d., 42s., 63s., 84s., and 100s.

THE AMATEUR'S PACKET OF CHOICE FLOWER SEEDS.
Price 3/6, Post Free.
(REGISTERED.)

Contains a Choice Assortment in 16 full-sized packets, with cultural directions.

Sweet Peas, Large-flowered Spencers, Four distinct and beautiful varieties ; one packet each—Aster, "Ostrich Plume," Choicest mixed ; Stock, Large-flowered Ten-week, mixed ; Phlox Drummondi, mixed ; Shirley Poppy, selected strain ; Nasturtium, Queen of Tom Thumbs ; Sweet Sultan, Giant mixed ; Godetia, Large-flowered, mixed ; Mignonette, Giant Crimson ; Clarkia, double, Orange King ; Chrysanthemum, Evening Star ; Larkspur, Stock-flowered, mixed ; Gypsophila, Elegans Grandiflora Alba.

FLOWER SEEDS IN TWOPENNY PACKETS.

1200 Alyssum, sweet	1234 Honesty, mixed	1266 Pea, Sweet, King Edward VII., scarlet
1201 Anemone, fine mixed	1235 Larkspur, double dwarf rocket	1267 ,, Lady Grisel Hamilton, lavender
1202 Antirrhinum, tall mixed	1236 ,, tall branching, mixed	1268 ,, Lord Nelson, dark blue
1203 ,, Intermediate mixed	1237 Linum grandiflorum rubrum	1269 ,, Mrs. Walter Wright, heliotrope
1204 ,, dwarf mixed	1238 Lobelia speciosa, blue	1270 ,, Queen Alexandra, crimson
1205 Aquilegia (Columbine), mixed	1239 Love-lies-bleeding, red	1271 ,, mixed, large-flowered
1206 Aster, Comet, choice mixed	1240 Lupins, tall mixed	1272 Phlox Drummondi, mixed
1207 ,, white	1241 Marigold, Legion of Honour	1273 Pink, Indian double, finest
1208 ,, Victoria, choice mixed	1242 ,, Lemon African	1274 Poppy, carnation-flowered, mixed
1209 Balsam, double mixed	1243 ,, Orange ,,	1275 ,, Shirley, fine, mixed
1210 Calliopsis Drummondi	1244 Malope grandiflora, crimson	1276 Pyrethrum (Golden Feather)
1211 ,, tall mixed	1245 ,, mixed	1277 Rhodanthe (Everlasting), mixed
1212 Candytuft, dark crimson	1246 Mignonette, sweet-scented	1278 Salpiglossis, fine mixed
1213 ,, white rocket	1247 Mimulus, choice mixed	1279 Scabiosa, sweet, large-flowered
1214 ,, mixed	1248 Nasturtium, Empress of India, crimson	1280 Schizanthus, mixed
1215 Canterbury Bells, mixed	1249 ,, Golden King	1281 Stock, Ten-week, purple
1216 Carnation, Margaret	1250 ,, King of Tom Thumbs, scarlet	1282 ,, scarlet
1217 Chrysanthemum tricolor, mixed	1251 ,, dwarf mixed	1283 ,, white
1218 Clarkia elegans, double mixed	1252 ,, tall or climbing, mixed	1284 ,, fine mixed
1219 Convolvulus major, mixed	1253 Nemophila insignis, blue	1285 Sultan, Sweet, mixed
1220 ,, minor, mixed	1254 Nigella damascena (Love-in-a-Mist), blue	1286 Sunflower, Giant Double
1221 Cyanus minor (Cornflower), mixed	1255 Night-scented Stock (Mathiola), lilac	1287 ,, Giant Single
1222 ,, dark blue	1256 Pansy, or Heartsease, mixed	1288 ,, Miniature
1223 Dahlia, single mixed	1257 Pentstemon, choice mixed	1289 Sweet William, choice mixed
1224 Delphinium, choice mixed	1258 Petunia, mixed	1290 Tobacco, White, sweet
1225 Dianthus Heddewigi, mixed	1259 Pea, Sweet, Black Knight, maroon	1291 Tropæolum Canariense, yellow
1226 Eschscholtzia, choice mixed	1260 ,, Dorothy Eckford, pure white	1292 Viscaria cardinalis, crimson
1227 Forget-me-not, blue	1261 ,, Evelyn Byatt, orange	1293 Virginian Stock, red
1228 Foxglove, mixed	1262 ,, Dora Breadmore, buff & pink	1294 ,, white
1229 Gaillardia Lorenziana, mixed	1263 ,, Gladys Unwin, pale pink	1295 ,, mixed
1230 Godetia, The Bride, crimson and white	1264 ,, Hon. Mrs. Kenyon, primrose	1296 Wallflower, blood red
1231 ,, Lady Albemarle, carmine	1265 ,, John Ingman, carmine	1297 ,, golden yellow
1232 ,, large-flowered, mixed		1298 ,, single mixed
1233 Helichrysum (Everlasting), fine mixed		1299 Zinnia elegans, mixed double

The COTTAGER'S Packet of Choice Flower Seeds, 12 varieties, 1s. 6d.

These collections, including Stocks, Asters and Sweet Peas, of which we sell a large number every year, represent the highest value possible to give, and can be confidently expected to furnish a good display for any small garden.

CHOICE FLOWER SEEDS IN MIXTURE. For Banks and Rockeries, per lb. 6s. ; per oz. 8d.

DANIELS' SUPERB GLADIOLI.

We would strongly recommend all who have not yet grown them to procure the new Giant-flowered hybrids, which can be highly recommended for making a display of rare beauty in the garden. The hybrids of G. Gandavensis are also well known and very popular. Plant the corms firmly, three to four inches deep and eight or nine inches apart, in clumps as required, and put a neat stake to each when the flower buds make their appearance. March is the best month to plant for blooming in July and August, and by a few successive plantings in April and the early part of May, a succession of handsome flowers may be had to the end of September. Gladioli are of especial value as cut flowers. If the flower spikes are placed in water just as the blooms are beginning to expand, they will all open in succession to the topmost bud, and will retain their beauty for a long time.

CHOICE NAMED VARIETIES.

ALBION. A charming pure white, with a tinge of carmine at the bottom of the throat.

Each 4d. ; per doz. 3s. 6d.

AMERICA. Lovely soft pink, magnificent spike.

Each 3d. ; per doz. 2s. 6d.

BARON HULOT. Dark violet blue Each 4d. ; doz. 3s. 6d.

BRIMSTONE. A fine new pale sulphur yellow, strong growing, long spike.

Each 5d. ; per doz. 4s. 6d.

ELECTRA. Brilliant scarlet with orange shade ; throat conspicuously blotched very pale cream. A fine variety.

Each 6d. ; per doz. 5s. 0d.

EMPRESS OF INDIA. Very dark rich maroon.

Each 4d. ; per doz. 3s. 6d.

EUROPE. Beautiful pure white, lightly pencilled lilac.

Each 9d. ; per doz. 8s. 0d.

FAUST. Crimson, lower petals pencilled blood-red.

Each 4d. ; per doz. 3s. 6d.

GOLDEN WEST. Orange red, overlaid with gold.

Each 4d. ; per doz. 3s. 6d.

HALLEY. Lovely salmon pink, blotched yellow. F.C.C.

Each 3d. ; per doz. 2s. 6d.

HOLLANDIA. Lovely rosy salmon, splendid. Each 3d. ; per doz. 2s. 6d.

LIEBESFEUER (Love's Fire). Striking coral scarlet, large flowers and very fine spike.

Each 6d. ; per doz. 5s.

LE MARÉCHAL FOCH. A grand new variety of strong growth. The flowers are of a lovely shade of flesh-rose, with a small yellow blotch on the lower petals. Very heavy spike, requires staking.

Each 1s. ; per doz. 10s. 6d.

L'IMMACULEE. Pure white, flowers of medium size, but opening eight or nine flowers on the spike at a time. One of the best for cutting.

Each 5d. ; per doz. 4s. 6d.

LOVELINESS. A finely formed flower on a strong erect spike, often carrying eight blooms fully open at one time. The colour is a beautiful shade of cream, faintly suffused apricot, deeper shaded throat ; one of the finest of the new varieties. Each 4d. ; per doz. 3s. 6d.

NIAGARA. Canary yellow, very tall. A.M. „ 3d. ; „ 2s. 6d.

PANAMA. Deep rose, large flowers and spike. „ 4d. ; „ 3s. 6d.

PEACE. White, blotched with pale lilac. „ 4d. ; „ 3s. 6d.

PINK PERFECTION. Extra large spike of soft rosy pink.

Each 4d. ; per doz. 3s. 6d.

PRINCEPS. A magnificent variety, bearing enormous flowers, often six inches across, of a dazzling scarlet colour, with a small white band on each of the lower petals. Each 4d. ; per doz. 3s. 6d.

PRINCE OF WALES. A quite distinct and very fine new variety ; colour a charming rose pink with salmon shading. Each 3d. ; per doz. 2s. 6d.

RED EMPEROR. Glowing scarlet, tinted carmine. Each 6d. ; doz. 5s. 0d.

SCHWABEN. One of the best all round yellows, the colour is a rich yet soft pure yellow. Each 4d. ; per doz. 3s. 6d.

WHITE GIANT. The finest of the whites. Immense blooms, loosely placed on tall spike. Each 8d. ; per doz. 7s. 0d.

WILLY WIGMAN. Enormous flowers, six to eight inches across, creamy white with large crimson blotches. Each 4d. ; per doz. 3s. 6d.

Collection of 36 in 12 Splendid Varieties .. 10/6) Our selection
„ „ 12 in 12 Splendid Varieties .. 4/-) only.

GLADIOLUS ALBION.

DANIELS' NEW GIANT-FLOWERED HYBRIDS, MIXED

Our own splendid and perfectly balanced mixture made from the very finest varieties, containing a good proportion of the most delicately coloured flowers. The growth is exceptionally vigorous, and the size of bloom, substance of petal, the length of time they remain in perfection, makes them unequalled either for garden decoration or cut flowers.

Per doz. 2s. 6d. ; per 100, 17s. 6d.

GLADIOLUS GANDAVENSIS.

Our mixture includes a splendid variety of the most beautiful colours, varying from the most intense scarlet and crimson through all the shades to the purest white.

Per doz. 2/3 ; per 100, 16/6

GLADIOLUS NANCEIANUS.

A magnificent class, producing large, brilliantly coloured blooms. Very Choice Mixed, in beautiful variety.

Per doz. 2/6 ; per 100, 17/6

GLADIOLUS BRENCHLEYENSIS

Splendid variety, of fine effect for massing ; the flowers are of a rich bright scarlet, and first-class for church & other decorations.

GLADIOLUS—GIANT-FLOWERED HYBRIDS.

Good flowering roots, per doz. 2s. 6d. ; per 100, 17s. 6d.
Extra fine roots, per doz. 3s. 6d. ; per 100, 25s.

GLADIOLUS LEMOINEI.

Hardy Hybrids. This fine new race blooms earlier than those of the Gandavensis section, and are much more hardy, so that their bulbs do not need to be lifted in Winter. The flowers are very striking and handsome in appearance, all having conspicuous blotches.

Choice Mixed, in beautiful variety. Per doz. 2s. 3d. ; per 100, 16s. 6d.

ANEMONES.

ST. BRIGID. A brilliant and very beautiful class of large semi-double flowers of the most striking and charming shades of colour, ranging from crimson and scarlet to rose, lilac, dark blue, &c., to the purest white. They are first-class for cut flowers, and if cut when the bloom is beginning to open, will retain their beauty for a long time.

Very Choice Mixed. In beautiful variety. Per doz. 2s. ; per 100, 14s.

GIANT FRENCH.

We can thoroughly recommend our strain of Giant French Anemones, the large flowers are of the most varied and brilliant colours ; vigorous.

HIS EXCELLENCY. A lovely large flowering variety of the Giant French Colour a brilliant deep scarlet, thick petals and strong stems.

Per doz. 2s. 6d. ; per 100, 17s.

SINGLE MIXED. Great variety Per doz. 1s. 6d. ; per 100, 10s. 6d.

DOUBLE-FLOWERED DUTCH.

A beautiful class of double flowers, very useful for garden decoration.

FINEST MIXED. Double .. Per doz. 1s. 6d. ; per 100, 10s. 6d.

SINGLE-FLOWERED DUTCH.

Beautiful large flowered varieties. Valuable for cut flowers.

FINEST MIXED. Single, fine roots .. Per doz. 1s. ; per 100, 7s.

Anomatheca Cruenta. A pretty little South African bulb, resembling a Freesia in habit of growth ; flowering in July and August, the colour being of the brightest crimson scarlet ; quite hardy.

Per doz. 10d. ; per 100, 5/-

LILIES (Lilium).

All the sorts mentioned in the following list are suitable for Spring planting out of doors. For pot culture, however, we strongly recommend the beautiful varieties of Auratum and Speciosum, with the addition of the fine Longiflorum Giganteum as the most suitable.

LILIUM AURATUM.

AURATUM (The Golden-rayed Lily of Japan). Large white with yellow stripes & brownish-red spots; deliciously fragrant, extremely hardy, very free bloomer, first rate for pot culture. Extra selected roots. Doz. 33/-, each 3/-. Very fine roots. Doz. 25/-, each 2/3
AURATUM, Large roots, dz. 16/- ea 1/6
AURATUM, rubro-vittatum. Immense; petals white, with distinct band of deep crimson. Each 3/3
virginale. Very large flowers, white with pale yellow bands; most beautiful. Each 3/6
platyphyllum (macranthum). Gigantic flowers, broad petals, white, with yellow bands. Each 2/9
BROWNI. Large, creamy white trumpet-shaped flowers, outside of petals being of a rich purplish brown colour. Each 3/6

                        each—s. d.

CHALCEDONICUM (Scarlet Turk's Cap). Splendid old variety, flowers medium sized, reflexed, and of a deep rich scarlet colour   3 0
CROCEUM. Light orange; spotted black   per doz. 10s. 6d.   1 0
DAVURICUM FULGIDUM. Orange red   per doz. 9s. 6d.   1 0
HENRYI (Orange-yellow Speciosum). Stems six feet high, bearing 15 to 20 flowers, of a rich deep orange-yellow colour   2s. and   2 6
LONGIFLORUM GIGANTEUM. Early-flowering species, trumpet-shaped flowers, pure white   per doz. 16s. 0d.   1 6
PARDALINUM. Bright scarlet shading to orange   per doz. 10s. 6d.   1 0
PYRENAICUM (the Yellow Martagon). Deliciously scented flowers, yellow, spotted black   per doz. 12s. 6d.   1 3
SUPERBUM. A fine yellow with purple spots   per doz. 15s. 0d.   1 6
SPECIOSUM. A fine hardy class; excellent for pot culture.
,, **Kraetzeri.** Pure white; finest variety   per doz. 12s. 0d.   1 3
,, **magnificum.** A highly improved form of Rubrum, with deep crimson spots, strong growing. Doz. 16/-, each 1/6
,, **melpomene.** Most beautiful variety; flowers of a lovely purplish crimson; heavily spotted. Doz. 16/-, each 1/6
,, **rubrum.** White, spotted crimson. Doz. 10/6, each 1/-
,, **roseum.** White, spotted. Doz. 10/6, each 1/-
THUNBERGIANUM ATROSANGUINEUM. Scarlet, spotted black Doz. 12/6, each 1/3
TIGRINUM SPLENDENS. Orange scarlet, black spots Doz. 7/-, ea. 8d.
,, ,, **FORTUNEI.** The finest of the Tiger Lilies. Orange scarlet, black spots. Doz. 12/6, each 1/3

LILIUM SPECIOSUM VARIETIES.

RANUNCULI.

The Ranunculi are very free-flowering and beautiful. They will succeed in almost any soil, and planted up to the middle of April will bloom abundantly during the Summer; very useful for cutting.

Per doz.   Per 100

GIANT TURBAN. A vigorous growing and free flowering class, giving a grand display in beds or borders, each plant when well grown producing forty to fifty large double flowers of the most brilliant colours; useful for cutting.
,, ,, **MONT BLANC.** A splendid pure white ..   1 3   8 0
,, ,, **PRIMROSE BEAUTY.** Lovely shade of yellow   1 3   8 0
,, ,, **VESUVIUS.** Fine scarlet ..   1 3   8 0
,, ,, **MIXED.** Flowers in great variety of colours   1 0   6 6
TURBAN, SCARLET. Admirably adapted for filling beds, ribbon borders, or massing   ..   1 0   7 0
,, **MIXED.** All colours; beautiful variety   1 0   7 0
PERSIAN. The Persian Ranunculi, though not so vigorous in growth as the other varieties, display the greatest diversity of colour, many of the flowers being spotted or edged in brilliantly contrasting colours, their form is also of the most perfect doubleness.
Collection of 100 in 10 choice named varieties   —   10 0
,, **CHOICEST MIXED.** In beautiful variety ..   1 0   7 0

TIGRIDIAS— TIGER FLOWERS.

These gorgeously coloured flowers are easily grown if planted in an open sunny border, in any rich, light, well-drained soil. Plant during the latter part of March and in April, three inches deep and six inches apart; a little sand round the bulb is an advantage. The flowers are short-lived but well-grown, plants will each produce a profusion of blooms.

Canariensis. Yellow, spotted with scarlet. Per doz. 1/10, 100 12/6.
Grandiflora Alba. Creamy white, spotted with red. Per doz. 1/10, 100 12/6.
Pavonia. Scarlet & orange. Per doz. 1/10, 100 12/6.
Mixed. All colours. Per doz. 1/3, 100 7/6.

RANUNCULI—GIANT FRENCH.

HYACINTHUS CANDICANS.

A splendid hardy bulbous-rooted plant, blooming in August, and throwing up fine spikes of white bell-shaped flowers three to four feet high. It makes a capital plant for pots in the greenhouse, and is highly effective when planted out of doors in association with Gladiolus Brenchleyensis, which blooms at the same time. Fine bulbs, doz. 2s. 6d., 100 17s. 6d.

YELLOW ARUM LILY.
(Richardia Elliotiana).

A beautiful pure yellow Arum, with large silvery spotted leaves, easily grown; stock limited ..   each 2s.

MONTBRETIAS.

Graceful spikes exceedingly useful for cutting. Planted in Spring they will bloom freely during August and September, and form permanent clumps. The plants thrive anywhere.

Per doz.   Per 100

California. Deep golden yellow, free flowering ..   1 0   7 0
Fire King. Glowing scarlet, large flowers ..   2 0   14 10
George Davison. Pale orange yellow, a very fine variety   1 0   12 6
Golden West. Pure golden yellow, large open flowers ..   4 0   30 0
King Edmund. Giant golden yellow, with brown markings   2 0   21 0
Lord Nelson. Deep orange scarlet, yellow eye .. each 6d.   4 0   32 0
Star of the East. Pure orange yellow, lemon eye. The finest variety, blooms often five inches across   each 1s. 0d.   10 6   —
Choice Mixed Seedlings, containing many beautiful colours   1 0   7 0

·NURSERY· DEPARTMENT

APPLES.

The great demand for all Fruit Trees experienced during the past five years, together with the difficulties in working stocks the latter part of the war period, have resulted in a shortage for this season of some style of trees, especially Standard Apples,—these are practically unobtainable in the Kingdom.

We are however able to offer an exceptionally fine stock of Bush, Pyramid, Espalier and Half-Standard Apples, Pears, Plums, etc. To enable our customers to select their requirements we have set out the Apples in sections, showing the Varieties of each style that we can offer with the prices attached.

We work our Apples on both the Crab and broad-leaved Paradise Stock, according to the varieties. Dwarf Apples on the Paradise Stock are of especial value for garden planting, and have come into favour during recent years. They are much dwarfer in growth, come into bearing and profit much sooner, are easier to thin and spray, and they produce almost continuously abundant crops of much finer fruit. For small holdings, or where the tenure is uncertain, they are specially recommended.

NEW APPLES OF SPECIAL MERIT.

HARLING HERO (Our Introduction). A most valuable addition to the late cooking varieties. It is a heavy cropper, a sturdy grower of a very hardy constitution, and thrives well on all soils. It possesses a remarkable beauty of colour and perfect shape; very large. Dec. to Feb. 2 years, 10/6 each.

MONARCH. A cross between "Wellington" and "Peasgood's Nonsuch." Very large, firm fleshed, handsome appearance, quality superior, and requires less sugar. Heavy bearer and good sturdy grower. Oct. to April. 2 years, 10/6 each.

NORVIC (Our Introduction). Large and handsome fruit, when ripe it is a greenish yellow; a first-rate cooking variety and of fine flavour; a most valuable acquisition both for private and market growers. Nov. 10/6 each.

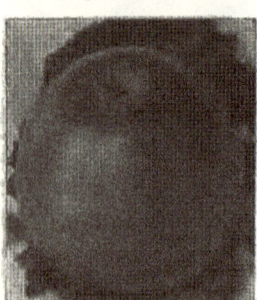

PEASGOOD'S NONSUCH.

GENERAL LIST OF SELECT VARIETIES.

D. denotes Dessert. *K. Kitchen.*

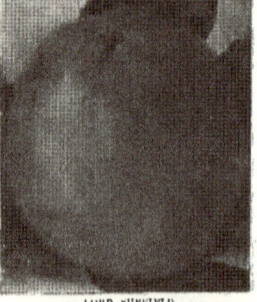

LORD SUFFIELD.

In all cases where customers leave the selection of varieties to us, they may rely on only good trees of the best kinds being supplied. It is most important, however, that the style or shape of trees required should be clearly stated when ordering.

PRICES OF APPLES.

BUSHES, 5/6 and 6/6 each, 60/- and 72/- doz. PYRAMIDS, 7/6 and 8/6 each, 84/- and 96/- doz. CORDONS, 5/6 and 6/6 each, 60/- and 72/- doz.

We have a splendid assortment of all the following Varieties in Bushes, Pyramids and Cordons. For Special Offer of certain of these Varieties in Horizontal Trained, Bushes on Short Stems, Half Standards, see following page.

ALLINGTON PIPPIN. A splendid medium-sized Apple introduced a few years ago, and which has taken a position in the front rank as a first-rate dessert variety and a reliable bearer. In form it resembles Cox's Orange. Pyramid trees only. *See also page 77.*

ANNIE ELIZABETH (K). Very fine late Apple; excellent keeping qualities. Dec. to May.

BEAUTY OF BATH (D). A very handsome early variety, has a brisk, sub-acid flavour. July and Aug. *See also page 77.*

BISMARCK (K). A very fine large Apple from New Zealand; one of the best varieties in cultivation for market or the private garden. Of great size, brilliant colour, a most profuse bearer. Oct. to Dec. *See also page 77.*

BLENHEIM ORANGE (D.K.). Well-known and splendid variety; large fruit. Dec. to Feb.

BRAMLEY'S SEEDLING (K). A large handsome fruit, resembling Blenheim Orange. Sept. to Jan. *See also page 77.*

CHARLES ROSS (K). A superb dessert variety. A cross between "Cox's Orange" and "Peasgood's Nonsuch." It has all the richness of flavour and handsome appearance of the parents, excellent bearer. *See also page 77.*

COX'S ORANGE PIPPIN (D). Medium, of delicious flavour, finest dessert apple; good habit, bears and grows well as Standard; A1 as a garden tree, succeeding in all forms, but prefers a warm rich soil. Best flavoured from low trees on Paradise. Nov. to March. *See also page 77.*

EARLY VICTORIA (K). Pale lemon-coloured, very early variety of the Codlin type; very free bearer. July and Aug. *See also page 77.*

ECKLINVILLE SEEDLING (K). A large and useful sort; flesh white and tender; a great bearer. Oct. to Dec. *See also page 77.*

ELLISON'S ORANGE (D). A delicious dessert Apple approaching in appearance and flavour to Cox's Orange Pippin; a good keeper.

GASCOIGNE'S SCARLET (K). Large, a distinct, richly coloured apple, extremely handsome, and a great bearer; prolific on Paradise, and a healthy grower. Prune lightly. Nov. to Jan. F.C.R.H.S.

HERRING'S PIPPIN. Delicious and of handsome appearance. Pearmain shape, flesh yellow, crisp, and sweet. Cordons, and Pyramids.

LANE'S PRINCE ALBERT (K). Large, extremely handsome striped fruit, very prolific, keeps six months; its fertility is remarkable. Cordons or Bushes, on the Paradise Stock, produce grand exhibition fruit. F.C.R.H.S. Oct. to March. *See also page 77.*

LORD DERBY (K). Large, handsome, heavy cropper; one of the best. Nov. and Dec.

LORD GROSVENOR (K). Large and handsome culinary Apple. Sept. to Nov.

LORD SUFFIELD (K). Fine variety of "Keswick Codlin" type. Early and prolific; one of the best cooking Apples. Aug. and Sept.

NEWTON WONDER (K). Large; a handsome fruit, keeping soundly, free grower and bearer; one of the best. In growth and sturdiness this surpasses all others. A sterling kind for orchard or garden. F.C.R.H.S. Nov. to May. *See also page 77.*

NORFOLK BEAUTY (K). A cross between "Warner's King" and "Dr. Harvey." Fruit large, pale green changing to yellow, in appearance intermediate between the two parents. *See also page 77.*

PEACEMAKER. A very large and handsome culinary Apple. The fruit is pale yellow, flushed with crimson, a heavy cropper.

PEASGOOD'S NONSUCH (D.K.). Very large and handsome, pale yellow, with bright crimson. Of diffuse growth on Paradise; requires its roots well pruned to induce fertility in a young state. We recommend it for garden culture and exhibition. As a standard it takes some years before it comes to profit. F.C.R.H.S. Sept. to Jan.

REV. W. WILKS (K). A very large, culinary Apple of fine form; good grower and free bearer.

RIBSTON PIPPIN (D). Medium; a well-known sort, succeeds best on Paradise stock. The finest fruit is produced on Cordons; not suitable for orchards, should only be planted in warm soils. Nov. to March.

STIRLING CASTLE (K). An early and free-bearing Apple; a great bearer, and well-suited for dwarf culture. Aug. and Sept. (K.) Sept. *See also page 77.*

WARNER'S KING (K). A very large and splendid Apple of first-rate quality; the tree is a free and vigorous grower, a great bearer, and not subject to disease. Nov. to March. *See also page 77.*

WORCESTER PEARMAIN (K.D.). Handsome early variety, suitable for kitchen or dessert; a great favourite in the market. Aug. and Sept. *See also page 77.*

APPLES.
BUSHES and HALF-STANDARDS
FRUITING SIZE.   SPECIAL OFFER.

BUSH APPLES on SHORT STEMS

We offer below a range including most of the best Kitchen and Dessert Apples in Bush trees with short stems. These trees possess many advantages for anyone having only a limited space for fruit growing ; they can be planted closer together and a heavier crop is thus obtained from a given area, they are handy both for spraying, pruning and gathering. Further, the fruit is, as a rule—given proper attention to the trees —of first-class quality. Bushes with short stems such as offered are also easier to treat in applying grease bands, the stem allows these to be placed without any difficulty.

The trees should be planted 15 ft. apart.

Allington Pippin (D). Nov. to Jan.
Annie Elizabeth (K). Dec. to May.
Bramley's Seedling (K). Sept. to June.
Beauty of Bath (D). July and Aug.
Barnack Beauty (K). Dec. to May.
Cox's Orange Pippin (D). Nov. to March.
Early Victo ia (K). July and Aug.
Grenadier (K). Oct. and Nov.
King of Pippins (D). Aug. and Sept.
Lane's Prince Albert (K). Oct. to March.
Lord Derby (K). Nov. and Dec.
Nowton Wonder (K). Nov. to May.
Norfolk Beauty (K).
Worcester Pearmain (K.D.). Aug. & Sept.

For descriptions of these Varieties see page 76.

Each 6/6, per doz. 72/-

EARLY VICTORIAN.

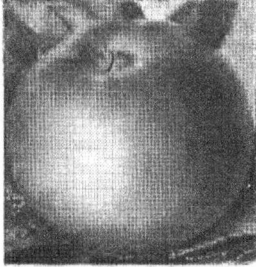

BRAMLEY'S SEEDLING.

HORIZONTAL TRAINED TREES.

We can supply 2 and 3 Tiers of the following varieties :

Allington Pippin	James Grieve
Beauty of Bath	King of Pippins
Bismarck	Lady Sudeley
Bramley's Seedling	Lane's Prince Albert
Chas. Ross	Lord Derby
Early Victoria	Newton Wonder
Ecklinville Seedling	Stirling Castle
Grenadier	Worcester Pearmain

2 Tiers 7/6 each, 3 Tiers 10/6 each.

We also can supply a few extra sized Trees, 4 and 5 Tiers. Varieties and prices on application.

SPECIAL COLLECTION BUSH FRUIT TREES.

This offer is made to meet the needs of those having small gardens or allotments, and who have not room for a large number of Fruit Trees.

4	RED CURRANTS.	2	APPLES, Bush.
6	GOOSEBERRIES.	12	RASPBERRIES.
8	BLACK CURRANTS.	1	PLUM, Bush.
1	PEAR, Bush.	40	STRAWBERRIES.

The above Bushes and Plants for 37/6, Packing Free, Carriage Extra.

We experience a large demand for this Collection. The selection of Varieties must be left entirely to ourselves, and no alterations can be made in any way whatever.

HALF-STANDARDS.

We give below a list of varieties of Apple of which we are able to supply half-standards, and we especially recommend these to those who desire to grow trees on stems.

Where the land is to be cropped between the trees they will be found most suitable ; they are also admirable for planting in ground which is used for poultry runs, the branches being sufficient distance from the ground to prevent the birds destroying the fruit.

The trees are all well grown, of fruiting size, and will quickly give a return. The varieties include all the best for cooking and dessert, both early and late sorts.

The trees should be planted 18 ft. apart.

Allington Pippin (D). Nov. to Jan.
Bramley's Seedling (K). Sept. to June.
Bismarck (K). Oct. to Dec.
Cellini (D.K.). Oct. and Nov.
Cox's Orange Pippin (D). Nov. to Mar.
Charles Ross (D). Oct. and Nov.
Early Victoria (K). July and Aug.
Ecklinville Seedling (K). Oct. to Dec.
Keswick Codlin (K). Aug. and Sept.
Lord Grosvenor (K). Sept. to Nov.
Newton Wonder (K). Nov. to May.
Worcester Pearmain (K.D.). Aug. & Sept.

For descriptions of these Varieties see page 76.

Each 7/6, per doz. 84/-

ALLINGTON PIPPIN.

CULTIVATION.

For small occupations and allotment gardens Dwarf or Pyramids are best planted eight to twelve feet apart on each side of the path, and about three feet from the paths.

The best situation for Fruit growing is a fairly open piece of ground, protected from the east and north-east if possible, as the winds from these quarters, when the trees are in blossom in Spring, often are most injurious, and ruin the crop for the whole season. A good deep loam is the ideal soil, and the preparation before planting the trees should receive most careful attention.

If the ground is heavy and cold, it should be thoroughly drained, and receive a good dressing of lime or ashes, which should be thoroughly incorporated with the soil to lighten it ; on the other hand, if a light sandy soil is the only piece available, a dressing of clay or brick earth will give body to it and be of much value.

Probably the cause of failure with most people is to be found in not using care in planting the trees ; too often the hole made for the tree is not large enough, and consequently the roots are crowded together in a bunch, and they cannot thrive as they should ; it is of the utmost importance that the holes should be sufficiently large to allow of the roots being laid straight out, and if this is done and the soil carefully shaken between the roots, being at the same time made gradually firm, and the stem quite secure, little fear need be entertained as to the future.

SELECT PEARS.

Pears should be much more freely grown than they are. The young trees come into bearing much earlier than is generally supposed, especially when worked on the Quince stock. Many of the varieties are exceedingly prolific, whilst the fruit are more valuable than Apples, choice sorts always finding a ready sale at good prices.

PRICES OF PEARS ON QUINCE OR PEAR STOCK.

BUSHES			5/6 and 6/6 each	60/- and 72/- doz.
PYRAMIDS. Selected			7/6 and 8/6 „	84/- and 96/- „
CORDONS			5/6 and 6/6 „	60/- and 72/- „
HALF AND THREE-QUARTER STANDARDS			7/6 „	84/- „
ESPALIERS. On Quince and Pear Stock			2 tiers 7/6 each, 3 tiers 10/6 each.	

Larger Trees, varieties and prices on application.

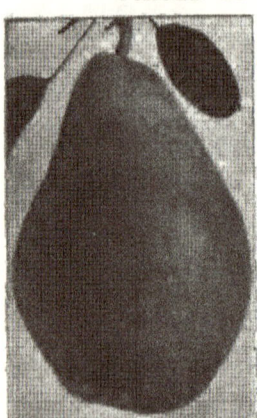

PITMASTON DUCHESS.

BEURRE D'AMANLIS. Fruit large, greenish white, fine grained, tender, melting, rich, sugary and agreeably perfumed. One of the best early pears for market. Sept.

BEURRE DIEL. Hardy and vigorous, first-rate quality. Flesh yellowish white, tender, a rich sugary flavour. Oct. and Nov.

BEURRE HARDY. A fine, large dessert pear of most excellent quality. As a pyramid it is a very great bearer. Oct.

BEURRE RANCE. Large, one of the late pears, of sweet, juicy flavour. Must be root pruned to induce fertility and prevent the fruit cracking; requires a south or west wall.

BLICKLING (new). Very fine late. Raised by Mr. W. Allan, Gunton Park, Norfolk. Ripens in January, is of most delicious flavour, good grower, free bearer; equal to " Doyenne du Comice " to flavour.

CATILLAC. Fruit large; one of the best stewing pears; does not succeed well as a pyramid or standard unless well sheltered, but is first-class for a wall. Dec. to April.

CLAPP'S FAVOURITE. One of the finest early. Medium size, rich yellow colour, flushed with crimson, juicy, delicious flavour. Aug.

CONFERENCE. Fruit large; skin dark green and russet; flesh salmon coloured; melting, juicy, and rich. Makes a strong healthy growth both on the pear and quince stocks; very prolific. F.C.C. Nov.

DOYENNE DU COMICE. Large, very handsome, ranks as the most delicious melting pear grown; it bears remarkably large fruit, and makes a fertile Pyramid, Cordon, or Wall tree. Oct. and Nov. Pyramid Trees only.

DUCHESSE D'ANGOULEME. Of great excellence. Large, greenish yellow, flesh white, buttery and melting, of a rich flavour. Abundant bearer and vigorous grower. Oct. and Nov.

GLOU MORCEAU. Fruit large, richly flavoured and juicy; a very fine dessert pear. Dec. and Jan.

JARGONELLE. Medium. Succeeds on walls or as an open Standard; makes a prolific tree on the Quince and forms a spreading bush. Aug.

JOSEPHINE DE MALINES. A fine pear of most delicious flavour; the tree is hardy and an excellent bearer. Jan. to May.

LOUISE BONNE OF JERSEY. Medium size, skin smooth and shining; colour pale green with deep chocolate crimson, flesh white, crisp and juicy, very sweet. Oct.

MARIE LOUISE D'UCCLE. Large useful pear of first-rate quality; great cropper. Oct.

MARGUERITE MARILLAT. Very large and showy, with aromatic flavour; handsome; the finest in its season. Sept.

PITMASTON DUCHESS. Very large, melting; bearing freely on Pear or Quince. Cultivated for market on a large scale, and succeeds admirably as Standards. Oct. to Dec.

UVEDALE'S ST. GERMAIN. A very large pear, first-class for stewing. Flesh white, crisp, juicy, and slightly gritty. Jan. to April.

WILLIAMS' BON CHRETIEN. Well-known splendid old dessert pear; very hardy and a good bearer. Aug. and Sept.

WINTER NELIS. One of the most delicious pears of its season. Fruit small and rich flavour. Nov. to Jan.

SELECT PLUMS.

DWARF TRAINED, 7/6 and 10/6 each.   STANDARDS, TRAINED (list of sorts on application), 12/6 and 15/- each.
HALF & THREE-QUARTER STANDARDS, 7/6 each, 84/- per doz.   BUSHES, 5/6 and 6/6 each, 60/- and 72/- per doz.

General List.   D denotes dessert.   K kitchen.

BELLE DE LOUVAIN (K). Very large handsome fruit of rich flavour. The fruit is red, and is a constant bearer.

BRYANSTON GAGE (D). Large, sugary, and richly flavoured; an excellent and abundant bearing sort. Aug.

COE'S GOLDEN DROP (D). Large oval fruit, pale yellow spotted with red; one of the very best plums for dessert. End of Sept.

COX'S EMPEROR (K). Large dark reddish-purple fruit, firm flesh, sweet, rich, and juicy; a very fine bearer. Sept.

DAMSON, MERRYWEATHER'S. Unlike other Damsons it commences to fruit as soon as the trees are two or three years old, after which it never fails. Two-year old trees only. 7/6 ea.

DENNISTON'S SUPERB (D). Large oval fruit, greenish-yellow blotched purple; a delicious dessert plum, and an abundant bearer. Aug.

DIAMOND (K). Large oval, dark purple fruit; excellent for cooking or preserving. Sept.

EARLY PROLIFIC (D). Hardy, and a certain bearer; very valuable market sort; ripens middle of July on a wall; one of the best. July.

EGG PLUM. This is the real " Evesham " variety, obovate yellow with golden tinge; a very useful cooking variety, a great bearer.

GIANT PRUNE. A very large, long, oval fruit of dark red colour, with yellow flesh of excellent flavour; and a good bearer. Fruit firm and does not split.

GOLDEN GAGE (D). Large fruit, of very rich and delicious flavour; a most excellent and prolific sort. Sept.

GREENGAGE (D). The very best and richest of all. This race requires vigorous root pruning, and then bears freely; as Pot trees they succeed in an orchard house. Aug.

JEFFERSON'S (D). A large and delicious plum, hardy, good bearer. Sept.

KIRKE'S (D). One of the very best of the blue plums, the fruit is medium-sized and richly flavoured; a first-rate dessert variety. Sept.

MAGNUM BONUM, WHITE (K). Large yellow fruit; an excellent kitchen variety.

MONARCH (K). One of the best late plums, of large size and splendid flavour, dark purplish blue; a heavy bearer and strong grower. Sept.

ORLEANS (K). A good cooking or preserving plum; a great bearer. Aug.

POND'S SEEDLING (K). Very large, good bearer and a steady grower. Forms a spreading tree; valuable for late market or garden culture. Early in Sept.

PRESIDENT (new). Very large, late purple, good and free bearer, deep purple with good bloom. Sept.

PRIMATE (Rivers). A splendid new late plum, purplish red in colour, dotted with good bloom; very large and late variety.

PRINCE OF WALES (K). Medium-sized purple fruit; a splendid plum for cooking. End of Aug.

REINE CLAUDE DE BAVAY (D). Large, round, greenish-yellow fruit of the " gage " type, rich and delicious flavour; the tree is hardy and a great bearer. Beginning of Oct.

SHEPHERD'S BULLACE. Large greenish round fruit, splendid for tarts.

THE CZAR (D.K.). Very large, purple fruit of rich flavour; an abundant bearer, most valuable to market growers on account of its earliness, fine appearance, and excellent quality. End of July.

TRANSPARENT GAGE (D). Large oval, greenish-yellow fruit marked with red; flesh rich, sweet, and juicy; superior to almost all other plums. Middle of Sept.

VICTORIA (K). A well-known and very fine variety; the tree is hardy and an almost constant bearer. The most useful kind of the season. Early in Sept.

WHITE BULLACE (K). A very prolific and useful culinary sort. End of Oct.

JEFFERSON'S.

STANDARD PLUMS.

We are only able to offer the following varieties in STANDARDS, each 8/6, per doz. 96/-.

Bryanston Gage	Coe's Golden Drop	Greengage	The Czar
Cox's Emperor	Farleigh Prolific	Merryweather	Victoria

APRICOTS.

DWARF TRAINED, 10/6 and 12/6 each.
HEMSKERK. Flesh tender, juicy, and richly flavoured. July and Aug.
LARGE EARLY. Very rich and juicy. July and Aug.
MOORPARK. One of the best. Aug. and Sept.
PEACH. Very large, rich, and juicy; one of the finest of all. Aug. and Sept.
ROYAL. Large, rich and juicy. July and Aug.

CHERRIES.

Cherries thrive on almost any free working, deep, sweet, well-drained soil, provided they have plenty of fresh air. Wherever the soil shows the slightest tendency to sourness, this should be checked by the application of lime.
All Cherries grow well as a rule upon an East wall. Where early crops are wanted a South wall is of course preferable. On a West wall, particularly in a wet district, the fruit is liable to crack.
DWARF TRAINED. 8/6 and 10/6 each.
STANDARDS. 7/6 each.
PYRAMIDS. 8/6 each.

GENERAL LIST.

BIGARREAU. Large and of first-rate quality; a capital bearer. July.
BIGARREAU NAPOLEON. Good bearer, hardy and excellent, follows the Bigarreau; valuable to extend the season; first-rate for market.
BLACK EAGLE. Fruit of good size and flavour; an excellent black cherry. July.
BLACK HEART. A capital early black cherry of good quality, free bearer.
EARLY RIVERS. Large, shining black, very handsome rich flavour; one of the best for forcing or cherry house, and valuable for wall.
ELTON. Large, rich and excellent. July.
FROGMORE EARLY PROLIFIC. A capital early sort, very prolific.
GOVERNOR WOOD. Large, yellow, mottled with red, sweet and rich; a good bearer; excellent. July.
MAY DUKE. Large, juicy, rich, and excellent; an abundant bearer as a standard or a bush. July.
MORELLO. Valuable for preserving and bottling. Pyramid trees produce fruit equal to that from a wall. Succeeds on north walls, and is occasionally planted as a Standard.
THE NOBLE. Very large, flesh firm, of rich flavour. A profuse bearer, and the fruit keeps well after gathering. Quite distinct.
WHITE HEART. Flesh firm, sweet and pleasant flavoured. End of July.

BIGARREAU NAPOLEON.

CRABS (Pyrus baccata).

The following varieties, which we consider by far the best and most useful, are excellent for making preserves. They are also very pretty as ornamental trees, the bright-coloured fruits hanging in abundance, as they generally do, for a long time in Autumn.
DARTMOUTH. Very handsome dark crimson fruit; an abundant bearer. Standards, 6/6 each; Bush, 5/- each.
JOHN DOWNIE. Bright crimson, conical fruit of good size and quality; very handsome. Standards, 6/6 each; Bush, 5/- each.

NECTARINES.

DWARF TRAINED, 10/6 and 12/6 each.
STANDARD TRAINED. Names and prices on application.

EARLY RIVERS. A Seedling Nectarine, raised by Mr. T. F. Rivers, ripening twenty-one days before Lord Napier. It is a certain and heavy cropper, and promises to be one of the most valuable Nectarines yet introduced.
DOWNTON. Fruit large, oval, skin greenish in the shade, dark red on sunny side; melting, juicy, rich, and highly flavoured; an excellent variety. End of Aug.
ELRUGE. Medium, pale green, flushed deep red, flesh melting, rich, and juicy; one of the best; an excellent bearer and forces well. Aug. and Sept.
LORD NAPIER. Medium size; pale cream with red cheek, flesh melting, very early, one of the best.
PINEAPPLE. Large, bright red on the sunny side, very rich and sweet. Sept.
PITMASTON ORANGE. Large bright orange, dark brownish-red on the sunny side; melting, juicy, and rich; an excellent Nectarine, a good bearer. Aug. and Sept.
RIVERS' ORANGE. Similar to Pitmaston Orange, but earlier.

PEACHES.

DWARF TRAINED. 10/6 and 12/6 each.
STANDARD TRAINED. Names and prices on application.

ALEXANDER. Medium sized, brilliant colour, early peach; skin yellow, almost scarlet next the sun; flesh pale yellow, very juicy. July.
BARRINGTON. Large fruit of rich vinous flavour, and first-rate quality. Sept.
BELLEGARDE. Large, handsome, deep red, almost black next the sun; flesh pale yellow, very juicy. Middle of Sept.
CRAWFORD'S EARLY. Very large, of splendid colour, very tender and melting. Aug. & Sept.
DR. HOGG. Large, fruit remarkable for its high colour; it is firm yet melting, and of rich sugary flavour. Middle of Aug.
DUKE OF YORK. Large free stone, fruit well coloured, of excellent flavour; ripe about same time as Alexandra.
DYMOND. Fruit large, skin greenish yellow; flesh white, rich, melting, juicy. Middle of Sept.
EARLY RIVERS. Large, pale straw-coloured fruit, very rich and fine flavour. End of July.
GOSHAWK. Large, of exquisite flavour, good bearer; pale with red flesh, very hardy. Sept.
GROSSE MIGNONNE. Large, pale greenish yellow, mottled red, deep brown red next the sun; flesh melting, very juicy, of delicious vinous flavour. Early in Sept.
HALE'S EARLY. Medium size, beautifully suffused crimson, flesh melting, juicy and delicious; forces well. July.
NOBLESSE. Large and handsome, remarkably juicy, with very tender, delicate flesh, sweet and luscious. Sept.
PEREGRINE. Distinct Mid-season variety of fine constitution, fruit large and handsome with brilliant crimson skin, flesh rich and highly flavoured.
PRINCESS OF WALES. One of the largest Peaches and best; skin cream with a rosy cheek, melting and rich. End of Sept.
ROYAL GEORGE. Large, very pale, speckled and marbled red, very juicy, rich and highly flavoured; a good bearer. Sept.
SEA EAGLE. Very large, good flavour; remarkable for colour and size. End of Sept.
STIRLING CASTLE. A fine hardy Peach of the "Royal George" type, large, skin deep red on sunny side, rich. Aug.

FIGS.

Figs will grow in almost any soil, but if it be too rich they produce a great deal of wood and very little fruit. Exuberance of growth is one of their chief characteristics. This can be restrained by limiting their rooting area and making the soil firm. They require a considerable amount of moisture when the fruit is swelling. Good drainage is also essential.
STRONG PLANTS, in pots, Trained flat.
FRUITING ,,
BROWN TURKEY. Most abundant bearer; the finest for out door.
BROWN TURKEY. Strong Plants, Fan-trained, from open ground. 12/6 each.
NEGRO LARGO. Very luscious, free bearer, strong grower; large rich chocolate purple fruit; splendid for second crop under glass, but not fertile outside. F.C.
WHITE ISCHIA. Small, sweet and delicious; produces three crops a year in fruit; forces well; great bearer; for indoor culture only.
STRONG [PLANTS, 10/6 and 15/- each

CURRANTS.

BLACK.

Black Currants thrive best in a deep cool moist soil. On a dry sand or gravel, and on hot shallow soils they are practically useless. They often grow luxuriantly on wet soil, but are liable to disease when the land is sour. A soil containing abundance of humus of vegetable matter suits them well, as such a soil is, as a rule, sufficiently damp for the moisture-loving rootlets, and sufficiently cool to prevent their over stimulation. The whole of our bushes are raised from young wood—a most important factor in the future success of the crop—they are also free from disease.

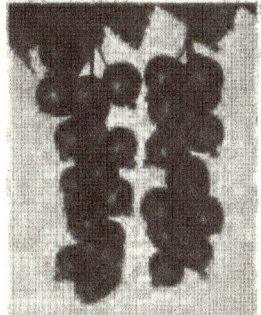

SEABROOK'S BLACK.

SEABROOK'S BLACK. A splendid Black Currant which possesses a strong constitution. A most prolific bearer. Our stock is perfectly clean. Those who are troubled with big bud or failing off in fruit are strongly recommended to try it. The best Market variety we know.
BOSKOOP GIANT BLACK. The finest Black Currant yet introduced. It is of extraordinary vigorous growth with long bunches of enormous fruit. Flavour, sweet and rich. A first-rate variety for exposed situations, and although it flowers late it ripens early.

Good, strong, Two-year old Stock, well-rooted, 1/- each, 10/6 per doz., 75.- per 100, £35 per 1000.
Good Planting Stuff, 9d. each, 7.6 per doz., 55.- per 100, £25 per 1000.

CURRANTS—RED.

FAY'S PROLIFIC. One of the best Red Currants. The bush is a strong grower, wonderfully prolific, and comes into bearing early. The fruit is large, bright red, and of excellent flavour.
RABY CASTLE. A strong and good grower, very large berries of rich crimson colour, hangs late on the bushes; great bearer.
RED DUTCH. Late, enormous cropper; one of the best Market sorts.
Good Strong Bushes, 1/- each; 10/6 doz.
PERFECTION RED. The finest and largest Red Currant in cultivation. The fruit, which is produced in long bunches, often having twenty fruits on a bunch, is of a beautiful glossy dark crimson colour; the flavour is excellent, sweet and juicy. Award of Merit, R.H.S. Bushes, 3/6 each. Limited quantity only.

CURRANTS—WHITE.

TRANSPARENT WHITE. The largest and sweetest of White Currants.
WHITE DUTCH. A good currant for general purposes; splendid for dessert.

Good Strong Bushes.
1 - each; 10/6 per doz.

We have a fine lot of Fan-trained Currants. Our selection from the above-named varieties, 33/- per doz.; each 3/-. Single and Double Cordons 33 - per doz.; each 3/-.

"The Currant Bushes you supplied me with two years ago produced 67 stone to the 1 acre."—Mr. E. A. DALE, Ludham, Gt. Yarmouth.

GOOSEBERRIES.

GOOSEBERRY, WHINHAM'S "INDUSTRY."

LANCASHIRE PRIZE VARIETIES,

A very fine class, much esteemed for the splendid size of their fruit and their value for exhibition or dessert. When well ripened they are of delicious flavour and equal to many forced fruits.

We can supply good sorts, our selection only,

Bushes, 2, - each, 21 - per doz.

GOLDEN DROP. Golden yellow, medium size, very early, delicious flavour.

WHINHAM'S INDUSTRY. A superb variety, bearing a wonderful profusion of large handsome fruit, which are of a dull red colour when ripe.

WHITESMITH. White, large fruit, splendid flavour, an exceedingly heavy cropper; early.

Bushes, 1 6 each, 16 - per doz.

We have a few Standards on about 3 ft. stems, our selection, 10 - each.

Fan trained, 3/- each, 33/- per doz.

From MR. J. CALDWELL, Blackvol.
July 22nd.
"Last Autumn you supplied me with Gooseberry Bushes, these I am pleased to say have done very well, and produced a fair quantity of fine berries."

ALMONDS.

Standards 5 6 each.

MEDLARS.

For the successful cultivation of Medlars an open situation sheltered from cutting winds is absolutely essential. A good moist well-drained loam suits them best; but with an occasional mulching they grow well on sandy soils.
Standards 7/6 each.

NUTS AND FILBERTS.

We have a very fine stock of these in good strong plants, comprising such varieties as Cosford, Kentish Cob, Filbert, white, red, purple-leaved, etc.
STRONG FRUITING DWARFS or BUSHES in first-class condition. 2/- each, 21/- per doz.

BLACKBERRIES.

Most of them are quite hardy, and succeed well under similar culture to the Raspberry. The fruits are large, handsome and delicious, either raw, cooked, or preserved.
PARSLEY LEAVED. Very ornamental cut-leaved variety, which bears large fruit, good and productive. 1/3 each, 12 6 per doz.
WILSON JUNIOR. Large fruit; delicious. 1/3 each, 12 6 per doz.

LOGAN BERRY.

Strong Plants from layers, the true variety.
2/6 each; 27/- per doz.

GRAPE VINES.

Many good crops of grapes are grown in greenhouses without any artificial heat, and often when other plants are cultivated in the same house. Great care must however be taken that plants are not grown which are liable to be attacked by Mealy Bug or Red Spider. Ferns, Palms, Bulbs, Chrysanthemums and Zonal Pelargoniums may however be grown in a vinery. The best position for a vinery is facing South or South-West, and a lean-to house is the best.

In making the border for planting, it is most important that ample drainage be supplied, especially so if the site is at all cold or wet.

To those about to plant vines we recommend the careful study of some good book, such as "GRAPES AND HOW TO GROW THEM," by J. Landsell, price 3/0 post free.

The fruiting canes we offer are strong and stout, from eight to ten feet in length; and if cultivated in pots will bear from eight to twelve bunches each next season.

H denotes those varieties that require a heated vinery.
C denotes those suitable for growing in a cool vinery.

BLACK ALICANTE (H). One of the largest and best grapes for late work, carrying a fine bloom.
BLACK HAMBURG (C). Juicy, sweet and rich; a well-known and excellent sort, sometimes ripens out of doors; the best for general use, pot culture, and forcing.
FOSTER'S SEEDLING (C). One of the finest and most easily cultivated of White Grapes; and a certain cropper.
GROS COLMAR (H). Berries very large, round, jet black with a beautiful bloom. Late and hangs well.
GROS MAROC (H). Large oval black berries, covered with a dark dense bloom; an extremely handsome mid-season variety.
LADY DOWNES' SEEDLING (H). A first-rate black late hanging Grape of excellent flavour.
MADRESFIELD COURT. A very handsome black Muscat, with large oval berries, covered with a dense bluish plum-like bloom, branches very long and tapering. An excellent variety for early use.
MUSCAT OF ALEXANDRIA (H). Rich amber; bunch and berries immensely large, with a deliciously rich, sweet Muscat flavour; requires a warm vinery; the favourite "Muscat."
ROYAL MUSCADINE. A fine hardy white; succeeds well on a south wall.
SWEETWATER BUCKLAND (C). A round white berry of good flavour and handsome.
STRONG PLANTING CANES,
In pots, 10 6 each.
FRUITING CANES.
In pots, very fine, 12/6 and 15/- each.

STRAWBERRIES.

BEDFORD CHAMPION. One of the largest fruits in commerce, 2½ to 3 ozs. in weight. Bright scarlet skin, flesh white. 13/- per 100, 7/6 per 50, 5/- per 25.
GIVON'S LATE PROLIFIC. Large, wedge-shaped fruit of rich colour, and splendid flavour. Award of Merit, R.H.S. 13/- per 100, 7 6 per 50, 5/- per 25.
HIBBERD'S KING GEORGE. This is a large late Strawberry. Fruit wedge-shaped, but some come pointed. 13/- per 100, 7/6 per 50, 5/- per 25.
KENTISH FAVOURITE. The heaviest cropping Strawberry yet sent out. The fruit is of a beautiful bright scarlet colour. 13/- per 100, 7/6 per 50, 5/- per 25.
KING GEORGE. A grand new early variety, equalling Royal Sovereign in size, but ripening fully a week earlier. 13/- per 100, 7 6 per 50, 5/- per 25.
LAXTONIAN. This new variety is the best maincrop yet introduced; the fruit is large, the centre ones wedge-shaped, the trusses are strong and bold. The flavour is first-class, and we do not know any other Strawberry equal in size so good. 15/- per 100, 8 6 per 50, 5/- per 25.
MONARCH. Large bright red wedge-shaped fruit, flesh firm. 13/- per 100, 7/6 per 50, 5/- per 25.
PRESIDENT. Great cropper, colour crimson, superior. 13/- per 100, 7/6 per 50, 5/- per 25.
RELIANCE. A fine firm fleshed medium maincrop. 13/- per 100, 7 6 per 50, 5/- per 25.
ROYAL SOVEREIGN. The best early variety, the best for pot culture. 13/- per 100, 7/6 per 50, 5/- per 25.
SIR JOSEPH PAXTON. Hardy early variety. The sweetest and most reliable Strawberry grown. 13/- per 100, 7 6 per 50, 5/- per 25.
"THE EARL" (Laxton). A much-improved "Vicomtess H. de Thury," larger in size of fruit, and more vigorous and free cropping in habit; the flavour is very rich yet juicy. 15/- per 100, 8 6 per 50, 5 6 per 25.
THE ADMIRAL. Maincrop, fine flavour, bright red, good grower. 15/- per 100, 8 6 per 50, 5 6 per 25.
THE DUKE. A really good early variety; it forces well, fruit oval, medium size, good flavour. 20/- per 100, 4/- per doz.

RASPBERRIES.

PERFECTION.

Ground intended for these should be deeply trenched and heavily manured. The canes should be planted (not too deeply) about 2 feet apart and the rows should be 5 or 6 ft. apart, and after planting, a mulching of well-decayed manure should be placed on the surface. Newly planted canes should be cut back to 2 feet to encourage the formation of suckers for the following season.

BAUMFORTH'S SEEDLING. A fine variety, fruit very large, of the most beautiful crimson colour; an abundant bearer of good habit.
30/- per 100; 4/- per doz.
HAILSHAM. A new Autumn fruiting Raspberry; the fruit is very large, of a rich crimson colour and excellent flavour; strong grower and heavy bearer. 48/- per 100; 6/- per doz.
HORNET (Rivers). A very fine Raspberry, fruit deliciously flavoured, and the most juicy of any variety. A splendid cropper, and will be largely grown when better known.
37/6 per 100; 5/- per doz.
PERFECTION. It is an exceptionally strong grower and makes a better plant the first year than any other variety. It is a good cropper, producing fruit from base to top of cane of a bold size, firm, flesh, arduous flavour, and brilliant scarlet colour, the high colour being retained even when the fruit is fully ripe.
30/- per 100; 4/- per doz.
PYNE'S ROYAL. A grand new Raspberry, the largest in cultivation. It is a strong and upright grower, quite distinct in habit and foliage; the canes are strong and sturdy and of most robust constitution. The fruit is borne on short trusses on which they are very thickly set. A limited number of plants only. 2/6 each; 27/6 per doz.
SUPERLATIVE. Fruit very large, mostly freely produced; an excellent variety.
30/- per 100; 4/- per doz.
THE DEVON. Grand new Raspberry, growth most robust; trusses have been found to carry as many as sixty fruits; an enormous cropper, brings all its fruit up to a large size. For jam making and bottling it is of the highest value.
1/- each; 10 6 per doz.
WHITE ANTWERP . . 37/6 per 100; 5/- per doz.

QUINCE.

Standards 7,6 each.

WALNUTS.

ROYAL EARLY FRUITING. These have already fruited two years, and will grow and fruit well in a small garden. It is a soft skinned variety. The trees are about 8 feet. 15/- each.
Fine Standards 10/6 and 12/6 each.

From Mr. J. T. GARTON, Dream.
Dec. 9th.
"I am glad to tell you I was very pleased with the Raspberry Canes and Gooseberries which I had from you last year."

COLLECTIONS OF CHOICE ROSES.

The Hybrid Tea Roses named in the following list are by far the most beautiful and useful for general cultivation in the Garden or for Table decoration or Exhibition. They commence blooming early in June and continue to furnish some fine bloom to the end of October. We have a fine collection of these, in good strong, healthy and well-grown plants, and would also draw attention to our fine stock of Climbing, Pillar, and other Roses. We beg to point out that in reducing our number of varieties we have eliminated only the older and less popular sorts.

MRS. WEMYSS-QUIN.

We anticipate a very heavy demand for all the choicer Roses this season, and to prevent disappointment, strongly advise our customers to send us their orders as soon as convenient after receiving this Catalogue.

The "NORWICH" Collection of
12 New and Good Bush Roses 24/-
Packed and Carriage Paid.

BETTY. Coppery rose.
DAILY MAIL. Shrimp pink.
GORGEOUS. Deep orange yellow.
HADLEY. Dark crimson.
LADY HILLINGDON. Yellow.
MADAME A. CHATENAY. Bright carmine rose.
MRS. H. STEVENS. White.
MRS. W. QUIN. Deep canary yellow.
M. D. HAMILL. Straw colour.
MME. M. SOUPERT. Pale saffron.
OPHELIA. Salmon-flesh.
RAYON D'OR. Pure yellow.

From Mr. W. BOUCHEN, Kelvedon.
January 22nd.
"Your Rose Bushes I received from you have turned out excellent."

MRS. CHAS. RUSSELL.

LIST OF STANDARD & HALF-STANDARD ROSES

Standards 7/- each, 75/- doz. Only a limited number of Half-Standards 6/- each, 65/- doz.

Please note we cannot supply any varieties other than those listed below. In ordering from the following list please give a few alternative names, to be sent in case of our being sold out of those first named.

COUNTESS CLANWILLIAM. Delicate peach.
DEAN HOLE. Silvery carmine.
FRAU K. DRUSCHKI. Pure white.
GEN. McARTHUR. Dark velvety scarlet.
GEORGE DICKSON. Velvety black crimson.
GOLDEN EMBLEM. Pure yellow.
GORGEOUS. Coppery fawn.
JULIET. Old gold.

LADY ASHTOWN. Pale rose.
LADY HILLINGDON. Fine golden yellow.
LYON. Salmon pink.
MARGT. DICKSON HAMILL. Straw coloured.
MADAME A. CHATENAY. Bright carmine rose.
MADAME E. HERRIOT. Coral red.
MADAME M. SOUPERT. Saffron yellow.
MRS. A. R. WADDELL. Reddish salmon.

MRS. G. MARRIOTT. Deep cream.
MRS. J. LAING. Soft pink.
MRS. W. QUIN. Deep canary yellow.
OPHELIA. Salmon-flesh.
RICHMOND. Scarlet.
SUNBURST. Yellow.
WHITE KILLARNEY.

MISCELLANEOUS ROSES.

MOSS ROSES, &c.
BLANCHE MOREAU. Perpetual, pure white, in clusters, well mossed.
CRIMSON GLOBE (HYBRID MOSS). Buds nicely mossed, flowers deep crimson, large, full, and globular, very vigorous.
COMMON MOSS. Rosy blush.
CRESTED. Rose, beautiful.
ZENOBIA. Satin rose, well mossed.

PROVENCE OR CABBAGE ROSES—
OLD PROVENCE. Rose colour, fragrant.
WHITE PROVENCE. White, beautiful.
The above varieties 2/- each.

HYBRID SWEET BRIAR.
ANNE OF GIERSTEIN. Dark crimson.
BRENDA. Maiden's blush, peach, dainty colour.
FLORA McIVOR. Pure white, blushed with rose.
LADY PENZANCE. Beautiful soft tint of copper.
LORD PENZANCE. Soft shade of fawn, yellow in centre.
MEG MERRILEES. Gorgeous crimson, very free flowering.
ROSE BRADWARDINE. Beautiful clear rose.
The above varieties 2/- each ; 22/- doz.

CHINA ROSES AND AUSTRIAN BRIARS.
AUSTRIAN COPPER. Distinct and beautiful, golden terra-cotta colour, flowers single. 2/6 each.
HERMOSA. Similar to Common China but more double, very effective. 2/- each.
PERSIAN YELLOW. The deepest yellow, fairly full bloom, the most double of this class. 2/6 each.

LADY HILLINGDON.

From A. GOODLET, Esq., Acton Hill, W.3.
October 31st.
"The Roses ordered from you have been safely received. They are in splendid condition and of first-class quality."

ROSES—TEA-SCENTED AND NOISETTE.
This beautiful class is distinguished by the peculiar and delightful fragrance of the flowers and the many charming tints and shades of yellow, rose and salmon colour, not to be found amongst the Hybrid Perpetuals. The individual blooms are of exquisite form, and invaluable for button-hole or bouquets. They are especially suited for pot culture in the conservatory. The following prices are for plants from the open ground.

GLOIRE DE DIJON. Yellow, shaded salmon, large, full, superb; one of the hardiest and best. 2/6 each.
HARRY KIRK. Deep sulphur yellow, passing to lighter shade. 2/6 each.
LADY HILLINGDON (T). Fine golden yellow novelty, a cross between Papa Gontier and Lady Roberts, with long pointed buds, producing a glorious effect. 2/6 each.
LADY ROBERTS. Rich apricot, shaded pale orange, buds long pointed, blooms large and of perfect form. 2/6 each.
MARECHAL NIEL (Noisette). Rich deep yellow, large, full and of perfect form; the petals are extra large, and of good substance, very sweet; a truly magnificent Rose. 2/6 ea.
MELODY. Deep canary yellow changing to primrose at the edge of the petals, fine full rose. 2/6 each.
MRS. HERBERT STEVENS (T). A hardy variety, faultless in shape and form, a flower of exquisite grace and refinement, colour white. 2/6 each.
MRS. PETER BLAIR. Lemon chrome, with golden yellow centre, lovely shape, deliciously perfumed. 2/6 each.
WILLIAM ALLEN RICHARDSON (Noisette). Fine deep orange yellow, very showy, and pretty for cutting. 2/6 each.

HYBRID PERPETUAL AND OTHER ROSES.
General List of New and Select Varieties.

In ordering from the following List, please give a few alternative names, to be sent in case of our being sold out of those first named.

GORGEOUS.

MISS WILLMOTT.

AUTUMN TINTS (H.T.). Coppery red, shaded orange and salmon. 2/6 each.
BESSIE BROWN (H.T.). Creamy white; the blooms are perfectly formed and of large size; highly perfumed. 2/6 each.
BETTY (H.T.). Coppery rose, overspread with golden yellow, perfectly formed flowers, a continuous bloomer. 2/6 each.
CAPTAIN GEORGE DESSIRIER (new) (H.T.). Vigorous grower of spreading habit, large full flower, globular, beautiful shell red shaded with crimson and fiery-red. Bushes 7/6 each.
CAROLINE TESTOUT (H.T.). Bright satiny rose, with brighter centre, large, full, and globular, very free. 2/- each.
CHAMELEON (new) (H.T.). Outside petals rosy pink, centre shrimp pink, edges of petals limblatol; a fine rose. 3/6 each.
CHRISTINE (new) (H.T.). The deepest and clearest yellow yet seen. Gold Medal. 3/6 ea.
COLUMBIA (new) (H.T.). Flower true pink, deepening as it opens to glowing pink, produced on stiff stems; very fragrant. Bushes 7/6 each.
COVENT GARDEN (new) (H.T.). Rich deep crimson, well formed flowers on stout stems, glossy and mildew proof foliage, very free and late bloomer. Bushes 5/- each.
CONSTANCE. A very fine variety, colour clear cadmium yellow, large exhibition flowers. 2/6 each.
COUNTESS CLANWILLIAM. Delicate peach, pink at base of petals, edged with deep cherry red. 2/6 each.
CUPID (new) (H.T.). Colour glowing flesh, single. Ground plant. 2/6 each.
EDITH CAVELL (new) (H.T.). A splendid variety for exhibition purposes, colour opening white tinged with cream, base of petals pale yellow, long pointed buds, robust grower. Ground plants. 3/6 each.
FLORENCE FORRESTER. Clear snow white, with lemon tinge, large, sweet-scented; the best white for exhibition. 2/6 each.
FRANKLIN (new) (H.T.). A fine bedding rose of the type of Lady Roberts, very free flowering, long pointed buds, colour salmon pink, with deeper apricot shadings. Bushes 5/6 each.
FRAU KARL DRUSCHKI (H.P.). Flowers large, perfectly formed, pure white. 2/- each.
FRIEBURG (new) (H.T.). Great well-shaped flowers of a lovely rose pink on the outside of the petals, and nearly straw white on the inner side. Bushes 7/6 each.
GEORGE C. WAUD (H.T.). Glowing orange vermillion that does not fade, flowers large and full, with high pointed centre. 3/6 each.
GOLDEN EMBLEM (new) (H.T.). A great improvement on Rayon d'Or, the colour being deeper and richer, with larger and more perfect blooms. It even surpasses the well-known favourite "Marechal Niel"; the habit of growth is splendid; it is mildew proof, very sweetly scented. Bushes only 3/- each.

GOLDEN OPHELIA (H.T.). A seedling from the well-known and justly admired variety Ophelia. The blooms are borne on a very stout upright stem of a good size, opening in perfect form, golden yellow in centre, paling slightly towards the outer petals. Strong plants 3/6 each.
GORGEOUS (new) (H.T.). Deep orange yellow flushed coppery yellow; a very beautiful variety. Bushes only. 2/6 each.
HADLEY (H.T.). A grand crimson, very free flowering and highly decorative. 2/6 each.
HENRIETTE (H.T.). Fiery orange crimson to soft coral salmon, shaded at base with glowing orange. Strong plants. 2/6 each.
HOOSIER BEAUTY. Glowing crimson with darker shading, exceedingly free. 2/6 each.
H. V. MACHIN (new). Scarlet crimson, very fine, large, full, well-formed flowers, with high pointed centre. 2/6 each.
ISOBEL (new). The most beautiful single rose in cultivation. It is carmine red flushed orange-scarlet, with a faint Austrian copper shading. Gold Medal. 2/6 each.
JULIET. Outside petals old gold, interior rich rosy red, base of petals deep yellow; large flowers, distinct. 2/- each.
KILLARNEY (H.T.). Flesh colour, shaded white, and suffused pale pink. 2/- each.
☞ **KILLARNEY BRILLIANT.** Deep rosy red, very large flowers; a fine rose. 2/6 each.
LOS ANGELOS (new) (H.T.). A very fine improvement on Lyon Rose, a much better grower and bloomer, colour flame pink shaded to yellow toned with salmon. Bushes 3/6 each.
LOUISE BALDWIN (now) (H.T.). Rich orange with soft apricot shading over the entire petal, a beautiful even colour, a big advance on all roses of the "Lady Hillington" type; very sweetly scented. Bushes only, 5/- each.
MADAME ABEL CHATENAY (H.T.). Bright carmine rose shaded to deep salmon; long pointed full-sized flowers. 2/6 each.
☞ **MADAME EDOUARD HERRIOT** (Daily Mail Rose). A very vigorous grower, quite hardy, coral red bud shaded with yellow on the base. 2/6 each.
MADAME MELANIE SOUPERT (H.T.). Colour pale saffron yellow, suffused with pink and carmine. 2/6 each.
MADAME RAVARY (H.T.). Golden yellow, shaded orange; a continuous bloomer and splendid bedder. 2/6.
☞ **MARGARET DICKSON HAMILL** (new) (H.T.). Straw-coloured, edged and flushed with delicate carmine. 2/6 each.
☞ **MILDRED GRANT** (new) (H.T.). Ivory white flushed with pale peach. 2/6 each.
MISS MAY MARRIOTT (H.T.). Sport from Daily Mail, colour a beautiful terra-cotta, sweetly scented and a strong grower. 2/6 each.
MISS WILLMOTT (H.T.). Colour soft sulphury cream with the faintest flush towards the edges, in shape and form this rose is a model of perfection. 2/6 each.
MOLLY SHARMAN CRAWFORD (T.). Beautiful continual white in the bud stage, and as the flower develops it is satiny white. 2/6 each.
MRS. A. R. WADDELL (H.T.). Rosy apricot, bud opening reddish salmon. 2/6 each.
☞ **MRS. CHARLES E. PEARSON** (H.T.) Orange, flushed red, apricot and fawn, a delightful combination of colour. 2/6 each.
☞ **MRS. CHAS. E. RUSSELL** (H.T.). Rose-carmine, with centre of rose-scarlet, fragrant; a large flower of good form. 2/6 each.
MRS. C. E. SHEA (new) (H.T.). Brilliant madder-red, shot with a glowing scarlet. Splendid garden rose. Bushes only, 2/6 each.
MRS. J. LAING (H.P.). Flowers large and finely shaped a beautiful soft pink. 2/- each.
MRS. BULLEN (H.B.). Colour cochineal carmine shaded with yellow, passing to carmine lake; a bright colour, and good bedder. 2/6 each.
MRS. C. V. HAWORTH (new) (H.T.). A beautiful decorative rose, colour a lovely combination of pink, orange and yellow. Bushes 3/6 each.
MRS. GEORGE MARRIOTT (H.T.). The colour is a deep cream and pearl, pencilled and suffused rose and vermilion, sweetly scented. 2/6 each.
MRS. HENRY BALFOUR (new). A strong grower, branching habit, a greatly improved Mme. de Watteville; free from mildew; colour flesh pink, edges of petals deep pink. Gold Medal N.R.S. Bushes 3/6 each.

MRS. HENRY MORSE (new) (H.T.). The most perfect in shape and form, a very free bloomer and grower. The whole flower has a clear sheen of bright rose deeply impregnated and washed vermilion veining on petals; the largest and most pointed of all roses; sweetly scented. Gold Medal N.R.S. Bushes only, 7/6 each.
MRS. REDFORD (new) (H.T.). Colour bright apricot orange, far the most striking variety in this lovely and pleasing tone of colour; a fine upright grower, foliage holly-like and mildew proof, and as perfect in shape and form as A. K. Williams; very free and sweetly scented. Bushes only, 7/6 each.
MRS. W. J. GRANT (H.T.). Imperial pink, flowers borne on good stems. 2/6 each.
MRS. WEMYSS QUIN (H.T.). Intense lemon chrome. Absolutely distinct. 2/6 each.
NELLIE PARKER (new). Pale creamy white with deeper centre flushed with blush at the tips of petals, very large and good. Gold Medal R.H.S. Bushes only, 2/6 each.
☞ **OLD GOLD** (H.T.). Vivid reddish orange with copper apricot shadings. 2/6 each.
☞ **OPHELIA** (H.T.). Salmon-flesh shaded with rose, large and of perfect shape. 2/6 each.
PHARISAER (H.T.). Rosy white shaded salmon, bud long, well-formed flower, growth vigorous. 2/- each.
☞ **PRINCESS MARY** (new) (H.T.). Single deep crimson-scarlet with bright yellow anthers; free flowering. 2/6 each.
PRESIDENT BOUCHE (Tertotiana). Coral red with rose, very large full rose. 2/6 each.
☞ **QUEEN MARY** (H.T.). Flowers medium size, fine form, colour lemon chrome, bordered deep carmine. 2/6 each.
RAYON D'OR (Pernetiana). Pure yellow resembling Persian Yellow; the buds are orange yellow with crimson flush, the flower is clear yellow. 2/6 each.
SOUVENIR DE GEORGE BECKWITH (Pernetiana) (new). Very large full globular flowers on stiff stems, colour shrimp pink, tinted chrome yellow with deeper yellow at base of petals. Bushes 7/6 each.
SUNBURST (H.T.). Long pointed bud; flower cupped form; yellow with orange-yellow centre. 2/6 each.
THE QUEEN ALEXANDRA (new) (H.T.). A startlingly brilliant flower of intense vermilion colour, deeply shaded old gold on reverse of petals, which fades to pure orange at base. Ground plants, 5/- each.
WHITE KILLARNEY (H.T.). A pure white sport from the well-known old pink. 2/6 each.
☞ **WILLOWMERE** (Pernetiana). A rich shrimp pink shaded yellow in the centre. 2/6 each.
W. C. GAUNT (H.T.). Brilliant vermilion, tipped scarlet and intensified by the deep crimson maroon reverse. Ground plants. 2/6 each.

CLIMBING, PILLAR AND WEEPING ROSES.

The following list of Climbing Roses includes the most beautiful and useful sorts in cultivation.

STANDARD WEEPING ROSE,

AMERICAN PILLAR. Very strong climbing Rose ; a lovely rose-pink colour. Vigorous.
AVIATEUR BLERIOT. Saffron yellow flowers, in clusters, very fine.
BLUSH RAMBLER. Beautiful soft blush.
CLIMBING DEVONIENSIS. Flowers creamy white with blush centre deliciously scented.
CLIMBING LADY HILLINGDON. A fine golden yellow variety of fairly good growth, glossy green foliage. 3/6 each.
CLIMBING RICHMOND. Pure bright scarlet, very free-flowering.
CRIMSON RAMBLER. A splendid free-growing variety, with bright glossy green foliage, and large pyramidal trusses of bright crimson flowers.
DOROTHY PERKINS (Hybrid Wichuriana). Clear soft pink flowers in large clusters, very fragrant and lasting.
EMILY GRAY. The finest golden Wichuriana Climbing Rose yet introduced.
EXCELSA. The Red Dorothy Perkins. This is without doubt the prince of Ramblers ; it is equally as brilliant as Hiawatha.
GOLDFINCH. Large clusters of yellow flowers.
HIAWATHA. Seedling from Crimson Rambler. Flowers are single, deep crimson, shading to white at base of petals.
LADY GAY (Wichuriana). A brilliant and lovely shade of rose-pink.
MADAME ALFRED CARRIERE. Pure white, sweetly scented, vigorous grower.
MARECHAL NIEL (Noisette). Beautiful golden yellow of lovely form and delicious fragrance.
MINNEHAHA (Wichuriana). Deep rose, very double flowers produced in small panicles, very large trusses ; extra fine.
MONSIEUR DESIR. Velvety crimson, shaded with violet, large and double good dark climber.
PAUL'S SCARLET CLIMBER (new). Flowers vivid scarlet shaded with crimson ; of strong climbing habit, with bright shiny foliage, flowering in great profusion, very large clusters, good sized semi-double blossoms, extra fine for Pillars and Pergolas.
WHITE DOROTHY PERKINS. A white sport from the well-known Dorothy Perkins, the same style of flower but pure white.
WILLIAM ALLEN RICHARDSON (Noisette). Fine deep orange yellow, very showy.

Plants from the open ground 2 6 each.

STANDARD WEEPING ROSES.

The varieties named below can be supplied on tall Standards. These are the very best and most suitable varieties for this purpose. All who have seen these charming subjects will at once acclaim their worth.

ALBERIC BARBIER.   GOLDFINCH.
AMERICAN PILLAR.   HIAWATHA.
AVIATEUR BLERIOT.   LADY GAY.
CRIMSON RAMBLER.   MINNEHAHA.
EMILY GRAY.   PAUL'S SCARLET.
EXCELSA.

4 to 5 feet stems, 10,6 each.

CLIMBING ROSES (in pots).

We have a very fine lot of Climbing Roses in 6-inch pots, with shoots 6 to 8 ft. long, to bloom this season, of the following popular varieties.

AMERICAN PILLAR. Single, rosy pink. 5/- ea.
CLIMBING NIPHETOS. Pure white. 5/- & 7/6 ea.
CRIMSON RAMBLER. Bright crimson. 5/- ea.
DOROTHY PERKINS. Clear soft pink. 5/- ea.
EMILY GRAY (new). The finest golden Wichuriana Climbing Rose yet introduced, bright glossy foliage, flowers as rich and almost as large as Madame Ravary, which is a beautiful orange yellow. Ground plants, 3/6 ; strong plants in pots, to bloom next season. 5/- and 7/6 each.

EXCELSA. Red Dorothy Perkins. 5/- each.
GLOIRE DE DIJON (T.). Buff, orange centre. 5/- and 7/6 each.
GOLDFINCH. Large clusters of yellow flowers. 5/- each.
HIAWATHA. Single, deep crimson, shading to white at base of petals. 5/- each.
MARECHAL NIEL. Beautiful golden yellow of lovely form and delicious fragrance. 5/- and 7/6 each.

MINNEHAHA (Wichuriana). Deep rose, very double flowers ; extra fine. 5/- each.
PAUL'S SCARLET. Vivid scarlet shaded with crimson. 5/- each.
PEMBERTON'S WHITE. Pure paper white. 5/- each.
WHITE DOROTHY PERKINS. A white sport from the well-known Dorothy Perkins. 5/- ea.
W. A. RICHARDSON (Noisette). Fine deep orange yellow. 5/- and 7/6 each.

HINTS ON CULTIVATION.

In planting Roses, select, if possible, an open situation, where they get the full benefit of sun and air, and at the same time are sheltered from strong winds.

Roses will thrive in any good garden soil, but they have a decided preference for loamy clay ; where the soil is heavy, a moderate dressing of coal ashes or coarse sandy grit will improve it, and if too wet drainage must be provided. November is the best month for planting, but this may be done in any favourable weather during the Winter months. In planting, make a good-sized hole, taking care to plant firmly ; dwarfs should be planted with the juncture of their stems below the surface, and standards should be firmly staked and tied to prevent their disturbance by the wind.

To ensure a vigorous growth and fine blooms, freshly planted, and indeed all hybrid perpetual and other outdoor Roses, should be closely pruned about the early part of March, or later according to season. When the leaf-buds begin to expand carefully thin out all weak-growing shoots or wood from the middle of the plant, and prune down the main stems to two or three eyes or buds on each stem.

A good top-dressing of well-decayed manure should be laid on the beds in Autumn, and may be lightly dug in in Spring. If the weather is dry when the plants are coming into bloom, give liberal waterings two or three times a week, and if fine blooms are desired for exhibition the buds should be thinned out, and liquid manure may be given freely once or twice a week.

Early in the season, when growth has fairly commenced, caterpillars should be carefully looked after and picked off by hand, and if the plants later on are attacked by green-fly, they should be syringed at night with Quassia Extract.

HARDY ORNAMENTAL TREES AND SHRUBS.

As we anticipated, last Spring we experienced a great demand for all kinds of Ornamental Trees and Shrubs for refurnishing the gardens and pleasure grounds which had perforce been neglected during the war.

The coming Season will doubtless see a continuance of this work, and we have made ample preparations for supplying the needs of our customers in this important department of our business.

So much depends on the work of planting Trees and Shrubs which have been regularly transplanted, and here we are able to say that the whole of our large stock of Trees has been transplanted during the past two years; we can therefore with confidence ask intending planters to place their orders in our hands.

During the past twenty years many most beautiful subjects have been added to the list of Flowering and Ornamental Trees, and in the following pages all the most charming subjects are included.

ACACIA INERMIS (Mop-headed Acacia). A magnificent circular head of handsome foliage for street planting, avenues, etc. A most attractive tree. Standards 10/6 each.
ACER (Maple). **COLCHICUM RUBRUM.** Very soft red-coloured leaves. Height 8 ft. 3/6 ea.
  ,, **DRUMMONDI.** Beautiful silver variegated leaves. Height 8—10 ft. 5/- each.
  ,, **PLATANOIDES SCHWEDLERI.** Very vigorous grower with leaves of a bright red colour. Height 8 ft. 3/6 each.
  ,, **NEGUNDO CALIFORNICUM AUREUM.** This is a specially good variety, with large, broad golden foliage. Standards, with 3—4 ft. stem, 3/6 each.
  ,, **ALBA VARIEGATA.** Silver, Leaf beautifully variegated. Pyramids, 3—4 ft. 3/- each. Standards 5/- each.
ALMOND (Prunus Amygdalus). Fine rosy flowers produced in great profusion, which are the first to greet us in the Spring. Standards 5 ea.
ANDROMEDA FLORIBUNDA. Dwarf compact growing shrubs, pure white bell-shaped flowers. Height 15 inches. 3/6 each.
ARBUTUS UNEDO (Strawberry Tree). Beautiful evergreen shrub, bearing an abundance of Strawberry-like fruit in Autumn. 3/6 each.
ASH (Fraxinus). **EXCELSIOR PENDULA** (Weeping). This is a splendid weeping tree. Standards 7/6, 10/6, and 15/- each.
  ,, **GOLDEN LEAVED** (Weeping). 7/6 each.
AUCUBA JAPONICA VARIEGATA. Splendid 1 ft. 3/6 each. Larger specimens 3/6 each.
AZALEA MOLLIS. These are excellent for forcing, or for outdoor planting. Mixed seedlings. Bushy plants well set with buds. Height 18-24 inches 3 - each, 33/- per doz.
  ,, **PONTICA.** Orange yellow, sweetly scented, very free. Height 18 inches 2/6 each, 27/- per doz.
AZARA MICROPHYLLA. A pretty, small-leaved evergreen shrub, covered with orange-red berries in Autumn. Height 2—3 ft. In pots, 3 - each.
BAMBOO (hardy), **AUREA.** Stems yellow, very straight, erect, growing close round the base. 4/6 each.
  ,, **FORTUNEII VARIEGATA.** Beautiful bright green leaves, striated white. 3/- each.
  ,, **JAPONICA** (Bambusa Metake). Dark green, sharply pointed leaves. 3/- each.
  ,, **SIMONII.** Tall, straight, slender stems, runs very freely at the root. 5/- each.
  ,, **NIGRA.** Stems glossy black after the first year. 3/- and 7/6 each.
BAY, SWEET (Laurel Nobilis), Height 2—2½ ft. 3/6 each.
BEECH (Fagus) **ATROPURPUREA.** Height 7—8 ft. 7/6 each.
  ,, **FERN LEAVES.** 7/6 each.
BERBERIS AQUIFOLIA. 1—1½ ft. 6d. each, 5/- per doz. 30/- per 100.
  ,, **DARWINII.** A densely branched evergreen, large yellow flowers. Ht. 2—3 ft. 3/6 each.
  ,, **STENOPHYLLA.** One of the best; very graceful, small evergreen leaf, covered with bright yellow flowers. Ht. 2—3 ft. 3/6 each.
  ,, **WILSONII.** Good hardy shrub of dwarf growth. The foliage is highly coloured in Autumn, and its long spines and coral red berries make it very attractive. Excellent for rockeries. 3/6 each.

From Mr. W. BINNING, Princes Risboro'.
March 17th.
"I was very pleased with the Trees sent."

ROW OF SPECIMEN MOP-HEADED ACACIA GROWING IN OUR NURSERIES.

BERBERIS THUNBERGII. Pretty early blooming species, white flowers; leaves in Autumn are tinted crimson. Height 2—2½ ft. 3/- each.
  ,, **VULGARIS** (Common Barberry). 2—3 ft. 2/- each.
BIRCH (Betula). **SILVER-BARKED.** Most beautiful. Height 9—12 ft. 3/6 and 5/- each.
BOX (Buxus). **JAPONICA AUREA.** A beautiful dwarf-growing variety with richly-coloured golden leaves; one of the best for Winter bedding or as an edging to large beds. 9—12 inches 1/6 each, 18—24 inches 3/- each.
  ,, **HANDSWORTHII.** This is the best of the green varieties of Box, close growing and of erect habit, foliage very broad, dense, and of the deepest green. Height 2—3 ft. 2/6 each, 3—4 ft. 3/6 each. Larger trees 5/- each.
BOX EDGING. One Nursery yard plants 3 yards. 1/6 per Nursery yard.
BROOM (Cytisus). **ANDREANUS.** This is perhaps the most distinct and beautiful Broom yet introduced, it is covered with maroon-crimson and yellow flowers. In pots, 2/6 each.
  ,, **COMMON YELLOW.** In pots, 2/- each.
  ,, **NIGRICANS.** Bright yellow, dwarf, compact habit, free flowering. In pots, 2/6 each.
  ,, **PRAECOX.** A beautiful free-flowering early variety. In pots, 3/- each.
  ,, **PURPUREUS.** In pots, 3/- each.
  ,, **SPANISH.** In pots, 2/- each.
  ,, **WHITE PORTUGAL.** Very free-flowering, one of the best, most effective if planted in a mass. In pots, 2/- each.
BUDDLEA GLOBOSA. Orange globose flowers. 3/- each.
  ,, **VARIBILIS VEITCHII.** In pots, 3/- each.
  ,, **MAGNIFICA.** 3/- each.
CALYCANTHUS (Allspice). Maroon-coloured flowers, very fragrant. Height 3 ft. 3/- each.
  ,, **PRAECOX.** Slender growth, producing in Winter large clusters of fragrant yellow flowers. Hardy, but succeeds best against a wall or in a sheltered position. 3/- each.
CHERRY (Cerasus). **JAMES H. VEITCH.** Said to be the finest variety yet introduced, flowers double rosy pink. Standards 5/- each.
  ,, **RHEXII FLORE PLENA.** Double white Cherry. Dwarf Bush 3/- each. Standards 5/- each.
  ,, **WATERII,** Double Rose. Beautiful rose. 5/- each.
CHIONANTHUS VIRGINIUS (Fringe Tree). Pure white flowers, very fragrant. Height 2 ft. 3/- each.

From Mr. E. KING, Plumstead.
Feb. 21st.
"The Lime Trees and Rose are grand, and I am very pleased with them."

CHOISYA TERNATA. Lovely white sweet-scented flowers. 2/6 and 3/6 each.
CORNUS, MASCULA ELEGANTISSIMA. A most beautiful tree. Dwarfs 5/- each.
  ,, **SPATHII AUREA.** Dwarfs 3/6 each.
COTONEASTER FRIGIDA. This variety makes an excellent hedge, covering itself with berries. Height 3—4 ft. 3/- each, Standards 5/- each.
  ,, **HORIZONTALIS.** Fan shaped, branches suitable for rockeries. Open ground. 2 ft. 2/6 each.
  ,, **MICROPHYLLA.** Fine for rockeries or walls; one of the best. Height 12—18 inches. 3/6 each.
  ,, **SIMONSII.** Tall growing variety, produces quantities of bright scarlet berries. 2—3 ft. 3/- each.
CYTISUS DALLIMOREII. 5/- each.
  ,, **PENDULA PURPUREA.** Rosy purple pea-shaped flowers. 5/- each.
DAPHNE MEZERUM. Fragrant purple flowers early in Spring, whilst quite leafless. 3/6 each.
  ,, **ALBUM.** Similar to above, but pure white and deliciously fragrant. 3/6 each.
DEUTZIA CRENATA. Single white, flowering during June and July. 2/- each.
  ,, **FL.** Beautiful double rose-coloured flowers. 2/- each.
  ,, **GRACILIS.** Pure white flowers, most useful for forcing. 2/- each.
  ,, **LEMOINEI.** Beautiful white variety. 2/- ea.
  ,, **SCABRA.** 2/- each.
DIPLOPAPPUS CHRYSOPHYLLUS. Nice deep yellow heath-like foliage, beautiful in Winter. Height 1 ft. 1/6 each.
ELDER (Sambucus). **GOLDEN LEAVED.** Height 2—3 ft. 1/6 each.
  ,, **SERRATIFOLIA FOLIUS AUREUS.** Magnificent fern-like leaf, bright golden in colour. Height 3 ft. 3/6 each.
ELM (Ulmus). **CAMPESTRIS, OR ENGLISH.** These are beautiful grafted trees, and splendid for parks or avenues. Height 7—8 ft. 2/6 each, 27/6 per doz.
  ,, **LOUIS VAN HOUTTE.** Golden. Standards 5/- each.
  ,, **CAMPESTRIS WEEPING.** The true Umbrella Elm, an excellent weeping variety, specially adapted for planting as specimens on lawns, or in public parks and cemeteries. 15/- each.
  ,, **DAMPIERI AUREA.** This is a splendid Golden Elm in habit and growth and colour. Height 3—8 ft. 5/- each.
  ,, **AUREA ROSSELSII.** A beautiful golden variety. 5/- each.
  ,, **WHEATLEYII.** A good Elm of upright growth. Height 10 ft. 3/6 each, 40/- per doz., 12 ft. 5/- each.

From Messrs. POWELL & SONS, Cardiff.
Dec. 16th.
"I received the Trees in excellent condition, and I was very pleased with them."

Hardy Ornamental Trees and Shrubs (*continued*).

BERBERIS AQUIFOLIA.

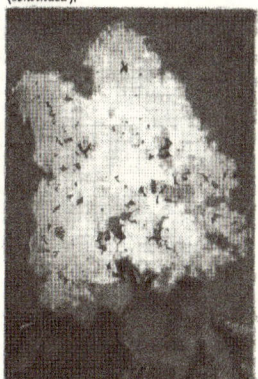

LILAC.

ERICA ALPORTII. The best crimson. 1/6 each, 15/- per doz.
" **CARNEA.** Abundance of reddish flesh-coloured flowers in March and April. 1/6 each, 15/- per doz.
" **ALBA.** White variety of the proceeding. 1/6 each, 15/- per doz.
" **HAMMONDII.** The lucky White Heath. 1/6 each, 15/- per doz.
ESCALLONIA MACRANTHA. Fine for seaside planting, beautiful foliage, covered with red flowers. In pots, 3/6 each.
" **INGRAMII.** Of erect growth, pink flowers. In pots, 2/6 each.
LANGLEYENSIS. Long slender branches, producing numerous small branches, each bearing flowers of a bright rose carmine colour, with dark lustrous oval green leaves. 2/6 each.
EUONYMUS EUROPÆUS (Spindle Tree). Very pretty in the Autumn when the fruit is ripe. Height 2—3 ft. 2/- each.
" **JAPONICUS.** Green leaf variety. Height 1½—2 ft. 2/6 each.
" " Gold variegated. 18 inches 2/- each.
FORSYTHIA SUSPENSA. Suitable for wall or rockwork, flowers very early. 2/- each.
" **FORTUNEI.** 2/- each.
" **VIRIDISSIMA.** 2/- each.
FUCHSIA RICCARTONI. One of the hardiest and prettiest of outdoor kinds. 1/- each, 10/6 per doz.
GENISTA HISPANICA (Spanish Gorse). Very free-flowering hardy shrub, flowers pale yellow. 2/- each.
GORSE (Ulex) **EUROPÆUS.** Double. In pots, 2/6 each.
GUM CISTUS (Cistus Ladaniferus). A handsome shrub, growing to about 4 ft. In pots, 2/6 each.
HALESIA TETRAPTERA (Snowdrop Tree). Pure white drooping flowers, somewhat resembling the Snowdrop. Height 3 ft. 3/6 each.
HAMAMELIS VIRGINICA (Wych Hazel). One of the most conspicuous of hardy winter flowering shrubs, gives a charming effect if several plants are massed together. It blooms from December to February, the branches being studded with bright yellow spider-like flowers. Height 3 ft. 3/6 each.
HAZEL, PURPLE LEAVED. Fine broad-leaved variety. 2/6 each.
HIBISCUS SYRIACUS. A useful late flowering shrub, flowers varying from pure white to mauve and blue. Height 2—3½ ft. 2/6 each.
HOLLY, ARGENTEA MARGINATA. Broad-leaved, silver, free grower and hardy. Height 2—3 ft. 7/6 each.
" **REGINA** (Silver Queen). 2½—3 ft. 7/6 ea.
" **GOLDEN QUEEN.** Height 2½—3 ft. 7/6 ea.
" **FRUCTO LUTEA.** Golden-fruited Holly. Height 1½—2 ft. 7/6 each.

HORSE CHESTNUT (Æsculus). **SCARLET.** Splendid subject for avenues or for planting as park specimens. Height 9 ft. 3/6 each. Specimen trees, 5/- each.
" **DOUBLE WHITE.** 7ft. 8 ft. 5/- each.
HYDRANGEA PANICULATA GRANDIFLORA. This is a beautiful plant and quite hardy, producing great drooping panicles of white flowers. 2—3 ft. 2/6 each.
JUDAS TREE (Cercis). Very ornamental and distinct in leaf and flowers. Height 2—3 ft. 1/6 each.
KERRIA JAPONICA. Very pretty yellow shrub, free flowering. 2/6 each.
" **FLORA PLENA.** A double variety of the above. 2/6 each.
" **VARIEGATA.** 2/- each.
LABURNUM ADAMI (Purple). Height 3 ft. 5/- each. Distinct yellow flowers. Bush
" **VOSSII.** plants 2/6 each. Standards 5/- each.
LAVENDER, COMMON (Lavandula). 9d. each, 8/- per doz, per 100 60.-
LAUREL (Laurus). **CAUCASICA.** Rich green foliage. Height 2—3 ft. 1/6 each, 15/- per dox.
" **COLCHICA.** One of the best varieties for the seaside. Height 2—3 ft. 1/6 each, 15/- doz.
" **LATIFOLIA.** Fine broad-leaved variety. Height 3—4 ft. 2/- each, 21/- per doz.
" **ROTUNDIFOLIA.** Height 1½—2 ft. 1/6 each.
" **PORTUGAL** (Lusitanica). Height 3—4 ft. 3/6 each. Clipped specimens, 7/6 each.
LAURUSTINUS. Height 2 ft. 2/6 each.
LILAC (Syringa) **ALBA.** The common single white Lilac. Height 3—4 ft. 2/6 each.
" **CHARLES X.** Single deep purple Lilac, extra fine trusses. 3/6 each.
" **MADAME CASIMIR PERIER.** Double creamy white, extra good flower. Height 3 ft. 3/6 each.
" **MADAME LEMOINE.** Double, compact, spike of the purest white. 4 ft. 3/6 each.
" **MARIE LEGRAYE.** Single white, very large flowers. 2—3 ft. 3/6 each.
" **MICHAEL BUCKNER.** Rosy lilac, double, compact spike. 2—3 ft. 3/6 each.
" **VULGARIS.** The common single purple Lilac. Height 3 ft. 1/- each, 9—4ft. 3/6 each.
LILACS. Standards in variety. 4 ft. Stems 5/- each.
LIMES, Red Twigged, from Layers. Standards 2/- each, and 7/6 each.
LIQUIDAMBAR STYRACIFLUA (Sweet Gum). Leaves very fragrant, and thrives well on damp situations, requires close pruning, flowers freely when established. Height 3—4 ft. 5/- each, 6—8 ft. 5/- each.

HOLLY.

MAPLES, JAPANESE (Acer), **ATRO-PURPUREA.** In pots, 7/6 and 10/6 each.
" **NORWAY PLATANOIDES.** This is a beautiful tree, very effective. Height 8—10 ft. 3/6 each.
" **FOLIUS AUREUS.** A beautiful type of Golden Norway Maple. Dwarfs 3 - each. Standards 5/- each.
" **SCHWEDLERI.** Leaves bronzy-purple, becoming as they mature a purplish green. Standards 5/- each.
MAGNOLIA CONSPICUA. White, reverse of petals suffused with purple. Height 2 ft. 7/6 ea.
" **GRANDIFLORA** (Evergreen). Large white flowers and very fragrant, requires a south aspect. In pots, 2—3 ft. 8/6 and 10/6 each.
" **SOULANGEANA.** Very fine sweetly-scented variety, bearing purplish tinted flowers with white centre. Height 3 ft. 7/6 each.
MOCK ORANGE (Philadelphus). **AVALANCHE.** Very free flowering, sweetly scented. 1/6 ea.
" **CORONARIUS.** Useful for shrubberies; flowers freely. 2—4 ft. 1/6 each.
" **FLORA PLENA.** Large double white flowers. 2—4 ft. 2 - each.
" **LEMOINEI.** Garden Hybrid. 2—4 ft. 1/6 ea.
" **BOULE D'ARGENT.** Dwarf habit, flowers very large. 2—3 ft. 2/6 each.
" **GERBE DE NEIGE.** Very large white flowers and sweetly scented. 2—3 ft. 2 - each.
MOUNTAIN ASH. Standards 8—10 ft. 3/6 ea.
OAK, COCCINEA (Scarlet Oak). The Scarlet Oak is one of the finest of our ornamental trees, the Autumn tints of the foliage being simply gorgeous. Height 8 ft. 3/6 each.
" **ILEX** (Evergreen). Grown specially in pots. Height 3—4 ft. 5/- each, 4—5 ft. 7/6 each.
OLEARIA HAASTII. A dwarf evergreen smoke-resisting shrub, covering itself with masses of grey bloom, fragrant and lasting a considerable time. Perfectly hardy. Height 12—18 inches. 2/- each.
OSMANTHUS ILLICIFOLIUS. Height 1½—2 ft. 2/- each.
PLANE, LONDON. This is a splendid tree for street planting. Height 8—10 ft. 5 - each. Specimens, extra good heads, 7/6 each.
POPLAR TREMULA, WEEPING. A very fine tree for lawns. 7/6 each.
PRIVET, JAPONICUM. Large, broad, shining green foliage. Height 2—3 ft. 3/6 each.
" **OVALIFOLIUM FOLIUS AUREUS** (Golden-Leaved Privet). This is the most showy hardy plant extant; foliage broadly margined with bright gold; useful alike for hedges, or for planting singly in borders it cannot be surpassed. Height 2—3 ft. 3/- each, 33/- per doz. Selected Standards 3/6 and 5/- each.

Hardy Ornamental Trees and Shrubs *(continued)*.

PRUNUS PISSARDI (Purple Leaf Plum). A handsome foliage tree with white flowers, quite hardy. Bushes 3—4 ft. 3/- each. Standards 5 ft. stems and good heads, 3/6 ea.

PYRUS FLORIBUNDA. Dwarfs 4—5 ft. 2/6 each. Standards 6—7 ft. 6 6 each.
" " **ATROSANGUINEA.** Pyramids 5—6 ft. 2/- each. Standards 5/- each.
" **MALUS, SIBERIAN Crab, Red,** 3/6 each.
" " **DARTMOUTH. Crab.** Very fine. Standards 6 6 each.
" **JOHN DOWNIE** (Crab Apple.) A beautiful variety. Standards 6/6 each.
" **SORBUS LUTESCENS.** A noble tree with silvery leaves, pure white underneath; bears large red berries when a large tree. Standards 5/- each.

RHODODENDRONS. For general effect in the borders they are most excellent, and being of very hardy and robust constitution are in very great demand. We strongly recommend them to our customers. Choice named Hybrids, Red, Crimson, White and Pink, well budded bushy plants 5/- each, 55/- per doz.
Choice **Hybrid Seedlings.** Height 15—18 inches 21/- per doz, 18—24 inches 24/- doz.
" **PONTICUM.** Good bushy stuff, well rooted. Height 12—15 inches 15/- per doz., 100/- per 100.

RIBES AUREUM (Flowering Currant). Flowers very early, bright golden yellow. Height 3 ft. 1/6 each.
" **SANGUINEUM.** Height 2—3 ft. 2/- each.
" **ALBIDUM.** White shaded with pink. Height 2—3 ft. 2/- each.
" **FLORA PLENA.** Flowers double red. Height 2—3 ft. 2/- each.
ST. JOHN'S WORT (Hypericum). **CALYCINUM.** Transplanted 9/- per doz., 60/- per 100.

SKIMMIA JAPONICA. Female variety. 1 ft. 3/- each.
" **FRAGRANS.** White, very sweet-scented. 3/- each.

VIBURNUM PLICATUM.

SNOWDROP TREE (Halesia Tetraptera). Height 3—4 ft. 3/- each.
SNOWY MESPILUS (Amelanchier). CANADENSIS. Standards 5/- each.
SPIRÆA AUREA. The golden-leaved variety. 2/- each.
" **ARGUTA.** Very early flowering, pure white variety. 2/- each.
" **CALLOSA.** Free flowering, red flowers. 1/6 each.
" **ALBA.** Pretty white flowers. 1/6 ea.
" **CONFUSA.** Slender habit, capital for forcing. 2/- each.
" **DOUGLASSI.** Rose-coloured flowers, free-flowering variety. 1/6 each.
" **ANTHONY WATERER.** A splendid dwarf-growing variety, covered with deep crimson flowers and keeps in bloom a long time. 2/- each, 21/- per doz.
" **AITCHISONII.** Long fern-like foliage, red bark, long panicles of pure white flowers. Extra good. 2/- each.
" **LINDLEYANA** (Himalaya). Very bold spreading habit, large foliage and white flowers. Height 2 ft. 2/- each.
SUMACH, VENETIAN (Rhus Cotinus). Lovely foliage, which deepens in Autumn. 3 ft. 2/- each.
" **TYPHINA** (Staghorn's Sumach). Fine bold foliage. Height 4—5 ft. 1/6 each.
SYCAMORE (Acer). **VARIEGATA** These are very beautiful trees and quite hardy. 3/6 each. Specimens 5/- each.
" **LEOPOLDI.** Beautiful purple flesh coloured. 5/- each.
TAMARIX GALLICA (Common Tamarisk). Very slender, graceful habit. Height 3 ft. 1/- each, 9/- per doz., 80/- per 100.
" **PETRANDRA.** Height 2—3 ft. 1/- each, 10/6 per doz.
THORNS (Cratægus). Double Crimson, Paul's, Pyramids 4/- each, Standards 5 - each. Single Scarlet, Pyramids 4/- each, Standards 5/- each.
Double White. Standards 5 - each.

TULIP TREE (Liriodendron Tulipifera). Large conspicuous soft green leaves, makes a fine ornamental tree. Height 6—7 ft. 3/6 each.
VERONICA BUXIFOLIA. Good strong hardy variety. 1/6 each, 15/- per doz.
" **TRAVERSII.** This is a most useful variety, stands well when planted near the sea, and makes a compact bush. 1/6 each, 15/- doz.
VINCA MAJOR. Large leaved variety with blue flowers. 1/- each, 10/- per doz.
" **MAJOR ELEGANTISSIMA.** With beautiful variegated foliage. 1/6 each, 15/- per doz.
" **MINOR.** Small leaves and blue flowers. 1/- each, 10/6 per doz.
VIBURNUM CARLESI. White shaded pale pink; sweetly scented. Height 1½—2 ft. 5/- each.
" **OPULUS** (Snowball Tree). Beautiful flowering shrub with large globular white flowers 3—4 ft. 2 6 each.
" **PLICATUM.** One of the best, a particularly showy shrub, flowers half the size of the Guelder Rose, pure white, splendid for planting on trellis or wall, forces well. Height 2—3 ft. 2/6 each.
WEIGELIA AMABILIS. Bright pink, strong grower and flowers freely. 1/6 each, 15/- per doz.
" **ABEL CARRIERE.** Rosy carmine, very free. 1/6 each, 15/- per doz.
" **ALBA.** Pure white. 1/6 each, 15/- doz.
" **EVA RATHKE.** A very beautiful variety, flowers dark red and carried in great quantities. 2/- each.
WILLOW (Salix). **AMERICAN WEEPING.** A fine weeping variety. 5/- each.
" **BABYLONICA** (Weeping Willow). Standards 6—8 ft. 5/- each.
" **KILMARNOCK.** This is a splendid Weeping variety. 5/- each.
YUCCA FILAMENTOSA. Most useful plant, flowers freely. 2/6 each.
" **RECURVIFOLIA.** Particularly hardy variety 3/6 each.

WEEPING ELM.

WEEPING WILLOW, KILMARNOCK.

SHRUBS suitable for Bedding and for Winter Decoration Outdoors.

We beg to draw your attention to the undermentioned Evergreen Shrubs, which we have pleasure in recommending for the purpose of winter decoration, and for the formation of permanent beds. By their compact habits, together with their capacity for being kept exceedingly dwarf, by being pruned to almost any extent, and by the many pleasing shades of colour that may be selected from amongst them, they provide both in winter and summer a most distinctive feature.

ANDROMEDA FLORIBUNDA ..	.. .. ..	see page 84	
BOX, JAPONICA AUREA ..	.. ..	" 84	
COTONEASTER MICROPHYLLA ..	..	" 84	
CUPRESSUS LAWSONIANA ..	.. ..	" 87	
EUONYMUS JAPONICUS ..	.. ..	" 85	
LAURISTINUS ..	.. ..	" 85	
OSMANTHUS ILLICIFOLIUS ..	..	see page 85	
RETINISPORA PLUMOSA ..	..	" 89	
" " AUREA		" 89	
VERONICA TRAVERSII ..	..	" 86	
VINCA ELEGANTISSIMA ..	..	" 86	

TRANSPLANTED FOREST TREES, HEDGING AND UNDERWOOD PLANTS FOR GAME COVERTS.

One of the most important lessons which this war has taught us is the absolute necessity of growing more timber in the United Kingdom, and the Authorities are already embarking on large schemes of afforestation, but much can also be done on small areas of land. Even where the land is unsuitable for ordinary cultivation many kinds of valuable timber trees will thrive and give a good return on the outlay necessary for trees and planting.

To meet the demand for Forest Trees we have considerably increased our Stock in this direction, and it will be found to comprise all the best varieties for Forest and Estate planting; further, we make it a practice to grow our trees thinly in rows which ensures their being thoroughly hardened when moved to exposed situations. We shall be pleased to give estimates, free of cost, for all kinds of planting, Forest or otherwise, and will carry out the entire work if desired.

Our prices, taking quality into consideration, are exceedingly moderate, and we are prepared to compete with any respectable firms in the trade. Extra Selected Plants, and smaller quantities than quoted, will be charged proportionally higher.

We shall be pleased to submit samples of any Forest Trees. Carriage Free.

ACACIA, Common. Very ornamental tree, growing freely on poor, sandy soil. Specimen Trees, 3/6 each.

ALDER, Common. Grows well on wet, undrained soils. Specimens, 2/6 each.

ARBOR-VITÆ (Thuya Occidentalis). Very compact growing tree, hardy, makes a splendid ornamental hedge. Height 2—3 ft. 2/- each, 21/- per doz.; 3—4 ft. 3/- each. Large trees 3/6 and 5/- each.

ASH, Common. Requires good land; timber valuable when well grown. Ht. 10-12 ft. 2/6 ea.

" MOUNTAIN. Very ornamental tree, most valuable for exposed situations. Height 5—6 ft. 6/- per doz., 8—10 ft. 3/6 each.

AUCUBA JAPONICA VARIEGATA. Grows well under shade of trees. Height 1½—2 ft. 2/6 each, 27/6 per doz.

BEECH, Common. Grows well on any good light soil, also makes a splendid hedge, retaining its foliage during winter. Height 2—3 ft. 25/- per 100. Specimen Trees, 3/6 ea.

BERBERIS AQUIFOLIA. Excellent for game coverts and shrubberies. Height 1—1½ ft. 5/- per doz., 30/- per 100

" DARWINII. Densely branched evergreen with large yellow flowers. Ht. 2-3 ft. 2/- ea., 21/- dz.

" VULGARIS. The common fruit-bearing Barbery. Height 2—2½ ft. 2/- each, 21/- doz.

BIRCH, Common. Succeeds in most situations, wet, undrained or bog land. Timber fine-grained and valuable. Makes the best charcoal for gunpowder. Height 10—12 ft. 3/6 ea.

" SILVER. One of the most beautiful of our forest trees. Succeeds in moist situations, wet, undrained, or bog land. Height 9—12 ft. 3/6 and 5/- each.

BOX, TREE. This forms a handsome hedge for ornamental purposes. Height 3 ft. 1/6 each, 18/- per doz.; 3—4 ft. 2/6 each, 27/6 per doz. 12/- per doz.

BRIAR, SWEET. Height 2—3 ft. 1/3 each, 12/- per doz.

BROOM, Common. Transplanted, 5/- per doz., 35/- per 100.

CHESTNUT, HORSE. Very handsome flowering tree. Splendid for avenues or parks, requires good land. Height 6—8 ft. 2/6 each. Specimen Trees 5/- each.

" SPANISH. Highly ornamental and rapid grower when planted in good soil. Requires a sheltered situation. Height 4—5 ft. 25/- per 100. Specimens 5/- each.

CUPRESSUS LAWSONIANA. The most popular of all Cupressus introduced by Messrs. Lawson, Edinburgh, in 1854; forms a fine evergreen hedge. Height 2—2½ ft. 2/6 each, 3—4 ft. 3/6 each, 5—6 ft. 5/- each.

ENGLISH YEW.

SPECIMEN ROW OF LIME TREES IN OUR NURSERIES.

ELDER, Silver variegated. 2—3 ft. 1/- each, 10/6 per doz.

ELM, ENGLISH. This is a tall and elegant tree of rapid and erect growth. Standards 3/6 ea.

FIR, DOUGLAS (Abies Douglasii). This is a fast-growing, magnificent timber tree, the foliage is a rich green. Grows freely on all soils. Height 12—15 in. 35/- per 100, 15—18 in. 40/- per 100.

" LARCH. Height 12 in. 12/- per 100, 90/- per 1000.

" SCOTCH. Height 12 in. 16/- per 100.

" SPRUCE (Pinus excelsa). Xmas trees in various sizes. Extra bushy 12 to 15 inches through. Height 12—18 in. 16/- per 100, 90/- per 1000, 24—24 in. 12/6 per 100, 100/- per 1000, 2 ft. 15/- per 100, 140/- per 1000.

GORSE, or FURZE. Seedlings. 20/- per 100.

HAZEL. Height 2—3 ft. 10/- per 100, 3—4 ft. 15/- per 100.

HOLLY, Green. Forms a beautiful hedge, if planted in double rows, leaving 12 inches between each row; also well adapted for mixing with thorn. Height 1—2 ft. 15/- per 100. 2½—3½ ft. 2/6 each, 24/- per doz.

HYPERICUM CALYCINUM. An excellent covert plant for growing under the shade of large trees, beautiful when in flower, and not liked by rabbits. 5/- per doz., 60/- per 100.

IVY, IRISH. Open ground. 12/6 per doz.

LABURNUM, Common. Very handsome early-flowering tree, covered with yellow blossom. Height 5—6 ft. 2/- each. Specimens 3/6 each.

LIMES, Red Twigged, from Layers. Very ornamental tree when grown sandy, most useful for Parks or Avenue planting, very hardy, and bear specimens transplant safely. Height 8—10 ft. 3/6 each. Specimen Standards 5/- and 7/6 each.

MAPLE, NORWAY. Specimen Trees 3/6 each.

OAK, ENGLISH. Specimen Trees 3/6 and 5/- ea.

PINE, AUSTRIAN. The Austrian Pine stands sea exposure well. Besides its great value for planting as an ornamental tree, it is one of the best for shelter. Succeeds on high, dry exposed situations, and on sea-shore. All well transplanted trees. Height 2—3 ft. 2/6 each, 27/6 per doz., 3—4 ft. 3/6 each.

POPLAR ABELE, Silver. Very valuable quick-growing tree, useful for exposed situations, with silvery leaf; grows freely on the coast. Height 4—6 ft. 9d. each, 7/6 per doz., 8—10 ft. 2/6 each.

" BALSAM. Large fragrant foliage. Height 10 ft. 2/- each. Larger Trees 3/6 each.

POPLAR BLACK ITALIAN. The most rapid growing of all our forest trees, grows fully in most soils; invaluable for shelter. Height 8 ft. 2/- each, 21/- doz. Specimens 2/6 and 3/6 each.

" DELTOIDEA AUREA. Is becoming a favourite, grows very freely, with rich golden foliage. Standards, Height 8—10 ft. 3/- each.

" LOMBARDY. Very ornamental upright growing tree, often introduced in Landscape with effect, grows well in almost any soil, and most useful for close planting to act as a block. Height 6—8 ft. 2/- each, 21/- per doz. Specimen Trees 3/6 each.

PRIVET, OVAL-LEAVED. One of the very finest evergreen shrubs for planting in town or country gardens; no plant stands smoke better, and it makes a beautiful ornamental hedge. It makes very fine specimens if kept clipped. Height 2—3 ft. 30/- 100. Specimens, extra fine bushy plants, grown 3 ft. apart. Height 3—4 ft. 3/- each, 30/- doz.; 4—5 ft. 3/6 each, 36/- doz.

SNOWBERRY. Height 2—3 ft. 15/- per 100.

SYCAMORE. Very hardy, and stands the sea winds better than most other trees; grows freely in any soil, very ornamental, and excellent timber. Height 6 ft. 20/- per 100. Specimen Trees 3/6 and 5/- each.

THORNS or QUICKS. This is the best of all plants for an ornamental hedge. Height 1½—2½ ft. 12/- per 100, 100/- per 1000.

YEW (Taxus), Common. The most Ornamental of all evergreen hedges, it should not be planted in any situation accessible to animals that might eat it. Hardy and a compact grower. Height 1½—2 ft. 1/9 each, 18/- per doz., 2—3 ft. 2/6 each, 27/- per doz., 3—3½ ft. 3/6 each, 40/- per doz. Specimens 5/- ea.

THE TRUE BAT WILLOW.

(Salix alba var. cœrulea).

The fastest growing, most profitable and best variety.

This fine Willow is a first cross between *Salix fragilis* and *S. alba*, and is known as *Salix alba cœrulea*. It was at first thought to be only a variety of *S. alba*, but is found to grow much faster than that variety, and that it occurs only as a female tree.

The true variety which we offer is grown from cuttings originally taken by Mr. Shaw, the eminent bat-maker, from a tree which he selected as being the best variety for making high-class cricket bats.

Fine selected standards, 10-12 ft. 18/- dz., 125/-100

CONIFERÆ.

All have been recently transplanted so as to ensure as far as possible safety in removal, abundance of room and attention have been given so that each tree may be a perfect specimen. Our trees are all hand pruned with a knife, which is a most important point.
We offer well shaped plants, suitable for potting or window boxes, in good variety, our selection. 18 inches, 1/9 each, 21/- per dox. 24 inches, 2/3 each. 24/- per dox.
We have a fine lot of Dwarf-growing Conifera, suitable for Rockeries, at 3/6 each.

ABIES CANADENSIS (Hemlock Spruce). Height 2—3 ft. 3/- each.
„ **NOBILIS.** Very fast-growing Fir; hardy. Height 2 ft. 3/- each.
„ **NORDMANNIANA.** Height 3 ft. 5/- each.
„ **PINSAPO.** Height 2—3 ft. 5/- each.
ARAUCARIA IMBRICATA. A most distinct tree. Height 1 ft. 10/6 each.
CEDRUS ATLANTICA. Fast-growing. Height 3 ft. 5/- each, 4 ft. 7/6 each.
„ **GLAUCA.** Glaucous-leaved. Height 3—4 ft. 7/6 and 10/6 each.
„ **DEODARA.** 3 ft. 5/- each, 4 ft. 10/- each.
CRYPTOMERIA ELEGANS. 3 ft. 5 - each.
CUPRESSUS ALBA-SPICA. Young foliage tipped with white. Height 14 ft. 3/- each.
„ **ALLUMII.** Height 3 ft. 3/6 each, 4 ft. 5/- each.
„ **ERECTA VIRIDIS.** Height 2 ft. 2/6 each.
„ **GRACILIS.** Very graceful, drooping habit. Height 2 ft. 3/6 each.
„ **LUTEA.** Height 2—2½ ft. 7/6 each.
„ **MACROCARPA** (in pots). Very handsome. Height 2 ft. 3/6 each.
„ **NOOTKATENSIS.** Very pretty. Height 3 ft. 3/6 each.
GINKGO (Maiden Hair Tree) (Salisburia adiantifolia). Height 2—3 ft. 2/6 each.
JUNIPERUS (Juniper). **CHINENSIS.** Height 2 ft. 3/6 and 5/- each.
„ **COMMUNIS FASTIGIATA.** Irish Juniper. Height 2—3 ft. 2/6 each.
„ **SABINA.** Very hardy, well-known variety. Height 1—2 ft. 2/6 each.
PICEA PUNGENS. Height 2—2½ ft. 2/6 each.

CEDRUS ATLANTICA.

We have a fine lot of Dwarf-growing Conifera, suitable for Rockeries, at 3/6 each.

PICEA PUNGENS GLAUCA (Blue Spruce). Height 2 ft. 5/- each.
PINUS CEMBRA. Height 3—4 ft. 5 - each.
„ **EXCELSA.** Height 3—4 ft. 5 - each.
RETINOSPORA OBTUSA. Light green foliage. Height 2—3 ft. 3/6 each.
„ **PISIFERA.** Height 3—4 ft. 3/6 each.
„ **AUREA.** Very fine golden variety. Height 2 ft. 5/- each.
„ **PLUMOSA.** Height 2—2½ ft. 2/6 each.
„ **AUREA.** Height 2 ft. 3/6 each.
„ **SQUARROSA.** Height 2 ft. 3/- each.
TAXODIUM DISTICHUM. Very ornamental, light feathery foliage, should be closely planted when transplanted, changing to rich brown in Autumn. Height 4 ft. 3/- each.
TAXUS AUREA (Golden English Yew). Height 1 ft. 3/6 each, 2 ft. 5/- each.
„ **FASTIGIATA** (The Irish Yew). Very dark foliage, with upright habit. Height 2 ft. 3/6 each, 3 ft. 5 - each.
„ **AUREA** (Golden Irish Yew). Height 1½—2 ft. 2/6 each, 2—3 ft. 5/- each.
THUJOPSIS DOLABRATA. Compact habit. Height 1½—2 ft. 5/- each.
„ **VARIEGATA.** Variegated form of Dolabrata. Height 2 ft. 3/6 each.
THUJA LOBBII. Height 2—3 ft. 2/6 each, 4 ft. 3/6 each.
„ **ZEBRINA.** Similar growth to Thuja Lobbii; nice golden variegated foliage. Height 2—2½ ft. 3/6 each.
„ **LUTEA** (Golden Arborvitæ). Height 2—3 ft. 3/6 each.
„ **VERVAENEANA.** Height 2 ft. 3/6 each, 3 ft. 5/- each.

HARDY CLIMBING & OTHER PLANTS.

SUITABLE FOR TRAINING ON WALLS, &c.

These are mostly grown in pots, and can be supplied and planted any time of the year with perfect safety.

AKEBIA QUINNATA. Purplish brown. 2/6 ea.
AMPELOPSIS (Creepers).
„ **LOWII.** Small Palmate leaves. 2/6 each.
„ **VEITCHII.** Small-leaved. 2/6 each.
„ **PURPUREA.** Dark-leaved. 2/6 each.
„ **Hederacea.** Virginian Creeper. 2/6 each.
„ **Sempervirens.** Evergreen. 3/6 each.
ARISTOLOCHIA SIPHO. Deciduous. 2/6 each.
AZARA MICROPHYLLA. Beautiful. 3/- each.
BIGNONIA RADICANS (Trumpet Flower). 3/6 ea.
BUDDLEA GLOBOSA. Orange flowers. 3/- ea.
CEANOTHUS, GLOIRE DE VERSAILLES. Panicles of sky-blue flowers. 3/6 each.
„ **Azureus.** Pale blue. 3/6 each.
„ **Divaricatus.** Very pale blue. 3/- each.
„ **VEITCHII.** Blue. In pots. 3/- each.
CHIMONANTHUS FRAGRANS. Sweet. 2/6 ea.

CLEMATIS.

DUCHESS OF ALBANY. Beautiful bright pink. July. 2/6 each.
DUCHESS OF EDINBURGH. The best of all the double white, deliciously scented. June to July. 2/6 each.
GRACE DARLING. A delicate tree of bright rosy carmine. 2/6 each.
HENRYI. Beautiful large creamy white. July to Oct. 2/6 each.
JACKMANII. Intense violet purple. July to Oct. 2/6 each.
JACKMANII ALBA. A grand pure white variety. 2/6 each.
JACKMANII, RED. A fine new red variety of true Jackmanii type. July to Oct. 2/6 each.
JACKMANII SUPERBA. Similar to Jackmanii, but the colour more intense. July to Oct. 2/6 each.
LADY BETTY BALFOUR. A fine, deep, velvety purple, a strong grower and free bloomer. 2/6 each.
LA LORRAINE. Colour a soft clear rose tinted with blush. A great acquisition. July to Oct. 2/6 each.
MARCEL MOSER. Mauve violet with red bar, very fine. 2/6 each.
MISS CRAWSHAW. Distinct softening pink. 2/6 each.
MONTANA—RUBENS. Flowers a soft bright rosy lilac with white. Most delightful climber for a trellis or arbour; quite hardy. 2/6 each.
MONTANA GRANDIFLORA. Large, pure white starry flowers. Splendid for covering trellises, porches, &c. May and June. 2/- each.

MRS. CHOLMONDELEY. Lavender. May to July. 2/6 each.
MRS. HOPE. Satiny mauve. July to Aug. 2/6 each.
NELLY MOSER. Light mauve, with bright red bars. July to Oct. 2/6 each.
PRESIDENT. Purple, suffused with claret, good. July to Oct. 2/6 each.
VILLE DE LYON. Bright carmine, red. July to Oct. 2/6 each.

CLEMATIS—JACKMANII ALBA.

COTONEASTER MICROPHYLLA. Scarlet berries in Autumn. 2/6 each.
CRATÆGUS LÆLANDII. Red-berried. 3/- ea.
ESCALLONIA MACRANTHA. Crimson. 3/6 ea.

HOP, Common Green-leaved. 1/6 each.
„ **GOLDEN-LEAVED.** Very rapid climber. 2/- each.
IVY (Hedera)—**Cavendishii.** Silver. 2/6 each.
„ **Clouded Gold.** Fine. 2/6 each.
„ **CHRYSOPHYLLA.** Sulphur yellow. 2/6 ea.
„ **Palmata.** Handsome variety. 2/6 each.
„ **DENTATA.** Dark green foliage. 2/6 each.
„ **Emerald Green.** Glossy leaves. 2/6 each.
„ **IRISH.** Fine, quick-growing variety, strong plants from open ground, 2 ft. - 12/- per dox. In pots, 4—6 ft. 3/6 each, 27/8 per dox, 10 ft. 5/- each.
„ **Tricolor.** Very pretty. 2/6 each.
IVIES, Variegated and Green. Strong staked plants. 3—4 ft. 2/6 each, 4—5 ft. 3/6 each, 6—8 ft. 5/- each.
„ 12 Ivies, distinct sorts, in pots, for 25/-; 6 varieties for 14/-.
JASMINUM (Jasmine)—
„ **Nudiflorum.** Yellow, blooms in December and January. 2/6 each.
„ **Beasiana.** Red flowering. 2/6 each.
„ **Officinale.** White. 2/6 each.
„ **REVOLUTUM.** Evergreen. 2/6 each.
KERRIA JAPONICA FL. PL. Yellow. 2/6 ea.
LONICERA (Honeysuckle)—
„ **Aurea reticulata.** Golden-veined foliage. 2/6 ea.
„ **EARLY DUTCH.** 2/6 each.
„ **Flexuosa.** Evergreen. 2/6 each.
„ **HALLII.** White, evergreen. 2/6 each.
„ **Late Red Dutch.** Well-known. 2/6 each.
PASSIFLORA CÆRULEA. Blue. 3/- each.
„ **CONSTANCE ELLIOTT.** White. 3/- each.
PERIPLOCA GRÆCA. Rapid climber. 3/- each.
POLYGONUM BALDSCHUANICUM. A splendid free-flowering climber. 3/6 each.
PYRUS JAPONICA. Valuable early Spring flowering plant, rich scarlet. 3/- each.
„ **ALBA.** White form of the above. 2/6 each.
„ **ATRO-COCCINEA.** Double-flowered. 2/6 ea.
„ **KNAPHILL SCARLET.** Bright vermilion, the best of this class. 3/6 each.
„ **RUBRA GRANDIFLORA.** In pots, 3/- each.
„ **MAULEI.** Red flowers in Spring, golden-yellow fruit in Autumn. 3/- each.
ROSES, CLIMBING. See page 53.
VITIS, Coignetiæ. The Crimson Glory Vine, brilliant scarlet in Autumn. 3/6 each.
„ **Purpurea.** Claret-coloured foliage. 3/6 each.
„ **THUNBERGII.** Handsome. 3/6 each.
WISTARIA MULTIJUGA. 5/- each.
„ **SINENSIS.** Lilac-mauve. 5/- and 7/6 each.
„ **SINENSIS ALBA.** 5/- and 7/6 each.

CHRYSANTHEMUMS.

JAPANESE AND DECORATIVE VARIETIES.

The following list includes the finest varieties suitable for exhibition and decorative purposes. All ready for sending out in March and April, in strong healthy plants from single pots.

A. V. BALFOUR. Rose pink, dwarf.
BALDOCK'S CRIMSON.
CHESTNUT WHITE. Large pure white.
CHURCH'S WHITE. One of the best of whites.
CRANFORDIA. Golden yellow, a fine variety.
DECEMBER PINK. Rose pink.
GENERAL NOGI. A lovely shade of soft pink.
JASEPHINO BERNIER. Large pink.
LA NEGRESSE. Bright crimson with gold points.
MADAME JULES VALET. Pure white.
MRS. G. DRABBLE. White.
MRS. J. GIBSON. Mauve pink.
MRS. R. C. PULLING. Deep yellow, large incurving florets.
N. C. S. JUBILEE. Pearly mauve.
PINK PEARL. A lovely pink variety.
QUEEN MARY. Opens with a shade of pink.
SNOWDRIFT. Fine white.
T. W. EDWARDS. Orange yellow.
WHITE WESTERN KING.
W. VERT. Rich dark crimson.

Strong Plants 1s. each ; 6 for 5s. ; 9s. doz. post free.

SINGLE-FLOWERED CHRYSANTHEMUMS.

These beautiful flowers are now very popular. Their long, wiry flower-stems and graceful Marguerite-like blooms make them of especial value as cut flowers for Table Decoration, and as pot plants for the greenhouse.

In March and April. Our selection, 1s. each ; per doz. 9s.

MADAME JULES VALET.

INCURVED EXHIBITION VARIETIES.

Strong Plants from single pots in March and April. Our selection, each 1s. ; 6 for 5s. ; per doz. 9s.

EARLY-FLOWERING LARGE-FLOWERED VARIETIES.

A splendid Class for Garden Decoration.

ALMIRANTE. Red with scarlet shading, a very taking colour.
BETTY SPARK. Rose pink, large handsome sprays.
BRONZE BETTY SPARK. Light bronze.
CRANFORD PINK. A beautiful shade of pink, fine for cutting.
EDEN. Bright rose with silvery reverse, fine.
EDNA MEW. Large yellow striped bronze.
FRAMFIELD EARLY WHITE. Very fine pure white.
GOLDEN DIANA. Lovely golden yellow, free flowering.
HESTON BRONZE.
HOLLICOT WHITE. Pure, glistening white, reflexed blooms.
J. BANNISTER. Lemon yellow, shaded reddish copper, fine.
MRS. J. FIELDING. A bronze sport from Goacher's Crimson.
PEACE. Lovely mauve.
PERLE CHATILLIONAISE. Creamy white, with rosy peach.
PROVENCE. Rose colour, with golden centre, very fine.
ROI DES BLANCS. Pure white, large flowers, splendid variety.
RUBY MEW. Large hairy deep pink.
SUNBURY BEAUTY. Large pink.
SUNBURY SUNSET. Pretty hairy golden amber.
WELLS' BLUSH. One of the best for cutting.
VICTOR MEW. Most lovely bronze.

Strong Plants in March and April. Our selection, 1s. each ; 6 for 5s. ; per doz. 9s.

FUCHSIAS—Select Varieties.

These are still amongst our most useful and beautiful plants for pot culture, and are well worth growing for their charming display of brilliantly coloured flowers. *Those marked (*) are double-flowered.*

*ALFRED RAMBAUD. Sepals lovely scarlet, petals deep violet.
*DUCHESS OF EDINBURGH. Sepals crimson-scarlet, corolla creamy white.
EARL OF BEACONSFIELD. Carmine, with deep carmine corolla.
FASCINATION. Long white tube ; corolla a lovely shade of rose-pink.
*H. DUTERRAIL. Tube and sepals scarlet, *corolla bluish-violet.
HENRI POINCARE (new). Tube and sepals scarlet, corolla purple.

*JUPITER. Sepals brilliant scarlet ; corolla violet.
*LA FRANCE. Sepals a bright rich scarlet ; corolla violet.
*MADAME BRUANT. Tube rich scarlet ; corolla lilac-mauve.
*MOLESWORTH. Tube and sepals a bright deep carmine-crimson.
MADAME ROZAIN. The tube and sepals a deep rich scarlet.
*MRS. E. G. HILL. Tube and sepals rich scarlet ; corolla creamy white.

MURIEL. Sepals a brilliant scarlet ; corolla violet-red.
*P. RADAELLI. Enormous double corolla of a rich bluish-violet.
PRINCESS MAY. Lovely creamy white ; corolla a brilliant carmine-rose.
PROVOST (new). Tube and sepals scarlet ; corolla pale blue.
ROYAL PURPLE. Corolla dark velvety purple, sepals clear crimson.

Twelve choice named varieties, our own selection, 1s. each ; 6 for 5s. ; 9s. per doz.

PELARGONIUMS—Zonal Single Flowered.

All Autumn Struck. Strong young plants from single pots.

BLENHEIM. Brilliant scarlet with white eye, large.
CALEDONIA. Blush pink, very large perfectly formed flowers.
COUNTESS OF JERSEY. Coral salmon, splendid flower.
DANIELS' ORANGE QUEEN. Brilliant orange scarlet ; quite distinct.
DR. NANSEN. Finest pure white.
DUBLIN. Bold flowers of a rosy magenta shade ; splendid dwarf habit.

FISCAL REFORMER. Colour clear salmon rose, fine habit.
LADY ROSCOE. Beautiful shade of pink.
MR. A. J. BELL. White and shrimp pink, very pretty.
MRS. L. STARES. White edged with pink.
SCARLET KING. Fiery scarlet, fine bold flower.
SNOWSTORM. A splendid dwarf-growing pure white ; first-class.
ST. LOUIS. Scarlet crimson, immense flowers.

VIRGINIA. Pure snow white ; flowers large.
WARLEY. Orange and white mottled ; a superb flower.
WINTER CHEER. Colour bright cerise impregnated with scarlet ; a charming Winter blooming variety.

Twelve in 12 superb varieties, our selection, 9s. Six in 6 extra fine varieties, our selection, 4s.

PELARGONIUMS—Zonal Double-Flowered.

DR. DESPRES. Purplish crimson, very fine trusses.
JULES LAFORGNE. Fine trusses semi-double purple crimson.
MADAME ROZAIN. A very fine double, pure white.

PAUL CRAMPEL DOUBLE. Magnificent variety.
PICOTEE (Fraicheur). Beautiful pure white.
SALMON QUEEN. Beautiful clear salmon-red.
THE SPEAKER. Of a salmon-cerise colour.

VIOLET DANIELS. A fine variety of immense size.
WHITE KING OF DENMARK. A very fine variety.
CHOICE VARIETIES, our selection, 1s. each. 6 for 5s. ; 9s. per doz.

PELARGONIUMS—Ivy-Leaved Double-Flowered.

ACHIEVEMENT. Double brilliant rosy carmine. 3 for 2s.
COL. BADEN POWELL. Soft blush lilac flowers.
CUVIER. Beautiful rich violet purple, distinct and very fine.
HIS MAJESTY THE KING. A lovely shade of dark cerise.
JAMES T. HAMILTON. A grand new hybrid, ivy-leaved variety.

KATE WILSON. Fine pure white, very free bloom.
LEOPARD. Clear lilac-pink, heavily blotched with crimson.
MAUVE BEAUTY. Good strong grower.
MILLFIELD GEM. Blush white with blotches of crimson shaded with pink.
PURITY. Splendid pure white, with large full double flowers.
QUEEN OF ROSES. Most beautiful rosy carmine.

RED CROUSSE. Rosy crimson, splendid for hanging baskets.
RYECROFT SCARLET. Very large bloom.
RYECROFT SURPRISE. Colour a lovely salmon-pink.
SOUVENIR DE CHARLES TURNER. A beautiful deep rose.
VICAR OF SHIRLEY. A beautiful shade of cerise scarlet.
CHOICE VARIETIES, our selection, 1s. each 6 for 5s. ; 9s. per doz.

DAHLIAS.

CACTUS-FLOWERED.—NEW AND SELECT VARIETIES.

The following varieties, which are all the true Cactus type, include what we consider the very choicest flowers for Exhibition or decorative purposes, and cannot fail to give the highest satisfaction.

ALABASTER. Purest white. The blooms are of large size and incurved in form.

ARGONAUT. Orange-scarlet, lighter centre, very fine and distinct.

BRITISH LION. Yellowish for the most part, but burnished with red, almost, it might be termed, tawny in colour.

CARONIA (new). A huge Cactus, unequalled in size by any variety yet raised. Colour clear medium yellow throughout. 2 6 each.

CARRIE HAMMOND. White to clear pink.

DOROTHY. The colour is a lovely bright silvery pink.

EDITH CARTER. Colour yellow, suffused rosy crimson.

ELECTRIC (new). An exhibition Cactus. The flowers are large and perfectly incurved in form. Colour pale lemon at tips to deeper yellow at base. 2 6 each.

FASCINATION (1914). Pure white deepening to clear pink.

FREDERICK WENHAM. Warm fawn pink with soft salmon.

F. W. FELLOWES. Bright orange scarlet.

GENERAL SIR DOUGLAS HAIG (new). A lovely combination of tints of pink, grading from almost white to deep pink, then to lighter again. The flowers are of perfect form and of good size.

GIGANTIC. Of enormous size, colour pure old gold.

GOLDEN CROWN. Bright clear yellow, good exhibition flowers.

GOLDEN RAIN. Clear yellow, form very incurved fine exhibition flower.

GUARDIAN. Glowing crimson scarlet, a most striking novelty.

HARRY CRABTREE. Colour purplish crimson at base of florets to yellow at tips; fine flower.

H. H. THOMAS. A deep rich crimson.

H. L. BROUSSON. A deep rich rose.

INDOMITABLE. A beautiful lilac mauve.

J. B. RIDING. Rich yellow, with apricot red petals.

DAHLIA—JOHN RIDING.

J. H. JACKSON. Brilliant crimson maroon.

JOHANNESBURG. Colour a bright rich golden yellow.

JOHN RIDING. Perfect form, great depth, and deep rich crimson.

KISMET. Cerise with rosy tips.

LIEUT. ROBINSON, V.C. Colour clear ruby, with amaranth at tips, and on older florets.

MARQUIS. Very fine flower, colour purplish crimson, florets very narrow and needle pointed.

MELODY. Base of petals pure yellow, tips pure white.

MISS STREDWICK. Soft yellow, changing to rosy pink.

MONARCH. Bright bronzy red with yellow centre; very fine.

MRS. ALFRED HARDY (new). A large full flower, with incurved florets gracefully arranged, and a beautiful colour; light salmon pink with deeper shading at base of floret. 2 6 each.

MRS. D. B. CRANE (new). Purest pearly white, the flowers being of good size, moderately and evenly incurved in form. 2 6 each.

MRS. HERBERT BLACKMAN. Colour pretty rosy-pink turning to white at centre, useful variety for any purpose.

MRS. H. SHOESMITH. One of the finest Dahlias yet sent out.

MRS. J. J. CROWE. Beautiful clear canary yellow.

MRS. MARGARET STREDWICK. One of the finest Dahlias ever raised, the colour is a combination of tints of pink with strong stout upright flower stems.

NEW YORK. Orange yellow in the centre, shading to deep salmon.

PIERROT. Deep amber, boldly tipped with pure white.

RED ADMIRAL. Rich fiery scarlet colour.

REV. T. W. JAMIESON. Yellow, edged with rosy lilac.

ROYAL SUSSEX (new). The blooms are of exceptional size, with long, slender, incurving and slightly whorled florets of glowing red shaded with orange. 2 6 each.

SATISFACTION. Rose pink, approaching to white.

SAXONIA. A splendid deep crimson.

SNOWDON. Flowers of the purest white.

SNOWSTORM. A magnificent pure white, dwarf and sturdy.

SWEET BRIAR. An exquisite soft bright pink.

THE IMP. Dark maroon crimson, almost black, quite distinct.

THE SWAN. The best pure white yet raised.

W. E. PETERS. Clear crimson scarlet throughout.

Those not priced, choice selected sorts, our selection 1s. each; 6 for 5s.; per doz. 9s. Strong Plants from single pots ready in May.

DAHLIAS—SHOW AND FANCY.

The following list includes the finest varieties. Strong plants from single pots in May.

S. denotes Show. F. Fancy.

BUTTERCUP (S). Yellow tinged with red, very fine.

COLONIST (S). Chocolate and fawn, very distinct.

COMEDIAN (F). Orange ground, flaked crimson and tipped with white.

DIADEM (S). Deep crimson, fine and constant.

DR. KEYNES (S). A pretty rich buff, having a reddish tint.

DUKE OF FIFE (S). Fine rich cardinal, large.

FLORENCE TRANTER (S). Blush white, distinctly edged rosy purple.

GOLDFINDER (S). Yellow, tipped with red.

GRACCHUS. Bright orange buff; splendid flower.

HARRY KEITH (S). Rosy purple, very fine and constant.

LOTTIE ECKFORD (F). White, beautifully striped with purple.

MATTHEW CAMPBELL (F). Buff or apricot, beautifully striped.

MONT BLANC (S). Pure white; large full flower, of exceptional beauty.

MRS. GLADSTONE (S). Delicate blush, with white centre.

MRS. N. HALLS (F). Bright scarlet, tipped with white.

MRS. SAUNDERS (F). Yellow tipped with white. Fine.

MRS. STANCOMBE (S). Canary yellow, tipped with fawn.

MURIEL (S). Clear yellow, a splendid flower.

PENELOPE. Fawn shaded amber, large flower.

TOM JONES. Yellow ground edged with rose.

WARRIOR (S). Intense scarlet, grand colour fine form.

Our own selection of popular and beautiful varieties, 1s. each; 6 for 5s.; per doz. 9s.

POMPONE DAHLIAS.

A brilliant and charming class, of a neat, compact habit of growth, with beautifully formed, perfectly double, miniature flowers, which are produced in profusion throughout the Summer and Autumn. Our list given below includes all the most distinct and beautiful varieties.

ADRIENNE. Crimson scarlet, small beautifully shaped flowers.

BACCHUS. Bright scarlet. One of the best.

CHEERFULNESS. Old gold, tipped scarlet crimson.

CYRIL. Bright crimson, very fine.

DAISY. Amber and salmon, a neat and charming flower.

DARKEST OF ALL. Very dark maroon crimson.

DOUGLAS. Rich deep maroon, shaded crimson.

ELEGANT. Primrose, prettily tipped with lake.

GLOW. Beautiful coral red, splendid form.

LORNA DOONE. Rosy purple, dark purple tip.

MERCURY. Reddish salmon, heavily tipped with white.

NERISSA. Soft rose, tinted with silver; good centre and outline, and of splendid habit.

QUEEN OF WHITES. Pure white, good dwarf habit.

SOVEREIGN. Beautiful bright golden yellow.

SUNNY DAYBREAK. Pale apricot, edged with rosy red.

THE DUKE. The colour is deep velvety crimson; habit very dwarf.

TOMMY KEITH. Cardinal red, tipped with white.

WHITE ASTER. Pure white, quilled flower of the most free-flowering habit; an extremely useful variety for cutting.

Very good varieties, our selection 1s. each; 6 for 5s.; per doz. 9s.

NEW PÆONY-FLOWERED DAHLIAS.

A remarkably fine and distinct new class, growing four to five feet in height, and producing enormous beautifully coloured semi-double flowers, which, at a short distance, resemble huge Pæonias. Massed in large beds, or in groups on the shrubbery border, they are splendidly effective.

ADMIRATION. Buff ground flushed with rosy carmine.

DR. K. W. VAN GORKOM. White shaded rose; fine.

DUKE HENRY. Rosy cerise, large splendidly formed flowers.

GERMANIA. Brilliant crimson scarlet, very showy; four feet.

HOLMAN HUNT. Deep scarlet, large, splendid flowers on long wiry stems.

KAISERIN A. VICTORIA. Yellow shading to white, very fine.

KING LEOPOLD. Canary yellow. A fine variety.

LANDSEER. Rich deep scarlet; very fine.

LIBERTY. Bright scarlet, very large flowers.

SNOW WHITE. Pure white, the blooms are of moderate size with pointed cactus-like petals. A charming variety for cut flowers.

SOLFATERRE. Soft rose. Distinct and beautiful.

SOUTH POLE. Pure white, large rounded petals.

THE GEISHA. Orange-red and yellow; very fine.

SIX BEAUTIFUL VARIETIES, our selection, including Snow White, 5s.; 1s. each; 9s. per doz.

HARDY PERENNIAL FLOWERING PLANTS.

Probably no section of the garden has suffered more during the past few years than the Herbaceous Borders. Where it was not found expedient to dig up the borders and plant Food Crops, little attention could be given to the cleaning, staking and manuring of the plants, and as a consequence most of the stronger growing sorts got quite out of hand and the more delicate ones perished.

In the years immediately preceding the war this beautiful class of plants had been brought to a high state of cultivation, and we are sure that from an ornamental point of view and for maintaining a supply of flowers for indoor decoration, it will be desired to lose no time in re-establishing the Herbaceous border, and there is no time like the Spring for taking this work in hand. In the following lists will be found all the most popular sorts, many of which may be had in strong flowering clumps to give immediate effect

A PORTION OF AN HERBACEOUS BORDER AT OUR NURSERIES.

ACHILLÆA PTARMICA—THE PEARL. Large double, pure white flowers; fine for cutting. 1/- each.

ACONITUM FISCHERI. Large heads of rich blue. 1/3 each.

ANCHUSA ITALICA, Dropmore Variety. This is undoubtedly the finest blue-flowered herbaceous plant in existence. 1/3 each.

  ,, **MYOSOTIDIFLORA.** Blue Forget-me-not flowers with broad leaves, quite distinct. 1½ in. 1/3 each.

  ,, **OPAL.** Sky-blue variety, a pleasing shade of colour. 1/3 each.

  ,, **PICOTEE.** White edged with blue. 1/3 ea.

ANEMONE JAPONICA ALBA. One of the best Autumn blooming plants. 1/- each.

  ,, **ROSEA.** Rose. 1/- each.

  ,, **RUBRA.** Rosy red. 1/- each.

  ,, **SYLVESTRIS PLENA.** Double snow-white flowers. 1/3 each.

AQUILEGIA CHRYSANTHA. Golden yellow flowers with long spurs. 1/3 each.

  ,, **MRS. SCOTT ELLIOTT'S VARIETIES.** Mixed, long spurred. 1/3 each.

ARTEMESIA LACTIFLORA. White flowers. ft. 1/6 each.

ASTERS (Michaelmas Daisies). Beautiful Autumn bloomers.

  ,, **AMELLUS, BEAUTY OF RONSDORF.** Large flowers. 2/- each. 1/3 each. 12/6 per doz.

  ,, **PERRY'S FAVOURITE.** Reddish-pink. 3 ft. 1/- each.

  ,, **CLIMAX.** Clear light blue flowers. 1/- each.

  ,, **CRENATA.** Dark blue, large flowers. 1/- each.

  ,, **DECORATOR.** Small white flowers on graceful stems. 1/- each.

  ,, **FELTHAM BLUE.** Clear dark blue, large flowers, with bright yellow centre; grand variety. 1/6 each.

  ,, **HON. EDITH GIBBS.** Pale lilac, extremely pendulous and branching. 4 ft. 1/6 each, 15/- per doz.

  ,, **MULTIFLORUS.** White heath-like foliage. 3 ft. 1/- each.

  ,, **NAMUR.** Clear pink, similar to St. Egwin, but flowering a fortnight earlier. 3—4 ft. 1/3 each.

  ,, **NOVÆ ANGLIÆ.** Large bluish-purple flowers; blooms in October. 1/- each.

  ,, **BELGII DENSUS.** Blue. Height about 3 ft. 1/- each.

  ,, **RUBELLA.** Deep rose, late flowering. 4 to 5 ft. 1/- each.

  ,, **SENSATION.** White, golden centre; branching habit. 1/- each.

ASTERS, SNOWDON. A most charming variety, about 4 ft. high, bearing in Autumn lovely bracts of almost pure white flowers with pale yellowish disc. 1/- each.

  ,, **SUB CŒRULEUS.** Very large blue flowers on branching stems. Height 1½ ft. 1/- each.

  ,, **TOP SAWYER.** Clear blue, large flowers. Height 3 ft. 1/3 each.

We offer clumps of some varieties 2/- each.

AURICULAS, ALPINE. Choice seedlings, self-coloured and laced varieties. 9d. each, 8/- per doz.

BUPTHALMUM SALICIFOLIUM. Golden yellow flowers; very showy. Height 3 ft. 1/- each.

CAMPANULA GRANDIFLORA ALBA. Very fine. 1/6 each.

  ,, **MARIESII.** Dark blue. 1/6 each.

  ,, **LACTIFLORA.** Pale blue. 2 ft. 1/6 each, 15/- per doz.

  ,, **LINDLEYII (new).** Light blue shaded purple, large bells on 3½ ft. stems. 3/6 each.

  ,, **PYRAMIDALIS (The Chimney Campanula).** Long spikes of blue saxifrage flowers. 1/- each.

CENTAUREA DEALBATA. Rosy-purple flowers, produced nearly the whole summer from disc foliage. 1/- each.

  ,, **GLASTIFOLIA.** Tall, with silvery foliage and yellow heads. 1/- each.

CHRYSANTHEMUM MAXIMUM, KING EDWARD VII. One of the finest varieties yet raised. Grows about 3 ft. high, and produces large, beautiful, pure white flowers. 1/- each.

  ,, **STAR OF ANTWERP.** Large flowers with broad straight petals and stiff stems grand for cutting. 1/- each.

  ,, **STAR OF THE EAST.** A grand variety. 1/- each.

  ,, **THE SPEAKER.** 1/6 each.

CIMICIFUGA SIMPLEX. Long spikes of pure white flowers. 1/6 each.

COREOPSIS GRANDIFLORA. Bright golden yellow; blooms from June until September. 1/- each.

DELPHINIUM BELLADONNA. Lovely sky-blue, one of the finest in cultivation. 2/6 each.

  ,, **GRANDIFLORUM.** Stronger stems and larger flowers than the above; a striking acquisition. 3/6 each.

  ,, **CORRY.** Double sky-blue tinged with red. 2/6 each.

  ,, **F. W. ELLIOTT.** Bright blue. 1/- each.

  ,, **LIZE VAN VEEN.** This variety is remarkable by the immense size of the single flowers, which have a pure blue colour. 3/6 each.

  ,, **MOERHEIMI.** White. 2/6 each.

DELPHINIUM, PERSIMMON. Beautiful bright azure-blue, with sulphur centre, extra fine. Height 3½ ft. 3/6 each.

  ,, **QUEEN OF SPAIN.** Semi-double pale blue and lilac. 2/6 each.

  ,, **REV. E. LASCELLES.** Dark blue. 4/- each.

  ,, **UNNAMED VARIETIES.** Good blooms. 30/- per doz.

  ,, **OUR OWN SELECTION OF SORTS,** 35/- doz.

DICTAMNUS FRAXINELLA (Burning Bush). This remarkable plant is one of the most singularly interesting herbaceous perennials in existence. 1/- each.

  ,, **ALBA.** A fac-simile of the preceding, but with pure white flowers; very showy. 1/- each.

DRACOCEPHALUM VIRGINICUM. Erect plant stems, 2½ ft. high, with numerous bright pink flowers. 1/- each.

  ,, **ALBUM.** Fac-simile of preceding, white flowers. 1/- each.

ERIGERON SPECIOSUM SUPERBUM. Large lavender blue flowers with yellow centre. Height 3 ft. 1/- each.

  ,, **QUAKERESS.** Large light blue. 1/6 each.

ERYNGIUM ALPINUM (Truel). The flower of the genus. The colour is a lovely metallic blue. 1/- each.

  ,, **GIGANTEUM,** The Ivory Thistle. 1/- each, 10/6 per doz.

  ,, **PLANUM.** Numerous small blue flowers, useful for cutting. Height 3 ft. 1/- each.

FUCHSIAS. Perfectly hardy. Set of 6 for 7/-.

FUNKIA SIEBOLDI VAR. Splendid foliage of green and gold. 1/6 each.

  ,, **LANCEOLATA.** Lilac. 1½ in. 1/- each.

GAILLARDIA. LADY EXETER. Yellow. 2/- each.

  ,, **MRS. McKELLAR.** Yellow and crimson. 2/- each.

  ,, **THE KING.** Deep red, margin bright yellow. 2/- each.

  ,, **CHOICE MIXED SEEDLINGS.** 10/6 doz.

GALEGA CARNEA FL. PL. Double flowers of lilac and white. 3 ft. 1/- each, 10/6 per doz.

  ,, **OFFICINALIS.** Numerous lilac flowers on branching stems. Height 4 ft. 1/- each.

  ,, **ALBA.** Similar to preceding, with white flowers. 1/- each.

GEUM, MRS. J. BRADSHAW. Double scarlet. 1/- each.

GYPSOPHILA PANICULATA. A fine border plant, and most valuable for cutting. 1/- each.

  ,, **FL. PL.** A pure white, double-flowered of the well-known G. paniculata. 1/6 each.

ANCHUSA OPAL.

Hardy Perennial Flowering Plants (*continued*)

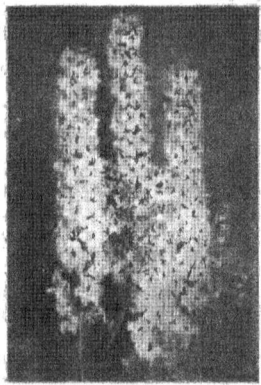

DELPHINIUM. *See page 91.*

HELENIUM PUMILUM MAGNIFICUM. This forms immense heads of soft yellow flowers, 2 to 3 inches across. 1/- each.
" **BOLANDERI.** Yellow. 3½ ft. July. 1/- each.
" **GRANDICEPHALUM STRIATUM.** Brown and yellow. 4 ft. 1/- each.
" **RIVERTON BEAUTY.** Lemon. Aug. to Sept. 4 ft. 1/- each.
" **RIVERTON GEM.** Brilliant terra-cotta red, a continuous bloomer from August to end of October. 1/- each.
HELIANTHUS, MISS MELLISH. Large single yellow. Height 5 ft. 1/- each.
" **SOLEIL D'OR.** A fine variety, with deep orange-yellow double flowers. 1/- each.
" **SPARSIFOLIUS.** Bright yellow. 1/- each.
" **TOMENTOSUS.** The flowers are of a rich golden yellow colour and 3 inches across ; very free bloomer. 1/- each.
HELLEBORUS NIGER. Christmas rose, white. 2/6 each.
HEMEROCALLIS, AURANTIACA MAJOR. Flowers large, trumpet shape, of a deep orange colour. Height 3 ft. 1/- each.
" **FLAVA.** Large umbels of beautiful Lily-like flowers of a bright yellow colour. 1/- each.
" **FULVA.** Bronzy-orange shading to crimson. 1/- each.
" **THUNBERGI.** Bright yellow. 1/- each.
HEUCHERA BRIZOIDES. A very distinct plant, forming tufts of dark bronzy foliage and splendid spikes of crimson flowers. 1/- each.
" **EDGE HALL HYBRID.** Large rose-coloured flowers. Height 1½ inches. 1/- each.
" **GRACILLIMA.** Elegant panicles of miniature rose-tinted flowers. 1/- each.
" **MACRANTHA.** White flowers. 1/- each.
" **SANGUINEA SPLENDENS.** Bright crimson. 1/- each.
IBERIS SEMPERVIRENS SUPERBA. White. 1/- each.
INCARVILLEA DELAVAYI. Height about 2½ ft., with large Gloxinia-like flowers of a lovely crimson-purple colour. 1/- each.
" **GRANDIFLORA.** Large flowers, deep rosy-crimson. 1/- each.
INULA GLANDULOSA. Deep yellow. 1 ft. 1/- each.
IRIS GERMANICA. May be planted any time from September to March. Choice named varieties, our selection. 1/- each, 10/6 doz.
" **ADONIS.** Blue and purple. 1/- each, 10/6 per doz.
" **BLUE SKY.** Pale blue. 1/- each, 10/6 per doz.
" **FLAVESCENS.** Soft yellow. 1/- each, 10/6 per doz.
" **GRACCHUS.** Yellow, reticulated purple. 1/- each.
" **MAORI KING.** Yellow and crimson. 1/- each, 10/6 per doz.
" **QUEEN OF MAY.** Lilac. 1/- each, 1/- each.
CRIS KÆMPFERI. Splendidly coloured. 1/3 each, 12/6 per doz.
Choice mixed. 1/- each, 9/- per doz.
Named Sorts. 16/- per doz.

IRIS SIBERICA. Blue, narrow foliage. 1/- each, 10/6 per doz.
" **ORIENTALIS.** Pale blue. 1/- each, 10/6 per doz.
" **SNOW QUEEN.** White. 1/- each, 10/6 per doz.
LATHYRUS LATIFOLIUS, WHITE PEARL. A superb variety of the well-known Everlasting Pea. 1/- each.
LAVATERA OLBIA. Rosy pink. 1/6 each.
LUPINUS ARBOREUS (The Tree Lupin). Yellow. Height 5 ft. 1/- each.
" **POLYPHYLLUS.** Blue. 1/- each.
" " **ALBA.** White. 1/- each.
" " **MOERHEIMI.** Rose. 1/- each.
" " **ROSEUS.** A charming variety of the Perennial Lupin, perfectly hardy, flowers of a soft rose-pink colour. 1/6 each.
LYCHNIS CHALCEDONICA. Height about 3 ft., brilliant scarlet, very showy. 1/- each.
" **HAAGEANA.** Mixed colours. 1½ ft. 1/- each.
" **VISCARIA SPLENDENS PLENA.** Rose. 1½ ft. 1/- each.
ŒNOTHERA ACAULIS VERA. A beautiful dwarf-growing species with large white flowers. 1/- each.
" **FRUITICOSA YOUNGI.** Golden yellow. 2 ft. 1/- each.
PAMPAS GRASS. White plumes. 3/- each.
" **ROSE QUEEN.** Enormous plumes. 4/- ea.
PAPAVER, MRS. PERRY. A peculiar shade of orange-chrome. Height 3 ft. 1/- each.
" **ORIENTALE, PERRY'S WHITE.** White. 1/- each.
" " **PRINCE OF ORANGE.** 1/- each.
" " **SALMON QUEEN.** Lovely salmon scarlet. 1/- each.
" " **SILVER QUEEN.** Lovely silvery white with a very faint blush hue. 1/- each.
PÆONIES, HERBACEOUS. 24 of the best varieties. 2½/- per doz.
Double and Single, choice sorts. 2/- each.
PHLOXES, PERENNIAL—
" **COQUELICOT.** Brightest of scarlets, with purple eye. 1/- each.
" **DR. CHARCOTE.** Pale violet purple. 1/- each, 10/6 per doz.
" **ELIZABETH CAMPBELL.** Pink and white. 1/6 each.
" **ETNA.** Brilliant scarlet, very fine. 1/- each.
" **FRAU A. BUCHNER.** Tall white with large pips. 1/6 each.
" **FRIEFRAULEIN-VON-LASSBERG.** The purest and largest white Phlox. 1/6 each.
" **G. A. STROHLEIN.** Orange scarlet. 1/- ea.
" **GRUPPEN KONINGEN.** Lovely pale rose, with carmine eye, very large flowers. 1/- ea.
" **IRIS.** Violet-blue; very fine. 1/- each.
" **LE MAHDI.** Rich violet-blue; very distinct. 1/6 each.
" **M. HUGH LOW.** Good crimson. 1/3 each, 12/6 per doz.
" **MISS PEMBERTON.** Salmon rose, enormous heads. 1/- each.
" **PANTHEON.** Rosy salmon, enormous flowers. 1/- each.
" **RIJNSTROOM.** Cerise pink. 1/- each, 10/6 per doz.

GAILLARDIA. *See page 91.*

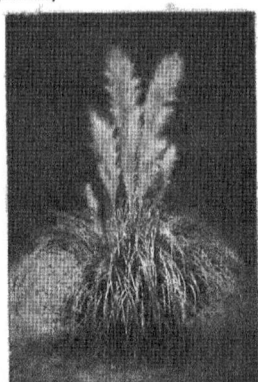

PAMPAS GRASS.

PHLOX, SELMA. Pink with deeper eye. 1/- each, 10/6 per doz.
PINKS. Choice named varieties. Our Selection. 1/- each. 10/6 per doz.
" **ALBUM.** White. 2½ ft. 1/- each.
POLEMONIUM CŒRULEUM. Jacob's Ladder. Blue. 1/- each.
POLYGONATUM MULTIFLORUM (Solomon's Seal). 1/- each.
POTENTILLA ATROSANGUINEUM, GIBSON'S SCARLET. Dazzling scarlet. 1/- each.
" **IN SIX VARIETIES.** 1/- each, 10/6 per doz.
PYRETHRUMS, DOUBLE—
" **CAPT. NARES.** Crimson. 1/- each, 10/6 per doz.
" **QUEEN MARY.** Pink. 1/6 each.
PYRETHRUMS, SINGLE—
" **AGNES MARY KELWAY.** Rose, telling variety. 1/- each.
" **COMET.** Crimson. 1/- each, 10/6 per doz.
" **JAMES KELWAY.** Scarlet. 1/- each.
" **LANGPORT SCARLET.** Good scarlet. 1/- each. 10/6 per doz.
Choice sorts to name, Double and Single. 10/6 per doz.
RUDBECKIA LACINIATA FL. PL. (Golden Glow). Large double golden yellow flowers. 1/- each.
" **NEWMANII.** Yellow, with black centre. 1/- each.
" **PURPUREA.** Reddish purple. 1/6 each.
SCABIOSA CAUCASICA. Large, handsome pale lilac-blue flowers. 1/- each.
" **ELATA.** Sulphur yellow. 1/- each.
SIDALCEA ROSY GEM. This is a distinct and pleasing plant, producing long graceful spikes of bright rosy flowers. 4 ft. 1/- each.
SOLIDAGO ALTISSIMA. A fine showy plant, growing about 4½ ft. high, with large panicles of deep golden yellow flowers. 1/- each.
" **GOLDEN WINGS.** Best golden yellow. 1/- each.
" **SHORTIA.** Long arching racemes of bright golden yellow flowers. Height 5 ft. 1/- each.
SPIRÆA ARUNCUS. A handsome, stately-growing border plant, with magnificent plumes of creamy white flowers. 1/- each.
" **ASTILBOIDES.** A beautiful species, about 2 ft. high, producing dense plumes of feathery white flowers ; easily grown in pots or borders. 1/- each.
" **FILIPENDULA FL. PL.** Corymbs of double white flowers and pretty foliage. 1/- each.
" **PALMATA (Crimson Meadow Sweet).** A fine border plant, flowers rich crimson. 1/6 each.
STATICE LATIFOLIA. Sea Lavender. 18 in. 1/3 each, 12/6 per doz.
STOKESIA CYANEA. Lavender blue flowers three inches across. 1/- each.
THALICTRUM ADIANTIFOLIUM (The Maidenhair Thalictrum). A beautiful plant rivalling Maiden-hair Fern in delicacy of foliage, and quite hardy. 1/- each.
" **DIPTEROCARPUM.** Rosy-purple with citron yellow anthers, of light elegant growth ; very attractive. 2/- each.
" **GLAUCUM.** Yellow. 1/3 each, 12/6 per doz.

Hardy Perennial Flowering Plants *(continued)*

PERENNIAL PHLOX. *See page 92.*

TRITOMA CAULESCENS. Bold plants, late flowering. 1/6 each.
,, NORTHIÆ. Scarlet and orange. 1 3 each, 12/6 per doz.
,, UVARIA GRANDIFLORA. Orange and red. 1/- each, 10/6 per doz.
,, TUCKII. Bright red changing to yellow. 1'- ea.
TROLLIUS ASIATICUS. Flowers bright orange. 1/- each.
,, EUROPÆUS (Potten's variety). Splendid variety; flowers nearly double the size of the old "Kuroneus." 1/- each.
,, HIS MAJESTY. Round flowers of deep orange. 1/- each, 10/6 per doz.
,, ORANGE GLOBE. Very large deep orange flowers; a strong grower and free bloomer. 1/3 each.
TROPÆOLUM SPECIOSUM. Producing a blaze of scarlet flowers in late Summer and Autumn; grows rapidly. 1/6 each.
VERBASCUM CALEDONIA. Grand spike of sulphur-shaded lake flowers. 1/6 each.
,, DENSIFLORUM. Flowers of a golden bronzy tint. Height 4 ft. 1/6 each.
VIOLAS. Choice named varieties. Our selection. 4d. each, 3/- doz., 21/- per 100.

We are able to supply extra sized clumps from the open ground, and we shall be glad to send a list of these to anyone wanting to obtain immediate effect.

From Miss COLLARD, Liphook.
December 21st.
"The Shrubs and Plants received in good condition, and are quite satisfactory."

From Mr. A. GREGORY, Ogmore Vale.
October 23rd.
"I am very pleased with the last lot of Plants that I received from you."

PÆONY. *See page 92.*

DANIELS' SPECIAL COLLECTIONS OF HARDY FLOWERING PLANTS.

We have much pleasure in recommending the following four collections, which contain a very choice selection of the above, specially arranged for a brilliant and varied display of colour and a long continuance of bloom in the open garden.

COLLECTION A. 100 in 50 fine varieties, our selection, 70/-.	COLLECTION C. 50 in 25 fine varieties, our selection, 35/-.
COLLECTION B. 50 in 50 fine varieties, our selection, 40/-.	COLLECTION D. 25 in 25 fine varieties, our selection, 21/-.
Our own selection, 10/6 per doz.	Mostly clumps from open ground.

VIOLETS—(Sweet-Scented).

SINGLE-FLOWERED VARIETIES.

ASKANIA. The freest winter flowering violet; an improvement on "Princess of Wales," the best of all single varieties.
PRINCESS OF WALES. A grand variety, producing very large, beautifully formed, rich violet blue flowers.
THE CZAR. Very dark and free.

DOUBLE-FLOWERED VARIETIES.

Most beautiful for button holes and are easily grown in frames during the Winter.
COMTE DE BRAZZA. Large, double, pure white flowers, deliciously scented.
LADY HUME CAMPBELL. Later and darker than Marie Louise.
MARIE LOUISE. Large double flowers, rich lavender blue.
NEAPOLITAN. Lavender blue, flowers very large and double, profuse bloomer.

Single-Flowered and Double-Flowered Varieties, 9d. each ; 8/- per doz. Carriage extra.

ALLWOOD'S HARDY PERPETUAL PINKS.

DOROTHY. Deep rose-pink with dark centre.
HAROLD. Large double white.
JEAN. White with deep violet centre.

MARY. Pale rose-pink with light maroon centre.
PHYLLIS. Lilac, free flowering and delightfully perfumed.

ROBERT. A delicate shade of old rose with a light maroon centre.

In small pots, 2/6 each ; 27/- per doz.

WALLFLOWERS.

DANIELS' DOUBLE VARIETY. Tall grand spikes of double blooms, about 2 ft. high, in April and May. 4d. each, 2 6 doz., 18 - 100.
DWARF MIXED DOUBLES. 12 inches high. 4d. each, 2/6 per doz., 18/- per 100.

WALLFLOWER. Blood Red. 2/- per doz., 14/- per 100.
,, Eastern Queen. Chamois, changing to salmon-rose. 2/- per doz., 14/- per 100.

WALLFLOWER. Fire King. 2/- doz., 14/- 100.
,, Golden Monarch. 2/- per doz., 14/- per 100.
,, Primrose Dawn. 2/- per doz., 14/- per 100.
,, Vulcan. 2/- per doz., 14/- per 100.

All the above are transplanted and grown thinly, and will therefore give good results.

SPIRÆAS—NEW PINK.

QUEEN ALEXANDRA. Bright pink. }
PEACH BLOSSOM. Pale pink. }
These grand varieties are suitable alike for forcing or planting in the open ground, when planted outside the colours will be much deeper.

These made quite a sensation when Exhibited at Holland House, and were awarded the Gold Medal of the Royal Horticultural Society.

Each variety 2s. each ; per doz. 21s.

PLANTS FOR SPRING BEDDING.

	per doz.	per 100.			per doz.	per 100.			per doz.	per 100
CANTERBURY BELLS—			HOLLYHOCKS—				POLYANTHUS—			
Double Blue	2 6	14 0	Double Cream	each 9d.	6 0	—	Mixed		3 0	—
Double Rose	2 6	14 0	Double Crimson	9d.	6 0	—	PRIMROSES—			
Double White	2 6	14 0	Double Pink Queen	9d.	6 0	—	G. F. WILSON'S Blue 9d. each	8 0	—	
Double Mixed	2 6	14 0	Double Rose	9d.	6 0	—	SWEET WILLIAMS—			
Single Blue	2 6	14 0	Double Mixed	9d.	6 0	—	Scarlet Beauty		8 0	16 0
Single Mixed	2 6	14 0	Single Mixed	9d.	6 0	—	Pink Beauty		8 0	16 0
Calceantherma Blue mixed	2 6	14 0	MYOSOTIS (Forget-me-nots)—				Prize Mixed		6 0	16 0
	2 6	14 0	Indigo Blue		2 6	15 0	Auricula-eyed Mixed		3 0	—
DIGITALIS (Foxglove)—			Sky Blue		2 6	15 0	VIOLAS (Bedding)—			
White	3 0	21 0	Ruth Fischer. The best grown	3 0	—	White, Mauve, Blue & Yellow.			
Spotted Mixed	3 0	21 0	PANSIES—				All Autumn struck cuttings.			
Monstrosa	3 0	21 0	Empress Mixed		3 0	—	Ready in March each 4d.	3 0	21 0	
			Giant Blotched		3 0	—				
			Giant Exhibition		2 6	16 0				

PLANTS SUITABLE FOR ROCKWORK.

This most delightful department of Hardy Plants is now represented in our Nursery by a wide range of all the most charming subjects suitable for Rock and Wall gardening. Those of our customers who desire to add a collection of Rock plants to their garden will find all the gems offered below.

Where space is limited very charming effects may often be obtained by forming a rockery, and if care is exercised in planting it a continual show of bloom may be had from early Spring until late in Autumn.

One great advantage of Rock Gardening is, that it may be introduced in positions where very often little else will grow, as the labour entailed in the upkeep of a Rockery is small and an immediate effect is produced. We strongly recommend this branch of gardening to our customers.

ACÆNA BUCHANANI. Beautiful glaucous
foliage. 1/- each, 10/6 per doz.
ACANTHOLIMON GLUMACEUM. The prickly
thrift. Flowers rose-pink. 1/- each, 10/6 doz.
ACHILLEA ARGENTEA. Silvery fragrant
foliage. Flowers white. 1/- each.
AGROSTEMMA ATRO-SANGUINEA. Crimson
purple, effective. 1/- each, 10/6 per doz.
ALYSSUM SAXATILE COMPACTUM. Dwarf
yellow. 9d. each, 8/- per doz.
,, Fl. Pl. Golden yellow. 1/- each,
10/6 per doz.
ANDROSACE CHUMBYI. Woolly foliage, rose
flowers. 1/3 each, 12/6 per doz.
,, SARMENTOSA. Large rosettes of woolly
foliage, yellow flowers. 1/- each, 10/6 per doz.
ANEMON SYLVESTRIS. White (snowdrop
Anemone). 1/- each, 10/6 per doz.
ANTENNARIA TOMENTOSA. Silvery foliage,
whitish flowers. 9d. each, 8/- per doz.
ANTHEMIS AIZOON. White flowers, silvery
foliage. 1/- each, 10/6 per doz.
ARABIS ALBIDA Fl. Pl. Invaluable rock
plant. 9d. each, 8/- per doz.
ARTEMISIA VILLARSI. Finely cut silvery
grey foliage. 1/- each, 10/6 per doz.
ASPERULA ODORATA. White flowers with
silvery foliage. 1/- each, 10/6 per doz.
ASTER ALPINUS SUPERBUS. Purplish blue.
1/- each, 10/6 per doz.
,, PEREGRINUS. Large violet blue, distinct.
1/- each, 10/6 per doz.
,, SUB. CŒRULEUS. Light blue, gold centre.
1/- each, 10/6 per doz.
AUBRIETIA ANTILASANI. White, compact
grower. 1/- each, 10/6 per doz.
,, DELTOIDES VARIEGATA. Distinct variety.
1/- each, 10/6 per doz.
,, DR. MULES. Dark violet. 1/- each, 10/6
per doz.
,, HENDERSONI. Rich violet purple. 1/- each,
10/6 per doz.
,, LLOYD EDWARDS. Glowing violet purple.
1/- each, 10/6 per doz.
,, PERKINSI. Large, deep violet. 1/- each,
10/6 per doz.
BETONICA SPICATA ROSEA. Spikes of rose-
coloured flowers. 1/- 1/- each.
CALAMINTHA GRANDIFLORA. Pretty rosy
pink flowers. 1/3 each, 12/6 per doz.
CAMPANULA CARPATICA. Neat growing, blue
flowers. 1/- each, 10/6 per doz.
,, TURBINATA. White Star. Charming.
1/- each, 12/6 per doz.
,, GARGANICA HIRSUTA. Distinct, light
blue. 1/- each, 10/6 per doz.
,, PORTENSCHLAGIANA. Pale blue, free.
1/- each, 10/6 per doz.
,, PUMILA ALBA. Fine companion to Pumila.
1/- each, 10/6 per doz.
CARDAMINE TRIFOLIATA. A compact plant
with pure white flowers. 1/- each, 10/6 doz.
CERASTIUM TOMENTOSUM. Stems and leaves
silvery white. 9d. each, 8/- per doz.
CHEIRANTHUS ALPINUS. Dense heads of pale
yellow. 1/- each, 10/6 per doz.
DIANTHUS CŒSIUS. Glaucous foliage, pink
flowers. 1/- each, 10/6 per doz.
,, DELTOIDEA ALBA. Flowers white with
narrow ring of crimson. 1/- each, 10/6 per
doz.
,, GALLICUS. Pretty ruby flowers, late. 1/-
each, 10/6 per doz.
EPIMEDIUM ALPINUM. Crimson and yellow.
1/- each, 10/6 per doz.
,, COCCINEUM. Ornamental foliage, yellow
flowers. 1/- each, 10/6 per doz.
,, NIVEUM. White. 1/- each, 10/6 per doz.
ERIGERON MUCRONATUS. Pink and white
daisy like flowers. 1/- each, 10/6 per doz.
EUPHORBIA CYPARISSIAS. A pretty plant
with yellow flowers. 1/- each, 10/6 per doz.
FERNS. Hardy, choice named varieties. 2/6
each, 27/6 per doz.
GENTIANA ACAULIS. Bell-shaped, intense blue
flowers. 1/- each, 10/6 per doz.
GERANIUM GRANDIFLORUM. Fine plant
with large deep violet flowers. 1/- each,
10/6 per doz.
,, MACRORHIZUM. Rosy purple, flowers
in profusion. 1/- each, 10/6 per doz.
,, PRATENSE STRIATUM. Branching stems
bearing a profusion of white and blue blooms.
1/- in. 1/- each.
,, SANGUINEUM. Showy ruby crimson flowers.
1/- each, 10/6 per doz.
GNAPHALIUM LEONTOPODIUM. The Swiss
Edelweiss) Creamy white. Easily grown.
1/- each, 10/6 per doz.
GYPSOPHILA PROSTRATA ROSEA. Very
pretty. 1/- each, 10/6 per doz.

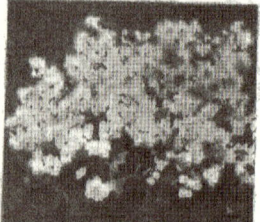

ARABIS.

GYPSOPHILA REPENS MONSTROSA. Pure
white, free. 1/- each, 10/6 per doz.
HELIANTHEMUMS (Rock or Sun Roses).
An exceedingly beautiful class of evergreen
trailing alpine Perennials. The flowers are
produced in such profusion that the plants
are a literal sheet of bloom for a very long
period. It is surpassed by no other for
modest beauty and grace when trailing over
stones and banks. Named varieties. 1/- each,
10/6 per doz.
HEPATICAS. In separate colours. 1/3 each,
12/6 per doz.
HŒMINIUM PYRENAICUM. Blue, and likes to
be in crevices. 1/- each.
HOUSTONIA SERPYLLIFOLIA. White. 1/- each,
10/6 per doz.
HYPERICUM CORIS. A graceful plant, with
glaucous foliage, yellow flowers. 1/- each,
10/6 per doz.
IBERIS SEMPERVIRENS. Little Gem. Compact,
pure white. 1/- each, 10/6 per doz.
,, SNOWFLAKE. Snow white, charming.
JUNIPERUS HIBERNICA PYRAMIDALIS
EXCELSA. 6—3 inches. In pots. 3/6 and
5/- each.
LITHOSPERMUM PROSTRATUM. Dark blue
flowers. 1/6 each, 15/- per doz.
,, Heavenly Blue Charming sky blue.
1/6 each, 15/- per doz.
LYSIMACHIA NUMMULARIA (Creeping Jenny).
1/6 each, 8/- per doz.
NIEREMBERGIA RIVULARIS. Dainty creeper,
large cream white flowers. 1/- each, 10/6 doz.
ŒNOTHERA RIPARIA. Golden yellow. Free
flowering. 1 ft. 1/- each.
OROBUS VERNUS. The spring Vetch. Blue
and purple. 1/6 each.
PHLOX MŒHRHEIMI. White flowers. 1/- each.
,, SUBULATA. Rich pink. 1/- each, 10/6 doz.
,, FRONDOSA. Rose, prostrate tufts.
1/- each, 10/6 per doz.
,, LILACINA. Lovely lilac blue, very
free. 1/- each, 10/6 per doz.
,, NEWRY SEEDLING. Pretty starch
blue flower. 1/- each, 10/6 per doz.
,, NIVALIS. Purest white of all. 1/6
each, 15/- per doz.
POLYGONUM BRUNONIS. Spreading plant,
rosy flowers in late summer. 1/- each, 10/6
per doz.
POTENTILLA ATRO-SANGUINEA. Bright
scarlet flowers. 1/- each, 10/6 per doz.
,, MINIMA. Creeping habit, yellow flowers.
PRIMULA PULVERULENTA. Crimson, orange
centre. 2/- each, 21/- per doz.
,, BULLEYANA. Lovely orange. Bloom spikes
covered with a white meal. 2/- each.
,, JAPONICA. Mixed Hybrids. 2/- each.
,, JULIÆ. A carpet of rosy-purple flowers in
April and May. 1/3 each.
SAXIFRAGA AIZOON. Panicles of white
flowers. 1/- each, 10/6 per doz.
,, APICULATA. Sulphur yellow. 1/- each,
10/6 per doz.
,, BATHONIENSIS. Scarlet crimson, large
flowers. 1/- each, 10/6 per doz.
,, CLIBRANI. Fine, deep crimson. 1/- each,
10/6 per doz.

SAXIFRAGA ELIZABETHÆ. Clear sulphur
flowers. 1/6 each, 15/- per doz.
,, HOSTII. Silvery leaves, white, spotted
purple. 1/- each, 10/6 per doz.
,, LINDSAYANA. One of the best whites.
1/- each, 10/6 per doz.
,, LONGIFOLIA. Queen of encrusted varieties.
1/6 each, 15/- per doz.
,, MAWEANA. Flowers white, on short stems.
1/- each, 10/6 per doz.
,, MUSCOIDES ATROPURPUREA. Red
flowers. 1/- each, 10/6 per doz.
,, NEPALENSE. Red stems, white flowers.
1/3 each, 12/6 per doz.
,, OPPOSITIFOLIA. Prostrate habit, rose
flowers. 1/- each, 10/6 per doz.
,, ALBA. 1/- each, 10/6 per doz.
,, PYRAMIDALIS (Cotyledon). Giant spikes,
white flowers. 1/3 each, 12/6 per doz.
,, RECTA. White flowers, close habit. 1/- each,
10/6 per doz.
,, ROSULARIS. White flowers, spotted pink,
incurved rosettes. 1/- each, 10/6 per doz.
,, SANCTA. Yellow, early to bloom. 1/- each,
10/6 per doz.
,, SANGUINEA SUPERBA. The best red.
1/3 each, 12/6 per doz.
,, STANSFIELDI. White, robust grower.
1/- each, 10/6 per doz.
,, UMBROSA. Pink. 1/- each, 10/6 per doz.
,, WARES CRIMSON. Intense crimson. 1/-
each, 10/6 per doz.
SCABIOSA ALPINA. Mauve, very pretty.
1/- each, 10/6 per doz.
SEDUM ACRE AUREUM. Very effective in
Spring. 1/- each, 10/6 per doz.
,, ALBUM. White flowers, bronzy foliage.
9d. each, 8/- per doz.
,, DASYPHYLLUM. Glaucous foliage, white
flowers. 1/- each, 10/6 per doz.
,, GLAUCUM. Plukish white flowers. 9d. each,
8/- per doz.
,, HYBRIDUM. Creeping, red margined leaves,
yellow flowers. 1/- each, 10/6 per doz.
,, KAMTSCHATICUM Fl. VAR. Good.
1/- each, 10/6 per doz.
,, LYDIUM. White, spreading carpet. 1/- each,
10/6 per doz.
,, MONSTROSUM. Resembling a cockscomb
in growth. 1/- each, 10/6 per doz.
,, RUPESTRIS. Yellow, bronzy red foliage.
1/- each, 10/6 per doz.
,, SPATHULEFOLIUM. Yellow flowers. 1/-
each, 12/6 per doz.
,, SPURIUM. Pink and white. 1/3 each, 12/6
per doz.
,, SPECTABILE. Pink, erect grower. 1/- each,
10/6 per doz.
,, TELEPHIUM. Erect leafy stems, flowers
pink. 1/- each, 10/6 per doz.
SEMPERVIVUM ARACHNOIDEUM (Cobweb
House Leek). 1/- each, 10/6 per doz.
,, FAUCONNETI. Reddish star-like flowers.
9d. each.
,, FIMBRIATUM. Red flowers. 9d. each,
8/- per doz.
,, TECTORUM (Common House Leek). 9d.
each, 8/- per doz.
SILENE ALPESTRIS. Starry white flowers.
1/- each, 10/6 per doz.
,, SCHAFTA. Bright pink flowers. 1/- each,
10/6 per doz.
SISYRINCHIUM ANCEPS. Grass-like foliage,
pale blue flowers. 1/- each, 10/6 per doz.
STACHYS LANATA. Woolly leaves. 1/- each,
10/6 per doz.
THYMUS CITRIODORUS ARGENTEUS.
Foliage variegated white. 1/- each, 10/6 doz.
,, LANUGINOSUS. Woolly leaved, good rock
plant. 1/- each, 10/6 per doz.
,, SERPYLLUM ALBUM. Fine for carpeting.
1/- each, 10/6 per doz.
,, COCCINEUM. Very effective. 1/-
each, 10/6 per doz.
TIARELLA CORDIFOLIA. Foam like flowers.
1/- each, 10/6 per doz.
VERBENA VENOSA. Hardy species, deep
violet flowers. 1/- each, 10/6 per doz.
VERONICA RUPESTRIS. Sheets of blue flowers.
Blue-mauve. 9d. each, 8/- per doz.
VIOLETTA CORNUTA, MAUVE QUEEN.
,, PURPUREA. Light purple. 6d. each,
5/- per doz.
,, GRACILIS. Rich purple. 9d. each, 5/- doz.
VIOLETTAS. In six distinct colours, our
selection. 5/- per doz.

Our Own Selection, 10/- per doz.; 75/- per 100.
All the above are grown in pots.

SUMMER BEDDING PLANTS.

SEEDLING PLANTS.

GIANT OSTRICH PLUME.

	Per doz.	Per 100
ANTIRRHINUM, TALL—		
Carmine King, brilliant carmine	1 6	10 0
Crimson King, fine	1 6	10 0
Fairy Queen, orange-salmon	1 6	10 0
Golden Yellow, clear colour	1 6	10 0
Lilac Queen, lilac and white	1 6	10 0
Orange King, orange scarlet	1 6	10 0
Princess Patricia, pale rose and chamois	1 6	10 0
Rose Queen, soft rose	1 6	10 0
Pure White, very fine	1 6	10 0
Very Choice Mixed	1 6	10 0
ANTIRRHINUM, SEMI-DWARF—		
Amber Queen, canary chamois	1 6	10 0
Apricot Queen, apricot pink	1 6	10 0
Crimson King, fine deep colour	1 6	10 0
Flamingo, deep terra-cotta	1 6	10 0
Golden Queen, golden yellow	1 6	10 0
Orange Queen, terra-cotta pink	1 6	10 0
Rosebud, rose, white throat	1 6	10 0
Scarlet King, brilliant colour	1 6	10 0
Sunrise, old rose and orange	1 6	10 0
The Bride, perfectly pure white	1 6	10 0
Choice Mixed	1 6	10 0
Tom Thumb, Crimson King, White Queen, Antique Rose, Yellow Prince, or Mixed	1 6	10 0

ASTERS.

	Per doz.	Per 100
Daniels' Giant Ostrich Plume. The very finest class for exhibition purposes—		
Azure blue, crimson, lavender, bright rose, delicate rose, white, or mixed, all colours	1 0	7 6
Daniels' Giant Comet. Splendid for cutting—		
Pure white, violet, salmon rose, crimson and azure blue	1 0	7 6
Choice mixed	1 0	7 6
Improved Victoria. Beautiful for bedding—		
Fiery scarlet, violet, pure white, blush rose, light blue	1 0	7 6
Choice mixed	1 0	7 6
Tall Branching. Late blooming, 2 ft. high—		
Scarlet, lavender, shell pink, white, and mixed	1 0	7 6
Single Flowered. Exceedingly useful—		
Scarlet, mauve, rose, dark blue, white, and mixed	1 0	7 0

	Per doz.	Per 100
Nemesia, Scarlet, orange, white, and large-flowered mixed	1 5	10 6
,, Compacta, Blue Gem and choice mixed	1 6	10 6
Nicotiana Affinis, White, sweet scented	1 0	7 6
,, Hybrids, great variety of colour	1 6	10 6
Pansy, Exhibition Giant, very choice mixed	2 0	14 0
,, Prize Blotched, many fine colours	2 0	14 0
,, Blue Emperor, rich ultramarine	2 0	14 0
Pentstemons, New Large-flowered Hybrids, mixed	2 0	14 0
Petunias. Our large-flowered strain of beautiful colours—crimson, white, brilliant rose, choice mixed	2 0	14 0
Phlox Drummondi, Rose, white, crimson, mixed	1 0	7 6
Verbena, Daniels' large-flowered Hybrids, mixed	2 0	14 0
Zinnias, Splendid double-flowered, mixed	1 6	10 6

	Per doz.	Per 100
Carnation, Marguerite, new large-flowered, choice mixed	2 0	14 0
Cosmos, Rose Queen or White Queen, fine for cutting	1 6	10 0
,, New giant-flowered, mixed, early blooming	1 6	10 0
Heliotrope, Large-flowered Hybrids, choice mixed	2 0	14 0
Kochia Trichophylla (Summer Cypress), decorative	1 6	10 0

STOCKS.

	Per doz.	Per 100
DANIELS' LARGE FLOWERED TEN-WEEK—		
Brilliant Carmine, splendid	1 0	7 6
Bright Rose, lovely shade	1 0	7 6
Blood Red, fine dark colour	1 0	7 6
Dark Violet, beautiful	1 0	7 6
Light Blue, delicate shade	1 0	7 6
Pure White, very fine	1 0	7 6
Splendid Mixed, from the brightest and most brilliant colours only	1 0	7 6
STOCKS, CHOICE NAMED VARIETIES—		
Azure Queen, fine light blue	1 6	10 0
Almond Blossom, white, delicately shaded carmine	1 6	10 0
Crimson King, brilliant fiery crimson	1 6	10 0
Mauve Beauty, delicate bluish mauve	1 6	10 0
Salmon Queen, beautiful salmon pink	1 6	10 0
Snow Queen, splendid pure white	1 6	10 0
Queen of Violets, lovely dark blue	1 6	10 0

Splendid transplanted sturdy plants.
Packing and carriage free.

STRONG ROOTED PLANTS
FROM CUTTINGS.

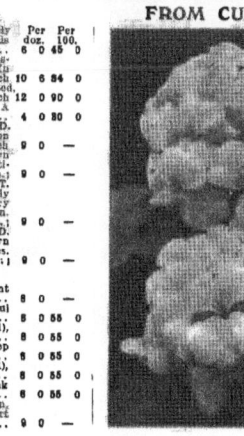

	Per doz.	Per 100
AGERATUM. Dwarf Blue, a lovely little plant for edgings of beds and borders, from single pots	6 0	45 0
BEGONIAS. Single, tuberous-rooted, beautiful varieties. In small pots 1/- each	10 6	54 0
,, Double, tuberous-rooted, selected, mixed. In small pots 1/3 each	12 0	90 0
CALCEOLARIA. Golden Gem. A splendid bedder	4 0	30 0
DAHLIAS. CACTUS-FLOWERED. Choice named sorts, our selection 1/- each	9 0	—
,, **SHOW AND FANCY.** Our own selection of popular and beautiful varieties 1/- each ; 6 for 5s.	9 0	—
,, **POMPONE OR BOUQUET.** Beautifully formed perfectly double miniature flowers, very good varieties, our selection 1/- each ; 6 for 5s.	9 0	—
,, **NEW PÆONY-FLOWERED.** Beautiful colours, our own selection of popular varieties. 1/- each ; 6 for 5s.	9 0	—
GERANIUMS. All from single pots.		
Daniels' Orange Queen, brilliant orange scarlet	8 0	—
King of Denmark, beautiful salmon	8 0	55 0
Madame Crousse (Ivy leaved), soft pink	8 0	55 0
Paul Crampel, the finest deep scarlet	8 0	55 0
Flower of Spring (Silver leaved), pretty	8 0	55 0
Verona, golden foliage, pink flowers	8 0	55 0
Victory (new). Lovely salmon, very fine for bedding, sport from Paul Crampel	9 0	—

	Per doz.	Per 100
GERANIUMS—continued		
Virginia, pure white	8 0	55 0
Souvenir de Charles Turner (Ivy leaved), deep rose	8 0	55 0
Mrs. Leavis, one of the finest pinks	8 0	55 0
Large Plants in 5½ inch pots for decoration.		
Paul Crampel, King of Denmark, Virginia, Madame Crousse, Souvenir de Charles Turner, 1/9 each	16 0	—
HELIOTROPE. Choice named varieties, from cuttings	7 0	50 0
LOBELIA. Mrs. Clibran, dark blue, white eye, dwarf	2 0	14 0
,, **Blue Stone,** sky blue. Very fine variety	2 0	14 0
,, **White Perfection.** The very finest white kind	2 0	14 0
,, **Tenuior,** trailing. Excellent for baskets or window boxes	2 0	17 6
MARGUERITE. Large single white, pot grown	7 0	50 0
,, **Boule de Neige,** double white	7 0	50 0
SALVIA. Pride of Zurich, dazzling scarlet. One of the very finest bedding plants	7 0	50 0
VERBENA. All splendid bushy plants from cuttings.		
,, **Miss Willmott,** salmon with white eye	7 0	50 0
,, **Scarlet King,** brilliant scarlet	7 0	50 0
,, **Mixed sorts,** all the best varieties	7 0	50 0
,, **Lemon Scented** (Aloysia Citriodora). Beautifully scented pot plant, in pots 1/- each	10 0	—

Orders of 40/- value, carriage paid; gratis plants included to help with carriage on smaller orders.

DANIELS' SUPERB BEGONIAS.

We have much pleasure in offering tubers of our grand strains of Tuberous-rooted Begonias. These have been grown and selected at our Nurseries during the past season, and for form, size, substance of flower, and beauty and variety of colouring are second to none.

DANIELS' DOUBLE-FLOWERED BEGONIAS
(Dry Tubers).

The Double-flowered Begonias are especially recommended for pot culture. The colours of the flowers vary from the darkest crimson and scarlet, through all the most beautiful shades of salmon, rose, and yellow, to the purest white. They are easily grown, and with their large massive blooms form strikingly handsome objects for the greenhouse or conservatory.

FOR POT CULTURE. A superb collection of choice sorts, equal to named varieties, the flowers being of the most perfect form, and of the most varied and beautiful colours. Highly desirable for conservatory or greenhouse decoration ... 1/- and 1/3 each ; per doz. 10/6 and 12/-
MIXED DOUBLES FOR BEDDING. A capital variety of large, full, double flowers, in beautiful variety of colour .. .. 6/- per doz.; per 100 **35 0**

DOUBLE BEGONIAS. In distinct colours for pots or bedding out.

Fine double flowers, carefully selected when in bloom, and first class for pot culture or the garden.
RED, YELLOW, WHITE, SALMON, ROSE .. .. 9d. each; per doz. 7/6 ; per 100 **50 0**

SINGLE-FLOWERED BEGONIAS (Dry Tubers). Pot culture.

FOR GREENHOUSE AND CONSERVATORY. A very fine mixture of choice selected flowers, mostly equal to the named sorts, the flowers being perfect in form and of the most beautiful colours .. .. 9d. and 1/- each ; per doz. 7/6 and 10/6

DANIELS' SINGLE BEGONIAS FOR BEDDING.
(Dry Tubers.) In distinct colours.

Distinct and beautiful colours, specially selected for effective bedding, all of the large-flowered erect growing class, and good strong tubers. Highly recommended.
RED, YELLOW, WHITE, SALMON, ROSE .. .. 9d. each; per doz. 7/6 ; per 100 **50 0**

SINGLE AND DOUBLE BEGONIA PLANTS.

In May and June we supply strong plants from single pots at the following rates.
SINGLE-FLOWERED. Choice Mixed .. .. 1/- each ; per doz. 10 6
" " To Colour .. .. 1/6 " " 15 -
DOUBLE-FLOWERED. Choice Mixed .. .. 1 3 " " 12/-
" " To Colour .. .. 1/6 " " 15/-

BEGONIA—DOUBLE-FLOWERED.

CARNATIONS—Perpetual or Winter Flowering.

A beautiful free-flowering class for Winter and early Spring blooming under glass. Invaluable as cut flowers for Bouquets, Button-holes, &c. The plants we offer are all growing in seven-inch pots and ready for blooming.

BEACON. Bright orange scarlet, large and free ; one of the best commercial scarlets.
CAROLA. The largest crimson ever raised, flowers of five inches diameter are no exception. A remarkably good keeper. Very strong grower. Should be cultivated entirely under glass.

ENCHANTRESS SUPREME. Clear pale salmon pink sport of " Enchantress."
LADY FULLER. Flowers large, deep salmon.
QUEEN ALEXANDRA. Rich salmon-pink sport of the well-known " Scarlet Glow."
ROSE PINK ENCHANTRESS. Rose-pink sport of " Enchantress," good habit, strong grower.

TRIUMPH. The best crimson market variety. The flowers are of the brightest possible crimson, and of large size. The shape leaves nothing to be desired, and the calyx never bursts.
WHITE ENCHANTRESS. White sport of " Enchantress." No better white can be obtained. Very good in every way.

Strong Plants, 3/6 and 5/- each ; 40/- and 57/6 per doz.

BORDER CARNATIONS.

We can offer strong plants of Border Carnations, choice sorts, our selection only. 1/6 each ; 16/- per doz.

GREENHOUSE AND STOVE PLANTS.

ARAUCARIA EXCELSA.

GREENHOUSE PLANTS
in choice variety.

Our selection, 35/- and 42/- per doz.

ARAUCARIA EXCELSA. A fine plant for the conservatory. 5/- each.
ASPARAGUS SPRENGERI. 3/6 each.
ASPIDISTRA LURIDA. 5/- each.
" VARIEGATA. 6/6 each.
AZALEA INDICA. We have a very choice collection, all good healthy flowering plants, varying from ten to sixteen inches across. 3/6 and 5/- each.
BEGONIA, GLOIRE DE LORRAINE. A profusion of bright pink flowers. 3/- & 5/- each.
CANNAS. Dwarf varieties. 1/6 each ; 15/- doz.
CARNATIONS, MALMAISON VARIETIES. In 5-in. pots, 3/- each. Colours :—scarlet, yellow, and various shades of pink.
COPROSMA BAUERIANA VARIEGATA. Beautiful variegated foliage, 3/- each.
CROTONS. A fine collection of choice sorts in nice young plants. 5/- and 7/6 each.
CYCLAMEN PERSICUM GIGANTEUM. Strong Transplanted Seedlings. In 5-in. pots, 2/6 each. 27/6 per doz.
" PURE WHITE. Very beautiful. In 5-in. pots, 2/6 each.
DAPHNE INDICA ALBA. Pure white, deliciously scented variety. 7/6 each.
" RUBRA. Very sweet. 7/6 each.
DRACÆNA AUSTRALIS. Fine for furnishing. 3/6 and 5/- each. Larger 7/6
" GRACILIS. Very useful for decorative purposes. 5/- each.
EUCALYPTUS CITRIODORA. Deliciously scented. 2/6 each.
EULALIA GRACILLIMA. Most elegant. 2/- ea.
" ZEBRINA. Very handsome. 2/- each.
FERNS, GREENHOUSE. Fine selection of the most useful and ornamental. 2/6, 3/6 and 5/- each.
FICUS ELASTICA (India-rubber Plant). 5/- ea.
" VARIEGATA. Beautifully variegated with yellow. 7/6 each.

GENISTA FRAGRANS. 3/6 each.
GLOXINIAS. In beautiful variety. Strong plants. 21/- per doz.
" CORMS. Very choice strain, ready in May. 10/6 per doz.
GREVILLEA ROBUSTA. 2/- each.
HOYA CARNOSA. A charming stove climbing plant, producing wax-like flowers. 5/- each.
LAPAGERIA ALBA. Lovely pure white, wax-like flowers ; beautiful. 7/6 each.
" ROSEA SUPERBA. Beautiful climber for the cool greenhouse. 7/6 each.
MYRTLES (Myrtus). Nice young plants. 2/- each.
OLEANDER (Nerium). Pink and White. 3/6 each.
PALMS. A nice assortment of choice plants suitable for the dinner-table and general decorative purposes, including :—Areca sapida, Cocos Weddelliana, Kentia Belmoreana, Kentia Fosteriana. 7/6, 10/6, 21/-, 31/- and 42/- each.
PASSIFLORA PRINCEPS. Large scarlet flowers. 3/6 and 5/- each.
PLUMBAGO CAPENSIS. Blue. 2/6 each.
" ALBA. 2/6 each.
SOLANUM CAPSICASTRUM. The well-known Solanum, with beautiful bright scarlet berries in Autumn and Winter. 2/6 each.
SOLANUM JASMINOIDES. 2/6 each.
STEPHANOTIS FLORIBUNDA. 5/- and 7/6 each.
STREPTOCARPUS. White, mauve and pink. 3/6 and 5/- each.
SWAINSONIA GALEGIFOLIA ALBA. White Pea-like flowers. 3/6 each.
TACSONIA EXONIENSIS. A fine variety. 3/6 each.
GREENHOUSE PLANTS, in choice variety, our selection, 35/- and 42/- per doz.

Please use this Form when sending an Order to

DANIELS BROS. LTD., (Seedsmen by Appointment to H.M. KING GEORGE V., and Nurseryman by Appointment to H.M. QUEEN ALEXANDRA) NORWICH.

Name..

Address ....

Post-town.. County.......................

Nearest Railway Station }
and distance from same } ....

☞ *⸪* In filling up this form it is of the greatest importance to write clearly the Name and Address of the sender.   The Railway Station should always be given.

Attention to this will save trouble, and prevent unnecessary delay.

For Terms of Business, &c., see inside front cover of this Catalogue.

Date...1921

Please keep a note of the date of this order, and should it become necessary to write us further respecting it, kindly quote such date in subsequent correspondence.

AMOUNT ENCLOSED:

CAUTION—Coins and Notes should be enclosed in a Post Office Registered Envelope. The Registration Fee is only 2d., and this ensures a safe delivery.

	£	s.	d.
Cheque ...			
Money Order			
Postal Order			
Coin } See			
Notes } caution ...			
Total			

KITCHEN GARDEN SEEDS, &c.

QUANTITY REQUIRED	NAMES OF ARTICLES	PRICE s.	d.	QUANTITY REQUIRED	NAMES OF ARTICLES	PRICE s.	d.
	Carried forward £				*Carried forward* £		

☞ Spaces for Flower Seeds, Potatoes, &c., &c., provided overleaf.

VEGETABLE SEEDS, &c. (continued).

FRUIT TREES, ROSES, PLANTS, BULBS, &c.

QUANTITY REQUIRED.	Brought forward £	s.	d.

QUANTITY REQUIRED.	Brought forward £	s.	d.

FLOWER SEEDS.
Numbers from this Catalogue will suffice.

No.	s.	d.	No.	s.	d.

POTATOES.

	Carried forward £		

	Total, £		

INDEX.

Flower Seed in Alphabetical Order, see pages 61—72.

CUT FLOWER DEPARTMENT.

All designs are most carefully packed in special cases, and our system is such that they will stand a journey of twenty-four hours, if necessary, and arrive quite fresh. It is much the best to keep the boxes closed and in a dark cool place until needed, so as to hold the moisture about the flowers, and thus retain their freshness for a longer period.

MEMORIAL WREATHS, CROSSES, ETC.

These are most beautiful and artistic in appearance, being made up of freshly cut flowers. They are composed either of white or coloured flowers, according to the wishes of our customers ; Violets, Roses, Carnations, etc., may be used when in season.

We are continually asked to make up special designs and emblems for Masonic and other funerals, and we shall be most happy to be entrusted with instructions for these special occasions.

Each 12/6 ; 15/- ; 21/- ; 31/6 ; 42/-, and upwards.

WEDDING AND OTHER BOUQUETS.

All orders for Bouquets are made up with the choicest flowers in season, and the important details of artistic arrangement and blending of colours receive most scrupulous attention ; we are glad to say we invariably give the highest satisfaction.

It is most important that instructions should be given at the time of ordering, as to whether "Shower" or hand bouquets are desired, also the colours of the dresses which the flowers used in the Bridesmaids' Bouquets are to match.

BRIDES', PURE WHITE FLOWERS. Either with or without "Showers." Each 21/- to 42/-.
BRIDESMAIDS', WHITE OR DELICATELY TINTED FLOWERS. Each 15/- and upwards.
PRESENTATION BOUQUETS FOR BAZAARS, FETES, ETC. Each 15/- and upwards.
GENTLEMEN'S BUTTON-HOLES, WHITE OR COLOURED FLOWERS, from 1/6 each.
LADIES' SPRAYS. Beautifully made up to order, any colour, from 3/- each.
LOOSE CUT FLOWERS AND FERN FOR WEDDING, ALTAR, VASES AND OTHER DECORATIONS, in boxes, from 5/- per box.

All the prices quoted for Cut Flowers and Floral Designs are strictly net. Package and Carriage extra.

IMPORTANT.

All orders are despatched promptly on receipt, if required, but customers should, if possible, give at least two days' clear notice before the flowers are required, also full particulars for forwarding. Orders from unknown Correspondents must be accompanied by remittance. We would suggest that orders for Wreaths, &c., should be marked URGENT on the Envelope.

FLETCHER & SON, LTD., PRINTERS, NORWICH.

for
AMATEUR
GARDENERS

SEEDSMEN AND NURSERYMEN
By Appointment
To H.M. KING GEORGE V.
& H.M. QUEEN ALEXANDRA.

DANIELS BROS LTD
Seed Growers
& Nurserymen
NORWICH

Spring 1921

www.ingramcontent.com/pod-product-compliance
Lightning Source LLC
Chambersburg PA
CBHW020808020726
47495CB00008B/2637